THE
SABRE
BRIGADE
UNITED NATIONS

For Mike Reid
with all ~~best~~ wishes
from the author,

Tom Preston
aka Derik L———

Ad Unum Omnes

P00-LATH

THE
SABRE
BRIGADE
UNITED NATIONS

Tom Preston

Si Vis Pacem Parra Bellum.

Tom Preston

To order additional copies of this book, contact:
Xlibris Corporation
1-888-7-XLIBRIS
www.Xlibris.com
Orders@Xlibris.com

CONTENTS

*I dedicate this book first and foremost to my wife,
son and daughter for hundreds of hours of their time,
assistance and understanding - without which I could never
have written it. Truly, it would have remained 'just an idea.'
I would also like to thank the following for help and support:
Bob, Maurice, Charlie, Paul, Stephen, Erl and Taffy.
"Pegasus-RIP 1999."*

PRIOR MEETING

"War should be long in preparing in order that
you may conquer the more quickly."
PUBILUS SYRUS, Senientiae

She was female and an officer! Born into a tradition and living by a code. Standing there in her uniform, one thing was apparent, even the drab uncomplimentary British Army uniform she wore could not hide the shapely curves of her body or her graceful athletic legs. At twenty-four years of age she was a beauty that all men, officers and enlisted alike, appreciated looking at—but her professional and icy stare had only encouraged the soldiers to create for her the infamous nickname of The Ice Maiden!

While the nickname had nothing to do with her sexuality or possible frigidness, none of the soldiers could know of any such personal details whether they existed or not, it was a nickname the troops concocted and bestowed upon her some time previously for her unsmiling and serious demeanour in conducting herself. She was very much aware of what they called her, knowing for some time now, but she didn't let it bother her. As she readied herself for her upcoming "rounds" in the company of the Regimental Sergeant Major as Duty Officer of the day, she took a moment and pondered on it some.

If only these stupid enlisted soldiers realized that this Ice Maiden is in fact a hopeless romantic just waiting for her knight in shining armour to come and carry her off, then maybe they might have a better understanding of her and even the female psyche, she told herself, looking into the mirror as she gave it one of her better frowns. *Hate to disappoint the troops,* she finally thought to herself, smiling wryly.

The Ice Maiden in question was in fact a recent addition to the Intelligence Corps and now newly attached to The Parachute Regiment. Jane Crenshaw had been a Commissioned Officer with the rank of Second-Lieutenant for just under a year now. She stood 5'6" tall and seemed a little on the leggy side. She had a full figure with a tan to her skin, which was surprising for one of her standing. It was unusual to find such a person in England (upper class and female) without a milky complexion. Her facial features were classic. She had wide bright blue eyes and lips that were not tight and drawn, but inviting. Her face was held regal by the French-braided hairstyle that brought her dark auburn hair straight back and accentuated her looks. In all, Jane Crenshaw was a very beautiful woman indeed!

All officers served as Duty Officer of-the-day on occasion and on this particular day it was Jane Crenshaw's turn. Ready, she went to meet up with the RSM at the Guard Room to first inspect the guard and those reporting for such duty. Afterwards, the two of them would start out on their associated rounds of duty for the camp.

Arriving in her customarily early time, just to be on the safe side (as no one ever kept an RSM waiting), Jane wandered outside of the RHQ Block for some fresh air. She walked leisurely around the side corner of RHQ out back of the Guard Room, enough for privacy and close enough to hear, if hailed. She was there basking in the freshness and solitude of the morning's glory when the noise of army boots pounding out a staccato rhythm on a tarmac road began to build in crescendo, thereby announcing the imminent arrival of the airborne soldiers before they were actually seen.

They were solid and powerful young men looking every bit like the modern centurions they were. They came running up toward Browning Barracks, nearing the Guard Room and RHQ block wearing their regular PT Kit of boots, OG fatigues and red T-Shirts. The Corporal in charge ran alongside mercilessly "beasting" them to stay the course and keep pace with him. Even if this was the modern army, beliefs and old habits died hard. This Corporal believed passionately and genuinely that at least the men under his charge should be as fit as their predecessors in the famous British Parachute Regiment.

He knew the army was changing and in transition. The rapid move toward a technological age was ever apparent in new equipment and training methods being constantly implemented. *Change is good,* he thought. *You can't stop progress.*

He felt strongly in the old axiom that if it ain't broke, don't fix it! He just couldn't understand or abide the current trend of obvious lowering of fitness standards that were the backbone (as he saw it) and very foundations that made British Paratroopers unique and special. Say what they like, he just knew instinctively that when the next dirty war or conflict came along, it would be *his* Regiment that got called to arms first—*not* those Cabbage Heads!

Next, they'll probably do away with P COY altogether or find ways to by-pass it. That will be a sad day, he continued in his detached thoughts as he ran. *Isn't P COY that common link that bonds us all together in this Airborne Brotherhood, as solid and reliable as the Pegasus he was wearing on his training top? If that day ever comes, I'm sure our badges and wings would surely follow next?* Shaking his head, he shuddered at these dark thoughts. He just knew that his own immediate task was to train these useless wankers until they were fit enough to even run himself into the ground. At least he knew had the fitness to do it to them. He smiled.

He was hardly in a sweat himself when his voice broke the rhythm of pounding boots when he shouted out for his section to halt on the road at the rear of the guard room. He knew his men were physically shattered for he ran them hard through Long Valley and the tank tracks for a good hour and half. Knowing their distressed state was mostly due only to lack of fitness that usually set in from these extended leaves, he let them break off and fall out, panting for their breath.

They all knew their Corporal was a fit bastard, but they respected him for it, even if with some it came begrudgingly.

For himself, Cpl. Ben Steele just wanted these men to all meet their potential as professional soldiers. He felt obligated to tradition that they meet a certain standard of fitness that he was proud to claim for himself. At least he knew he would never have the "Old 'n' Bold" look on them in shame and hang their heads low. He believed in and liked tradition, ensuring The Parachute Regiment were "Simply The Best" was one he enjoyed keeping alive. Cpl. Ben Steele was a fair man. He did feel his men under his charge were as good as their predecessors, so he would do his part to keep them ready, fit and capable as best and honourably as he could.

Besides, as long as they're moaning and groaning at me, I must be doing something right, he grinned.

He watched distractedly as they mingled and chatted, when suddenly from the corner of his eye, he caught the most amazing sight. A beautiful female soldier (an officer by her insignia) the likes of which he had only ever read about but never seen was leaning up against the brick wall observing them, watching him intently.

When he turned to face her full on, she quickly turned herself, moving gracefully away. As suddenly as she had appeared, she was gone! She glided through his thoughts of vision in sudden slow replay, as he just couldn't believe her stunning beauty.

He knew he had been smitten in that instant—which scared him to his very boots by its fact! Her presence and effect had caught him totally off guard. Cpl. Steele was virile, healthy and he liked women, but he was a dedicated soldier and found little time for them in life in the realms of meaningful relationships. He was never comfortable being "looked over" by women and so it bothered him when one took time out to look and take stock of him. Being insecure only in this area of his own good looks, he just didn't get it at all—that his modesty and indifference in this regard was just an added attraction and "turn on" for most women. This fact just never ever registered with him at all, or the possibility that the look-over he had received himself was even remotely in these realms.

By this time, however, his men had slowly walked the length of the road behind RHQ block and were instinctively falling themselves back into formation, out of habit and training. Cpl. Steele liked these TOMS. His thoughts faded as he heard them muttering to themselves about her too.

"Okay, listen up lads, twenty minutes to shower or change, then the last man to get his arse over to the NAAFI before me, buys me a cuppa!"

Yelling exhubilantly in the deranged and excited childish mentality that they all possessed, they all tore off in an unorganized wild run, but by far the fastest most had moved that morning. As Cpl. Steele moved off to follow them at his own leisurely pace, he thought again of the female officer. This instant attraction bothered him greatly. He had no idea who she was or if he would ever see her again, but he knew the sight of her was locked favourably away in his memory forever . . .

Meanwhile, a variety of other duties and activities had occurred and were being carried out by thousands of men in the garrison. After two hours of parades, inspections and other duties being performed simultaneously around the camp that morning by all the soldiers, the time close approached 1000hrs. It was the usual custom of all British soldiers at this time of the day to take a NAAFI break, a British Army term for the military canteen. It was the place where troops usually attended for morning tea or coffee, and in the evening to drink beer. In effect, it was the Regimental canteen and bar where the enlisted soldiers met to socialize.

In addition, this particular canteen was located inside the barracks of The Parachute Regiment for 1, 2, 3 Para Battalions and other Para Logistical units of the British Army. "Para" was the universal abbreviated term used by all of the men here, for those not in the know, it just meant they were all British Paratroopers.

So, in the canteen, all the Paras were lining up along the stainless steel counter moving along collecting their morning tea or coffee and bun or cake. In attendance was the Orderly Officer of-the-day, Lt. Crenshaw, with the RSM. They were stood to one side trying not to intimidate, yet observing all who entered, reprimanding those who warranted such for any dress code infractions and the like.

Eventually, the same section of men who had just returned from an earlier morning run that Lt. Crenshaw recalled seeing, had entered the NAAFI with most still in their PT gear. The men were milling around in an unorganized queue as the subject of their fascination and conversation once again was the female officer present, whom they called The Ice Maiden! Their comments were lewd and bawdy with no inhibitions as they were laughing and quite noisy now, but basically in your typical boisterous good mood. Then a few of them made the stupid, fatal mistake of making some of their loud comments about the Ice Maiden, in close proximity and ear shot to which she and the RSM both overheard. This brought the obvious cold icy stares from the Lt. herself, but it was the RSM who turned his own withering gaze and attention upon them first! Fixing them all with his glaring eyes now, the RSM slowly and purposefully approached and asked testily, "Who's in charge of this unruly lot?" as if he didn't know the answer.

Fear is a powerful motivator in the right hands. It gripped all present as the RSM slowly breathed in to expand his chest as he slowly paced up and down amongst them, deliberating. The TOMS present looked on in new awareness which bordered on pending doom for them, they all knew. The customary silence of the moment issued respectfully, automatically and almost instinctively prior to an RSM's "supreme bollocking" was also in effect now, and they waited with taught breath in the stillness, like sheep to the slaughter.

Suddenly, moving away from the men who had now lined themselves up in orderly fashion, a lone Para stepped forward to announce, "I am Sir."

"Come here then Corporal Steele," bellowed the RSM, who, by the very nature of his position, "unofficially" knew *all* the names of his NCOs, junior and senior alike. Then as his men looked on at him guiltily standing alone in front of the Lt. and the RSM, Cpl. Steele awaited their wrath.

"Explain!" was all that the RSM demanded.

"No explanation or excuses Sir."

The RSM knew these facts, of course, for he was all wise and all knowing, but he carried on regardless, "Did you yourself make any of the comments Corporal Steele?"

"No Sir."

"Then if it wasn't you, it must mean that you can't control this rabble."

"No Sir!"

"I don't believe you Corporal. I want you to get yourself off to your barracks right now "on the double" and changed into battle dress. Then go directly to the Guard Room by 1100hrs and await us there. Do you understand?"

"Yessir!"

"As for the rest of you Toms," the RSM shouted, "I hope you all feel it was worth it," then pointing to a Lance Corporal the RSM stated bluntly, "You, take over."

Then without waiting for a reply, barked out his command.

"I'm sending you all out on another 6 miler. Now you sad looking lot, move your arses outside, NOW!"

Later, in a quiet area by the steps at the side of the Guard Room, the Duty Corporal was talking to the newly arrived soldier just sent there in full battle dress order by the RSM himself.

"How in hell did you get yourself into this mess, Ben?"

"Well Dave, I think it has to do with the fact that one of my lads said too loudly something or other about the female Duty Officer being an 'Ice Maiden'!"

"Oh shit, I wouldn't want to be in your boots right now!"

"That's about what I figured," he replied, thoroughly pissed off himself.

As they talked for a few more minutes, they broke apart quickly upon the arrival of the Lt. and the RSM.

"Corporal," started in the RSM right away, "Do you think it wise for your men to call out derogatory names against a female *and* an officer like that?"

"No Sir."

"Then what do you have to say for yourself or them?"

"Well, I wasn't part of the conversation Sir. I also didn't know those comments were directed at the Duty Officer. But if so, I'll take full responsibility and apologize to the Lieutenant on my own and on their behalf Sir. I will never allow it to happen again!"

Ignoring the apology for now, the RSM barrelled on, "I don't like it, Corporal, when I think an officer in my company has been insulted. If I could prove it, I'd use Queen's Regs and Court Martial the lot of you, you understand me"?

"Yes Sir," and he knew the RSM could and would too, if he saw fit.

"I will not let these things pass in my Regiment. As we speak, I have already sent your section out on another six miler to repent their smug ways. As for you, I want you to get yourself a rifle and await the Sergeant of the Guard who will give you a little reminder from me with some drill out on the square."

Looking at the RSM and then glancing at the female officer for the first time since his previous encounter from the run, the Corporal came to attention once more, before saluting the officer and replying to the RSM.

"Yessir!"

As he stood there at attention, the Lt. and RSM were talking apart from him while they awaited the Sgt. of the Guard. It was no longer than five minutes before the big burly Sgt. arrived.

"Sergeant, I would like you to take this soldier out onto the square with the ammo pack and rifle and drill him rigorously until we return in a half hour. Is that understood?"

Grinning from ear to ear, the big burly Sgt. said, "Yes RSM."

As the Lt. and the RSM turned and left, the Lt. couldn't help herself to glance back at the Cpl.

The Sgt. looked to Cpl. Steele and said gloating, "Well Steele, they say all good things come to he who waits?!"

Neither looking nor replying, Cpl. Steele just stood there at attention with his gaze fixed front and centre, as taught. "I think you know the drill. Pick up the rifle over by the Guard Room along with the ammo pack and march out onto the Parade Square, then I'll just have to see if I can shake some of that cockiness outta yah, now move yourself!" barked the Sgt.

. . . Cpl. Steele had been at it for well over an hour and a half now. The noon day sun was beginning to swelter while the sweat was pouring down his neck and back, burning the raw cuts and abrasions that the thin metal ammo re-supply pack had cut as it swung on his back by the thin straps that held it there. The pack consisted of four plastic canisters filled with wet sand weighing anywhere in total from 50-75 lbs. The Parachute Regiment used these mostly for training purposes, running from hill to hill with them to simulate real shells, as if they had been parachuted into the area under war conditions. This was a drill simply called "ammo re-supply."

It was effective training under different circumstances, but also a very effective punishment that the duty Guard Room personnel liked to use to punish soldiers by making them "drill" with them. The thin, "tinny" metal frame that the plastic shell cases filled with sand were attached to, with its thin webbing straps, made it awkward and hurtful to march and drill with, at least when on the back. Trying to ignore the digging and rubbing pain burning into him, Cpl. Steele concentrated only on the commands the Sgt. shouted out.

"A leaft right, leaft right, leaft right, lee-eaft!"

"About turn!"

"Leaft turn!"

"About turn!"

"Right turn!"

"Attention!"

"Ground Arms!"

"Pick up Arms!"

"Stand at ease!"

"Attention!"

"Shoulder Arms!"

"Quick march!"

"Double time!"

These commands rang out to break the silence of the summer morning air, and the only other constant sounds were those of Cpl. Steele's boots crunching on the dark grey gravel below, as he was put through these paces.

"Attention!"

Walking slowly up to Cpl. Steele, spittle came flying out of the mouth of the big burly Sgt. as he spoke.

"So, how are we enjoying ourselves so far, Steele?"

Fatigued with the pain but refusing to let it show, he replied, "I thought the RSM said something or other about only a half hour or so, Sergeant?"

"Well now, he's not here to remind me, is he?" the Sgt. spat out nastily.

Then, just as the Sgt. began to drill him once more, the RSM and Lt. returned. Seeing the condition of Cpl Steele, it was their turn to feel a little guilty now as the RSM angrily said, "I told you no longer than half an hour, Sergeant White. What's been going on here?"

"I guess I got carried away and forgot what time it was Sir!" he lied, showing no facial expression that could hint otherwise. An experienced soldier in these subtle matters, as even he believed you should rule with an iron fist, the RSM was also a fair man, and knew what to expect. He decided that it would be easier to handle this now if he put the Sgt. out of the way for the time being.

"Sergeant, I'd like you to attend to the NAAFI canteen and observe the normal rounds of the roving guard, we'll catch up with you there later. You, Corporal Steele, right now into the guard room and unload that rifle and unhitch that pack!"

They both replied, "Yessir!" in unison.

Once into the Guard Room, Cpl. Steele began trying to remove the pack without scraping the abrasions or letting on that his back was hurting, but he wasn't having much success. It was not the first time that he or anyone else had suffered at the hands of the brutal and sadistic Sgt. As the Lt. and the RSM stood in the Guard Room with the rest of the duty guard watching him remove his pack, the RSM asked, "How long were you kept at it out there, Corporal?"

Looking at them both he replied hesitatingly, "Since you left Sir!"

"Damn him!" uttered the RSM under his breath.

"Take off your shirt Corporal and let's have a look at your back," said the RSM.

"If you don't mind, Sir, I'd rather not—not with the Lieutenant watching."

Lt. Crenshaw involuntarily blushed at Cpl. Steele's sudden discomfort with her presence and prospect of showing them his back. She felt a sudden pang for him and for the first time since her return, took stock of him once more.

She guessed Cpl. Steele to be at about 6'1". He's also a very well-built muscular-looking type on closer inspection, which was deceptive from a distance. He looked tanned himself and had dark brown or black hair, she couldn't decide. He had a clean trimmed moustache, straight white teeth, a strong chin and looked no older than herself. Again, she blushed involuntary as she admitted to herself that she found him to be excitingly good-looking.

The RSM's words startled her. "Besides being female, she's also an officer in the British Army, Corporal Steele, don't forget that. Now, off with that shirt!"

The words jolted Cpl. Steele into action this time too, as he carried out the order. He turned slowly around when ordered to do so, but not before looking directly at the Lt. with a look as if to say, "I'm sorry!"

Lt. Crenshaw couldn't contain her gasp of surprise, as did the others watching, when she saw the blood and the oozing laceration the length of Cpl. Steele's back.

"Hell," thundered the RSM, "You're a mess Corporal Steele."

I suppose I could also say it wasn't my fault to have you out there on the Parade Square for that length of time drilling, but hell WOULD freeze over if I did that — not to mention my reputation down the tube, too, mused the RSM, conveying no look to reveal HIS thoughts.

The RSM liked Cpl. Steele, so all he said was, "You plonker!"

'That's okay Sir!" Cpl. Steele said grinning, but feeling a little embarrassed now, especially since getting the kind word and compliment from the RSM like this.

"Will I need a dressing or something, Sir?" he added.

"I'm afraid so. Look, I'll get the duty driver to get you over to the hospital emergency and have them see to you right away, alright?"

Not knowing why, but Lt. Crenshaw found herself saying, "Look RSM, I'm doing nothing anyway, so why don't I ride down to the hospital with him, to see he's okay?"

"Good idea, Lieutenant. I'll just wait here for the Sergeant to call or return!"

As Cpl. Steele climbed into the duty driver's jeep followed by the Lt. which was parked out in front of the Guard Room anyway, Lt. Crenshaw spoke directly.

"It's probably of no consolation to you, Corporal Steele, but I wouldn't like to be the Sergeant right about now!"

Cpl. Steele looked across to smile directly at her for the first time, then leant forward in his seat being unable to lean back into it, even for the short ride that it was to the hospital.

The following morning, as the duty nurse came to change his dressing, she said to him, "There's a lady officer out there para. Come to visit you, and real pretty too!"

"Hello Ma'am," said Cpl. Steele sitting up in bed beaming as she entered.

"Hello Corporal. Sorry they had to keep you in overnight for observation, but the good news is that after they change your dressing one more time, they'll discharge you!"

"That's a relief. So tell me Ma'am, what brings you in here?"

"Just wanted to make sure that you were okay, even the 'Ice Maiden' has feelings you know!" she said watching him carefully.

"Yes, well, I'm really sorry about that. Fact is I just wasn't aware of what went down, um, or aware of what they called you, if you'll forgive me Ma'am?"

"That's not your fault Corporal, but tell me, do all the men have "pet names" for their officers then, like with me?" she smiled.

"Oh they have a couple of standards they normally just use on everyone, but yes, some do get special ones Ma'am. But I was thinking as I lay here last night, yours must be more for your stare than anything else, no offence intended."

"None taken, but yes I think you're right. So now tell me, do you find me snooty or whatever Corporal, I mean we're about the same age, correct? So if you met me for the first time out on the street, do you think you would like me?"

She saw that the comment really threw him. She liked his composure though, for he never panicked like some might have done.

"That's a tough question to ask me Ma'am, seeing as I don't even know you."

"Give it a go," she urged him on, not quite knowing why.

"Well, I can assure you of one thing . . . "

"What's that then Corporal?"

"Are we still talking off the record Ma'am?" he smiled hesitatingly.

"Yes."

"Good! Then I'd have to admit to one thing and that is you're incredibly attractive!" Smiling proudly to himself, he thought that sounded a heck of a lot better than if he had come out and said, *Well, I wouldn't kick you out of bed for eating crisps!*

So, pleasantly shocked and a little giddy from the suddenness of his compliment, Lt. Crenshaw threw back, "That's quite a compliment for a any girl, especially dressed in this uniform!"

The informality then began, as the two of them laughed and chatted casually and comfortably together for awhile, soon forgetting all about time, their rank, or positions, to which they only returned to the present on the arrival of the nurse. After the nurse finally exited the room, Lt. Crenshaw said, "Well Corporal, I doubt very much that our paths will ever cross again, so, it's been awfully nice meeting you, under the circumstances. I hope from here on in it's less trouble for you. Best of luck to you!"

"Yes Ma'am thank you. Best of luck to you too!"

. . . The story, as you might have guessed, does not end here though, in fact it's just the very beginning! In the days and weeks and even months that followed, both Lt. Jane Crenshaw and Cpl. Ben Steele secretly searched for that elusive sight or glimpse of each other, constantly alert and looking out for opportunities to meet, if only by accident. But as fate would have it, they failed to connect so soon. Lt. Crenshaw remained attached with the Airborne Brigade but, unknown to her, Cpl. Steele was soon promoted to the rank of Sgt. and after completing the most gruelling physical selection course anywhere in the world, was accepted into the 22 Special Air Service Regiment (22 SAS) based in Hereford.

Then the Gulf War came and went. They did their duties to the best of their abilities, but always the two of them, quiet confident loners. Until one day, fate decided, in her strange roundabout-way, to cross their paths and bring them together yet again. So it would be far better to begin this story where it all really started, back there on that hot British summer day . . .

PART 1

He had just been bluntly informed by his Commanding Officer of D Squadron, 22 SAS Regiment, that due to his poor re-hab record and long convalescence at the military hospital after his recent "covert operation," or "black Ops" as they were being called nowadays, that he was being "spelled off" for awhile! He was being given the cushy task of EP detail on the VIP squad for the security of some Staff General out of the War Office. The general, he was told, was heavily involved with sensitive command structure intelligence for NATO and ARRC (Allied Command, European Rapid Reaction Corps) whose regular HQ was in Sarejevo but whose special current tasking and involvement had him working this end of things in England right now.

Not often impressed, he found he liked the profile for this job he was being assigned and was actually looking forward to the change. He put his things in order and went about the business of collecting his papers and personal documents and then departed from the Regiment with little or no further fuss. He took a cab from Stirling Barracks in Hereford to the train station and caught an early morning return commuter to the Aldershot District, heading for a town called Basingstoke.

Upon his arrival in Basingstoke, he had missed the bus connection to his final destination and was also informed by the station-master that there were no taxis running either. Thus, he returned to the ticket booth where they told him the next bus would not arrive or depart for at least another hour. He decided to leave his luggage there at the Basingstoke train station, opting to walk the approximate twelve miles to his new posting. *Besides,* he thought, *nothing like a brisk walk in the English countryside!*

In just under two hours he had arrived at his destination, hardly having broken a sweat. Just off the road there was a large black ornate gate that was swung open and secured to the right of the roadway, as an ornate sign was saying that this was indeed #7 Coach-house Mews.

Standing there in the fresh summer air for awhile, he leant on the gate and just stared up the path at what he could make out beyond to be this large and impressive red bricked building. It was a large Victorian mansion perched on an angle facing north and located at the top end of the gradually climbing gravelly driveway he was standing at below. The driveway was lined on the right side with large oak trees that you just knew in winter would shed their leaves to make a colourful burnt orange and golden brown matte. Running parallel to this bumpy stony road was a typically British rock wall with a rockery garden of perfumed flowers that sat atop and also wound its way along. It was a most pleasant and delightful sight and aroma, perfect for such a bright sunny day.

He walked up the roadway and at the top in the "natural" courtyard area in front of the mansion house there was another large gravelly area which was obviously used as a parking lot. Rather than approach the front entrance, he instinctively followed the line of the house to the rear, looking for a staff entrance.

To his left he spotted an open doorway while opposite this was a fenced horse paddock. Beyond the paddock was an opening in the treed and hedge growth, where three young men were leaning against a small green sports car, laughing and pointing at something in a field beyond. For just a brief moment, the young men all glimpsed over in the direction of the house at his arrival, then moments later, looked again.

After their stare, of which he was more than casually aware, each of them then looked away seemingly content as they continued with their light banter and laughter and going about their own pursuits. He himself returned his focus to the doorway where happy voices of children and that of an older woman could be heard. Making his way toward the voices as they grew in volume, he caught the distinct smell of cinnamon and baking apple pies. Entering the doorway, he surprised them all as their thoughts and actions were obviously preoccupied elsewhere.

"Hello there!" he said in his rich tenor voice.

"Oh my gosh, but you clear near scared me and the tiny ones here to death," a laughing and vibrant lady with a Cockney accent replied through squeals of surprise. "What can I do for you young man?" she enquired with a smile.

"Sorry to bother you Ma'am, but I'm looking for Sergeant Major Steele, is he here?"

"Over there by the assault course he is," she pointed. "There behind that gap, in front of those three idle young men."

Looking back at this happy and pleasant lady and the two smiling children, he said as politely as he could, "Thank you very kindly Ma'am, sorry to interrupt your baking!"

As he walked away from the doorway and the grey haired elderly lady, she in turn wiped her floured hands on her apron as she smiled and said to herself, "Now there's a handsome one."

"Hello there," he spoke on approaching the men still leaning and laughing around the sports car, "I'm looking for Sgt.Major Steele. Can any of you direct me?"

"New recruit are we then?" one of them enquired as his cohorts laughed.

Ignoring the remark as well as their laughter he repeated his question, adding, "I understand that Sgt.Major Steele is somewhere in the vicinity?"

One of the men stood up and asked, "Who's looking for him?"

"I am!" he replied, again ignoring the silent request for his particulars, which this time brought another guffaw of laughter from the other two. As this fellow looked at him all red faced and angry ready to reply, from the area of the gap in the hedge that he could see now led into some kind of field, approaching them was a young lady, with a very good figure and looks (at least on first glance) with dark brunette hair that seemed to be gathered in the back into a French braid of some sort.

Does she look familiar?

Accompanying her were two older men both wearing military uniforms. On closer inspection he saw that one had the insignia of Brigadier General on his epaulets whilst the other was wearing the familiar crown of Sgt.Major on a leather wrist strap which was proper identification when in summer short sleeve issue.

"Hello," said the General on arriving amongst them, "Who do we have here then chaps?"

"Don't know, Sir!" said the red faced man who had previously been ready to continue his questioning. "We did enquire though," he volunteered, looking right at this new arrival, adding, "only he seems reluctant to co-operate with us!" He now leaned back, feeling proud of himself for seemingly putting this person on the spot.

Looking at Ben closely, the Sgt.Major was the first to speak.

"What's your name then son?" he asked in his best authoritative army voice that carried traces of his own Cockney accent.

An instant before Ben replied, the corners of his own eyes seemed to crinkle just a little as a smile seemed to spread across his face raising the corners of his moustache ever so slightly and running back up to his clear hazel eyes. Then, with a smile on his face he spoke. "My name is Steele, Sgt.Major—Corporal Ben Steele."

At the mention of his name, the countenance of the two older men, the General and Sgt.Major, changed remarkably. Again the Sgt.Major was the first to speak. With a malicious grin as though he sensed the tension that was beginning to develop between the original group of young men and the new arrival before he got there, as much as he would like to have seen it play out, he looked at Cpl. Steele saying, "If you'll just follow the General and myself into the house, we'll get you sorted."

Ben gave the brunette one more quick glance, liking what he saw, and turned and followed the General and the Sgt.Major into the house.

Lt. Jane Crenshaw was not quite yet aware that she was staring at Cpl. Steele as he left with her father and the Sgt.Major, until one of the group laughingly chided, "Jane, didn't anyone tell you it's rude to stare?"

She ignored the remark and found it gave her a sudden rush when she realized that she knew this Corporal. Her heart pounding, she hid her excitement and turned and joined in the laughter of her guests, but caught the snideness in the tone of voice of one of them when he said, "Yes, especially when it's the hired help!"

"What's that supposed to mean then, Jeremy?" asked Jane.

"Oh never mind poor old Jeremy, he's just miffed that the Corporal, whoever he is, just seemed to start to get the better of him, right Jeremy old boy?"

Above their laughter, Capt. Jeremy Smythe stated, "I don't particularly care for a smart mouth, especially in the hired help."

"Jeremy, there's that awful term again. Really, you're such a snob these days."

Looking directly at her now, Capt. Smythe spoke. "Jane, we're having a cocktail party over at our Officers Mess this weekend, can we expect to see you there?"

"Is my father invited?" she teased.

They all climbed into the small sports car that belonged to Jeremy as Jane replied to all their pleading and laughter, "We'll see. I may remain at home and try to improve my stamina by training on the assault course here a little more."

One of the other men called David spoke up this time. "Jane, you really are serious in your bid to join the ranks of the Army Airborne then, aren't you?"

"Of course I am David. I always was, only you three jokers never took me serious until today!"

As the car was started and then reversed in an arc, it drove at about a speed of no more than five miles per hour until it reached the gravel area in front of the house. Shouting their farewells from the car to a waving Jane, they sped off then with gravel spitting up from the rear tires. They veered to the left and disappeared down the driveway. As Jane heard them roar away from the property, she walked slowly over to the house.

Ben followed the two older and higher ranking soldiers into the Mansion House through the kitchen doorway he had visited earlier. He found the elderly lady and the children were still there, but watching as he entered. Looking directly at him, the elderly lady said with a smile, "I see that you found 'im then?"

Returning her pleasant smile he said, "Well sort of!"

"Not even close," interjected the Sgt.Major, looking at Cpl. Steele to add, "We found him first!"

Ben shrugged his shoulders at the woman as she looked on with her friendly smile which also brought a chuckle from the children.

"If you'll just be kind enough to follow me, Corporal!" said the General as he walked on through the adjoining doorway.

As the General left the room with the Corporal following, Jane entered the kitchen, throwing her sweaty sweatshirt at her younger brother and sister as she did so. Amid their outraged but friendly squeals, Jane could not hold back, and asked the Sgt.Major and his wife, the cook, "Why is that soldier here?"

Looking serious the Sgt.Major said, "New staff!"

"Oh cut that out Sgt.Major," she said smiling, "Really, who is he? Some relation of yours you never told us about?"

Looking fondly at this beautiful young lady whom he had known all her life and whom he cared for as though she were his own daughter, the Sgt.Major said, "The name's a coincidence. As it happens, he's the new bodyguard and driver your father requested from the Ministry!"

This seemed to make them perk up and garner everyone's attention. They seemed to ask their questions all at the same time. To tease them a little further and to feed their curiosity, the Sgt.Major said, "Actually, on the other hand, he could just be the new gardener Mrs. Crenshaw requested too!"

Amid howls of, "Oh come on, please?" and the inquisitive smiles of Mrs. Steele, whom he knew would get the information out of him one way or the other, he continued for one last try, "Actually, he's just the Regimental Courier delivering some papers to your father!"

"Yeah, then how come he's dressed in civilian clothes?" young Tom queried.

Before he could continue his teasing, Mrs. Steele gave the Sgt.Major one of those serious glances, while Jane playfully poked him in the ribs.

"Okay, well just keep what I originally said under your hat until your father speaks to you all!"

Sgt.Major Steele then left the room himself, heading in the same direction the General and Corporal had just taken.

When Ben followed the general, he noticed the right hand side of the hallway was a thick oak panelling that carried the heavy scent of lemon wax. Each walled panel framed large portraits that were of historic battle scenes. The left side opened up onto an antique dining room with a large table set for ten and dressed with silver plates and candelabra.

A wall separated the hall foyer that held a traditional coat rack and cane stand with a Grandfather clock commanding vigil in its place near the front entrance. The other side of the hall foyer led down into a sunken living room with bay window. The room was large, at least 30' x 80', and round a fireplace closer set to the bay window was a seating arrangement of comfortable-looking couches. He did not know what was beyond the living room wall to the opposite end but could only guess there were more rooms. Directly opposite the main entrance was an open staircase that led up to the second floor bedrooms. Just next to this stairway was an office door that the General opened and led the way into, pausing to say, "If you'll just follow me into the study here, Corporal."

Once inside the room, Ben looked around and liked what he saw. Bookcases lined one of the walls while a leather couch and armchair with a small table hugged another wall that had another painting of battle scenes above the fireplace. In the centre of the room directly behind a window that appeared to leave the room well-lit with enough natural light, was a large oak desk. On the walls behind the desk and to the side of the windows were plaques of the different regiments and units that he assumed held a close and sentimental attachment for the General.

The desk itself was tidy and uncluttered as though someone cleaned it as the General would not expect a less-than-tidy workspace as he would be so used to. As the General took his familiar position behind the desk, he invited Cpl. Steele to hand him over his package which contained his files and to take a seat. As he sat there in silence while the General read quietly to himself, Ben took stock of his surrounds. The study was covered in books as he first observed, yet he needed no further looks to know here was also a first class intellect that was well read indeed. He tried picking out some of the titles but could barely make them out, instead being pleasantly distracted by their ornate and colourful bindings. As he waited, he saw the General's bemused look of recognition that his library had impressed this soldier.

There was a knock at the door then and the Sgt.Major popped his head into the doorway to say, "Mind if I join you?"

"Of course not," said Gen. Crenshaw. "Saves me having to repeat myself."

"What I figured, Sir."

After a few minutes' reading, Gen. Crenshaw handed the file over to the Sgt.Major who had pulled a chair up to the side of his desk. When the Sgt.Major nodded to the General that he had finished reading the file also, the General spoke.

"Pretty impressive record, Corporal."

"Thank you Sir," he proudly responded.

"Tell me, Corporal, how old were you exactly when you went to Northern Ireland for the first time?"

"I was seventeen—but turned eighteen there, Sir!"

"And you won the military medal there, is that right?"

"Yessir."

"And you picked up the Queen's Commendation in the Gulf war just over seven years ago, is that right also?"

"Yessir."

"And you have been 'out of country' on a number of assignments since, with your present unit I see."

"Yes, I have Sir."

"You're a highly decorated soldier—for a British soldier, Corporal Steele," said the Sgt. Major, adding, "How many years have you been in the 22 Special Air Service Regiment?"

"Well Sir, I was inducted into Sabre Squadron just over eight years ago now Sir, right after I made it to Sergeant in the regulars!"

"In very short time too, so I see," mused the General.

"Yes Sir, it was considered quick."

"I see. So how come you have dropped back in rank though to Corporal since, were you punished or reprimanded in some way?"

"Well sir, when you enter the Regiment, 22 SAS, you automatically revert to the rank of trooper and have to earn it back. I guess for one reason or another I have been slow in picking my previous rank back up again!"

"Of course, I should have known. Well, your records also say here that you were due for promotion a few times but declined to take it. Would you care to elaborate on that for us?"

"Well sir it's the same old story, having far too much fun out there in the field to be brought back into barracks and shoved behind some counter I guess!"

Looking knowingly at the Sgt.Major the General then turned back to Cpl. Steele and asked, "How do you feel about this assignment then?"

"Actually Sir, I was kind of looking forward to it for a change of pace, if you know what I mean?"

"It says here in your files that you have been slow to re-hab regarding your wounds received "in theatre" somewhere. Is Bosnia a good guess?"

"Pretty good," smiled Ben, "But you'd be wrong!"

After a few chuckles, the Sgt.Major Spoke, "How are they healing?"

"Well Sir, I can function as well as anyone else in the Regiment on short or immediate action, but ever since my leg wounds they don't seem to think I have the stamina or the strength for the really long range stuff anymore."

"I see."

"Tell me Corporal, it says here on your record that you're an ex Bisley champion and small arms expert — are those skills still current?"

"Yessir."

"Says that you also spent a fair amount of time on the anti-terrorist squad and even helped train members of the German GSG9 on VIP/EP security, having also served time with the Embassy courier detail and that you're an expert in the martial arts."

"Yessir."

"Phew, that's a lot, did we miss some skills or is there anything you're *not* good at?" he joked.

"Making coffee?" was his quick answer.

"Guess I walked into that one," laughed the general, joined by the Sgt.Major.

"So, did the Regiment give you any details of the position or duties you are expected to assume here for us?" inquired the General.

"Only the basic stuff, Sir. I'm the bodyguard/driver. In my executive protection role I am also expected to be vigilant for the entire family, assist the Sgt.Major here with other staff duties and be your personal guard to and from any staff meetings etc. and be flexible and versatile—did I miss anything General, without going into specifics?"

"No, that about covers it mostly, except the fact that the position is a promotion for you to the rank of sergeant!"

"I was waiting for you to say that part yourself, Sir," smiled the newly promoted Sergeant Steele.

"Well, other than the title, it will not have a lot of bearing on the position very much at all, as it will be kept very low key with you mostly wearing civilian dress."

"If there is occasion for you to wear your uniform, Sergeant," said a smiling Sgt.Major, "We may as well have you correctly dressed, so just hand the spare uniform you were told to bring over to Mrs. Steele and she'll have those stripes sewn on perfect for you by morning."

"Talking of Mrs. Steele," said the Sgt.Major, "She has readied your room for you, which is just off the stairs by the kitchen and down the hall from our own quarters."

As if to answer the new Sgt.'s question, the General said, "The Sgt.Major has been with me since we fought together in Borneo. He has been my right hand man ever since. He came to serve in my household before my children were even born, and yes, besides being the best cook there is, Mrs. Steele is also our housekeeper!"

As if that explained everything and put it all into place, General Crenshaw went on, "Well, welcome to our little family Cor.. Sergeant Steele," the General corrected himself, adding an aside, "I hope you like children Sergeant, as my little lot will definitely keep you busy and even sometimes have a habit of getting in your way. As for running errands, the Sgt.Major's wife, Mrs. Steele, and especially Mrs. Crenshaw, will not only keep you busy but will use you as much as they can. Trust me, it's a difficult assignment," he laughed.

"Sir, you will find that not only do I like children, but I have a habit of making myself a pretty useful errand boy also!"

"Well that's settled then, Sergeant," smiled General Crenshaw.

"By the way, other than the Sgt.Major here and myself, I will just be telling the rest of the family and anyone else who enquires for that matter, that you came here from your parent company of the Parachute Regiment, as per standing orders for the 22 Special Air Service, keeping their duties and assignments as secretive as possible!"

"Yessir."

The standing orders that all personnel from 22 Special Air Service Regiment, whether on active duty or detached, keep their activity silent and secretive has been in effect since their inception. So to now state that it would be so, was only a formality by the General.

"Well Sergeant," he said reaching across his desk to shake hands, "Welcome!"

Just as the Sgt Major and the new Sgt. were rising to their feet, the General leaned back away from his desk to say, "One last thing Sergeant, where is your luggage and stuff, you didn't come empty-handed did you?"

"No Sir."

"So your stuff, where did you leave it then?"

"The buses were running quite late and seeing that it was such a nice day, I thought I would take a walk here, so I left my gear in the bus station in the left-luggage security lockers!"

Startled, he said, "But that has to be a good twelve miles away at least!"

"That's what I estimated as well," smiled Ben.

As they all walked out of the General's office with the General shaking his head at the Sgt's long walk, the Sgt.Major spoke.

"Well what say we head back into the kitchen and see if there's any of that apple pie left?"

Ben had been sat there at the large kitchen table for some time now talking and eating his apple pie, as he found himself surrounded by the entire Crenshaw family, minus Mrs. Crenshaw who was in London visiting. Mrs. Steele plus the Sgt.Major and himself were holding the conversation.

"So how long have you served in The Parachute Regiment, Cpl. Steele?"

"Twelve years Ma'am."

"I hear they are going into this 'new' Air-Assault Brigade formation for the future?" she said, looking over at Jane Crenshaw, a look he didn't miss.

"Which Battalion were you in then?"

"2 Para."

Before anyone could ask the next question for the sudden confusion was on a few faces, the Sgt.Major spoke up to explain, "It is second nature with the men of The Parachute Regiment to call each of the different Battalions in their Regiment simply by its number and 'Para' am I right Sergeant Steele?" he said, his crinkled eyes showing his humour.

"Yes, you have it right of course."

"I thought you were a Corporal?" young Tom chirped in.

"I was!" smiled back Ben, "But your father just promoted me!"

"Hooray!" cheered the children to everyone's laughter.

"Yet you speak and sound like you have an American accent," said Mrs Steele.

"Yes, where are you actually from then Sergeant?" asked the Sgt.Major.

"Born and made in Canada, Sir, at least my tattoo says so, but my father immigrated from here in England before I was born. That was enough to give me a dual Canadian/British citizenship birthright, so I could come back and, well, here I am!"

"So how old were you when you initially came here to England from Canada?"

"Just sixteen."

"That makes you how old now?" asked young Amy looking at all of her fingers to everyone's laughter.

"Twenty-eight and holding."

The two children, Tom who was twelve and Amy who was eight, seemed to be pleased that they had a guest eating in their kitchen as they sat with hands propping up their chins, just staring at him, enthralled. He didn't let the stares bother him as he periodically raised his eyebrows and twitched his ears in between bites to their giggles of amusement. Refusing a third slice of pie from Mrs. Steele, Ben said to no one in particular that he should be getting back to the bus depot to reclaim his belongings.

"You may as well take the jeep from the rear garage, it'll be quicker for you," said the Sgt.Major, stating the obvious.

Leaning against the kitchen counter observing all the preceding, Jane spoke up for the first time since the Sgt. first sat down at the table.

"If you like, I could come along with you, strictly to show you the way?"

Ben raised his eyebrows in his quizzical look and smiled as he looked up at her finally for the first time. There were also some muffled giggles from the children with instant smiles and not too subtle and furtive glances of surprise which passed between the others seated there at the table. Realizing this while involuntarily blushing, although looking directly at her father, with her hands on her hips Jane stated, "Well someone has to show him the route, how else is he going to find his way into town?"

Rising from the table to leave, her father smiled and casually threw at her, "Funny, but I thought he did a remarkable job of finding his way here to begin with!"

Before anything else could be said on the matter the children said, "Daddy, we've finished here with aunt May so can we go along with the Sergeant too?"

The General grinned looking at the Sgt. as though to say, "Well, you see what you can look forward to?"

Ben himself spoke first though, "That's perfectly okay by me, as long as we can fit everyone safely into the vehicle, including seat belts!"

Jane rightly suspected that her father somehow respected this Sgt. as a trusted and worthy soldier, and it astonished her! This *was* a big deal, as she knew exactly how demanding and discriminating her father was. It all just gave her an added excitement and attraction to the chemistry brewing that stirred and fuelled her desires. Jane Crenshaw was already hooked, all this Sgt. had to do was reel her in and she knew it. She was very much interested in him, the mystery angle etc., but didn't quite know why, she just knew she wanted to be close to him. So, to climb out of the hole she had seemingly begun to dig herself into, and to cover her initial eagerness, Jane added, "Of course they can come along, plenty of room!"

Receiving a nod of approval from the General, Ben said loudly, "Okay then, let's all get our shoes on and be on our way!"

Looking at Mrs. Steele he said sincerely, "Thanks again for the pie Ma'am!"

"You can call me May, or aunt May, whichever suits you!" she said beaming.

"Okay, aunt May it is," he agreed, looking at the children as he winked at them, then looking at the Sgt.Major for his approval of this familiarity with his wife. As he received a warm and welcome nod of approval back, he asked, "The only question then is where are the keys?"

While they were driving down the road into Basingstoke proper, Jane looked at Ben sitting next to her, in fact she had been stealing illicit glances ever since she first saw him. Her memory told her that standing, he stood about 6'1" while she could easily tell he was of muscular build with a slim waistline. He was dark tanned in complexion and his face and skin reminded her as though he had just returned from a sunny locale. *Had he? Is this the mystery angle?*
He had hazel eyes and dark brown hair that looked black and being cropped on the short side, it still appeared as though it couldn't decide whether to be curly or wavy or remain straight. His moustache suited him and it was neatly trimmed to the ends, giving him a friendly appearance. He was dressed in dark blue summer cotton slacks, a maroon golf shirt which had the Airborne Pegasus/Bellerophon crest embroidered on it, which fitted snugly. Finally, he was wearing dark brown fringe loafers.

Her visual "stock inventory" over, she saw no wedding band on his fingers as his hands gripped the steering wheel as they drove along, to which she cursed herself for looking there the instant she did so, for she hoped her interest wasn't that obvious. Suddenly, Jane could contain it no longer and said while looking at him as he drove, "You don't remember me at all, Sergeant?"

Laughing now, he replied, "Of course. I'm sorry, you're the Ice Maiden!"

Taken aback but more than pleased he remembered, Jane replied, "That's not quite how I was expecting to be remembered after all this time!"

"I'm sorry Ma'am, I didn't mean it that way, in fact I have a rather nice opinion of you. I thought it was nice of you to visit me in the hospital I mean," he blurted, trying not to be obvious and hide his feelings. *Heaven help me if she only knew how seriously I looked for her after that*, he thought to himself.

Looking at him once again she said kindly with her disarming smile, "No offence taken then Sergeant!"

"Thank you for that Ma'am, because none was meant."

"So, to change the subject somewhat, if I understand correctly then, you'll be our personal chauffeur when my father doesn't require your services, taking these obnoxious children here to school and back?"

Fending off the feigned slaps and swats from them she laughingly added, "And you're to also run errands into town for everyone and occasionally even give me a lift?"

"Yes Ma'am!" was his smiling polite answer.

Somehow, even though she was twenty-eight and a female officer with the rank of Lieutenant in the Army Intelligence Corps, Jane never really came to accept this Ma'am title so comfortably as her peers.

"If memory serves me well, we're nearly there," he exclaimed.

"Looks like you didn't need us after all Sergeant."

"Are you kidding?" he said, looking at the uncertain faces of the children. "You really don't think I could handle all this baggage on my own do you?"

"You mean we get to carry your bags?" asked Tom.

"All the way to the jeep."

"What do I get to do?" asked Amy.

"Well, you get the most important job of all!"

"What's that?" she squealed excitedly.

"Well, do you think you could carry my guitar?"

"A guitar?" she said, out of awed breath.

Looking at each other, Jane and Ben began laughing.

Jane made the statement, "I think someone is going to be expecting someone to sing or serenade them from now on, I wonder who that someone could be?"

"Over here, let's just get my gear first okay?" he laughed.

With the Sgt.'s bags and guitar in the jeep and a few grocery items picked up for aunt May, they headed back to Coach-house Mews, but not without singing some songs for the General's two younger children. When the songs died out, Ben asked of Jane, "If you don't mind my asking, Ma'am, what exactly were you doing out there in that field you came from earlier today? Were you riding your horse?"

"No, I don't mind telling you. There's an assault course back there, of sorts anyway. It came with the property."

She felt obliged for some reason to add, "Anyway, I was practicing for my own upcoming parachute course at P Company, looking to get my wings and then transfer over to the section of my Corps officially assigned to The Parachute Regiment!"

"That's quite a task for a lady, no insult intended, but I never knew they accepted women in the British Airborne."

"They don't!" she smiled, "But unlike in that other country of yours, Canada, women here are not allowed to have a line Infantry combat role, but they *have* allowed us to apply for certain qualifications that in the past were off limits to us. Anyway, I'm in the Intelligence Corps, remember. I'm not after joining The Parachute Regiment proper, just after my wings."

"So how many women have actually qualified for their Airborne wings then?"

"To date, I do believe there has to be about a dozen," then quickly added as if inspired, "You're a Para yourself aren't you?" she half asked, half stated.

"Yes Ma'am," he beamed.

"So how hard *is* P Company? No, don't answer that silly question, just tell me if you have ever been an instructor, as I could sorta use some help?"

He glanced her way and just seemed to be looking at her, sizing her up, as she got the goosebumps and went on hurriedly, "Then seeing as you're going to be our new bodyguard and we're going to be seeing a lot of each other when I'm home, maybe you might be able to take a little time out to train with me occasionally, show me what it takes, that sort of thing?"

"What about your three friends I met today?"

"You mean Jeremy, the one who questioned you don't you?"

"I surely do Ma'am. I have no reason to make enemies or anger any of them, I mean, I don't particularly want to make your suitors jealous or have reason to start trouble for me here, Ma'am."

"They're just friends Sergeant, I promise I won't let Jeremy scare you or bully you again, okay?"

Having observed the Sgt.'s demeanour and quiet confidence he seemed to portray all day, Jane never for a moment believed her statement about the Sgt. letting himself be bullied, but added it more out of mischief than anything else. Not letting the remark ruffle him, the Sgt. said simply, "It would be a pleasure to help train with you Ma'am," adding himself mischievously, "and thanks for the offer of close protection for me against your friend."

They then looked at each other and laughed heartily.

"That's that settled then!" she just said matter of factly.

Later that evening, just before dinner, the Sgt. was introduced for the very first time to Mrs. Crenshaw, who had just returned from her trip to London.

"I understand that you're our new driver now, Sergeant Steele?"

"Yes I am Ma'am."

"I also understand that you have made an immediate impression on my family?"

"As long as it's a good one I hope Ma'am!"

"Yes, I believe it is," then added, "After dinner, maybe we can chat and I can get to know you better? I do so like to know our staff."

"Not a problem Ma'am."

"Well then, I'll talk to you later."

Later that evening while the Crenshaw family ate in the dining room, the Sgt. ate his meal in the kitchen with the Sgt.Major and his good lady, while the maid and other household members were sent to their respective barracks nearby. Their duties being complete for the day, the Sgt.Major and his wife and the Sgt. it seemed, were the only members of the household staff who slept and ate on the premises.

"She's really a very nice lady once you get to know her," said aunt May.

"Yes, don't be nervous or anything about talking with her, okay?"

"Okay."

"Good, then let's enjoy this lovely meal."

Later, as that evening came around and after meeting and talking with Mrs. Crenshaw, Sgt. Steele was asked to come to the General's study with the Sgt.Major.

"Thank you for coming, Sergeant. I was hoping that we might be able to get you to tell the Sgt.Major and I about your Gulf War experiences, old nosey soldiers that we are."

Thinking on it for just a short moment, Ben replied grinning, "Only if you assure me that what is said remains in this room, Sirs."

Laughing uproariously, the General added, "I thought I'd ask, but would you mind awfully if I let my daughter Jane in on this? She is in the military, too, as you know."

Ben said uncomfortably, "So I've been informed, Sir. But I'd hate for her to consider me a braggart or anything like that."

"Of course she wouldn't boy, would she Sgt.Major?"

"Well, it could be embarrassing for him, nevertheless, Sir..?"

"Yes, I see what you mean. Well okay, let's get on with it then," urged the General, not wanting to miss out and eager to hear first-hand accounts of war.

"Where would you like me to start, Sir?"

"I was wondering, before you go and tell us all about your first deployment or engagement, how about you tell us what you know of those damned Scud Missiles we heard so much about?"

Ben walked over and took the offered comfy seat on the couch by the fireplace. He tried to relax and search his memory for the knowledge of those Scuds he knew were in there. It seemed so very long ago, but he started to talk, repeating what he was told prior to his deployment out to Saudi Arabia.

" . . . The use of rocket-propelled ballistic missiles in the Gulf War by the Iraqis is a very serious threat. It's not an original idea though, using ballistic missiles. In fact, during World War II, the Germans used the world's first ballistic missile known as the V2 bombs. Then after the war, the United States and the USSR began development to improve and perfect short and long range ballistic missiles.

"At the time, both the super powers developed their own capability for strategic ballistic missiles that would take hydrogen bombs even over longer distances of thousands of miles, to be able to deliver these pay loads with incredible accuracy. As you know, these strategic missiles could only be built on a large scale for fuel and they were very intricate and complex in design, so much so, that only the major super powers in the world had the capability to produce them. Because of costs and size and design problems, most countries then successfully adapted their own technologies to build smaller rockets and shorter range versions of their bigger brothers, with the idea to use them as tactical battlefield weapons. These smaller ballistic missiles could also be adapted, and were, with the capability to deliver not just conventional high explosives, but nuclear warheads.

"The USSR were the first to develop their own series of biological and chemical warheads for not only long range ballistic missiles, but also these short range battlefield versions. That's what we have been doing ever since the Cold War— building up our arsenals of nuclear capable payload missiles! Then, after arming Iraq to combat the Ayatolla in Iran, it suddenly came about that in the early 90s, Iraq was well equipped with its own tactical ballistic missiles to wreak havoc! Which under Saddam, the forces in Saudi Arabia and elsewhere could be attacked with. Saddam had amassed hundreds of them. His favourite missiles were the Scud B and they were acquired successfully over the years from the USSR."

"How big were these missiles then, Sergeant?"

"They were approximately thirty-seven feet long by three feet in diameter, weighing close to 14,000 pounds at lift off, all powered by liquid propellent rocket engines."

"Wow, do they train you lot to memorize these sorts of things Sergeant?"

"Comes natural, Sir. I was always good at math."

"Really, well carry on."

"Well, the rocket propellents are just liquids at normal temperatures and can even be stored in canisters like gasoline. The Scuds though, are transported ready for firing on a large eight wheeled truck called a MAZ-543. All the 'spares' are then towed behind on an articulated trailer. This Scud B missile also carries an 1100 pound warhead."

"What range do they have then?"

"I was just getting to that Sir. They have a maximum range of 185 miles. But without a nuclear warhead, the Scud's could and were, only be used against large targets such as airfields, cities, large supply dumps, all those sorts of targets."

"That's pretty effective, but NATO thought different didn't they?"

"Yes, indeed they did Sir. In the NATO context of things, they all made the tactical error of deeming them not to be very effective at all. But back whenever, the political and military leaders of Iraq thought that they still were, at least Saddam did! Let me say this here and now too Sir, as it was clearly pointed out to us— It was and still is, a very real mistake to think of the Muslims or Arabs as a people incapable of any intelligent thinking or analysis, that theory is just all wrong! If they can take our Nuclear technology itself and adapt it, under such scrutiny, well need I say more?"

Thoroughly enjoying this military dialogue, the General eagerly added, "Of course not, point well made , but do go on Sergeant, don't stop!" he was really into this now.

"Well Sir, the biggest mistake the West made with the Iraqis which we all know, is the way in which they portrayed them in the media constantly. It was like they were nothing but stupid or ignorant fanatics. In fact the total opposite is true, they are extremely intelligent and very sophisticated and philosophical people in a lot of areas."

As Sgt. Steele paused to ponder on some more aspects of his experiences, the General spoke, "The world knows that in every war that Iraq has had with Israel, the Israeli Air Force quickly gained the air superiority. The Israelis could strike with seeming immunity, but the Scuds changed all this though, am I correct Sergeant?"

"Absolutely Sir! While the Iraqis had the weapon and the range to use it against Israeli airfields and cities, their missile launch sites could be attacked, but being highly mobile, they could also easily be hidden to make themselves difficult to locate. Actually, the Scud missiles that the Iraqis used in the Gulf War were a modified version of the USSR models. Clones right off their own production lines, called the AL-HUSAYN which had 400 pound warheads and a range of a few extra hundred miles too.

"These missiles and their devastating fire power could not be underestimated, as during the war between Iraq and Iran, on Feb. 29, 1968 both countries began missile attacks against each others' cities. This 'War of the Cities' as it was called, lasted over fifty days. Over 500 missiles, 200 of them these AL-HUSAYNS, were fired directly at Tehran and accurately too, for most reached their targets. This strategy as well as accuracy and reliability worked, for the Iranians showed they had no stomach or worse, any defense at all against this massive and concentrated missile attack. Heavily outnumbered, Iraq's ballistic missiles won them the war in the end despite that, all due to its Scuds. Taking all those factors into account very seriously, the obvious move to all of us troops in the Gulf War was one of 'search and destroy', for we had very little knowledge about them still and needed to either gather it quick or find some way to eliminate their use."

"So we can assume that the Scuds were your first mission?"

"Yessir, they were indeed Sir!"

"Then come on," smiled an urging General, "tell us all more about it."

Ben pondered here awhile, searching deep in his memory again of where to start, then his thoughts and mind went back to that very first briefing.

. . . "Gentlemen," continued the briefing Officer, a Major Montague, who was standing next to the seated Brigadier Davies.

"As you all know and realize, the importance of neutralizing these scud missiles is imperative! As of midnight tonight, our entire command of units will be tasked to search and destroy these missiles and their transports with every means available to us. Some teams will be international. We've all visited and trained each other's personnel, so now let's see if we have the ability to work together, shall we?

"We recalled all you long range scouts, observers and FOOs," then in afterthought added, "and you American roving patrollers on your dunebuggies," amid howls of laughter adding, "a toy which everyone now wants! But we recalled you men in particular in an effort to have you seek out and destroy the EL-TARIQ radar station viaduct."

Amid the hushed silence he continued. "If we could get our hands on one of those Scud Missiles and even one or two field officers from Saddam's Red Guard on your return run, we would be most appreciative." Closing out the speech, the Brigadier himself stood and said, "Best of luck chaps." As he raised his back straight, cinched his belt and with swagger cane tucked firmly under his arm, marched stiffly out of the hangar with his entourage . . .

"Nothing like being direct. That's some request they made. So who led the patrol you were on Sergeant?" asked the Sgt.Major.

"Well Sir, our combined patrol consisted of six four-man battle squads formed into a section, led by an American Captain and his 2IC being an American Top Sergeant."

"Kind of unusual for British Operations, no?" queried the General, seemingly surprised for the very first time.

"Not in that theatre of operations Sir. International relations and co-operation and all that stuff."

"Utter nonsense!" said the General. "Should just leave the fighting to our own lads, we'll soon sort them out, heh Sgt.Major?"

"Yessir!" said the Sgt.Major, trying to suppress his tears of laughter.

So left to pondering his recollections once more, the Sgt. tried to imagine those early days of Gulf War combat and to continue on with his train of thought.

. . . "For crissakes Jonesy, you know better, keep the volume down will yah?"

"I can't 'elp it Ben, it's me eyes, all this fuckin' sand and shit blowin' in 'em all the time!"

"Then use that whatsit-called scarf round your neck to keep it off!"

"It's rat-shit if you ask me, can't figure out what blinkin use it is?"

"It's no matter Ben, blind as a bat he is anyway!" laughed another voice buried away in the murky darkness.

Then another voice spoke in, "Makes no matter, in fact it sort of proves a popular belief we Americans have always held about you Brits."

"What's that?" someone else asked.

"That you Brits are like the blind leading the fuckin' blind!" chuckled the voice of Sgt. Ridgeway, a big American Special Forces Sgt.

After more hushed laughter, someone else said, "Oh, I get it, an analogy!"

"OOH, big words over here!" someone else chuckled.

With no time delay another voice in the dark spoke, "It's sorta similar to what *we* British Forces also perceive your American Forces to be like too mate!" baited another.

"What's that?" said Sgt. Ridgeway, knowingly taking the bait.

"All fuckin' Chiefs and no fuckin' Indians!" as all the Brits laughed and said together.

Amid the hushed laughter the voice of Gunny Ridgeway said, "Goddam Limeys, I've heard of combined operations before, being Allies and all that shit, but jeez, couldn't I once just get the Frogs once?"

"Excusez moi, mon Capitaine?"

"Aye, does anyone know why the French carry a frog in each pocket?" laughed another voice. Amid even more laughter to the obvious combined answer of "I.D." the laconic and friendly big Sgt. Steve Ridgeway said to his Captain, "You did request this sorry lot didn't you Sir?"

Captain Ed Stacey felt he was too far away to give a reply, but he thought about that, his mind quickly recalling his own briefing three nights previous in Control Centre. Take six four-man squads in a combined Allied section out on an extended seven day recce joy-ride. Simple task really, penetrate as deep as possible behind enemy lines to observe, map and detail enemy troop placement and movement, gathering as much information as possible transmitting back everything through their satellite link-ups by splurging their encoded signal in the usual short splurges, not forgetting the task of taking out EL-TARIQ viaduct and looking for a Scud Missile launcher to just "bring back" with a few prisoners for fun. Hell, this mission was a regular walk in the park. I think not!

Being playfully jostled by one of the men, Sgt. Ridgeway "nicked" his thumb on a sharp jagged edge of a can of his K-rations he was attempting to open. "Shit damn!" He cursed.

In mock accent one of the British troops said, "Heck Gunny, now's you can file for another gong to go with the ones for cutting yourself shaving and standing in line at chow!"

"Which only proves," added Gunny Ridgeway, "that besides being the richer nation, we honour and recognize our heros!"

"How you figure that then?" asked another Brit.

"Well, seeing as you guys mostly only give your medals or

gongs out to your officers, whilst the rest of you peasants get to pick straws, yeah, I can see why you'd all be jealous of me now!"

"Sez who?" came from another Brit.

"That's okay," continued Gunny Ridgeway in his mock aloof humour, "When you have your little parades and ceremonies after this campaign to collect your one single solitary lonely gong as you Brits call them, I'll be there waving from the stands with my chest full of medals. In fact, I may even have some spares if you ask nicely," he laughed.

"Eez more than right you know. Reminds me of me Bruvver and that stupid Jubilee Medal Fiasco back in the 70's . . . "

"Ow's that Ted?"

"Don't wind him up and get him going again, please?" muttered Ben.

"Didn't I tell anyone?" grinned Ted.

"Just tell the fuckin story Ted!" another voice said from out in the night.

"Well, me bruvver, a senior NCO in the Navy, had to do exactly what the Yank said; pick stupid straws for that medal with the junior NCOs and the ratings! Ain't that a fuckin waste for a good gong."

Quietly, Gunny Ridgeway asked, "Now that story can't be true Ted?"

"It's true Gunny!" some of the Brits said together.

"Why don't they just be fair and give it to everyone, especially the career men?"

"What, and deprive us the privilege of nights like this, bitching and taking the piss out of each other?"

When the laughter died down, Gunny Ridgeway moved along the gully aware his Captain had not responded to him earlier, so he settled in next to him. After a moment of silence he whispered, "I don't get it Sir, some of these Brits are the most disciplined and wild ass bastards I have ever stood and fought beside, yet as much as they are all seasoned and experienced veterans, they all seem to be low in rank and don't seem to have more than two medals between the bunch of them?"

"Politics Gunny, politics," said Captain Stacey. "What most don't know, is they were all mostly Corporals and Sergeants in their previous units before joining the SAS, which rank they lose on joining and therefore, have to earn it back if they're accepted, so at least that accounts for their ranks."

"And the medals?"

"Hell Gunny, how should I know? Cost maybe, budget restrictions."

Thinking of what Colonel Molinsky had told him he added, "Plus I guess as much as maybe they love to fight, maybe they don't like to advertise or make a big fuss over it."

"But what about that unfairness like that trooper just said?"

Agitated by Gunny's line of questions, Capt. Stacey said, "Hell Gunny a lot of what the Brits do is different to our ways, to each their own huh?"

Feeling a certain empathy for the British soldiers who were under his command on this operation, Captain Stacey changed the topic of conversation which was niggling him, by saying, "Hell Gunny, get these men back to reality quick, we're in the middle of a fuckin war here!"

Knowing immediately that the down time respite was finished, and aware that all the soldiers here were the elite professionals of the British and American Forces who had heard his Captain's orders also, Gunny Ridgeway knew before he even spoke that he would have complete compliance of his orders.

"Ben?"

"Yes Gunny?"

"Bring your men in to the centre here, just leave the outward sentries."

"Done!"

"We'll go over this just one more time, then I want your men to get in place ready for our attack, it's nearly zero hour." . . .

Of course, Sgt. Steele never repeated the preceding events word for word as the recollections came flooding back to him, but he did try to highlight the exciting points. Just before he actually went into the details of the battle itself the General said, "Sergeant, it's getting late, I'm sorry for taking up so much of your time, but how about you tell us all about the details of the battle on another evening?"

"I think I can do that no problem Sir."

"Yes, thank you Sergeant," said the Sgt.Major, adding, "If you want to follow me, I'll show you to your quarters if you haven't already had a chance to see them."

"Saw them earlier this afternoon Sir, thanks."

"Then we'll be off to bed, see you bright and early in the morning Sergeant. Have a trip scheduled already for the War Office in London. We'll take the Mercedes."

The following morning, the Sgt.Major gave the Sgt. his uniform, "Here, Mrs. Steele sewed them on early last night, but the General said just wear your everyday Army work dress and woolly pully, would you?"

"Sure, and tell Mrs. Steele I say thanks too Sir."

"No problem. Listen, Mrs. Steele was wondering if it would be okay for her to call you Ben, seems to be far too many Steeles around here, if you know what I mean?" He said smilingly wryly.

"Not a problem at all Sir, in fact I would prefer it."

"Good, that's settled then Ben, now let's get some breakfast before you're off."

The following few weeks just seemed to fly by with Ben being kept busy driving the General to and from his staff meetings around the country and at different barracks and watching over the General's children and running errands for Mrs. Crenshaw and aunt May — and getting familiar with the General's daughter.

A big factor in Ben's arrival at the Mews was that General Crenshaw had decided finally he wanted to put the Sgt.Major into semi-retirement. Advancing in years now, he could see the demands of the job were catching up and taking its toll of him. It was a tough decision for the General to make as they were close friends and companions after all the years spent serving together. For himself, Ben had just assumed correctly too, that the duties he was now doing were previously handled by the Sgt.Major.

Now replaced as such, the Sgt. Major rather liked his new found lesser pace of limited hours and duties. The change had not come as a surprise, but had been openly discussed and mutually agreed upon; a courtesy the General extended to him out of respect as he could easily have ruled it so and the Sgt. Major could not have disputed it, but that was the way the General was, a true gentleman. Not the idle kind of man either, he still kept himself busy at the Crenshaw household running the place as there were still other household staff to monitor, plus lots of little jobs and daily administration to keep himself occupied and out of his wife's hair. He barely asked for any assistance from Ben but when he did, he thoroughly enjoyed the company and the working relationship and level of respect he was receiving, so the Sgt.Major was quickly becoming like everyone else, quite attached and fond of Sgt. Ben Steele.

They had logged a lot of hours travelling these past weeks and on this particular night, Ben was driving the General back from yet another one of his late staff meetings. It was also one of those rare occasions when with just the two of them together in the car, the rules be dammed, the General insisted on sitting up front, too! It usually signalled to Ben when he did this, that the General also wanted a more informal and personal conversation. One of his insightful mind probes Ben insisted on calling them with the General being in Intelligence and such, much to the General's own pleasure and amusement. As the car sped into the night on its homeward journey, along a stretch of British Motorway called the A40, the General knew they would just cruise along at a set speed now for some time. So with little or no distraction as the roads were good tonight, he took this opportunity and started right in on the topic he wanted to explore.

"Tell me Ben, you being Canadian, have you spoken to your

relatives back home recently about this new trend nowadays of their government sending policemen into war zones for UN Duty, as another form of Peacekeeper?"

"Yes Sir, I have," stated Ben, who admittedly phoned family and friends in Vancouver on a not too frequent basis, but still enjoyed reading the local papers they sent him periodically.

"So tell me, how do feel about it then."

"Well, I like policemen Sir, my uncle is even one, but I don't agree with them being used as peacekeepers."

"Why's that then Ben?"

"Well Sir, call it different mind-sets, but I don't think they're any more suited for being soldiers or peacekeepers, anymore than soldiers are as police. They're too by the rules and methodical. Plus their way takes far too much time and energy in the negotiation process. Soldiers on the other hand like instant results. Using a blunt instrument to whack your enemy on the head to get their attention with in true 'ABI' fashion will work wonders in seconds too, so we've found!"

General Crenshaw laughed at this reference to the gifts of being a Para and their ability for using "ABI" improvisation.

"The peace movement may want that argument, not me," he grinned.

"Bring 'em on—as my uncle would say."

"This is your people I'm trying to figure out, you continue."

"Well I think they're making the switch partly because their troops' hands are tied every time they now go in and the tyrants do see this as a weakness, thus they take full advantage of the situation and act up even more."

"You think?"

"Of course! Just look at the record. Today's adversaries shoot the peacekeepers as openly as their chosen enemy, and everyone knows the UN and NATO doesn't condone fighting back!"

"Since peacekeepers are not supposed to shoot or fight back and because the public now also perceive them as policemen, not soldiers, is that it?"

"Exactly!"

"So, you're saying most Canadians feel there is no longer a need for soldiers to be peacekeepers anymore, the role should just be given to policemen and that's why they are now using them as such?"

"The public at large not entirely, those in power who call the shots, yes!"

"Interesting. Very interesting, go on please."

"Okay, well just look at Bosnia and Haiti Sir. I honestly believe this trend will continue to escalate until the role of the soldier-peacekeeper actually evolves into one of the policeman-peacekeeper."

"It does seem that way I admit, but these policemen, do you think they mind being used like this, as peacekeepers then?"

"Mind? No, not really. I'd bet even they get a little excited too at the prospect of some action. Add a sense of adventure and all that, plus a medal for their efforts, I think they'd probably enjoy going off to a place like Bosnia or Haiti for a little tour.

"So you think the public there in Canada prefers this option then?"

"I think they never gave it a second thought Sir. One day, it just sorta all changed. I believe the public think it's sort of a brave, noble and humanitarian thing to do anyway, so they don't really question the political ramifications. But you watch this closely now to see just how often 'when and where' these policemen are removed from their designated community policing roles, then used to replace your conventional soldier peacekeeper in the future."

"So overall, you don't agree with sending them off on these types of duty then."

"No Sir, I don't believe a policeman will ever replace a professionally-trained soldier, at least not out in the field or in a combat war zone. It's a trend that disturbs me."

"Why's that then?" the general really wanted to know.

"Simple really, Sir. Fact is, good soldiers are destructive buggers!

We enjoy blowing the crap out of stuff with as much noise and bang as possible, also relishing all opportunities to shoot the shit out of anything that moves given half a chance."

"And police?"

"As I said Sir, we have different mind-sets. I think it comes down to the fact which you know in war and conflicts just as I do Sir, that it can get ugly, brutal and deadly real quick—to which you have to be prepared at least to respond in kind! It's not their strong point, plus it conflicts with their role and training."

"Conclusion?"

"Policemen are great as policemen, but lack the deadly aggression of a soldier."

"Well Ben, thank you for a rather enjoyable insight on a segment of Canadian society. It has been an eye opener I must admit, with some good truths there I'm sure. Well, if Scotland Yard or the FBI do get themselves involved like this down the road, I shall have to remember our little conversation!"

"Wouldn't that be prophetic and scary though."

"Prophetic maybe, but why scary?"

"It would just mean that more of them than us would be doing our jobs, heh Sir."

"True I suppose," concluded the General. Then deciding it was over now, he stated, "Well look now, we're still a good hour or more from home by my reckoning, so as soon as you get us off this stretch of the motorway, how about a stop at the nearest layby or cafe to stretch the legs?"

"Will do Sir."

They exited the A40 at a ring-road junction, which then put them on a new road, being the A34. Ben then looked for and found a suitable place to meet their needs before continuing on the final leg of their journey home to the Mews. In the cafe, their conversation over coffee was limited and was not of matters military. They were also feeling the fatigue from the long hours in the schedule they had been keeping, but there was after all, a time and place for everything—and a public setting was not one for debate over matters they dealt in.

With days off and what free time was allotted to himself, Ben would find that his life and time would still revolve around the Crenshaw family. But he made time for himself to exercise or practice his songs and guitar playing, which the children loved to hear. On one of those days when he was exercising, as he ran along the field and over the assault course, his mind started to wander to the General's daughter, Jane. Against his better judgement he still found himself pleasantly counting the days until her next leave from her military unit and trip back home. The strong feelings and attachment that he knew he was developing for her was bothersome to him, for so far in his life, he had never afforded himself the luxury of any permanent emotional attachment simply due to the nature of his work. But in this instance he found himself attracted to Jane in a way that excited him and stirred something deep within, giving him feelings of genuine apprehension, which of course, was due to the fact that she was an Officer *and* a general's daughter to boot!

Surely nothing good could ever come of that? Just my over-active imagination and flights of fantasy being indulged, he chuckled. *Just? Enough to have me put up against a wall and shot! What is this feeling, anyway? Like I have a yearning for something so forbidden, the temptation is intoxicating.* He knew he had to get a grip on himself and get control of these feelings before the Lt. found out herself and became indignant or even worse, insulted! He promised himself that he wouldn't let his guard down or let it slip anymore, putting it out of his mind. He was good at that, putting things out of his mind so they never bothered him, *all that escape and evasion training,* he grinned.

As he ran on just a little faster now, lengthening his stride, with the sweat pouring from him, he saw that he was getting toward the gap in the hedge that once through, would let you see the house at last. As he ran through, he automatically came to a stop and put his hands on his hips and began his deep breathing routine.

"Hi there," said Jane. She had been standing there watching for how long he didn't know. She was dressed for the very first time in weeks (at least for him seeing her this way) in her military uniform. The kakhi uniform she wore did not take away from her natural beauty though as it did for most women in uniform, as she had a bright face with good features and he liked the way she kept her brunette hair tied back in that French braid look nearly most of the time. What he noticed for the first time was that even though she hardly ever wore make-up, she had a tinge of lipstick that just accentuated her looks. He didn't need to guess for he "knew" that her clothing hid a full figure. Yet she looked lithe, slim and athletic standing there in front of him. *She dressed out so prettily* he thought, looking at her in the afternoon sunlight. He lost himself somewhere in her eyes as they just sucked him in with desire and longing. She was as beautiful as he had ever seen her.

"Oh, hi there Ma'am."

"There you go again with that awful reply," she laughed.

"What's that?" he asked all confused.

"Ma'am," she repeated mockingly. As he stood there she continued, "Don't you realize I come home to get away from the Army?"

Not knowing if she herself was teasing him he said, "You have to understand you are the General's daughter, not forgetting that you are also an officer in your own right."

"Ma'am just makes me feel old, and I don't want to feel old."

"What else can I do?" he said smiling.

"I would much prefer that you call me Jane if no one else is around, it would just make me feel at ease is all, if you don't mind?"

"What about your father, not to mention Mrs. Crenshaw?"

"Like I said, when no one's around!"

"That could cause problems."

She repeated, gritting her teeth, "Like I said, when no one's around?"

"Okay, Jane," he said hesitatingly.

"Thank you Sergeant," she beamed, triumphant!

"Uh, if I'm to get familiar and start calling you Jane, don't you think you ought to at least be able to call me Ben?"

For some unexplained reason which was maybe the newly found closeness and friendship that was developing between them, as well as the mysterious rugged quality to him that she found incredibly attractive, Jane found herself blushing. Looking straight ahead but past him in her attempt to hide it she just said, "Okay Ben."

Alone like this at last, they instinctively knew in their newly-found familiarity that they both felt this sweet swell of intoxicating closeness, that is but an instant in time that conjures prayers and wishes of contact or intimacy, but transcends words. With this sudden awareness, both of them feeling the excitement and awkwardness of the situation, they walked back to the house in silence, yet closer.

They were sat in the kitchen discussing Jane's training methods for her impending course at The Parachute Regiment which she would be doing over at P Company, and having a cup of tea and a sandwich along with further discussing her plans for the upcoming weekend. They were joined by the rest of the Crenshaw family returning from an afternoon of shopping.

"Look what I got to wear for my upcoming birthday!" exclaimed young Amy, showing off her new summer frock to her older sister.

"My, isn't that just smashing!" she replied to Amy's cries of delight at her approval.

"What did you get?" the Sgt. asked young Tom.

"Same old boring school clothes," was his dejected reply as the General and Mrs. Crenshaw looked on, shaking their heads and rolling their eyes behind him.

Trying to console and cheer the young lad up, Ben said, "Oh well, consider yourself fortunate that you have them anyway. I have to go into town for some new guitar strings soon, do you want to come along with me Tom?"

Looking around and up at his father, young Tom asked, "Can I please Father?"

With a relaxed smile the General said, "Of course you can, as long as you promise to behave yourself for the Sgt. and not create too much of a fuss."

Young Tom hugged his father affectionately and said, "Thank you!"

"Sergeant Steele," asked Mrs. Crenshaw. "I've been meaning to ask you, young Amy's birthday is coming up and when we asked her if she wanted a clown or anything like that to entertain herself and her school friends she asked us instead if we could entice you to play your guitar for them all?"

The pleading look on young Amy's face was enough to make Sgt. Steele crack up laughing and say mischievously, "Only if everyone else helps me out?"

Giving him one of her patented "I'll get you for this" stares, her older sister Jane laughed also and said, "Of course we'll all help!"

"Yippee! Yippee!" shouted Amy as she ran off upstairs.

"Thank you for making Amy happy," said Mrs. Crenshaw to Sgt. Steele.

"My pleasure Ma'am."

"What were you two laughing and talking about before we arrived to interrupt and spoil your conversation?" asked the General.

"I was just trying to bribe the good Sergeant here with a late lunch and get him to agree to help train me for my upcoming P Company Parachute course!" replied Jane.

"What an absolute brilliant idea!" enthused the General, "Don't you think?" he asked, turning to Mrs. Crenshaw.

"I most certainly do, yes, I'm all in favour." she agreed.

"There you are!" grinned Jane looking at Sgt. Steele. "Now you have to help me!"

"Okay, I know when I'm out-voted," laughed Ben. "Just be up and out there then, for 0600hrs, sharp!"

"Ouch!" laughed the General.

"You can laugh," she cried, "It's me he's going to punish!"

"Just make sure you do as he says and that way you'll get to pass, can't have a Crenshaw failing on us now, can we?" said the General.

"Oh thanks father, nothing like a little family moral support!"

Laughing in his deep rich voice the General added, "Think nothing of it dear," as he left the room.

"Is the course really very hard Sgt.?" asked Mrs. Crenshaw.

"No lying about it—yes it is Ma'am!"

Looking worriedly over at her daughter Jane now she asked, "Are you sure this is what you want to do dear?"

"Of course it is Mother!"

"I just worry, I don't particularly want to see you sad or have to fail?"

"Don't worry Ma'am, I give you my word she won't fail!"

Giving him a quick and hard stare now, Jane looked over at the Sgt. smiling, and trying to reassure her mother.

Why did he do that? she wondered.

"And what if I let you down too, Sergeant?"

"You won't!" was his confident reply.

"Why do you say that? And so confidently too?" asked Mrs. Crenshaw.

"Yes?" added Jane.

"Because she's a Crenshaw isn't she?" said Ben, matter of factly.

Laughing, Mrs. Crenshaw said, "This one's been listening to your father!"

"Besides," added Ben confidently, "She has *me* training her now."

Jane turned and stared deep and hard at him now, liking the newly found confidence he seemed to display in her, it was refreshing after all her nights of quiet tears and doubt she had indulged in. *What* did *he see in her that she couldn't in herself then? Was he just bluffing?* She hoped not, as she really did want to succeed.

Jane liked succeeding, especially in a male-dominated institution like the Military. She hoped he saw something more than just an athletic or military ability as an officer. What would the handsome, good looking and kind-hearted sergeant do if he knew that Lieutenant Jane Crenshaw was feeling more excitedly attracted to him, or bluntly said, had the "hots" for him?

She had fantasized about this many times now, but figured his discipline would probably make him run a mile. She laughed and disparaged at her thoughts, *not* the appropriate feelings for a female officer to have about an NCO, heh?

Not at all in fact a most taboo arrangement, but Jane slowly admitted to herself staring across the kitchen table and blankly listening to the Sgt. talk to her mother, how she would like to feel the touch of his lips and wondered how it would be to be held and caressed by those strong and muscular looking arms and touched and . . .

"Jane?" asked her mother.

"Oh, sorry, I was just distracted for a moment, thinking about some business I have to attend to, see you all later!" she said as she hurriedly got up and left, hoping that her Sgt. had not caught her longing stare. She did not want to see him upset or embarrassed by the affection of a lonely female Army officer!

It was six a.m. sharp when they both left the manor house and walked slowly through the morning chill and over the grassy dew, over to the assault course.

"What's your personal best for this poor excuse for an assault course Jane?" he started in with a grin.

"3:57," she retorted.

"Don't do it, it's not worth shooting yourself over," he grinned.

"What?" she began, then laughed back. "Oh, the 3:57 thing, very funny Ben!"

He set the stop-watch aside.

"Okay, first we do some limbering-up exercises, then I want you to just follow my lead, okay?"

Fifteen minutes had elapsed, before he spoke once more.

"Okay, now listen closely to me Jane. All I want for you to do is run the assault course. While I run along side of you, I want you to remember just not to take what I say or shout at you personally. It's just, well, it will probably just go this way when you're on course for real. You understand?"

Receiving a nod back he shouted, "Okay, let's go!"

Immediately after they started running, it seemed to Jane that her Sgt. began tearing verbally into her rather quickly. She wasn't liking this sudden assault at all.

"Get the lead out of your ass and let's move it there girl! What kind of a poncey trot is that? Open that stride NOW, and move it up there soldier! Move, move, move," he screamed as they went up and over a wall, then over a water obstacle.

"What the hell kind of a pansy crawl is that? For crying out loud get that rear end down, do you want it shot off? Move faster, faster!" he kept yelling, but also urging.

These and other profound accolades he kept bestowing on Jane throughout her assault course run, which had her nearly in tears. Toward the finish she was gritting her teeth but running and stumbling on in anger and frustration at the embarrassment of the insults he was bellowing out for her seemingly pathetic effort, then as suddenly as it had all started the ordeal came to an abrupt stop.

Lunging for the end of the assault course, Jane then leant over gasping and spitting up puke as well as crying for breath. As Ben came toward her, she suddenly reared up and punched him in the mouth shouting through her tears and anger, "You bastard!"

The blow, besides being a complete surprise, sent Ben back a pace and blood now trickled from the corner of his mouth.

He looked at her hard, then spoke, "One more thing, don't ever slack off and don't ever say I quit, okay? Here, catch."

Jane reached out instinctively for the stop-watch and caught it from the air as he tossed it to her. He added coldly but calmly, "By the way Jane, that really is the way it may go, just thought you should know."

Ben walked quickly away, as Jane looked from him to her stop-watch for the very first time. It read 3:29!

Looking up flabbergasted, all she saw was the back of him walking away and then she herself ran quickly past him and into the house in tears. It wasn't that Jane was a softie, far from it, she was in fact quite hard (beyond the obvious physical boundaries of her femininity) but as aggressive and determined as any prospective recruit is to pass. Everyone at some stage who goes through the Airborne P COY Selection will have their determination and resolve challenged in many ways. What Jane was unaware of at this defining moment for herself, was that this type of experience was one of those intangibles that just can never be explained—the "why" of why some stop or quit, and others find the courage and resolve to continue? Jane had experienced one of those moments and she had made the grade, albeit unknowingly!

In the house, they both went their separate ways but were showered and back for breakfast as the others in the house were just stirring awake or already up and joining them. They sat across from each other at the table, just glaring, not saying a word. Aunt May and the Sgt.Major entered. Soon, the smell of frying bacon let them all know breakfast was not far away. They were soon joined by the General and his wife. The Sgt.Major said innocently enough, "Looks like a lover's quarrel to me!"

A comment to which Jane then rose from her chair and stormed out in silence.

"I say, Sergeant," began the General, "You two seem to have become so close and friendly these past few weeks, I hope there's no truth to the Sgt. Major's words?"

In anger himself now, Ben mocked, "What, that a lowly Sgt. may find it in him to find the General's daughter more than a Lieutenant in the army? Have no fear Sir!"

The silence that followed for Ben was earth shattering! Having said the words, he regretted them instantly but awaited the General's wrath, which he felt would be harsh. Surprised at getting no response, he himself rose from the table and quietly left the kitchen. Get going while the going's good, he thought wisely.

The General turned to his wife. They looked at each other bewildered, as aunt May said something to the effect, "They just had a little disagreement, not to worry, they'll be the best of friends again soon."

Looking to the Sgt.Major for some backing up, he in turn added more to the truth than any of them would ever know, "Yes, they were out there on the assault course this morning you know. Maybe the Sergeant just overdid the realism a bit too much for Jane's liking?"

Not one for being hung up with propriety on rank or position, Mrs. Crenshaw was genuinely concerned for them as she knew they enjoyed each other's company. She was also preoccupied with her youngest daughter's party arrangements.

"I do hope they can patch this up and get along by this afternoon," said Mrs. Crenshaw, "as that's young Amy's birthday party, if anyone here happened to forget?"

"No-one will forget dear, and I'm sure the Sergeant will keep his word and not let her down either!"

"Here, here," spoke the Sgt.Major.

That afternoon in the rear hall of the Mansion House, Ben was moving wires about and setting up the microphones and speakers which they had rented for the party. Coming into the room, just off the main lounge, Jane approached him directly to whisper meekly, "Will you forgive me please Ben?"

Looking at her eyes closely he smiled and said, "Sure."

"I won't blame you if you hate me, but I truly am sorry. It's just, well no one has ever spoken to me quite like that, or in that manner before, that's all. It really surprised me. It takes some getting used to you know!" She looked pleadingly.

Grinning now, he said, "Jane, I said it's okay, I understand."

Her eyes watered then and not knowing why, she instinctively just reached out and touched his cheek on the side where she had seen the blood on his mouth earlier that morning, to gently place her hand there, in a look that spoke volumes.

Her surprise touch was like an electric shock! It just bolted and riveted him to the floor. Waves of euphoria flowed over him then as he felt the gentleness of her touch and soft fingers and he knew then he wanted more. He wanted to reach up and touch or hold them then, even kiss them. He resisted the urge, catching himself just in time, for as Jane removed her hand from his face, Mrs. Crenshaw suddenly entered the room.

There was an awkward silence in the big room for a long moment as Mrs. Crenshaw saw them standing there, very close, staring at each other.

"Everything all fine between you both now?"

"Yes Ma'am!" "Yes Mother!" They both replied simultaneously.

"Good. By the way Sergeant, just what kind of songs do you sing for a small girl's birthday party anyway? We never did discuss it."

Laughing now, he exclaimed, "From where I come from Ma'am there was this guy called Raffi. Ever heard of him?"

"Not that I can recall, why?"

"Well, let's just say that you're all in for a major treat, for when it comes to kids' songs, Raffi was the king! But what makes him special is that he gets all the children to join in!"

Now he was wickedly looking at Jane Crenshaw.

"Oh no you don't, no way!" she started to say . . .

Amy's birthday party was the success they all wanted for her and her friends. Long over with now and Amy tucked away tiredly into her bed, they all sat around the warm kitchen in the large mansion house laughing and joking over their coffees.

"Play that song again for them you made me sing!" laughed Jane.

"Which song?" teased Ben.

"You know, something about, down by the bay where the water melons grow, did you ever see a whale with a polka dot tail, down by the bay?"

"Yes, that really was quite the song," interjected the General.

"You sang it beautifully too dear," laughed Mrs. Crenshaw, looking fondly at her husband.

"You really are quite good with that guitar, but can you sing more grown up serious songs?" enquired aunt May.

"Yes, you know I can sing grown up serious ones," he mocked.

So as they all teased the Sgt. and laughed and cajoled him to play the guitar, he said, "Okay, one of you get my guitar and I'll sing for you."

Before he could change his mind, Jane rushed out of the room and returned with his guitar to ask, "What are you going to sing, we've never actually heard you sing serious yet, or at least I haven't you know?"

"What would you like?"

"That good, heh?" laughed aunt May. "Okay, how about that song by that other Canadian, Adams is it? You know, that Don Juan de Marco song. I really like that one. What's it called? Oh yes, 'Have You Ever Really Loved A Woman?' "

As she offered up her suggestion, aunt May levelled him quickly with a secretive kind of knowing stare, then panned it across the table to Jane as if to say, "Let's see how you both handle that one?"

Everyone seemed to get clued in and also began smiling and frowning looking back and forth from Jane to Ben because of her request. They both withered and folded under their collective gazes. Jane began blushing and covered her face in her hands. Ben narrowed his eyes in jest and said between gritted teeth, "I'll get you for that aunt May!"

They were all laughing when Mrs. Crenshaw smiled and chided in fun, "Just sing your song, soldier!"

"Yes!" They all said banging the table, "Let's hear you sing!"

"Okay, okay," he laughed and positioning his guitar he closed his eyes and softly, slowly began to strum as he started singing the ballad. The flamenco aspect of the song was well suited to his rich tenor voice to which, when he finished, the ladies were all looking at him with their moist eyes. He could not avoid making eye contact with Jane. She tried to avert in case anyone present in the room caught his obvious looks of longing and desire. He still knew he had to seriously mask his feelings from them all, especially Jane who was, after all, a Lt. in the Army Intelligence Corp and an officer. He tried to do this by quickly talking and asking for more requests. He then in turn played a few more ballads and upbeat songs for them he knew and liked, including a request for "Rockabye Sweet Lady Jane" by James Taylor, then finally ending his singing with a favourite of his own by Bruce Springsteen, a song called "My Home Town."

With the evening still young, the Sgt.Major said, "I've an idea, why don't we all go down the road to that nice little pub, The Rose and Crown, and have a pint or glass of brandy. It's still not late."

With everyone in agreement and in a festive and merry mood, as the ladies grabbed their coats and purses, the men decided to pass on the walk and take the station wagon for the short drive there.

The Rose and Crown was a fine establishment. As you entered the rustic and quaint country pub, you saw how it was bedecked with framed hunting scenes and copper and brass and other paraphernalia adding to its charm. The main room was divided and separated in part by a railed-off upper landing that held a large warm and cozy fireplace. The ambience and atmosphere was traditional and sentimental which kept the place a very popular habitat indeed. As their small group entered, they found that while the place was alive with people chattering and laughing, it was not really noisy. They made their way to a back table against the wall with a direct view of the bar on the upper stage behind the railings.

"Honestly, you men and your need to keep your backs to the wall," mentioned aunt May.

The evening itself was going quite well and they had already enjoyed two drinks each when just before they were ready to leave a group of loud motorcycle gang members entered the premises and began to push their way to the bar and soon took over the area with their obnoxious loutful behaviour.

"Louts," grunted the Sgt.Major.

"I concur," muttered the General.

"This lot were in here last week and really gave everyone a bad time. Better to avoid them though, they really look like they are a hard bunch," said Jane as she added, "Well, if you'll excuse me, I need to go to the ladies room before we leave so can I squeeze past you here aunt May? Thanks."

They sat finishing their drinks and waiting for Jane to return. They were engaged in small talk while instinctively glancing and watching anxiously at the noisy rabble at the bar. Then they heard Jane yell, "Let me go you pig, or you'll be sorry!"

What they all saw was a large burly leather jacketed gang member, who seemed to have grabbed Jane by her purse as she was returning from the ladies room. This man had let go of her purse but held her by the arm, much to the enjoyment of his noisy fellow gang members.

Time seemed to stand still for Jane, but Ben needed no prompting or urging, for out of nowhere he appeared by Jane's side and placed his hand on the wrist of the gang member and said directly to him, "Let her go now please. She's with me."

The large fellow threw back his head and laughed, as his fellow gang members laughed with him. He turned to face Ben.

"And what if I don't, you puke?"

He got his answer instantly! Somehow Ben twisted the man's hand off Jane without hurting her, then pushed the bully away while he moved Jane behind him, at the same time admonishing to his potential foe, "Don't even think of it."

"Or what?" asked the humiliated gang member whose position of authority had just been taken away from him much to the astonishment of himself and his fellow members. Ben was a trained and experienced martial artist, but had learnt this type of down and dirty fighting through experience. He wasn't kidding when he retorted, "You really don't want to know!"

Moving slightly, the large leather-clad fellow made his move as if to go away from them, then whirled and swung a huge meaty fist at the face of Ben—but it never connected. Ben had obviously expected one of the oldest tricks of the trade. He easily ducked under it and came up with a vicious short jab to the ribs that was followed by a two-handed under-hand arm grab on the arm that was meant to hit him.

Holding onto it, while twisting the arm of his assailant with one hand and placing his other against the shoulder to lock him into a bent-over position, Ben then raised his outside leg over the head of his trapped and bent-forward assailant. He brought his leg backward over the head and kicking down on the back of the neck and in a blur, he brought his leg back up again from the bent knee position to thrust it forward and flush into the face of his assailant.

The motion of these two quick and short vicious kicks were fast and violent and extremely effective. The last upward kick brought the assailant to an upright position with Ben still holding onto his outstretched hand and arm. Turning and pivoting, Ben thrust the elbow of his left arm into the solar plexus of his assailant which brought a grunt and gasp as you could hear the air leave his chest and collapse.

Still holding onto the arm of his leather-clad assailant, Ben twirled back completing the motion and grabbed him by the hair with his now free hand and with a little leverage from the other, along with a sweeping leg thrust, his assailant was easily flipped up and over! As he landed, the impact knocked what remained of his air out of him. Still holding his assailant's arm, Ben twisted it and put a foot in a stepping motion, on the side of his assailant, who was now in the prone position. He said very coldly, but nonchalantly to his startled friends, "Who's next?"

Seconds passed with shocked surprise. They came alive and shouted, "Let him go!" then yelled, "He never did anything to you!"

Looking around at the group of them Ben said, "Yes he did. He assaulted this lady, and if you or he ever try that again, I promise you I'll rip your hearts out!"

Ben then threw the arm aside. He turned to Jane. Quite pale

but eyes narrowed and staring at what had just transpired, she grabbed Ben by the arm in instinct and for protection. Sensing her fear he spoke softly, "Sorry to scare you, are you okay Jane?"

Trying to smile she looked up and muttered, "Yes," while still clinging to his arm.

When his assailant had initially grabbed Jane, on the other side of the room the General and the Sgt.Major, with their wives, also suddenly felt vulnerable, afraid and longing for their youth, all at the same time! Their reaction time was also far slower than Ben's, for he was already up from his position and gone, leaping across the rails to come to Jane's rescue, before they could even move. At first, the two older men spilt their drinks rising suddenly from their table. In fairness, somewhat also aided by their own wives' panic and clinging. By the time they had realized or considered looking to Ben for help, he had already moved into action. Like the other patrons of the pub, they were only able to witness his response to this display of bothersome bullying by these thugs in their intimidating-looking leather jackets, with their own array of silver studded ornaments and chains.

The resultant cheer by the pub's regular patrons to Ben's timely intercedence, not to mention the Crenshaw party, was raucous and loud. The landlord, who had observed the entire altercation himself from his vantage point at the bar, shouted at the motorcycle gang members in fury.

"Get out of my pub now and don't you ever return or else I'll call the police!"

As some of the gang members lifted their fallen leader from the floor and they all left subdued or defeated, the whistles and roar of the crowd was deafening. Jane, still clinging to Ben and beginning to realize what he had just done for her, flushed with excitement as the landlord gave him his thanks stating, "I've been waiting for someone to do that to them for a long time!"

The Sgt.Major had appeared at their side by this time, quickly being followed by the General and their wives and said, "Well done son. Now let's leave, enough for one night, heh?"

There was no sign of the gang in the parking lot as they left the pub and made their way to the car. The ladies were concerned and fussing all over Jane asking if she was alright while she tried to convince them she was just fine. All the while though, she kept her eyes on Ben.

The General and the Sgt.Major were far more relaxed and animated about the incident, and let their excitement show.

"I say Sergeant, that file of yours wasn't exaggerated when it said you were capable and qualified in the area of fighting," gushed the General, "Even sort of reminds me of the Sgt.Major here in his younger days!"

As they rode back to the Mews, after the initial excitement had died down and they coasted along in silence for awhile, Mrs. Crenshaw said firmly, "Sergeant Steele, that was a very brave thing you just did, but would you have moved as fast if that were the General himself you were protecting," and looking mischievously at Jane added, "and not his beautiful daughter?"

With his face straight but eyes twinkling, Ben looked over at Mrs. Crenshaw, then her daughter, and said, "Ma'am, if it were the General, I'd be obligated to move faster!"

In relief they all started laughing again. In the dark of the rear of the car they were all squished together. Jane was next to Ben. Quietly, she slipped her arm through his and by doing so, moved closer, to rest her head against him as she also gently and softly slid her slender hand into his . . .

The successful graduation of Lt. Jane Crenshaw from her parachute course she completed at P Company came along with her full transfer over to the Intelligence Wing at The Parachute Regiment. It was indeed to be celebrated at the Crenshaw residence in regal style, befitting the daughter of a Staff General and his wife, who herself was a most distinguished lady.

The large manor hall situated just off from the end of the equally large sitting room (where Amy had her birthday party) was more than capable of handling upward of 100 guests. The stewards themselves were members of the nearby Officers Mess who had volunteered their time in return for time off from their own C.O.

The catering as usual would be supervised by the more than capable Mrs. Steele, while her husband, the equally capable Sgt.Major, would competently do as he had on many previous and similar engagements, direct and supervise all the waiters.

The whole event was designed as a surprise by Mrs. Crenshaw and Jane's friends. She wasn't very fond though, she had to admit, of that Jeremy Smythe. His friends were nice, she just didn't care for him. That group were Officers of the Coldstream Guards from the nearby training depot.

The General, as did most senior officers, always liked the childish energy the younger officers constantly displayed. He found their exuberance and desire to fete his daughter too appealing an occasion to dismiss, so found the time and gave it his blessing. Jane arrived home for the weekend expecting to share her recent success privately with her family (inclusive of the Steeles and Ben). She was shocked and surprised beyond belief at the reception awaiting her.

Composing herself quickly and professionally, she proudly strutted amongst her peers and friends and her father's military friends, displaying for all to see her airborne insignia down a little on the right shoulder of her tunic. The famous white parachute in the centre with the pale blue wings either side of it, her "Wings," as they were universally called in the British Army.

Jane moved around the cocktail party mingling with people and even popping into the kitchen to visit with aunt May, yet her eyes were always searching for Ben. Seeing him nowhere so far, a little bit of panic came over her, when shocked and surprised, she suddenly saw him in the most unlikely of places. He was dressed in a waiter's white jacket—casually walking amongst those here, but serving her guests! Excusing herself from her present conversation, Jane made a bee-line straight for him. Uncaring of her surroundings, Jane went straight to it.

"What the bloody hell's going on Ben?"

Knowing exactly where *he* was, he spoke calmly, "Sorry Ma'am—staff shortage. I'm helping out serving!"

"Couldn't they get someone else?" she barrelled on.

"They were understaffed on the waitering side. Like the decent guy that I am, I volunteered my services to the Sgt.Major. Sort of getting him out of a sticky situation, if you know what I mean?"

"I was just hoping, well I wanted to see you, have you to see me, but not quite like this" . . . she trailed off.

Just then Capt. Smythe appeared at her side and scolded her, grinning, all the while watching Sgt. Steele closely.

"I see you have a habit of chatting up the hired help when I'm not around Jane," he said, looking between them deviously and not without a little contempt toward the Sgt.

"I was . . . " she began, but was interrupted by Ben who quickly said, "The Lieutenant was just telling me about her jump wings Sir, nothing more!"

"Something yourself can only dream about, heh?" he replied nastily.

"Jeremy, that was not called for!" Jane said angrily as she turned to face the Captain. Capt. Smythe had been very impatiently waiting a long time for this moment to get even with Sgt. Steele, ever since their first meeting at his car that very first day when he could not intimidate or best him. It was misplaced and unwarranted anger, but for some grudging reason, it seemed to fester in him.

Not having knowledge of his background or what his duties really were here around the Mews for the General and family, he was even a little more resentful, if that were possible. He saw him as a challenge for Jane's affections and he resented it. When he heard through the grapevine that he had even taken over helping to train Jane for her Parachute course, which she had now passed (and it being something he had always envisioned for himself doing all along) this "new" opportunity presenting itself to humiliate, insult or degrade him in her presence and eyes was more than appealing. To him, it was long awaited, something he would relish and achieve successfully, so he arrogantly presumed.

"Well, I meant to say, as the real soldier here, an Infantryman and Captain in the Coldstream Guards, seeing as my own Batman is on leave maybe your waiter friend here may be willing to clean my Sam Brown and the rest of my uniform, and polish my Gulf War medal in time for next week's Armistice Parade?"

In those choice snide comments, the magnitude of the difference that still existed and separated officers from the enlisted ranks, was so openly tossed into his face with a clarity like never before. Jane seemed more embarrassed. She felt the anger well up in her, but for the very first time was sorry and embarrassed for the lower rank and position that Ben held. She was also, for the first time that evening, at a total loss for words and could only stand by Capt. Smythe looking ashamed.

Always aware of these barriers and distinctions that separated them, but ever the consummate proud and professional soldier, through narrowing eyes and gritted teeth Ben fought to contain his composure. It only took a few seconds. Taking a deep breath, he replied, "Thanks for your generous offer, Captain, but the General will be attending the ceremony himself, so I do have other duties to attend to and I might attend myself."

"That will be interesting to see, sort of curious how the hired help looks in a plain old uniform!" sneered the Capt.

By this time a small crowd close by, including Mrs. Crenshaw, had the opportunity of overhearing the remarks of the Captain. Mrs. Crenshaw made a mental note to have a talk with her husband immediately following Jane's surprise affair. Looking over at her daughter with this pompous officer and poor Sgt. Steele, she heard the Sgt speak.

"Then if my duties allow, I promise to greet you at the parade, Captain, and allow you that opportunity to laugh at me in uniform. Now if you'll excuse me?"

"You really are a glutton for punishment aren't you?"

"Please, can we end this now Jeremy?" pleaded Jane.

Another young officer, Capt. David Pritchard, who had happened to be one of the three by the car on Ben's arrival, was now in the group behind them with Mrs. Crenshaw. He had also overheard Jeremy going at it with the Sergeant. After receiving a nod from their own C.O. who was also part of that same group Capt. Pritchard walked over to join them.

"I say, is my friend trying to have a pissing contest with you? Never mind him, he picks on everyone, don't you Jeremy?"

Looking directly at the Sgt., then staring at Jane, Capt. Smythe replied, "Not a pissing contest old boy, just putting this cheeky little sod in his place!"

"I don't think he looks that little," he smiled, "Will you be a good chap and go back into the kitchen and refill that tray you're carrying, the other guests are looking a little thirsty?"

Instantly understanding and respecting the ploy to remove him, Ben replied, "That will not be a problem Sir!" He turned sharply on his heel and left.

"I say Jeremy, you were a little hard on the poor chap there, weren't you?"

"That Corporal, or whatever his rank is, was in dire need of being put in his place. Also of which I may add, I do not care for his manners and attitude and will be reporting him to my superiors and to your father, Jane!"

"For your information then Jeremy, know that the Corporal as you called him is in fact a Sergeant and I know he had not done anything that remotely deserves him being reported to my father. But if you do so, I will tell father that it was you who started all this with your needless bullying!"

"Be that as it may, but I will be reporting him nevertheless."

In a huff, Jane also spun on her heel and left them both standing there to follow Ben in the same direction to the kitchen. On entering, she found him there engrossed in conversation with the Sgt.Major and aunt May, probably retelling them what had just transpired. They all turned and saw her approaching them. If Jane's behaviour confused him before, Ben didn't mind. Looking at her he was completely distracted by her beauty anyway, but he knew he had to be alone to clear his head. With a last quick glance, Ben just turned away and left out the rear kitchen door. Jane made to follow, but aunt May caught her arm and softly chided, "Let him go dearie!"

"I just want to apologize to him aunt May for what happened out there."

"No need to girl," said the Sgt.Major, "He just got put in his place is all, sort of happens in his job and standing in life, if you understand?"

"No, I don't understand," she blurted out angrily.

"Look Jane, you may be a pretty girl, but you have to realize that you are an officer in the British Army. Sergeant Steele out there is just that, a Sergeant!"

"Is that what this is about then?" pleaded Jane.

"My dear girl, this is *all* of what this is about. Your station in life and your rank as an officer puts you off limits to the Sergeant. You're like the forbidden fruit for him in the garden of Eden, Jane. Surely you can understand that?"

Jane Crenshaw had fallen against the kitchen counter listening to the Sgt.Major's words echo in her ears. She looked over at aunt May for comfort but received the same reply by her sadly nodding accent. As much as she was angry to hear these words spoken by them both, she realized their simple truth. With her emotional nerves jangling and feelings ripped apart, when the tears welling in her eyes finally flooded over as the dam burst open, she ran right past them in a blur between her flowing tears and sobs, right past her mother who had just entered the kitchen and looked worriedly on. By looking at the Sgt.Major and his good wife she knew what had taken place and silently understanding, turned herself to follow her out of the room. . . .

The days that followed passed quickly now and found Ben standing alone in the General's study awaiting his arrival. They had become good companions travelling together and the General fondly called him by his given name when alone, or even around the house now. Ben wasn't quite sure why he had been summoned, but he could only imagine what the topic of conversation would be, for he had suspicions believing that Capt. Smythe was up to no good, he wondered how the General would react.

Ben turned as the General opened the heavy door and entered his study alone. Quietly, he walked round his dark oak desk to sit himself down. He slumped tiredly into his leather chair and just seemed to sit there awhile pondering, when letting out a sigh, he looked up at Ben fondly.

"Ben, regarding that incident the other week between the Captain and yourself, I am sure it will be a relief for you to know that I at least from my end am doing nothing about his complaint and shall try to extend that to your boss at Hereford!"

"Yes Sir, it is a relief of sorts, but why get involved, if I may ask?"

"Ah yes, the why of it all!"

"Exactly Sir!"

"Well, as it so happens, I was made privy to the truth of the matter which besides making the Captain's complaint unfounded, quite ticks me off! But, I felt I had to act on it and so I am." Smiling, he went on, "I am ignoring it for two reasons. The first is that personally I can't stand the poxy, smarmy, little snot-nosed bastard!"

"I see," grinned Ben more than slightly pleased and in agreement, but most surprised at the General's sudden need for candor.

"Secondly Ben, I am ignoring it because it will serve no purpose to add such an unfounded reprimand to your excellent military record. Especially since we have finally come to the end of it, or I should say, near to the end of your service with us here."

It was a little bit of a shock to Ben on hearing that his six month posting had come to an abrupt end. *Had time passed that quickly?*

"I totally forgot about the time factor Sir!"

"Don't feel bad Ben, so did I. So did the whole bloody lot of us!"

"When do I have to leave by then, Sir?"

"Well actually Ben you are able to leave us anytime. Due to the fact you also have holiday leave we have neglected to give to you."

"I see Sir."

"Umm Ben, I have a request to make of you."

"What kind of request Sir?"

"Well I think you know what an impact your presence has had upon my entire family and the Sgt.Major and his wife . . . "

"Yes Sir," he smiled fondly.

"Well Ben, I would consider it a personal favour if you would agree to stay on with us for a few more days here at the Mews. Just so our little family can say our farewells like we had planned. Plus there's another important reason."

"What would that be Sir?"

Breaking into a wide grin for the first time now, the General continued, "Ben, the Remembrance Day parades are coming up next week, on Wednesday. I, that is we, the Sgt.Major and myself, would consider it a great honour if you joined us for our parade. We would also like to see you in your regular Regimental uniform before you leave us, if you would be willing?"

"Yes Sir, I can and will join you. Besides, it will afford me that opportunity to say hello and good-bye to our friend the Captain!"

"I considered that thought in my equation," beamed the General. "By the way Ben, your record will be added with the highest recommendations possible. We will not forget you here, not any of us! Um, well is there anything else you want to ask?" the General fidgeted, uncomfortable with handing out such personal compliments.

"Yes Sir, I would just like to take this opportunity to thank you. It has been my great pleasure and privilege to serve you and your family. It has been genuinely nice to get to know them all, as I am sure you realize I like them very much." Pausing, he continued, "I also thank you for your respect and understanding, especially of my rank, position here, and feelings for your daughter!"

Rising up and coming round from his oak desk, the General smiled fatherly while putting a big arm across Ben's shoulders, "Ben, my daughter is her own person, she has made that crystal clear to us on many an occasion. She is also quite grown, free to make her own choices in life. He grinned, then he said, "But being a General as well as her father, hurt her in any way and I shall have you shot, then hung and quartered, understood?"

"Absolutely!" smiled Ben, knowing more than just an element of truth lurked in those words.

"Now, what do you say we go into the kitchen and see if we can beg or steal a piece of aunt May's rhubarb pie without the ladies balling their eyes out knowing you'll be leaving us soon."

Laughing with him Ben said, "I think I'll be able to handle that General."

With the General leading the way, the two men headed for the kitchen.

It was already dark now and raining miserably. A standard evening for the English November climate of Autumn. It was about 5 o'clock. The Crenshaw family were eating a casual tea in the warm kitchen. The Sgt. Major, aunt May and Ben were also seated. They could hear the rain pelting down. By this time, they were all basically finished and there were at least three different conversations going on simultaneously which was not unusual for this household!

"Will Jane be coming home soon mummy?" shouted out young Amy.

"I'm sure she will be dear."

"Is Janey going to join you in the parade tomorrow too Daddy?" asked Tom.

"She had better!" laughed out the General, in his booming voice.

Just then, the rear door to the kitchen suddenly flew wide open. Jane stood there completely soaking wet while a pool of water quickly formed round her feet on the floor.

"Didn't you drive home dear?" asked her mother, peering over her tea cup.

"Are you serious, this is just getting from the garage to the house, it's pelting cats and dogs out there mother!"

"Come over here then, close by the fire where it's warm and I'll get you a towel to dry yourself off dearie," aunt May said kindly and thoughtful as ever.

Jane surprisingly was not dressed in uniform and somehow, maybe it was the fact she had been gone this entire past week, but she looked positively gaunt now and even a little run down and tired out.

"Are you all right Jane?" asked her father concerned, "You don't look it."

"I'm fine daddy, just a little tired is all, it's been a particularly busy week."

"We thought you may not come home Jane and that way you'd have missed our going-away party for the Sergeant!" little Amy told her bigger sister, smiling with glee.

Looking at Ben now, seeing him looking back at her, Jane wished with all her heart that she was neither the General's daughter nor an officer in the British Army. For all she longed for was to run into his strong arms and have him caress away all her fears and longings and achy feelings that she still harboured for him! She managed a feeble hello to him, or at least in that direction, before the flood gates opened once more and tears streaming, she ran off, out of the room and upstairs to her bedroom.

This vision of Jane in distress set them all off in a dither. One of the hardest things for women to control were their emotions. It was and always shall be something as unpredictable as their prerogative to change their mind or mood. Crying herself now, poor aunt May could only repeatedly say, "Poor thing, God bless her!" then turned away to busy herself at her kitchen sink in make believe chores and sniffles. It was contagious, as Mrs. Crenshaw joined her in this sniffling. The Sgt. Major coughed loudly, excusing himself before anybody noticed the tear that came to the corner of his eye. The General looked on apologetically, then stood and mumbled something or other about needing to do something in his study. The only ones baffled and slightly confused by all of this performance, were of course, young Tom and Amy.

Ben took all of this in as he rose slowly from the table. After he said his polite thank you's for the evening meal, he then stepped out through the rear kitchen door, the same way Jane had entered not minutes before. Doing so just in time so that none of them would see how troubled he looked. He left silently with no further comments in parting.

Staring over the top rail, leaning up against the paddock fence near the overhang of the barn, watching Jane's mare frolic about in the rain which had tapered off into nothing more than a light drizzle, he felt a soft and gentle touch against his hands. Turning, he saw Jane standing next to him looking distraught.

"I don't want you to go Ben. I don't want to lose you. You have no idea what you have become to mean to me," she half sobbed, half pleaded.

Absolutely stunned at this open admission, he struggled to put his feelings aside. "It's probably for the best Jane. Besides, you'll get over me in no time."

"Do you care for me Ben, I mean do you more than just like me?"

"Since I first set eyes on you!" he said softly, partially turning away.

"Then why, why did you never tell me, do something about it?"

"Come on Jane, get a grip here, think about that for awhile. I'm a Sergeant, you're an Officer and your father *is* the General . . . " He let it trail off.

Looking straight at him defiantly, her eyes blazing, Jane replied, "Then if you're going to leave, take me in your arms to hold and kiss me, so you'll know what it is you're leaving behind," as the tears just rolled silently, as she left him with that plea.

I'm a rotten bastard, he thought. *I'm breaking her heart and yet I don't want to. What the hell is going on and what am I afraid of?* There was a sinking feeling in his gut to rival the Titanic! He looked at Jane's beautiful face and saw the sadness trickling from her eyes— *you rotten miserable shit*, he thought to himself one more time.

He had so much he wanted to say, to share. He had dreams and plans. So much more now. He knew he could not keep her, instinct told him this was just not their time, not yet anyway. Lovingly but with a tenderness he had kept hidden and not displayed until now, he reached up and touched her for the very first time as he gently moved a wisp of hair out of her face.

At that point, her perfume and femininity was intoxicating! After caressing the side of her cheek in the same hand that reached to her hair, he let it slip to her neck and gently brought her toward him. The kiss was a battle to keep it modest and gentle, for when their lips met their passions erupted. A hot pulsing urgency and their searching tongues urged them to reach out instinctively with their arms and hold onto each other desperately. As they stood there embracing and kissing, Jane's tears mingled with the rain, their lips that found one another so instinctively mashed and ground against their teeth as they struggled to manoeuvre their bodies, feeling the heat, all to get closer with their embrace which lingered on, as desires grew with every passing second . . .

It was an overcast morning but they were snuggled warm inside for now. The military members of this household, the General and Jane, with the Sgt. Major, stood there in the kitchen with aunt May and Mrs. Crenshaw fussing over them and trying to remove every last piece of lint from their uniforms. A little tugging here, a little patting there and another downward tug and straightening out. Then there were the medals with their familiar clink every time they moved. A time-honoured ritual that was really nothing more than passing away of time, but it made all feel purposeful.

Waiting impatiently for Sgt. Steele to come down it was still only the General and Sgt.Major who were aware of his 22 Special Air Service Regiment connection, so none of the others had any idea of what to expect. They all just expected to see him come downstairs in his uniform as a member of The Parachute Regiment, which was impressive in its own right, although they had never seen him in complete uniform anyway.

It was Mrs. Crenshaw who spoke, "Shush, I think that's him coming now!"

The unmistakable heavy clumping of boots coming down the stairway and the distant familiar clink preceded his arrival. When he turned the final corner and made his entrance into the kitchen they gasped, to stare in awe and surprise.

"Do I look that bad?" he laughingly chided.

"That uniform, YOU'RE in the SAS? But how? And just look at those medals?" Jane could only mouth her astonishment!

"Sorry to you all," the General spoke, "But it's those bloody orders and standing policy type things, but at least we all get to finally see how the Sergeant really fills out in uniform don't we?" he understated.

"Wow, look, he nearly has as many medals as the Sgt.Major!" burst out young Tom, while at the same time and grinning from ear to ear the General said, "Ben, I would consider it an honour if you would be an escort for Jane at today's ceremonies?"

"It would be my greatest honour and duty to perform Sir." Looking directly into the adoring eyes of Jane he added, "If that is agreeable with the Lieutenant?"

Walking slowly over to Ben, Jane looked at him lovingly and secretly and said "The honour will be all mine soldier, not to mention the thrill I will get for seeing our Captain's face!"

She and everyone else laughed good-naturedly, for they all

knew by now the perception the Capt. had of the Sgt. *This would surely shock the shit out of him,* Jane laughed contentedly to herself.

"Ben, I want to pass on my old red sash to you as a gesture of friendship and all that sentimental bullshit," the Sgt.Major spoke up.

"Thank you Sgt.Major."

"Colour Sergeant it is then!" interrupted the General.

Jane reached up to kiss her father on the cheek. Aunt May then said, "I guess I should best be off and get the bloody old red thing then, heh?"

With the women's help in having a go at tugging and straightening him out, Ben put on the red sash of the Sgt.Major's. He really looked the part, smart and professional.

"It is such an enjoyable occasion and event for me, of having another soldier in this household having to undergo the rigours and torture of this family inspection, the only ones I'll ever undergo now, anyway," quipped the Sgt. Major.

"What are *your* medals for Sergeant Steele?" asked Tom.

"These two are my bravery medals. The Queen's Commendation Medal, this is the Military Medal. These two are my campaign medals, Northern Ireland and the Gulf War. This one is my NATO Medal and this one a United Nations Peace-keeping Medal, with Clasps!"

"Wow!" said little Amy and Tom together.

Walking over to place her hand on his chest and to touch and admire his medals, Jane added unnecessarily, "You've been around some there soldier!"

"Some I guess!" He added warmly, then laughed, "Well Sirs, what say we get this show on the road?"

"Good idea."

"Sgt.Major, lead the way . . . "

Some time later, standing in the British Legion hall lobby directly after the church ceremonies, parade and cenotaph salutes had been earlier achieved, Mrs. Crenshaw said to Jane, "There's that Captain Smythe, don't you think now is as good a time as any to walk over and introduce him to our Sergeant?"

"I think you're absolutely correct!" she replied mischievously.

The Sgt. Major and aunt May were there in the lobby also holding the hands of the Crenshaw children. Mrs. Crenshaw looked on encouragingly at Jane and her ruggedly handsome escort, Sergeant Steele.

Jane, with Ben at her side, walked straight for Captain Smythe and his group. They saw them walking from a distance and as they came closer, you couldn't mistake the surprised look on their faces when they became aware of the known but rarely seen sand-coloured beret of the SAS with its winged dagger cap badge and the motto of "Who Dares Wins," not to mention the very distinctive airborne wings on the right shoulder sleeve unique only to the SAS, along with Sgt. Steele's bright red sash and his own full set of medals!

Their combined beauty and presence, even in uniform, was the kind that just doesn't get passed unnoticed. You just knew everyone in the place had picked them out, as the word "distinctive" would have been an understatement. All eyes were constantly watching, for it was a rare sight indeed to see any member of the 22 SAS in dress uniform, especially with such an officer by his side.

"I thought it would be a perfect opportunity to bring Sergeant Steele over here to see your lonely War Medal Jeremy, allowing for the fact that you considered him incapable of even having that at the time, also not forgetting how you wanted to laugh at him in his plain old uniform! Like I said, if your memory serves you well?"

You could cut the ensuing silence with a knife. When Jane had been speaking, she made it a point of making eye contact with all those in his little group, ensuring for herself that they all fully understood the implications of Captain Smythe's previous insults, and how they were obviously now backfiring six-fold. Hence, the number of Sergeant Steele's own medals, which were, obvious further embarrassment to the Capt.

Jane made it a further point of being vocal enough so that all in the obviously close and nearby vicinity could overhear her comments. Looking at Ben with her prettiest smile Jane added, "Not only is the hired help much better looking than you Jeremy, but it is obviously clear to anyone he was the only gentleman and quite distinctly, is by far the superior soldier too!"

In her final look of punishing scorn worthy of the Ice Maiden of yester-year, she told the Capt., "Rank and power is a privilege to be used and not abused Jeremy, but that aside, I think the Sergeant here has more character and soldier in his little toe than you have in your entire body. Let's face it, in a man for man pissing contest you lose big time."

Looking back at Ben she added sweetly and demurely, "If there's anything I forgot to say, please let me know Sergeant?"

Studying the thoroughly deflated countenance of the Capt., then over to the positively glowing spirit of Jane, Ben gave his famous smile, "It appears to me Ma'am that your comments were heard and understood!"

Amid the choked off guffaws and splutterings of officers and men alike who were nearly choking on their ales as they let fly with uncontrolled mouthfuls of beer spray, there were also some cheers from the surrounding officers and men alike too! So the verbal thrashing finished, with a final look at the public humiliation of the Captain, Jane turned to Ben and with eyes sparkling wildly, offered for all to hear, "Well, now that I'm finished here, would you escort the General's daughter over to the bar and buy her a drink?"

Looking proudly at her now and in a whole new light Ben replied, "It will be my most pleasurable duty to perform Ma'am!" They left the Capt, red-faced and standing there alone, like the ridiculed nit-wit he deserved to be!

As the General and Sgt.Major were standing a respectable distance away talking to some old comrades, a retired Brigadier approached him to say, "General Crenshaw, it's good to see that daughter of yours is made of fine British upright stock. By Jove, I haven't quite enjoyed myself in years until I heard that speech and telling off that she gave to that uppity snooty Guardsman. Damn fine show, tell her, damn fine!"

"Thank you Brigadier, thank you, I'll be sure to tell her!"

"Damn fine looking young man and soldier with her too, if you don't mind my saying so, they look damn well together, reminds me when you were a cock-sure dashing young rogue too, heh?" He walked away jovially and waving his free arm, shouting his hello's to some other long ago veterans and friends!

The next hour or two passed pleasantly but fast. Jane was hoping that time could and would stand still for her and Ben, for she knew that with their leaving for the Mews and to home it would mean Ben would have his final meal with them all before his departure. The Sgt.Major would then drive him to the Basingstoke train station, to leave them for Hereford.

The Crenshaw family were kind enough to ensure that Jane and Ben were left alone in the kitchen in privacy to say their final good-byes. Not being judgemental either of the fact that their daughter Jane was an officer and that Ben was an enlisted soldier, for them it was immaterial! Her happiness was their major concern. They had long ago deferred to the fact that their daughter was her own person. Not to mention a mature, fully grown woman, capable of making her own friends and the like in her life. Besides, it was obvious to all that everyone was attached to the very likeable Sgt. Ben Steele.

Alone with Ben and with tears flowing down her cheeks liberally now, Jane turned from the kitchen counter having had her back to him and the room. Trying to hide pitifully her sadness and all the future tears she knew she would shed in her state of distress with hands and arms clasping, holding herself tightly, in despair her shaking frightened voice and tired weary eyes said, "You're breaking my heart Ben Steele, why are you leaving me?"

"You know I have to Jane!" was all he could manage to say.

Hesitating for just an instance she asked, "Then just tell me this, the other night, did you mean it?"

He replied simply and honestly, "Yes."

Crying more now, Jane asked, "Tell me Ben, could you have ever loved me?"

Surprised, Ben said, "I've always loved you, Jane. Ever since I first saw you, truth!"

The groan that seemed to come from within Jane at that admission was nearly enough to make him stay, but Ben knew he couldn't of course.

"Oh my, aren't we a pair of odd sorts then?" was all she could manage when she had composed herself a little better.

"Jane, it's for the best, it would never work out for us the way things stand. Call it duty, unfinished business, but whatever this is within me I have to get it resolved Jane. This is just not our time, as much as we both wish it was. "

"What about a future then, do I get one with you or do I never get to see you again, ever?"

"I just don't know right now, Jane. I want it to be with you! I even have some property left to me in Canada. Maybe one day I can sell it off and start a different life, one with you, but right now, like this, the two of us, it would just be an embarrassment and difficult for you and your family to explain. Especially your father. You know I'm right!"

"Yes! That's why I hate you. For being so right. Just come and hold me Ben one last time before you leave and convince me that I will see you again and you will not forget me—my life would be over if you did that to me!"

Ben brought her closer to his chest and whispered "hush" as he gathered her up in an embrace and cuddled her and tried to kiss her tears away. With no more words left, just exhaustion and resignation, Ben knew he would at least dream of her forever . . .

PART 2

Even as the storm played out and raged in the sky above, you could not help but hear on the ground below the many flags atop the building snapping against its drag. As the rain came down in sheets and beat against him mercilessly streaming down his face, forcing him to squint, he leant into it just a bit harder, as the rain's icy wind tried to push him back.

The night's silence was again broken by another loud crack from the flags above as the wind raged through them. For some reason, the sound of those flags on this wet night crossing this deserted square of the United Nations Plaza seemed unusually comforting. The autumn leaves he so liked to see float and dance and decorate the avenue had lost their crispness and now just became the soggy mat that muffled their steps. His mind, normally ever so alert and vigilant, briefly wandered from the seriousness of his impending duty looking around as they walked briskly, pushing into the sheets of rain.

Next to him, the younger man had his own thoughts. *How is it every kid loves rain and adults come to detest it,* he thought? Then, to confirm his distraction had been noted, the muffled sound of the voice next to him startled him to attention.

"I hope that smile on your face doesn't indicate you're ready to go into a bloody Gene Kelly routine and start dancing on me?! . . . " the voice trailed off.

"Actually Sir, I was thinking of . . . "

"Well, whatever you were thinking of, hold that thought son, we have company ahead!"

Heading up the steps leading to the entrance of the United Nations General Assembly building in New York City, they barged into the building foyer through the large glass doors and went over to the sentry stationed in the main lobby, just slightly behind a four star U.S. General. Frank D. Clarke, touted as a "top candidate" for being the next NATO Supreme Allied Commander of Europe (SACEUR) and who was also a "past" commander of IFOR in Bosnia and Herzegovinia (COMIFOR).

Exchanging courteous but half-assed salutes, their be-

draggled attire seemed to have priority right now over proto-
col. They started stomping and shaking off the rain and went
about yanking off their issue raingear. General F.D. Clarke was
first to speak.

"Blasted rain, reminds me of my honeymoon up in
Vancouver, Canada." After the expected chuckles and laughs
died out, he went on. "Well gentlemen, if you'll be so kind as
to get your passes and follow me to the office, we have business
to attend to!"

One star General MacKenzie Logan, a highly decorated current Pentagon strategist and a veteran of Bosnia and the U.S.'s first
involvement there with Operation Joint Endeavour, looked at his
partner and asked of him, "Captain, did you bring my file folder
down with you as I asked?"

"Yes Sir, General!"

"Well then son, let's follow the General and see what's so important as to bring us out on such a lousy night, heh?"

"Yes Sir, General!"

General MacKenzie Logan leaned over to speak close to the
ear of his partner on this night and said, "Captain Rance, just
one thing, before we arrive at the good General's office, would
you please decide just which title you wish to address me by,
you're getting me nervous," he said with a good-natured wink.

"Yes Sir, Gen . . . Yes sir!" he quickly corrected and stammered
out.

As they walked briskly passing through each and every elevator and hallway on route to their destination, there were also stationed military Marine guards who did their customary and necessary identity card checks.

As these three officers of the United States Army made their
way through these necessary checks, they eventually reached the
corridor of UN Command, then stopped at a solid oak door which
led into the General's office. The General himself led the way pausing long enough to throw a smile at his efficient clerk/secretary
and miracle worker only to plead, "Maggie, can a cold wet stray on

a night like this with no place to go get a steaming hot mug of coffee?"

"Coming up as we speak Sir," she answered with her genuine fond smile.

"What a girl that one is," the General nonchalantly threw at General Logan.

"I wouldn't know how that is Sir, I just have Cpt. Rance here," he grinned.

As Cpt. Rance coloured and the two senior officers laughed at his obvious embarrassment, the General said kindly, "Relax son, the General here was just being sharp with his wit as he always has been!"

"Captain Rance," General Clarke continued, "if you will be so kind as to wait out here, General Logan and I have some business to attend to."

"Yessir, General," spoke Captain Rance as he quickly proffered the manila envelope and looked to the General in guilt.

Receiving the package and shaking his head in unison and grinning to himself, General MacKenzie Logan followed, as General Clarke went to taking his position behind his desk. Maggie, familiar with his idiosyncrasies, immediately followed them in. She brought the General his coffee in his favourite oversized mug, not forgetting coffee for his guest. Mumbling his thanks to Maggie over a gracious sip of his steaming brew, Maggie left the room quietly and the door closed.

General Clarke spoke. "Well, may as well get down to business. Pull up a chair, I don't want you falling over when you hear me out."

With the mood suddenly very serious, General Clarke slowly removed a large pale blue folder from his desk, opened its pale pages and, looking across his desk, began to talk . . .

"You should know, Mac, that with the culmination of the Gulf War, followed by the major relief operations in Somalia which became a minor conflict in itself, the ensuing problems with Haiti and then the ethnic cleansing in Rwanda that went unchecked and will haunt the UN for years when the truths finally do come out, we have had this constant troubling war in the Balkans in Eastern Europe to contend with, namely Bosnia and Herzegovinia. Just when it finally looked like all armed conflict had come to a halt in Bosnia, which we both served in theatre and know so well, things go and explode in Bosnia all over again! The civil war there has been over some years now but it has meant that the deployment of all UN troops quietly took a back seat to the NATO-led IFOR, which became SFOR, up until the sudden and recent eruption in Kosovo which have left them badly compromised and under-strength in this region.

"The bombing and air campaign we allies conducted of strategic targets in Yugoslavia for invading Kosovo, has had the NAC+N and UN Security Councils politically concentrating all their time and energies into this one area, terrified of it spreading like wildfire and starting the next major war, the 'big one' they're all afraid of. It isn't so much 'where' it is going to happen Mac, it's just that none of the military or even politicians wants to be the person responsible for starting it all. Quite frankly, I think this is making everyone over-cautious! Every time there's a conflict or war now where we're needed, everybody wants to 'get stuck in' but nobody wants to be the first one to do it—in case it all goes to hell in a handbasket!

"In Washington D.C. on Feb.14th of this year, our President offered to send 4,000 of our own US troops to Kosovo, about 15% of which was for an intended approximate 30,000 troop NATO force. The peace talks in France stalled as you know, NATO then again threatened their usual air strikes 'if' the Yugoslav Serb Army and the Albanian Muslim-led KLA rebels failed to reach a brokered peace deal. They didn't deal, it fell apart and you know how things have developed from there too!

"Mac, as I speak, all our military leaders gather in The Hague to try and find a solution to contain this awful mess in Kosovo—

and now on top of it, the shock of Bosnia to contend with, all over again! The British Defence Minister is struggling in partnership with our own Secretary of State to get past the hysteria and schizophrenia of an impending 'All-Out' Balkan War!

"The NATO Kosovo verification we put in place and know as Operation Eagle Eye, became in its turn, Operation Determined Guarantor, which prompted the NATO insertion of the relatively new Rapid-Reaction Force troops with Operation Determined Force. As you know, this last force became the quagmire and opening that the Bosnian and Yugoslav Serbs have waited patiently for, otherwise, the man has to be a raving lunatic to even consider going into Bosnia all over again. They may have even orchestrated this whole Kosovo scenario just for that, Mac. Anyway, the one thing we do know for certain this time though is that they are the aggressor here on this latest one.

"The approximate 32,000 troops of SFOR we sent were decimated in numbers in Bosnia by shifting them to Kosovo, to back NATO's Rapid-Reaction Force. The approximate 10,000 remaining troops of SFOR's Operation Joint Guard, our own Big Red 1, were badly outnumbered by the Serbs, they were forced into defensive manoeuvres and the humiliating pull-outs were reminiscent of the last days of Vietnam. In their fears about the Balkan war spreading and even overflowing into Macedonia and Albania and everywhere else de-stabilizing the entire Balkans commands greater fears have been realised, as we are now at war with Yugoslavia.

"The build-up to all this Mac, is that the Serbs were always getting stronger, getting their footholds to re-group and short of the UN or our allies admitting defeat, the Serbian forces have constantly harassed and prevented any of the UN peacekeeping forces from driving them out of Bosnia anyway. These are facts that don't make the evening news back home Mac, like when the Serbs put a ban on all our military convoy escorts in late 1998-99, which was only done to give aide to Sarejevo and some of the other hard-to-reach but strategic locations in Bosnia. These set-backs were just crippling. Therefore Mac, I can sum up our peacekeeping mission in Bosnia as 'marking time' in a sort of void waiting for this inevitable new war, which is, a most unpleasant conclusion.

"This Bosnian President is a very charismatic leader Mac, at least to his own people. He seems to hang on the popularity of the majority every time he starts another war or conflict. The same can be said for that Serb President character. But they are competent adversaries, not stupid people as the media like to portray. They have done remarkably well making sure the remaining UN and NATO-led troops in Bosnia were continually harassed, attacked and fired upon. A big part of the problem, I am afraid, is also our own reluctance not to do what our instincts and training teach us, namely, engage the enemy! It is also a problem that whenever we called for air-strikes as we should under the Rules of Engagement, like has happened before in Bosnia, they were denied. This angers me Mac, when our UN Commanders fail to pass on these requests to NATO, causing repeats of the 'Dual Key' errors of the past.

"Mac, this isn't rocket science! It doesn't take a lot of smarts to figure out that as long as the UN or NATO were *never* going to fight, only defend, all the Serb forces needed to do was wait with these problem-delaying tactics. My assigned counterpart over in the UK, General Thomas Crenshaw, is arguing this very same point. His own reports and Intel have constantly been over-looked and ignored by the politicos there too. Shit, I wish they would just listen to history for once and leave the fighting decisions to us. The largest peacekeeping mission in the post-war world has been made ineffective through intimidation by the Serbs, can you believe that—and by a lack of will power and resolve by the West. This Radovan Karodzic is organized and damn bloody-minded. He is *not* a stupid, illiterate moron as some of the UN Command have labelled him. He is an intelligent determined adversary and opponent Mac.

"His General, Blavic, is his right arm and they have *both* taken this thing back to square one. Right where we were all those years ago even before we joined in. They have the remnants of the SFOR troops and the Bosnian Army surrounded and under siege in Sarejevo and other isolated places. All we can handle right now is diplomacy and aid 'air-drops.' We can also eliminate air strikes as too many civilians are there and we know how the public responded to those on Kosovo, they were just not behind us. On top of all this, all the refugees in the region are in mass migration once again.

"We have other serious problems to contend with here Mac, if you ever thought that all that's been said here was more than enough! Because back then when the multi-national military Implementation Force, IFOR, flatly refused to search for suspected war criminals as indicted by the International Criminal Tribunal in The Hague after the Peace Agreement, their number one suspect and most wanted, one Aleksander 'The Gorilla' Dobrilla from the Krajina region, is now a major player. He is one of their golden boys. To jog your memory in case he escapes you, he is also the man responsible for the 'suspected' atrocities, not yet proven, of Srebrenica. We now know he was involved and that he was the right-hand man, right there alongside Blavic. He started out as Blavic's bodyguard and driver at the start of the war in 1992, and has risen rapidly ever since. He is said to have also been the architect and source of the 'BZ' chemical agents used, but little is still known about that and we have yet to prove it.

"To compound the equation, just a few short years back, the IAEA received notification that as 'Yugoslavia' was no longer a Member State due to its break-up, it was now a free zone and player if you will. Mac, we always suspected that the former Yugoslavia had nuclear missile silos all over its territory in some former pact with Russia. If they did, and Serbia now get those nukes from them as we sit back and let them consolidate, we have another monster and potential disaster to contend with. Letting tyrants like these get their hands on Nukes is not good notions to go to bed to sleep on at night, Mac. We have to make sure it doesn't happen or hasn't already.

"Mac, we are losing our credibility! To regain some face, respect and the backing of the free world once again, we have to prove to this world we are capable of making the tough choices and will not be cornered, bullied or compromised by these opportunists because of our own decencies. We did that once before, a long, long time ago! Mac, our own people are not prepared to let that happen, or this excursion into Kosovo, or the retaking of most of Bosnia and Herzegovinia by the Serbs. It will not be left unchallenged. We have argued our case and been given the green light. We have less than a year to put it all into place and show them our plan is the only way.

"It is time for the UN to kick some badly needed ass! We are going to revamp our past policies and re-deploy troops. All these issues and change in geographic boundaries have brought an ever increasing rise in global conflicts and the opportunity to push or to change those geographic borders. This has meant that the deployment of those UN troops and the profile of the United Nations has never been higher nor the demands that accompany it been greater."

Peering over his folder now like a hawk but with no noticeable movement of the head, watching for any reaction from General Logan, he continued.

"There is a major philosophy and power struggle going on here at the UN, Mac. The people of the United States have long refused to wear the blue beret of the international peacekeeper, yet will only get involved in these conflicts if we call the shots all the time and remain totally independent. Our allies see us as control freaks and quite frankly, are getting tired of always having to do the dirty stuff on the ground to then watch the US come in after the fact, then take charge. It is an issue we need to address real fast, or we really will be out on our own! The positive is that most recognize the need for us to police the globe and still come crying to us with their problems to bail them out. But there is also an ever-growing acceptance and 'push' for the United Nations as being the first choice as that peacekeeper for us all, before any of the so called individual super powers are called in, or go in alone. To be the ones to respond to hostile warlike situations is a task and responsibility with its very own, unique political problems."

Taking a long warm gulp of his hot coffee and over the rim of his cup through the rising steam, the General paused once again to look for any change or excitement in Mac. Disappointed, he went on.

"To continue, at this time Mac, many Member States of the UN Security Council feel it is, and should be, their own elite fighting units as that initial combat unit of the United Nations that are sent to diffuse these conflicts now and into the future. It is this very present 'status quo' of sending so many mixed nations that create time delays, leadership problems, logistical problems. They all waste valuable time in responding to these conflicts in general, not to mention the many language difficulties this also creates.

"So this desire and jockeying we have *always* had going on here politically to be that sole fighting force of the UN, to represent them, is causing some furious debate and thinking regarding policy change, I can tell you Mac. With all its logistical problems aside which we needn't mention at this time, imagine the prestige involved, if you will, to any and all those nations of the UN who want to become or be that single unit? It was and is fast becoming a problem out of control of its very self!"

The General was really enjoying this, for now he knew he finally had his hooks into Mac's expectant attention. Without faltering or sounding excited himself, he continued on further.

"So, under the direction of the Secretary General himself, the top brass of the five most powerful nations' military have agreed, through bitter dialogue but nevertheless agreed, to create a selection process they will all abide by, honour and respect, and in so doing, agreed that this selection process is again necessary and vital to establish who! Whoever is chosen for the next three years will be *that* strike force Mac, the chosen spearhead and the sword of the United Nations!"

He wondered if his words had sunk in. He knew he had to continue now and press on regardless.

"In 1999 Mac, the results of years of tense, secret meetings are in. The major obstacle is finally cleared. We knew we needed a unit of Divisional strength but could just not get the necessary approvals or commitments. Instead, we found a way to actually side-step the problem and all the official red-tape as well as circumvented all the beaurocrats by beefing up a Brigade so that it at least rivals a division in strength. We needed the Command Structure we desired and we also needed enough reserves to operate independently. Not to mention the logistical arms and sappers. We both know that we do the fighting mostly, but nothing else happens in any theatre without them. You still need them to do their part to win the 'hearts and minds' of these wars and conflicts afterward for you."

Looking up, the General beamed when he spoke with finality.

"General Logan, the fruit of their labours rests on *your* shoulders now. The creation and formation of a competent, *S*trategic *A*ction *B*attle *R*eady *E*ntity as it has been called, but all the same a quick reaction fighting unit, is *your* responsibility to create, answerable only to me and the Secretary General of the United Nations himself."

Ah hah, finally shocked the bastard, thought the General as he leaned contentedly back in his leather chair and looked at Mac's apparent countenance of bewilderment. The look on General Logan's face, with slack jaw just hanging and head tilted askew as he also looked back, was priceless! Laughing, the General broke the silence by saying, "Come on Mac, this silence is not you, challenge me on this or say something, heh?!"

Slowly and deliberately forming his words, Mac finally spoke. "General, when you called me in to New York a few wet nights ago and saddled me with Captain Rance, no disrespect to the Captain out there, but I just naturally assumed that it was for the usual statistical purposes, for that is all Captain Rance outwardly seems to have an interest in besides that computer of his!"

"Surprised the bejabbers out of you, heh?" understated the General grinning from ear to ear!

"Surprised doesn't quite cut it, Sir. With all due respect I think you have the wrong man."

"Like hell I have," thundered General Clarke slamming his desk with a meaty fist and pointing his finger, "When the Pentagon assigned you to me for this project, you came highly recommended by *all* the Joint Chiefs. You should also know that final selection for this assignment was approved by 'the man' himself Mac—along with me getting the final say-so!"

Leaving time for those words to sink in he went on, "That pioneer of all modern special forces, Colonel Fredericks, held a staff position similar in nature to what you have now and look how he turned out. Face it Mac, it's that once-in-a-life-time chance to get back into the saddle again and do what you do best—kick some ass!"

"I respect the General's faith in me, but aren't my skills in the combat role a little rusty?"

"The reason we, and why I specifically chose you Mac, is that no matter how rusty they may be, they were the best. Just like riding a bike, you never forget those skills. Besides, we were more impressed with your administrative and motivational abilities combined Mac, because whoever takes this job is going to need every damn blasted ounce of tact and diplomacy he has!"

"It seems too good to be true Sir. At last, the formation of a true independent military unit, only taking orders from and only answerable to the United Nations—I'll be dammed!!"

"That you will be, Mac, that you will. But these next points I make are important for you to remember and don't ever lose track of it, because as I speak we are *still* trying to convince those within the Security Council with tunnel vision that a need for a Brigade this size is absolutely necessary. Half the problem with the UN is response time which you yourself identified for us Mac while the other half is having a Brigade large enough to actually fight in any theatre realistically and have enough in reserve also without having to wait or go begging to Command for more manpower to contain this break point, or that risk area.

"If you ever need an example, just look at those Brits. Courageous bastards and they have some great units for sure, but they *need* allies only because the size of their units are so small now. I don't believe you could cut or scale them back much further. If they were to take serious losses in any theatre of operations acting alone, their only option would be to bring in another Brigade of similar size. This still takes time and has its own logistical problems, other commitments or tasking. My point being, what if their new fancy Air Assault Brigade took serious losses or was compromised in one of those scenarios? As good as it is, they have no other reserve troops on the same level of training or ability to instantly replace them out there in the field.

"So having a Brigade large enough to do the job without relying on outside reserves of manpower and equipment is every bit as important as speed, trust me on that! There is one thing you will hear 'over and over' in this position Mac, that is the words, 'Give me more men!' Most conflicts have eventually required a peacekeeping force anywhere from 20,000 to 50,000 troops in size—eventually. New tactics due to equipment and technology demand speed, but it also demands a Brigade capable of having enough men to go in and get the job done without waiting for less trained or qualified personnel from your own or other country, which in most instances due to political reasons, can realistically take months. Look at the formation schedule and timetable to get *this* Brigade operational. Thankfully, once it's in place, we never have to worry about this part again. The time delay will only be for the formation, once it is complete, we will not be stopped by long delays totalling months. We can and should be able to go in a moment's notice as soon as the word comes, a headache I can do without and will certainly not miss Mac."

"So when do you start this Brigade Sir?"

"You General, you, remember?"

Mac grinned. "I meant to say when do we get the troops and equipment and location and set it all up?"

"That was what we fought so vigorously 'for' and 'over' Mac, don't you recall? That whoever had the task of the formation of this unit would do so totally independent of all Member States. That's for you to put in place and do Mac, on our behalf of course. After all, you are now the new Commander of the United Nations' very own armed service, namely The Sabre Brigade!"

Like a little boy who had just received a new train set, the General's excitement was growing and contagious. "How long have you known this sir?"

"Not five minutes before I had you paged and ordered to meet me here."

"And Captain Rance?" General Logan asked again.

"Ah yes, Captain Rance. Well Mac, the young Captain out there is a graduate of MIT down in Boston and a veritable genius with computers so I'm told, especially with logistical and statistical material. This task is going to be difficult enough and you have to start with a core compliment of staff somewhere, so I thought, why not? Hence Captain Rance—my gift to you!"

"If he's that good I'm sure he'll have ample opportunity in the near future to prove it to us, but there's just one little question nagging at me right now General, which is, if I am to be the new commander . . . "

" . . . AM the new commander!" interrupted the General.

"Yes, well, as the new commander, where do I base this unit or brigade, where do I get my men, how many men do I get and as I said before, where do I get our equipment?"

"It's all here in these blue pages, Mac. When you leave this office you take this folder along with you. Maggie will be giving you and the young Captain waiting outside one-way airline tickets to your destination and future barracks! From there on Mac, you're answerable only to me and the Secretary General himself— best of luck son!" General Clarke smiled as he came up from around his desk and proffered one of his great big meaty hands for a firm handshake! The grip was strong and warm and conveyed all the sincerity and desire for success that he felt, as the General moved his arm in two short pumping motions of his shake.

"Don't let us down son, you're our last chance to see that this works, just go out there and do it—remember, 'Rangers Lead The Way!' "

Mac left the inner office with the General right behind him. Outside in Maggie's territory sat a bewildered and confused-looking Capt. Rance. As he entered, Capt. Rance jumped to his feet and this time he had it just right. "Sir?" he enquired and getting no reply and not knowing quite what to say now, Capt. Rance stared back and forth between the two Generals, waiting.

"Captain Rance, here are your papers. As of this moment you are now assigned to General Logan indefinitely. Any further questions, you are to direct them to your new boss, do I make myself clear?"

"Yessir General!"

Captain Rance's instincts told him he was going to be part of something important at long last! Looking directly at General Logan with a huge grin he asked, "Well sir, what next?"

"Are your bags packed like we were ordered?"

"Sitting in the hotel room by the door as we speak Sir."

"Okay Captain Rance, just give me a moment with the General here and I'll be with you right outside."

"Right Sir, I'll be waiting!"

Turning to General Clarke for his final farewell, Mac didn't quite know what to say. This man had been like a father, friend, and mentor all rolled into one this past year as they worked on the project assigned to them by the Brass at the Pentagon. He was as close and familiar with the General as one can get. He never thought in his wildest dreams this day would become a reality, or expected to be the one chosen for this task and duty. He had also along the way managed to get on good personal terms with Maggie, being able to call her by name and he even thought she harboured a deep interest in him! She knew what they had discussed, she was, after all, the top General's secretary. Becoming sentimental and letting her emotions show through her tears, she managed to give him a hug, and looking over her shoulder as she did, Mac thought he saw the corners of the General's eyes glisten as well. The big heavy-set General reached over and patted his shoulder saying, "Okay, enough, go on, get out of here Mac, but keep in touch. I'm still your boss and if anyone gives you any great problems call me, I'll see what I can do. No promises mind you, but I'll see!"

Picking up his issue raincoat that wasn't yet dry, and putting on his hat, he came to full attention and threw the General a crisp salute, then making a smart about-face, he stepped out into the hallway.

"Well Captain Rance, let's pick up our bags on our way to the airport, shall we? And by the way Captain, if you have a first name, now would be a good time to share it with me."

"It's Theodore sir, but I would be grateful if you just called me Chance."

"If that's what you prefer but you'll have to explain that one."

"Never played it safe if you know what I mean Sir?"

"Well Chance, this isn't particularly a safe bet either so welcome to the unit!"

As the taxi stopped at their respective hotels long enough for them to retrieve their luggage, they soon emerged and continued on to the airport. Even though New York has one of the busiest airports in the world, somehow, they all look and feel the same. From ticket counters, magazine stands, souvenir and duty free stores, bar and restaurants plus the self-serves, they all have their usual array of resting, waiting and anxious passengers. In New York's La Guardia Airport the two soldiers had barely enough time to use the men's room before their flight was called. Once they were through the usual security and boarding procedures, they were then finally onto the plane itself.

Mac was grateful that Maggie had placed them in business class besides being anxious and eager to go over his files. *I can really use this extra peace and solitude this type of luxury affords me,* he mused to himself, *so to hell with the tax-payers' money,* he grinned, *on this occasion I warrant it!* After the stewardesses had completed their life-jacket demonstration and procedure, which for some reason always kept him enthralled, they were finally airborne. With the lights dimmed, he waited patiently for his coffee before opening his file . . .

The second flight of their trip was on a small commercial carrier which landed at their destination airport on the outskirts of Helena, Montana. Taking the shuttle bus over to the southside terminal, they looked for and awaited the arrival of their transport that was meant to take them to their new barracks. Mac and Chance sat on a bench near the steps out front of the terminal building. Waiting and squinting into the morning sun they observed the sound and then sight of a familiar vehicle coming into view. Their pre-arranged jeep screeched to a halt right at the steps in front of them as the driver, an Army Airborne Special Forces Major, smiled at them and threw a crisp salute, "Sorry I'm early Sir!"

"Is that statement some kind of cowboy humour Major?" asked Mac.

"Was told to be here at seven a.m. Sir, as you can see, it's 0655."

The new Commander glanced at his watch but said nothing. As the Major threw Mac's bags into the rear of the jeep, leaving Chance to care for his own, he turned to ask, "Where to, General?"

Suddenly realizing that he and only he new the final destination, Mac smiled, saying, "To headquarters Major!"

Coolly the Major smiled back and replied, "I hope the General's Aide can lead the way?"

"What's your full name Major?" was Mac's next inevitable question.

"Galloway Sir, Major Luke Galloway."

"Ah yes," his memory sizing up the Major.

"What unit were you first with Major?"

"Originally, 82nd All American Sir!"

"And presently serving with . . . ?"

"5th Special Forces Sir!"

Smiling broadly Mac responded, "Not anymore, Major."

"I don't understand Sir?"

"I'll explain as we drive."

All now seated in the jeep and driving away from the airstrip, Major Galloway looked at Chance and said, "Which direction then Captain?"

"Just take us out of here and head north for the mountains."

As they had been driving in silence for about thirty minutes steady now, Mac turned to Maj. Galloway, saying, "I suppose all they told you Major was to pick us up in the jeep and drop us off, heh?"

"In a nutshell, yessir."

"Well then, let me start by telling you we are forming a new unit up here in Montana. There will be an initial HQ core of personnel that have been specially selected, like yourself, who will be arriving within the next few days and weeks to start it all up. We will all be the very first members of that unique force. Certain personnel such as yourself were assigned because of their special military skills. I understand that your particular special skills, befitting someone with an MA in logistical planning and having warehousing/purchasing management knowledge as a military officer of stores, is running a first class quartermaster operation. Or have I been misinformed?"

Laughing at the General's humour, Maj. Galloway emphatically volunteered, "Sir, it's the good old Irish in me, a master scrounger it is that I am, but let's not forget I am also a damn fine Infantry Line Officer!"

"If I had Major, you wouldn't be here!"

As they all laughed, Mac broke up their little aside by saying, "I hope you are that good Major, because if what I read in my report on the flight up here is true, this camp we're heading to is just about non-existent, and you're going to need every ounce of those skills and the luck of the Irish to build us a camp we can live in, acquiring all the necessary materials and supplies for an initial encampment of some 500 men, then possibly later, even women."

"Whew! That's some task you just set General. Whereabouts is this camp of ours going to be?"

"Like I said Major, north! Up there on those plains at the foot of those mountains on Military property is the very old shell of an encampment of the original Special Service Force. The old Devil's Brigade itself! We're going up there to find it and restore it Major, resurrect it from out of the ashes like the Phoenix, what do you say to that?"

"I say heaven help us all, heh Captain?" adding, "Is the Captain here joining us too, General?"

"Yes he is. He's to be our resident computer and logistical technological wizard, with maybe a helping hand or two from our other comrades joining us all in due time. But only after you have built us a camp Major!"

As their jeep continued its journey and crossed through the city of Helena and headed north winding its way upward, there at the foothills to the mountains across the plain it stood—nothing! Just like the General said. Mac asked Maj. Galloway to park the vehicle for a moment so that he could get out and take a view of the surroundings and place with his binoculars. As he climbed out, the tiredness from so many hours of travel began to catch up and he afforded himself a few moments to bend and stretch his legs, inviting Maj. Galloway and Capt. Rance to join him likewise.

As the other two began to laugh and joke with each other getting acquainted, Mac walked a few metres further away to have his look. At first he really couldn't see anything. Then, focusing for better vision, it eventually came into his sight, the remnants of a ghost camp. Actually, it was just an old broken down dilapidated shell. Some of the concrete pads still looked to be in place where the wooden huts and office building complex were once situated, he decided. *My God*, he thought, *this is where all those men trained and lived, all those American and Canadians troops from World War II who were the original Special Service Forces!* He suddenly felt goose-bumps. It was hard to imagine that they had actually existed looking at this wasteland before him. He thought back to his childhood where even he sat enthralled at their black and white T.V. screen as they watched "The Devil's Brigade."

He was quickly hit with the realization that they were once a real unit too, not just a movie. Here though, looking across this wasteland before him he wondered how on earth he could manage to do this. To quote an understatement, he knew it would not be easy! As his two officers approached him he handed the glasses to the Major, saying, "Whatever you need Major, just get it! Manpower, supplies, equipment, anything! Remember, we have the authorization to requisition whatever it takes. On this little job we have less than three months before the first intake of our main body of troops start to arrive."

"I have never built a whole camp before General, but then there's always a first time for everything, heh Captain?"

Chance nodded.

"General, now that we're here, just exactly where are we going to be eating and spending the night, or nights?"

"Good question. Well Captain, being experienced Boy Scouts, we're going to bivouac right down there under the night sky in them tents the Major has stashed in the jeep and just like in the movies, the Major here is going to shoot some rattlesnake for our supper!"

They all went back to the jeep laughing. Before they could go any further there was the matter of the locked gate around the fenced property with the sign stating that trespassers can and would be prosecuted.

"Do you have those bolt-cropper cutters that they supplied you with for this trip Major?"

"Sure do General."

Using a given name for the very first time the General said, "Here, let Chance do the honours—and bring us just a little luck there Chance!"

"Hold on Chance," said the Major, "This is one of those Kodak moments!" as he ran to get his camera.

Chance "posed," then cut the heavy rusted chain away, and after doing so, he waved his arm in a wide but low sweeping gesture for them both to enter. The General and Major both in the jeep, moved it slowly through, pausing just long enough for Chance to close up the gates and hang the chain over them. As he jumped into the back of the jeep, they sped off down the hillside in the late day sun, and the beginning of their own unique military history . . .

Maj. Luke Galloway was thirty-eight. He had been promoted to Major just before he was sent to Bosnia as a member of the multinational Division North area of Operations, at Tuzla Eagle Base, coordinating efforts with the UN Mine Action Centre there. In the Eastern region alone over 600,000 mines were known to exist!

Luke started out his military career as a rookie Lieutenant and with a baptism under fire almost immediately. It seemed he was hardly out of West Point when as a newly arrived member of the XVIII Airborne Corps 82nd Airborne Division, he found himself in the thick of the fighting during the Panama conflict to capture Noriega and his drug smuggling cartel. He was also one of those who made the combat jump in.

Besides his warehousing and management skills, he found that he held a natural gift for being a skilled and effective combat soldier, so one Bronze Star later and soon after Panama, he transferred over to Special Operations Forces (SOF) joining the 75th Ranger Regiment, 2nd Ranger Battalion.

Soon Lt. Galloway was promoted to Captain and found himself as a "detached" observer and member of the Reagan/Bush anti-drug smuggling Task Force which worked out of South American locations trying to break the Medelline drug cartel. On occasion, even having some "cross-training" help from those British 22 SAS guys (man but they seem to be everywhere don't they?) with very little mention of those operations being made public by the DOD—which is as it should be. How the heck can you task individuals to do "secret assignments," yet letting the media get their hands on the info and blabbing to the "bad guys" about their intention? *That* part of "freedom of the press" *always* amazed him.

Those missions were a whole new aspect to Special Operations for the Ranger Battalions, as they were trained and most suited to a more different version of Special Operations such as seizing key locations in surprise covert or overt battle attacks. Or a variety of hostage rescue procedures, and last but not least, counter terrorism. Special Forces are trained to work behind enemy lines and after transferring to Special Forces when the Gulf War was in its early stages, Lt. Galloway played a pivotal role working with a special combined force consisting mostly of the world's most renown and elite fighting unit—the British 22 Special Air Service Regiment.

He had to admit to himself, his early impressions and perception that the 22 SAS soldiers were over-rated, were very, very quickly dispelled. They were without doubt, the ultimate fighting machines! What left the biggest impression on him from serving with these men was their ability to follow orders implicitly, yet at the same time, think independently—a living oxymoron. They truly had mastered and honed the art of the soldier to a fine edge. He was also quite surprised that far from being aloof and cold hearted, they were very warm and colourful and full of life with the sharpest of wits. When and how he had his first "real" meeting and joint service with these 22 SAS members was on a biting cold sand stormy evening in a corner of a hangar out on some desert airstrip out in Kuwait at the beginning of Saddam Hussein's "Mother of all Wars!" They were selecting personnel and assigning them for missions behind enemy lines. It all started for him when he entered Command HQ, but that was long ago he thought . . .

Their jeep made its way down from the hilltop and across the plain to where the once proud camp-site of the first Special Service Force was spread before them. What Mac had seen magnified through binoculars was now before their very eyes. Well, what remained at least!

"Wow!" exclaimed Chance, "Other than a few pieces of dried out rotten wood all that remains here are those few concrete pads!

To rebuild this camp it would seem that the Major here will have to start anew!"

Shaking his head at what he also saw, but in agreement with Chance, Luke replied, "I hope you meant what you said about being able to requisition all the manpower, equipment, and materials we need to build this camp General?"

"And more Major!" After a pause he went on, "That goes for you also Captain Rance, until the remainder of our 'start-up staff' arrive, you're on your own in setting up our computer and phone lines and even satellite link-ups when they arrive. I do not expect it to be easy on you both but understand this, you have the backing of the Pentagon and the United Nations to see that we get set up and running, as the saying goes."

"General, you said on the drive down here that those initial 'core' set-up staff will be arriving here tomorrow in a convoy of vehicles to get started?"

"Yes I did."

"I thought you said we were the first General?"

"In a manner of speaking you are, you're part of the first! You're part of a squad of approximately 300 hand-picked men as an initial Headquarters Company that will get this show up and running and be responsible for setting up an outfit and making it viable. Once we have this camp built, initially to hold a contingent of 500 officers and men, we will continue building, growing and recruiting at the rate of 2000 per month, more if possible, until we reach Brigade strength of nearly 30,000!"

"Other than the initial manpower to build this camp and the 300 or so men pre-selected for HQ Coy, am I reading you right when you say the balance of the men for this Brigade as you called it, will be recruited?"

Acknowledging his agreement with a smile Mac said, "All volunteers, but not only that Major, *all* of HQ Company, including us three here, are going to have to pass some initial training to prove we can do it together. Now, do I hear a request to transfer?"

"Hell no Sir!"

"I was hoping to hear you say that, besides, I would never allow it so soon!"

"Well let's leave the rest of this conversation 'til after we set up camp and get some food down our necks, what do you say men?"

"That's a go General."

Mac went about helping Maj. Galloway unpack the jeep and set up the tent. The task of setting up the stoves and preparing dinner fell to the junior member of the group, Capt. Rance, "How do you like your K-rations done sir?" he laughed.

Before he could answer though, Luke spoke, "If you look in that blue Coleman cooler of mine Chance, you'll see that I took the liberty of packing a few steaks and some cold ones, unless you prefer the first option?"

Mac laughingly said, "I was beginning to wonder if we had the right man for the job Major, now I'm convinced!"

"I'll eat to that!"

"And I'll be happy to drink to your health."

A few hours after having set up their camp and having eaten their steaks, they sat back and, sipping on a cold one, Luke was the one who bridged the subject once more.

"General, this Brigade that you're responsible for forming, where exactly are the men coming from, and what units? I mean are they our own?"

"Fact is Major, we are going to be a genuine multi-national Brigade with the bulk of the initial manpower being volunteers from the Americans, British and French, possibly others. Also HQ Coy, which as I told you both earlier, is the hand-picked bunch including us, as we have to start somewhere."

"The 300 men from HQ Coy, are they to be the Americans then Sir?"

"Again, hand-picked multi-nationals and volunteers. From the best fighting units the world has to offer us!"

"Are they all starting to arrive in the a.m. as you said earlier Sir?"

"The Americans will be arriving with the vehicle supply convoy, the French will be arriving by train on that track that runs parallel to this camp and I have no idea at this time how the British contingent will arrive here, other than to say that they were informed to be here no later than noon tomorrow."

"We will all be bivouacking until our Army Engineer tradesmen that are due to arrive with all our American troops, have built the pre-fabricated buildings we need, with us moving into them as quickly as they get built."

"So my job isn't so much then the construction of the base camp, but more a case of setting up Quartermasters Stores and being responsible for the basic military needs of the Brigade."

"That's it Major, but even you know that making sure you have all that you need on hand is easier said than done." With all in agreement Mac continued, "Besides Major, at least initially, until you can designate a suitable replacement, the construction of this camp does need a qualified project manager. Something you are capable of overseeing. In other words Major, we can't afford to fall behind on our schedule or come up short on materials and such."

"But you do know the red tape we face in requisitioning what we need sometimes Sir?"

"That is why they gave me *you* Major. Apparently you are the best there is at circumventing that route. By barter, beg, borrow or stealing, I don't particularly care how you get what you need Major or how you acquire it, I just want it here is all, is that understood?"

"You have my word sir!" said Luke, and he meant every word of it too.

"I suppose that goes for me too?" said Chance.

"Especially you Captain. Without the technological equipment we need for everyday communications and satellite link-ups with the Pentagon and United Nations, we just may as well not bother with it at all!"

"Who will be in charge of my section of Command then General?

"You will be of course Captain."

"I'm just a Captain Sir, won't that cause problems?"

"You'll just have to handle it, and their egos, whoever they are, won't you?"

"Yessir," he said not too assuredly.

After a moment Luke said, "It seems to me, Sir, that we just might have a little problem with a thing called language?"

"Well Major, that was one of the trickier issues in setting all this up. It was eventually decided and agreed upon that the official language of this Brigade be and remain, English. Every last man assigned or volunteering for this unit will have an understanding of English, but interpreters will be available, as are in all SF type units."

"Well that's a relief," said Luke.

The talk then just drifted off from there into where they were from, what units they had been with and Mac getting familiar enough, for the moment at least, to allow them to call him Mac.

"Luke, if you and Chance here want to carry on yacking for a bit more you're welcome, but it's been a long two days for me and I don't think I will be getting a better opportunity in the next few days either, so if you don't mind, I'll excuse myself and get bedded down, as I can use all the sleep I can get."

"We'll be right behind you Mac," said Luke slightly merry.

Somewhere in the night hours they were woken by the lonely howl of a coyote which kept up his serenade for a good half hour.

"What the hell is that?" exclaimed Chance.

"Just the great outdoors!" laughed Luke.

"By the sounds of our General over there, I'd bet money he never even heard it."

Sleepily, Mac stirred enough to say, "You'd lose that bet."

Then as the laughter and howling died out, they all drifted back into their separate sleeps . . .

Being experienced soldiers, getting up early was not out of the ordinary, thus they were up and ready at the crack of dawn. As they were going about their ablution business of the universal three S's (shit, shave and shampoo) in the distance they could all hear a low rumble. Looking far off, they saw dust clouds and eventually a convoy of unmistakably Army vehicles winding down the hillside route they themselves had passed just the previous afternoon. Making a rough guess, they figured it probably meant that they had about a good half hour at most to get finished up here and ready for the first arrivals.

The convoy stretched for at least a good half mile by first guess and the lead vehicle was just about upon them. Coming to a stop not metres from their encampment, a Deuce and a Half pulled up short. Jumping down from the passenger side was a big burly man who asked for General Logan, and not missing a second, continued his approach to state, "I'm Major Biggle of the Army Engineers Sir, arriving with your men, equipment and supplies as ordered!"

"Thank you Major Biggle," Mac saluted back as he offhandedly passed his coffee mug over to Capt. Rance adding, "I'll leave you in the capable hands of Major Galloway here who is to be your project manager. He will direct you as to where he wants all the supplies and equipment off-loaded." Mac added, "If you could, I'd like you now to direct me to whichever part of the convoy my men are located?"

"Pulling up the rear sir!" said Major Biggle, now standing with Maj. Galloway.

As Mac left them, he began to walk his way to the rear of the convoy while the lead vehicles already began to start moving away. He continued to walk, and approaching him from the rear of the convoy in the opposite direction was a no-nonsense looking soldier in combat fatigues with a strong stride.

Mac was the first to speak as they neared each other. "You must be Major Ed Stacey?"

"Yessir!" A crisp salute from the soldier followed.

Taking the Major aside he said, "Major Stacey, before I go any further, let me ask you some questions. Were you and your men informed of any details?"

"Only what we needed to know, as per regulations General!"

"Which is?" asked Mac with a smile.

"Which is, Sir, that we are to be a mixed group, selected and deployed to this location as soon as possible, to be part of the formation of a very specialized unit Sir!"

"That is good. Now what is the breakdown of the men you brought with you Major?"

"Do you mean which parent units are they from Sir?"

"That's exactly what I mean Major!"

"Well Sir, I have with me about 50 Special Forces types including myself, broken down into about 30 Special Forces and 20 or so Seals. I also have about 25 Marine specialists and Recon Marines and the same contingent of Rangers, 82nd Airborne and 101st Airborne Sir!"

"How many officers in your group Major?"

"About 10 Sir, 2 Captains and 8 Lieutenants Sir."

"NCOs?"

"4 Sergeants and 10 Corporals Sir."

Major Stacey didn't have long to wait for General Logan to make a decision as to what he was to do next. "Major, for now because I just don't have anyone else, I'm putting you and your men in charge of the camp!"

"What camp Sir?" the Major asked befuddled, looking around.

Mac, grinning his white teeth said, "The temporary tent camp we are all going to live in over there Major," pointing in the general direction of where his own tent was located.

"I want you to take charge of keeping these men busy erecting the tents we'll all be living in, until we get the rest of our men, or you complete the job, understood?"

"Yessir, but a question?"

"Go ahead Major."

"How long will we be living in the tents Sir?"

"Your guess is as good as mine Major, but as long as it takes until we get this camp built."

"What about food sir, my men have already missed breakfast."

Laughing, Mac said, "Major we both know your men can go

without food for at least a few days, but I'll make sure that as soon as we find the cooks who better well have come along, they get organized right away. In fact, deploy some of your men to assist them, alright."

"Right on it Sir, and one last question Sir?"

"Go for it Major."

"Sir, when will we be debriefed?"

"Once I get all my officers and men here today, then I'll hold an officers' briefing. All right Major?"

"That's understood Sir!"

As Mac walked away, he stopped, "Oh and Major Stacey?"

"Yes Sir?"

"Welcome aboard!"

"Gunny?" called out Major Stacey in search of his top Sergeant.

"Yessir Major?" replied a large approaching man.

Before he made his request, Major Stacey smiled and said, "Gunny, I know I haven't held the rank of Major for too long, what, maybe only a few weeks?" and upon receiving a nod from the Sergeant he continued on, "Well Gunny, give me a break on the Major bit for a while, heh?"

"Only way I'll ever get used to it Sir. Don't want to make a mistake and call you Captain again in front of the men, Sir!"

In sublime resignation the Major threw up his arms and said, "Okay Gunny!" then continued, "Well Gunny, better get some men to help the cooks and the rest of the men over to that Maj. Galloway and ask him where he wants us to build this tent city."

"Yessir, Major!" said a beaming Gunny, adding personally, "Reminds you of the Gulf just a little, heh Sir?"

"The Gulf? Don't you mean Bosnia Gunny, all this greenery, there was nothing but sand in the Gulf for crying out loud."

"I meant this Tent City thing Sir?" he said, ruffled at having to explain himself.

Got him! thought Maj. Stacey, laughing to himself.

Being reminded about the Gulf, his own mind started wandering. The Gulf, that was where he received his Silver Star, due mostly to that British SAS Corporal, what was his name again? That was it, Steele.

Going back some, Maj. Stacey was a career officer who was forty and received his commission just prior to the Panama invasion. He was a young green Lt. back then, in his mid twenties. Good job he had Gunny along there as a "Sgt. in the making" to help him on his way before the Gulf War, that was a whole different matter. The Gulf War all started for him as he walked into that distant hangar. The one they all knew was used for briefings and was designated the Special Forces Command Operations Centre . . .

You had to love the pompous bastard though, smiled Colonel Molinsky reflecting on the recent debriefing by the British Officers. He had a liking for the British, dating to his father's past, a man who had been a Polish officer and Paratrooper under Montgomery during World War II and his operation "Market Garden."

Ever since he was a little boy his father had told him of how brave the British really were under that stiff upper lip! *What had this Brigadier Davies called this one? Operation Scavenger Hunt? I love their sense of the dramatic,* he mused to himself. *Well, this will be one for the grandchildren, if that daughter of mine* ever *marries,* he laughed silently. In the office and "prep" room set up in the rear corner of the hangar, Colonel Molinsky idled over to the map and just stared and observed the terrain areas as "possibles." Also now staring at this same map and mulling over his coffee holding a stale sandwich (ahh, the taste of food) he squinted his eyes and poured over what was before him. Colonel Molinsky had received very little sleep himself in the past forty-eight hours of operations and briefings since his arrival in Saudi Arabia. He had been busy monitoring his Special Forces and Ranger Units out on forays and patrols. With the above briefing seemingly over, Capt. Ed Stacey of 5th US Special Forces approached his Colonel to ask, "I'm a little confused here Sir."

"About what?" said the Colonel tiredly.

"About who exactly is running this here Op."

"We all have a role, a job if you will Ed. Remember, there are nearly as many Allies as there are us out here, and they are not exactly incompetent! Some of them, like the Brits and the French for instance, have the upper hand over us when it comes to Desert Warfare, so let's give them some leeway and cut them some slack on this one alright?"

"I'll have my men ready and rolling Colonel!"

"Not on this one you don't Captain, remember? You're the invited guest here.

"Sir?", he said grudgingly.

"Combined Ops Captain! That's what this was all about. Scavenger Hunt is technically a British gig which the Brigadier kindly allowed a few of our best men to participate in!"

"But Sir!", he began to protest.

"I know what you're about to say Captain Stacey, so I'll only say this the once. There isn't a country in the world today that has a better combat trained Armed Force than the British! Call them Paras, Royal Marine Commandos, any other famous Infantry unit, or those cloak and dagger SAS types, there is one thing they all have in common with us, do you know what that is Captain?"

"No Sir. What is it the Colonel thinks I should know Sir?"

"That they are simply on your side Captain! Be proud of that fact and when you get to know them under combat conditions as I have, I guarantee, you also will not sleep at night without saying a little prayer for that blessing!"

"I get what you're saying Colonel, it's just, well my own men were hoping? . . . "

"Shit, they'll probably have my balls for this, but what the hell, I take it you want Sergeant Ridgeway?"

A smile was all the Captain needed to answer.

"That's all you get Captain, remind Sergeant Ridgeway for me that he also volunteered for this! And those wonderful British troops you yourself have just personally selected to lead, you can nod yes here Captain and smile, are waiting for you and looking on right now as we speak, over there on the far side of the hangar!"

This time with a wide grin, Capt. Ed Stacey came to attention and gave his new Commanding Officer a crisp salute. "Will that be all Sir?"

"You have your orders, Captain. Just bring me something interesting back!"

Yeah, the Gulf was a whole different story . . .

"How's it going there with the tents Maj. Stacey?"

"Pretty good Sir, nearly finished them in fact, but the men here are beginning to get a mite hungry and are beginning to squabble a little bit amongst themselves. Though I do think most of it is due to working in all this heat!"

"That's still not acceptable for experienced professional soldiers Major Stacey!"

"No Sir!" added the Major.

"Well, let's call for lunch then. Why don't you get your men on over to Major Galloway then and see where they decided to locate the mess tent, then you can get these men of yours fed at last."

"Will do Sir!"

It was getting close to eleven a.m. and Mac was getting just a little bit edgy as to when the other troops, the British and French, would be arriving. Suddenly in the far distance, someone heard the distinct hoot and whistle of a train.

"What's that noise man?"

"You hear that?"

"Was that a train?"

"Over there, look, over there, a train!" someone else yelled out.

Everyone then seemed to drop what it was they held, or stop whatever it was they were doing to make their way over to the tracks for a better view. Slowly, the train pulled up close to the encampment. Suddenly, like ants coming out of the woodwork, bodies, equipment and kit-bags began disembarking from the train.

What made this spectacle just a little out of the ordinary were the uniforms, accents and voices, which were distinctly French.

"Hey, mon ami, you be careful with my bag, it contains very good French wine from Paris."

"Hey, do not open my bag, American pig!"

These and other such epithets rang out loud and often from the soldiers who also brought their own personal weapons which were presently being piled upon kit-bags along with their webbing, with great abandon. The uniforms were quite varied and different too. For starters, they wore a different shade of combat fatigue and some even had their sleeves rolled up, like the US Marines.

Other soldiers wore a combat issue of uniform that had crests bearing the French Flag. There was also an array of colours to the Berets that these men wore. Mostly, the red of Paratroopers and the black of Frogmen and the green of Marines. But no green was more distinct than that worn by the Foreign Legion! The Legionnaires not only wore their berets at a slightly different angle to other troops but also the badge was over their right eye as opposed to being on the left, as the other troops. The winged arm of their badge, bent and holding sword, was inspiring in itself!

So, amid this disembarkment and the playful hoots and hollering from the American soldiers and rude gestures from the French already in progress, one impressive-looking soldier ignored this performance and asked the nearest American officer for the Commanding Officer.

"Could you be so kind, mon ami, and direct me to the General?"

After receiving a pointed finger for direction, he continued his pace and ignored the commotion the arrival of his troops had caused as he marched directly up to Mac and saluted.

"General, I am Major Lefleur at your service!"

"Thank you Major," said Mac, returning the salute and adding, "It is good to have you here!"

"Thank you General," adding, "but I think our arrival could be debated, non?"

As Mac looked around at the commotion and also to the Major's gesturing sweeping arm, the colonel added with his own smile,

"I do think it is just the good- natured fun of all soldiers for one another Major, nothing more!"

"I hope you are right General."

"I'm sure of it Major, now let me ask you, what were you told of your assignment before coming here?"

"Only what I was needed to know General. That our men were specially selected for this assignment and upon our arrival to this location, you yourself would debrief us."

"I see, well let me start by asking you, how many men have you brought us here today Major?"

Pausing and looking around for a brief moment he continued, "The requested amount General, approximately100 men."

"And their breakdown?"

"What is that term General?"

"I'm sorry. What different units are they all from Major?"

"Ah yes, I understand now General. I have 50 Marines, 25 frogmen and 25 Legionnaires from 2e rep of the French Foreign Legion."

"2e rep?"

"The English speaking detachment General."

Pausing for just a moment Mac then asked, "And what ranks are they all Major?"

"Their ranks consist of 8 officers, 2 Captains and 6 Lieutenants, with 2 Sergeants, not including Sgt.Major Brassard, the requested unarmed combat instructor, and 8 Corporals with the rest making up the enlisted ranks, totalling 100 men."

"Unarmed combat instructor?" interrupted Major Stacey who had overheard the conversation like others, but couldn't help speaking out loud his own curiosity, but then regretted his outspoken comment for the angry stare the General quickly gave him.

Looking directly at Maj. Stacey, Maj. Lefleur said, "I think you will find that Sgt.Major Brassard is an experienced and capable man Major!"

"The Major was not questioning Sgt.Major Brassard's abilities, were you Major?" said an angry Mac.

"No sir, General," he said, chided.

"General, where do you want to camp my men?" asked Maj. Lefleur.

"They will be camped over there in Major Stacey's tent city."

"With the Americans General?" said an outspoken French officer this time.

"What's wrong with my Americans Major?" asked Maj. Stacey testily.

"Just look at them Major. They are uncivilized and undisciplined!" replied Lefleur.

Shrugging off the urge to laugh, Mac looked straight at Major Lefleur and said, "Unfortunately for all Major, tent city is all we have until we can build this camp. Besides, if we're going to serve together we may as well start to learn to get along with each other starting now!"

"Yessir, will that be all Sir?" asked Maj. Lefleur.

"For now Major. Just get your men together and assign them to the tents with their gear and advise them we'll all be ready for lunch, so get out their eating utensils!"

Giving a crisp salute once more, Maj. Lefleur called out for Capt. LaPerriere.

"Mon Capitaine get the men on parade now and tell them to stand tall and erect and proud and march them over here on parade before you fall them out and assign them to these tents. Let's show these rabble Americans what professional soldiers can look and should act like, do you understand?"

"Yessir Mon Major!" came the swift and curt reply. As he walked off he shouted out for Sgt.Major Brassard.

"Yessir Mon Capitaine?"

As Capt. LaPerriere repeated what he wanted from him, he walked away to the other officers who were watching and waiting and began to talk to them while Sgt.Major Brassard walked over to the men and began shouting out his orders!

Coming to attention, the French troops then marched proud and erect over to the compound in front of their Major and came to attention in perfect formation, but not without being distracted by the American troops making fun of them still, with some retaliating of course! With his men at attention, Maj. Lefleur reminded them that they would uphold the honour and tradition of the French people and their trust in them not to let them down with a lack of discipline. Maj. Lefleur re-iterated his command by giving Sgt.Major Brassard a long and knowing stare that all assembled there caught. After being dismissed and assigned to their tents, they were all back out in front of this new encampment with their eating utensils awaiting their lunch hour meal.

Looking at his watch, Mac's concern now was solely the seemingly late arrival of the British troops. *Where the hell can they be?* he wondered. But as they were all mingling and standing around the tents, they heard the unmistakable roar of two Hercules C130 transport planes, flying parallel, at about 1,000 feet. Looking skyward, all the paratroopers present seemed to make instant approval for the "perfect" weather conditions. They then all saw a perfect parachute insertion with full scales of equipment.

The paratroopers were rapidly exiting as they came flying out of both the side doors of the aircrafts in simultaneous sticks. They were using the British Irvin LLP Mk1 style parachutes that are also capable of allowing for the low-level insertion for combat jumps (to get under the enemy radar). For some, this was also their first jump, which you would never have known. The reason for doing the whole drop so quick was to minimize dispersion on the drop zone. Once the canopies of these paratroopers were safely deployed, the sky around checked, their equipment containers (CSPEP) were released to hang from the five meter rope. In less than a minute they were on the ground.

This was the arrival of the British contingent. Trust the Brits to arrive here in style. Mac grinned, they were stylish indeed! The British troops were already gathering in their chutes as fast as they were landing on the drop zone (DZ) and disentangling themselves from the harness. They, including the assembled American and French, then heard the unmistakable shrill sound of a hunting horn breaking the noon air. Out on the plain not 800 metres away the British soldiers were being called in to their points. What they had all just witnessed was an abnormally exceptional spectacle of precision parachuting! At the distant sounds of the horn and the strong voices of command, Paras were all now gathering to one specific spot.

Within a few minutes these airborne soldiers had all arranged themselves into a group formation with an officer at the front. Bergens were on their backs now and the personal weapons they had brought along were in plain view. Some had SA80's with x4 SUSAT sights in hand while others had the same, only with iron sights. When they were all gathered together, they then commenced to march in the direction of Mac and his American and French troops. As the British marched, they were being piped along by four Highland pipers. To the side of this marching unit, which were in columns of three, was an array of Colour Sergeants and one Regimental Sergeant Major (RSM) barking out commands.

"By the cen-tre, a quick maa-rchh!"

"A left right, left right, left right, leeaft!"

"Look lively there laddie!"

"Keep in step!"

"Youu!"

"Lift those arms laddie before I rip 'em off and beat you to death with the soggy ends!—Never mind adjusting the weight of those packs, pretend they're pillows!"

As the British contingent's smiling faces came into full view, you couldn't help but notice that more than a few could better be described as "orthodontically challenged!"

"Right whee-al!"

"A left right, left right, left right, leeaft!"

"Compan-nyy, halt!"

"Aa-leeft, turn!"

A short silence and pause as the Colour Sergeants then took their designated places in with this group of assembled rank and file. The officers took to the front, shuffling to assume their position and place by rank. Only then did the lone RSM march to the front of this parade and come to attention. Looking at his clipboard, he then started a roll call, but to the playful heckles from the American and French troops combined this time! As he and each of his men ignored their heckles, the RSM even barked out his commands louder over their combined noise. When he was satisfied that all his men were present and accounted for, he marched up to the officer in front of his paraded men and came to attention once more, only this time in front of him. As he wheeled to face the officer at the same time, he drove the heel of his boot into the earth with a thud. He immediately saluted the officer shouting, "Company all present and accounted for Sir!"

"Thank you RSM."

Giving the RSM time to take his allotted place, the officer marched over to General Logan and said, "Sir, Lieutenant Colonel Price here with the British contingent, awaiting your orders Sir!"

At the conclusion of his little speech, the whole camp erupted into a loud cheer and hand clapping for the British troops. Unable to contain his smile Mac said to the British officer, "Colonel Price, it's been a long time since I held the pleasure of your company!"

"Yes, it has been a while there General."

"Let me ask you Colonel, what were you told of this assignment, if anything at all?"

Without hesitating Lt.Colonel Price replied, "Only that you yourself would give us our next command instruction upon arrival, seeing as we were specially hand-picked for this little caper with yourself in charge. How am I doing so far?" Lt.Colonel Price asked a little cheekily.

"You're about the same I guess!" laughed Mac. "Now let me ask you. How many men have you brought us in your British contingent, Colonel Price?"

"As requested, 100 Sir, not including officers."

"Breakdown?"

"10 officers including myself. 2 Majors, 3 Captains and 4 Lieutenants!"

"Enlisted men?"

"1 RSM, 2 Sgt.Majors, 1 RQMS, 1 Staff Sergeant, 5 Colour Sergeants, 10 Corporals, 10 Lance Corporals."

"What units are they from Colonel Price?"

"Let me see, RSM do you have that clipboard?"

As he marched briskly forward he halted and saluted. " 'Ere it is Sir!"

"Thank you RSM. Okay now let me see, ah yes, starting here from the top we have 8 from 22 SAS, 32 from The Parachute Regiment, 20 from Parachute Logistical Support Squadrons; 9 Para Engineers, 7 Para RHA, 216 Para Signals, Airborne Logistics, 23 PFA, RMP Provost Unit. Then we have 20 from the Royal Marine Commandos, 20 from 'assorted' Infantry including Scottish Regiments."

"That's a pretty impressive lot you have there Colonel Price!" said General Logan, having dropped the added Lt. part to his rank out of courtesy.

"Thank you Sir!"

"Well, if you'll just direct your men over to Major Stacey waiting over there, he'll assign you all to where your quarters are in Tent City, for officers and men alike," adding, "Tell your men to drop their gear in their tents and be on parade for chow." Adding with an affable smile, "I mean lunch Colonel!"

"Yes I know, will do Sir!"

" RSM?"

"Yessir?"

"Take over please."

"Yessir!"

As the RSM started directing the men over to Maj. Stacey's direction, Mac approached Colonel Price and said, "Oh, Colonel Price?"

"Sir?"

"I will be holding a debriefing for my officers and Senior NCOs immediately after lunch."

"Understood Sir."

He turned before walking away, "Just one last thing there, Colonel Price."

"Sir?"

"Nice to have you aboard."

The two huge mess tents that were looking more like circus tops, now that Maj. Biggle's Engineers had erected them, with some help from Maj. Stacey's men, were located in the centre of the camp and were the unofficial dividing line between the two tent cities, for those of the men and officers of the soon-to-be-formed UN Brigade. There was also another tent city that was erected, although in a separate area, for the Engineers and tradesmen. For these men would build more permanent structures of the encampment, but also needed somewhere to stay themselves while they achieved this task.

Mac entered this mess tent along with Maj. Galloway who had spotted him earlier and had joined him to discuss some logistical matter. As they entered they saw that the officers were seated at tables that had been placed in a longways position across the width of the tent at the top end while those tables for the NCOs and enlisted men went down either side of the tent, thus leaving a huge and long centre aisle to walk down.

Heading over to his officers who were already seated and eating, Mac took the vacated and empty spot they had reserved for him directly in the middle and in full view of the men. The clatter of mess trays and the commotion of good-natured banter and playful jostling did not encourage him, for looking out onto his newly assigned men he saw signs of isolated glares of doubt and antagonism between them all. He expected better quite frankly, hoping that they would make the effort to assimilate rather than to remain independent. He had grave concerns for their ability to interact and gel as one efficient unit.

As he ate, he surreptitiously looked up occasionally and glanced down at the men whom he could see stuck very independently and strongly to their own countrymen trying wherever possible to get the seating arrangement just so. This could pose problems in the future, he guessed correctly, if the men don't learn to act as one unit rather then staying in their separate groups. He was quite disappointed actually.

Maj. Lefleur said to the General, "Sir, please can you have your officers restrain your American troops from hassling and stealing the equipment from my men? It's already causing some minor irritation."

"Like his French troops aren't exactly innocent?" spat back Maj. Stacey in defence of his men, adding, "Besides, maybe if he checked those Brits out, he might find the missing gear he's moaning about?"

"I'll have you know Major," said Colonel Price, the newly arrived second-in-command of the brigade, "That my 'Brits' as you so rudely refer to them as, were civilized while yours were still running around the woods half-naked. So look elsewhere with your complaints!"

The snickers this comment brought opened up the flood-gates as insults starting flying back and forth across and round the table until Mac himself had to interject.

"It's bad enough with all the enlisted men arguing, so I'm going to ask that at least for the duration of our existence, which at this rate will not be long at all, if all my officers can refrain from this petty squabbling and at least set an example?"

With embarrassed silence amid the muffled apologies of, "I'm sorry there!" and of "Me also old chap!" they continued on eating their very first meal of the Brigade in silence. After the meal, Mac asked all his officers to remain behind in the tent and to send runners to bring forth those who were not present so that all his officers received the benefit of his debriefing with no exceptions.

The debriefing itself lasted no longer than an hour with General Logan telling them all only "part" of what he knew, that they were a quick reaction tactical battle-ready response force, described at the United Nations as a *S*trategic *A*ction *B*attle *R*eady *E*ntity, for the sole directive of the United Nations.

To the hushed silence from the amassed officers of this combined force he conveyed to them that he had the philosophy that *all* his men would be made aware of the awesome responsibility that rested on their shoulders and not just his alone. He detailed to them that while equipment and transport was to be mostly American, it was decided long ago that the breakdown and military structure of the Brigade be set on the same lines and standard of rank and file echelon as that of the British and French. Hence the very fact that they were joining a Brigade and not a Division!

The Brigade would be much larger in numbers than the conventional standard would be. Broken down into nine separate battalions consisting of approximately 3000 men each. Being further broken down into respective Companies and Troops and with the remainder of the Brigades complement making up the HQ Company. The Logistical Support such as transport troops, REME, RE, cooks etc, would be a complete separate battalion, but deployed in support, as was their usual role. HQ Coy itself would eventually grow with the influx of more troops which would include the remainder of the men in the Brigade not assigned to a Battalion. He started to wind it down by informing them all that they had to be up and running within the remainder of the year, which left less than eight months! Every last man in the Brigade would be quickly retrained by this first advance party of pre-selected initial HQ Coy, until others could take over, so these men would have to train themselves—and then be prepared for those who followed. So that was it, they were the very first, and it was up to them to set the standard and example for others to follow.

Mac concluded his briefing with, "Gentlemen, I'll allow you a half hour to inform your senior NCOs of the set-up and who they report to and have them back here with you with those tables set out like I asked, ready for the men's briefing!"

The air was abuzz with the excitement as the 300+ assembled

officers and men awaited the arrival of General Logan. The tall and equally stocky British RSM Whittle, who looked most impressive in his beret and insignia of the Coldstream Guards, declared the General's arrival by shouting in his booming voice, "All right you 'orrible lot, look lively and pay attention as your Brigade Commander is now present!"

After the initial surge and stare of excitement, this seemingly strange mixture of the international elite of military fighting forces of the western world, a veritable sea of uniform, began to settle down and take stock of their situation. If the looks of acknowledgment that here were amassed SAS, Green Berets, Paras, Commandos, Marines, Infantrymen and Legionnaires, as consummate professionals, none of them showed their surprise (or were all hiding it extremely well!).

"Gentlemen," the voice of General Logan shouted, "The first and foremost criteria for your presence here is that we are all professional soldiers and do speak English. So, before I continue, let me say welcome to you all."

"Well now, let's understand first and foremost while you're all here, shall we? I understand in your own part of this world *you're* the best?" at which point, even Mac looked out to smile at an SAS soldier to state in his direction smilingly, "Okay soldier, there may be grounds to prove your parent unit's claim to that title, but even here in this mixed company you may get a different opinion, heh!? You're here because you are the best, not to prove which parent unit is, is that clear? So, no Top Gun bullshit here, best of the best, I'll make you better crap! You'll complement and make each other better, including making me better. Let's hope so people, for we really are it! This is what you *all* volunteered for, correct?"

To the snickers that came forth for knowing that most or all were more than probably assigned he said, "You want elite? This is it men, it gets no higher!" Following this he made the cheeky statement, "Unless I or one of my fellow officers or Sergeants ask you to jump!" After the laughter died down he said, "So we are here, and right now it starts!"

"Whose uniform do we get to wear then, Sir?" some bright soldier asked.

Mac suddenly realised the validity of this soldier's question, that even this Brigade had to have a uniform, so he answered spontaneously, "Okay then, it's going to be mine. That's the one luxury I'll afford myself!" Looking around on instinct that he felt would go over well with the men he added, "I'll leave the insignia up to the RSM and the input of you lot!"

Above the sudden looks and hushed mumbling amongst the men he added, "Besides my indulgence, I will also let you men keep one piece of insignia off your own uniforms, I recommend you make it your country's parachute wings! In fact I insist, for no other reason than I like the fact that it is the one thing we all seem to have in common. Let's start there. Oh, and when you Paratroopers get your light blue berets, you will wear them!"

After the laughter hushed once again he carried on with his speech. "The only other concession is that in dress uniform, Military Decoration in the form of Bravery or Campaign Medals only, will be worn! We are a military unit here men, that is official and as such, we shall continue to act the part. The up-side to all of this is that it is like I said, a voluntary posting!" After more laughter he said, "Any such requests for RTUs not from the decision of this Command will be frowned upon!"

"I expect the insignia the RSM and you men design for the uniform of this Brigade will be respected and worn proudly, as both you and it will symbolize a most unique, gifted, and as you all prefer, elite unit! I do want warriors men, but I also want and need people with a brain as well as courage."

Pausing for breath, and to think of anything more he may be missing he went on. "They assured me that you *all* qualified! Let's prove it and make history for this Brigade as I know you, from now on, will be the standard that all or most armies and Special Forces try to emulate! Make us proud and may God have mercy on all of you!" Amid the cheering and whistles from all the troops, Mac turned to Colonel Price and feeling a little more confident, said cheerily, "Take over your Brigade Colonel!"

"Gentlemen," began Colonel Price, "I wish to remind you that not unlike your previous experiences on induction into an elite unit, any rank that you may presently hold is forfeited with the exception of the Sergeants and above and just a few selected Corporals. Only upon graduation of the Brigade's training will it then be reinstated, if we see fit, or if we decide not to keep you and return you to your parent unit!" He went on, "As the General stated, I will emphasize we are a military unit. Not mercenaries. No disrespect intended to you Legionnaires. We are not without jurisdiction and civil laws can and will apply for such violations, if you are caught—or fortunate enough to escape our own punishment!"

"Oh, one more thing. From this moment on, your rank is that of trooper and officers and NCOs will still be spoken to and recognized as such by rank. That is all, and by the way, my name is Colonel David Price!"

"RSM?"

"Yessir?"

"Carry on."

RSM Whittle was your time-honoured and thoroughly British Senior NCO. A veteran of the Falkland and Gulf Wars, he was a truly dedicated and talented soldier. He was a WOI (Warrant Officer 1st class) which was equivalent to the Sergeant in Charge. A top Sergeant of all Sergeants. This was the highest of the ranks in the British Army. The only step up from this rank was to take a Commission as an officer and start all over again! Very few RSMs ever did this, for besides a substantial drop in the level of respect afforded to them and their rank as compared to junior officers, there was also a substantial pay drop. Besides, RSM Whittle had served and worked all his career for this position. For him, it was the realization of all his dreams and ambition. Fearing no man, rather gifted at instilling fear and trepidation in others, this was a role that RSM Whittle seemed born into!

"Well now, look at what I have! A puffed-up bunch of primadonnas if ever I saw 'em in a bunch! I bet you lot can't even remember a 'square' aye? Not by the sights of what I saw earlier today! My, but we will have fun won't we? . . . Okay, look lively then you 'orrible lot, when Gunny Sgt. Ridgeway calls your name I want you to look lively, front and centre and report to the area he directs you."

"I thought these dicks could speak English," muttered a big black US Recon Marine. Wasting no time, RSM Whittle approached the outspoken individual.

"Queen's fuckin' English to you, grunt!" he said, nose to nose. "Why ain't you moving? You want it in rap or something?" at which point he slowly rocked and chanted, "When I culls yo name, answer yo, falls in with the rest, moves along slow!"

Amid the howls of laughter from the British and even some of the Americans and getting bewildered stares from some others, RSM Whittle was quick to say, "Told you we had primadonnas Gunny!"

Returning his stare to the poor Recon Marine who was still glaring at him, the RSM shouted, "Gunny?"

"Yes RSM?"

"Call the British troops first so that this soldier can see them set an example by doing what they do best!" Sensing what was coming, Gunny asked the question anyway. "What's that RSM?"

"Queuing up!"

It soon had everyone laughing! Making eye contact with the worried-looking Marine, RSM Whittle gave him an okay wink of the eye before turning to the crowd again, only to bellow, "Come on, look bloody lively, we don't have all bloody day, you're like a bunch of bloody Girl Guides!"

A few minutes later they had about ten orderly lines consisting of about thirty men each. The RSM spoke up, "The Sergeant seated at the table in front of you is your new Troop Sergeant. He will be in charge of you and will take you for any uniform issue or equipment to the RQMS if and when available! And furthermore, you are not rookies, so my task to maintain order and discipline in this Battalion should be a breeze. Considering the calibre of professionals we have, anything to the contrary like today's fiasco at mealtime will not be tolerated. In fact, as we speak, the offenders are right now being returned to their parent units in disgrace! We are an international unit here remember? You can still be proud of your parent countries, to which you will *all* return eventually, if God and I allow it. But right now, for the next three years at least, this is your home! This is *your* Brigade men, so the buzz word is team-work, save the nasty stuff for your assignments!"

The RSM looked at Gunny Ridgeway and said, "Anything you care to add Gunny?"

"Only that the future of this Brigade also rests with all of you and how you perform. Think about that. There may be better out there, but remember, we are the chosen ones, so let's set a standard that ensures our future existence!"

"Couldn't have said it better myself!" beamed the RSM adding, "As the General said, this is it lads. It just doesn't get any higher, as we all decide together whether or not this unit functions or if it fails. Sleep on that, 'cos tomorrow I will challenge your skills and commitment!"

Tent city was awakened early the old fashioned way, by a bugler! Reveille was a thunder of noise to those deep in dreamland. For others, it was late, as they were quietly lying there anticipating their wake up. It was played by one of the four Scottish Highland pipers with the British contingent, a gifted bandsman also, doing double duty.

Amid the moans and groans of stirring bodies, RSM Whittle, Gunny Ridgeway and Sgt.Major Brassard strode up and down the gaps in between their tents shouting out their commands at the top of their lungs helping in their own subtle way to stir everyone awake. Sgt.Major Brassard was hollering through a loud-hailer, Gunny Ridgeway was accompanying him with a dustbin lid and baseball bat, as RSM Whittle threatened all with just his booming voice, which was *always* enough!

As the respective soldiers of these assembled countries awoke and made their way over to the wash areas in different states of dress, the situation in the officer's area was similar, only the three top soldiers helping all with the waking, were if anything else, just slightly more respectful!

It was 0530hrs when everyone was assembled on parade. They were being informed that before they could have breakfast a six mile run was in order. Thus, in their three separate troops they left the compound heading down the dusty road. There was no particular order or choice as to who led the way on this run. It just so happened the British were in the area closest to the roadway so they led off first with the Americans bringing up the rear being farthest removed, leaving the French sandwiched in the middle. With morning runs like this being a usual occurrence for most of these elite troops (or at least it should have been) the run was easily paced out and returned. There were a few bodies breathing heavy and struggling, but on the whole, it was a relatively easy run.

After the men of the newly formed Brigade had re-entered the camp, the RSM informed them all that their next run would be slightly different. After being dismissed they were then allowed roughly a half hour respite before a breakfast lasting from 0630 hrs to 0700 hrs after which they were all once more required back on parade.

"When you see the RQMS will you ask him to please come and see me RSM?" asked the Brigade 2IC, Colonel Price.

"Yessir, I believe I saw him by the mess tent, just finished eating his breakfast. I'll tell him when I pass by there."

The RQMS had been standing outside the mess tent talking to his equivalent from the French contingent, Sgt. Belfour. In the British Army while an RQMS had the same pay qualification and standing as an RSM, the similarity ended, for where the RSM was also an administration specialist on a day to day basis, the RQMS was a specialist trade. In this particular instance though, RQMS White was also a Warehouse and Stores expert who was logistically trained in Airborne re-supply. RQMS stood for Regimental Quarter Master Sergeant and was the title and rank used predominantly by the British Forces for their senior rank in charge of stores which handled all supplies and equipment. After being told by the RSM who needed to see him, he said his good-bye and left.

"QM White, just the man I've been looking for!" said Col. Price.

"What can I do for you Sir?"

"Your assignment QM!"

"Been wondering when it was coming Sir," he smiled.

"Yes, well Major Galloway of the American contingent is in charge of all stores, you and your core group of men will work for him from now on. This means QM, that from now on you take all your orders and direction from him, do I make myself clear?"

"Yessir!"

Holding out his hand to shake, Col. Price said, "Thanks for all your help on preparing and getting us British here QM. Now let's see you do just as terrific a job for the Brigade!"

"I will endeavour to see that I co-operate and do my duty sir, don't you worry!"

"That's what I wanted to hear. So, just find a Major Galloway then and the best of British to you QM," he said as he walked off.

"Major Galloway?"

"Yes?"

"I'm the British RQMS White, reporting for duty Sir."

"RQMS?"

"Quartermaster of Stores Sir."

"Ahh. How do your own men address you then?"

"Enlisted ranks RQMS or just QM, officers the same and friends a nickname of Chalky, Sir!"

"Chalky?"

"Refers to the name Sir—White?"

"I'll try to remember that, for now though QM will do just fine, if that's good enough for you?"

"Perfectly acceptable Sir," he smiled back.

"Well QM, if you will take this list of names I was given that I have already compiled by rank and position with yourself heading up the list, round up the following men on it so we can have our own little pow-wow and get this show off the ground. We have to decide QM, which men will be in charge of their respective Battalion stores and later respective Company stores. Also, which will be HQ? I understand it will be the first hut or building actually going up, even before our HQ, so we had better get a move on."

"I'll get on it right away Sir."

"ASAP QM!"

"Yessir!" he saluted, walking away at his own brisk pace.

"Captain Rance?" shouted Mac.

"Sir?"

"How was your run?"

"Bit of a struggle, in fact I found I had muscles I never knew I had, but I'll live!"

Laughing, Mac said, "Just you wait until they turn up the pace on you." He then changed the subject, asking, "Have Captains Pierce, Bryce and Lieutenant Maroi reported to you yet with their respective specialists?"

"Sort of Sir!"

"What the hell do you mean sort of?" exploded Mac.

"Well Sir, I tend to think they might feel a little resentment in reporting to another Captain!"

"Is that so?" eased off Mac.

"Yessir!"

"How?"

"Well sir, I'm working on my third request as we speak!"

"Well we'll quickly fix that!"

"How's that Sir?"

Smiling and grinning from ear to ear Mac put out his hand and said, "Congratulations on your new promotion, Major!"

Incredulously Chance just stared at him and spluttered something about thanks.

"It's not unwarranted Chance as I should have seen this coming sooner and done this beforehand. Now get your men in order, that's an order Major!"

Beaming the biggest smile since they had met, Chance said, "Thank you General."

Having a fondness for the young man, Mac returned his smile and said, "Just don't ever give me reason to regret it Chance."

"I won't Sir!"

"Good, now get your men together as we are already behind schedule. Use as much of the temporary equipment and supplies that you have, but for now get me a line through to General Clarke as soon as possible. I'm sure he's having conniptions waiting to hear if we're all here, and whether or not we have killed each other yet, heh!?"

Laughing, the newly promoted Major walked off, only on this occasion shouting for the missing Captains with a lot more authority!

Love to hang around and catch the looks on their faces, Mac mused, as he went on about his business. *What was it I was doing?* he thought. *Ah, got to get over to that Biggle and his Engineers.* As he walked along acknowledging the salutes and courtesies from passing men of the Brigade throughout the compound, he thought how he liked the style and ability of that Biggle, wonder if we can find a way to hang onto him after his duty? *Have to look into that!* Continuing to look around him everywhere, he was becoming excited at seeing what they were creating and what he was an integral part of as catalyst and leader of the Brigade. *What a unit we have the potential capability of being,* he mused. *I sure hope it works— for all of them as much as me!*

On his arrival, Mac was able to see Maj. Biggle shouting and coercing the maximum effort from his men as they were still unloading stores from the vehicles.

"Ah General, I could use some extra manpower unloading here. Free up my Engineers to do what they came here for, to build!"

"Request understood Major. I will make sure I have some men sent over to you as soon as I get back and see Major Galloway, but first I just want to see what you're doing here as you to start to build my camp."

"Well Sir, I already have the carpenters putting up the boards and bracing for our cement foundation pads for each building hut as per your prior designs that were forwarded to my division."

"Any problems figuring them blueprints out Major? I don't know how to read them so well myself, as computers and CAD programs are not my strong points. Good job those architects working for the Pentagon do though, as one of them designed them!"

"No problems there General. We have enough tradesmen and experts amongst us with blueprint expertise to figure these plans all out. The biggest problem we have actually, is identifying all these prefabricated panels for walls and such sent to us, as we never really had a chance to work with it a whole lot, more a civilian construction material and use. Besides, our first job is to get all the tools required for use for when the giant cement trucks arrive, we have to get off-loaded so we can get to work immediately on those concrete pads."

"How long do you expect that to take?"

"No telling Sir, but a lot longer without any extra manpower."

"I don't care how much extra it takes Major. I'll see that you get it, but I just wanted to ensure that my orders were being carried out and that the pad and building for our supplies and stores were built or assembled first."

"Yes, I received that request Sir. It's not a problem, the large stores building goes up followed by their smaller counterparts, then the HQ building, then the TT&C, Technology, Telecommunications and Command Centre, then the Hospital, then Dining rooms followed finally by all the single living quarters."

"How long will it all take do you think?"

"It's fairly quick with this pre-fab equipment, matter of days, just have to quickly pour the cement pads and wait a few days for it to set hard first!"

"As long as that?"

"Have to, Sir. Mind you, we do have an additive or quick-set compound, plus in this heat we may be able to shorten the waiting time."

"How many stories high will the buildings be Major, as it's been some time since I saw those plans myself?"

"Well the stores building will be the largest. Stand about five stories high, be as tall as any large commercial warehouse. By the way Sir, there will be smaller stores buildings, single level, built at the head of or on the site of each Battalion, the large one is the Central Stores, the first one we're building for the Brigade itself."

"That's good," said General Logan, asking further, "what about the other buildings?"

"Mostly single dwelling, at least the living quarters will be, Sir. Again with the exception being HQ and TT&C, with all that latest electronic, computer and satellite gadgetry and wizardry!"

"How high is that building blueprinted to be?"

"That's just a little three storey job Sir, but a lot more difficult to build though, as it's three floors of walking, usable office space, not just three floors high at the outside walls like the Stores building. Also, it has a lot of wiring that the other buildings don't require."

"Can you give me your estimation for completion Major, looking at the plans?"

"Well Sir, they were pretty well-planned out. Barring no hitches, I'd have to say that we'll have the Stores building up within two weeks, the next buildings shortly thereafter, and the whole camp up within three months!"

"Terrific, just about right and according to schedule, Major."

"Thank you Sir."

"What about the electrical lines and cable we need setting?"

"The Electrical and Mechanical men, with the help and direction of your own specialists, are already preparing to set all that up and it's in progress as we speak Sir. Shortly, we'll be having vehicles arriving on a daily basis now, too, for digging and laying cable while on the other side water and sewage culverts are being laid in ground by the plumbers, pipefitters and welders. Just need to get close enough to the big civilian commercial electrical grids and lines of power and supply to afford a hook up."

"Know where that is Major?"

"Not exactly Sir, but I figured that we would be able to call in the local city planners and check their plans."

"Good idea Major, for now though, just take us as far as you can before we need to do that, I don't see any point in having civilians wandering around here, even if it is organized chaos."

"Right Sir, I see your point."

"So, how are your men holding up so far Major, any problems?"

"Nothing that can't be sorted out. Just the usual curiosity mostly as to who your men are exactly that will be living here once we build the camp for them, is all."

"That's understandable, but I'm sorry I can't tell yourself or them more than you need to know right now, hope you understand."

"Sorta Sir, still curious though," he laughed.

After chit-chatting awhile longer with the Major, Mac said, "Well, I'll leave you now, Major. See about that extra manpower for you and a few other things that need taking care of."

"Drop by anytime Sir. That Major Galloway of yours has already come by a few times to take a look and make sure things are going the way they are meant to."

"Good old Galloway, glad to see he's taking his role seriously," muttered Mac as he walked off.

He reached the compound of Tent City, as it had already become known as, while still in his search of Col. Price. As he passed by the mess tent, he spotted him talking with Maj. Lefleur.

"Any of you seen Major Stacey?"

"No Sir!"

"Well if you can find him, grab yourselves a coffee and meet me over in the HQ tent within ten minutes."

"Yessir!"

It was obvious a runner was sent for Maj. Stacey as he was there almost immediately and Mac knew he liked his coffee and he was the only one arriving without one!

"Welcome Gentlemen!" spoke Mac.

"Good morning Sir!"

"Well, let's get right to the quick. As you may be aware, I have deliberately refrained from mixing the men, and left them in the units they arrived with—for now. At least until we have a better chance to become familiar with each other and we have had a chance to see where everyone's skills and abilities lie. What I want from you starting immediately is to all set in place the respective programs we outlined yesterday, regarding the on-going training and development of this Brigade. You all have your specialist Sergeants with you. Let's start getting these men organized and familiarized with their primary role and function which, if anyone has forgotten, is the reason we're all here—that of a combat infantry soldier!"

"I have spoken with Majors Stacey and Lefleur Sir, but you haven't had the pleasure of meeting, or of being introduced personally to, their British counterpart, Major Buxton-Smith Sir," said Col. Price.

"Pleased to meet you Major!" smiled Mac, realizing that the British and the French were a lot more on formal customs and ceremony than the Americans were.

"My pleasure Sir!" said Maj. Buxton-Smith, nodding and shaking hands.

Formalities over, Mac wasted no time. He spoke immediately.

"Well, as the direct and immediate leaders of the men from your own country's contingent, I am relying on your own sense of impartiality in the evaluation of your men. We can't afford any biases to cloud our decisions on this, as we will all eventually be working as one unit gentlemen, am I understood?"

In one voice or form of another, they all acknowledged that *that* was clear.

"That's fine gentlemen, just make sure you have your lists completed then for each skill level that your men attain, handing them back to Col. Price to collate. By that, I do mean separate and evaluate, at least this way we should get a fair and detailed idea of what calibre and skill level and categories all our men fall into. We can eventually assign them to their mixed units accordingly. By the way, we have only started integration with the officers and Senior NCOs until we know our strengths.

"In the next day or two Colonel Price and other officers will be giving you all a briefing on our strengths and weaknesses, on what equipment exactly will be arriving and what we'll be using overall. From radios down to fighting vehicles, to artillery, tanks, helicopters, anti-tank weapons, the complete list gentlemen. Know it and memorize it for, in turn, you will be passing this info along later to your own Battalions when they start arriving. I want everyone on the same page with this. For now, that will do. Very well, you're all dismissed, excepting Colonel Price and Major Lafluer."

"Pull up a chair David, Marc. I have a lot of confidential information I would like to share with you both regarding what's been behind this movement to form this Brigade and how it evolved and how its hierarchy is structured. Outside and beyond this gathering of men for the Brigade, I believe this should be available to my Second-in-Command and Intelligence Officer and Field Commander."

They both looked at him quizzically now, not knowing what was coming next.

"David, you knew you would be my 2IC, but neither of you knew you would be promoted to full Colonel. Yes, that includes you too, Marc. You get the prize in that regard, for you will be our Brigade Commander 'in the field' for you have the most experience. Besides, I need you to take charge out there. David and I will have our own hands full with the over-all Command duties. Congratulations to you both!"

He proffered his hand to them. Handshakes and smiles later, he said, "Okay, let's get to business," and he meant it.

"You never know what dangers lurk out there David, Marc. There's a very influential and political partisan effort going on right now on the part of some of the Member States of the UN Security Council and even NATO. Also, some of my own country's politicians, as well as British and French, want to see that this Brigade is nixed even before it has a chance. There is a big reluctance from Americans to wear the Light Blue Beret as part of a UN Peacekeeping Force. Hence the accelerated schedule set out for us by the Pentagon's military liaison to the United Nations and our immediate superior, a 4 star Commanding Staff General by the name of General Frank D. Clarke.

"If you want some good reading on the subject of Peacekeeping, check out one or two written by past Generals with the UN in Bosnia, maybe then you'll get a better grasp of this beast."

"Thanks about the books, we will read them, of course, when time allows, but to understate the present situation, I was kind of looking forward to this little moment in time if you know what I mean?"

"I also," agreed Marc.

"Of course! Well, let's start by you both calling me Mac."

Smiling broadly, David said as an old friend would, "Okay Mac."

Followed by Marc's now familiar French accent, "Mac."

Moving his coffee mug aside, Mac leaned across the table looking at his two highest ranking Brigade Officers and began talking more . . .

Mac knew he had to get his senior officers who were in charge of set equipment and units prepared and up to speed ASAP when the remainder started arriving en masse. The best and only way to do this was with specs and even an OrBat. First, before he gave that order, he wanted to find out where the Sabre Brigade stood with a most important and often overlooked unit and its equipment, communications.

So, once deciding he needed to get that aspect settled and in order first, he advised his orderly Cpl. to locate Maj. Rance. Later, while still waiting for Maj. Rance to arrive, Mac was sitting in the tent discussing the communications and tactics with his two new Colonels, Price and Lafluer. Mac knew from the discussion as well as his own advanced military tactical and battle training courses at West Point that the classic method of mounting *any* infantry attack was to rain down an advance barrage of shells by battery or plane on the enemy position.

You would then attack the enemy by advancing as close as 400 metres behind this barrage which had to be directed by Forward Observation Officers (FOOs) kitted out with the necessary night viewing aids, laser range finders and any other possible equipment. They would be tasked with instructions to use radio or satellite splurge for the incoming artillery or plane attack several miles back or above them. In back of them, the support of the Forward Artillery Computing Equipment (FACE) would be carrying out the calculations to direct the firepower quickly and accurately. But if the FOO's instructions failed to get through, it could prove disastrous for the attacking infantrymen, therefore good communications in this potential engagement was of the essence.

"Ah, Major Rance, just the man we need right now," said Colonel Price as Maj. Rance entered the office. "Come over here and join us, Chance, and tell us what exactly our communication set-up is."

"Well Sir," started the Maj. as he came over to the desk to join them, "our current Brigade signals equipment is geared for operations over relatively short distances for your general climatic condition and terrain."

"We know the terrain. What kind of equipment is what we need to know."

"Well Sir, the majority of the equipment we have on hand to issue has primarily been used and tested and geared to a NATO role."

"Then it is imperative and obvious that a degree of improvisation is in order, wouldn't you say so?"

"I'd say yes, it is essential, especially with the need for satellite communications!"

"In what way? Explain."

"Well, I just have to ensure we're hooked into the U.S. Defence Satellite Communications System, known as the DSCS. That way, once on the ground, I assure you General, and your HQ Colonel, will have access via a station that has been established as a necessary priority!"

"How large is this system going to be?"

"Well Sir, I have already discussed this with my men and we are in agreement that we use the new Air-Portable installation in any confrontation. It can offer both digitally transmitted speech as well as Teletype facilities."

"This *is* a ground station we're talking about here, correct?"

"Yessir, this station was designed specifically to be air and ground portable, and is also of relatively light weight, considering what it is made of—but we have a serious problem!"

"As in?" asked Mac.

"Well Sir, most battlefield communication systems now use secure satellite connections as I mentioned and we all know, but to make them all work, you need a Crypto Fill that is usually changed on a weekly basis for security measures."

"And . . . " Mac prompted.

"Well the Gun, as it is called, is a small hand-held unit about the size of your common mobile phone which you program with your secure 'Fill of the week' coordinates by selecting set switches on it. The Gun itself doesn't need to be changed, just re-programmed with a new setting each time you make the adjustment."

"How does this make the satellite system work again?" one of the enraptured audience members asked.

"Well, once programmed this way, with the Gun, the unit is

connected to your computer radio equipment and the encrypted fill is then splurged and uploaded into your system itself."

"So where's the problem then?" Mac wanted to know.

"Well Sir, the problem is that on occasion the computer or system will just 'drop a fill' with its coordinates. This will prompt a warning message that then gets displayed on your screen 'WARNING, UNSECURE COMMUNICATIONS'."

"And?"

"Well refilling the system rectifies the problem!"

"AND," repeated Mac, getting irritable he still didn't "quite" know what the problem was.

"Well I'm sure we have some of these Crypto Guns available to us Sir, but for our specific needs, the only one we can use is presently on trials at Stirling Lines in Hereford with the SAS."

"So what are you telling us Chance?"

"I'm saying that these Crypto Guns are classified Top Secret, so we need somebody from our Brigade to physically go and collect ours, in a special courier detail or whatever, as it isn't so much the info as it is the item itself we physically need."

"Okay, that we'll take care of. What about the rest of the ground communications, how do we talk Chance, explain?"

"Clansman, Sir."

"What is that?"

"Man portable and static wireless radio equipment, Sir."

"Can you explain it to us Chance without getting too technical, after all, this is your Brigade Commander, not your own technical staff."

"Yessir," he grinned, "The Clansmen family of radios consists of nine distinct units, 3HF, 5VHF and 1 UHF, which operate on frequencies of 1.5 to 75.9 MHz and 225 to 399.5 MHz bands."

"How easy are they to use?"

"All these different sets share similar design characteristics which greatly simplify operating procedures for the soldiers and are compatible in maintenance."

"I suppose we have to know these things," David muttered,

adding, "I am familiar with them, but go ahead, they need to know," nodding in the direction of Mac and Marc. Mac, leaning back in his chair smiling at his nearest counterpart, Marc, confirmed David's remark, "Go ahead Chance and give us the details!"

"Well Sir, the 3 HF sets are the 320, 321 and 322 with the first of these being man portable. During daylight hours it holds a range of approx twenty-five miles, which can be dramatically increased at night by the use of 'Skywave' technique, that is, bouncing your signals of the E-Layer up in the atmosphere. Using 'Skywave', the 320 model also offers ranges of up to several hundred miles. The 321 and 322 are the vehicle mounted equivalent of their sister and all three operate on the HF band. The VHF elements of the family comprise the 349, 350, 357, 352 plus the VRC 353."

"This could be dangerous," Mac threw out, "I'm actually finding this easy!"

After the laughs and banter subsided somewhat he looked at Chance, "Go ahead, Chance, continue."

"1. The 349 is the smaller of the radios, it is intended for personal communications at infantry *section* level, up on the front lines. It weighs 3.3lbs with a range of .6 miles on the MHz band.

"2. The 350, 351, 352, are all man portable and carried on the radio operators' backs and also operate on the MHz band but on a different frequency setting. The 352 is essentially a 351 but with an added power unit to boost range and signal strength. Both use a 4' whip aerial and the former offers a ten mile range, while the latter can reach five miles, give or take, in certain terrain. Again, both can also be connected to others of their like kinds by land lines General, of up to 1.8 miles themselves. This feature is used to further provide more secure signals traffic down the lines and the second unit re-transmitting it.

"3. The final set in the group, the 353, is vehicle mounted with a range of twenty miles and can be used for voice, Teletype, and digital transmissions," concluded Chance.

"Which were the ones again that the men use and carry on their backs?" asked Colonel Lafluer, a little bit confused by it all.

"The 349, 351, 352 were the radios Sir. They are the ones we have decided long ago to use, and will be the ones the men will carry on their backs. The use of the radios lets a Field Commander exercise tight control on his men sir. Battalion Commanders use the 352 to talk to their Company Commanders, they in turn use the 351 to talk to their Platoon Leaders, who in turn use their 349s to talk back."

At this information Colonel Lafluer came alive, and with eyes narrowing like a hawk, said, "In this area Major, I will get a better explanation from you later, yes?" Half asking, half stating.

"No problem Sir," said Chance, "I am always ready to help."

"Excellent Chance. Now, what's that last and final one on this list do?"

"That final set would be the 344 Sir. It's a UHF man portable set used for ground-to-air communications between ground troops and close support aircraft or transport helicopters, and in this mode has a range of up to 100 miles."

"The FOO's bread and butter!" said David.

"For sure Sir, without this little baby, we can't guide them in!"

"Excellent, Chance, excellent!" said Mac.

"So can this Clansman family of radios and signal equipment withstand the rugged terrain and weather conditions of Bosnia?"

"Well it proved itself in the Falklands for the British Paras and Commandos, just ask the Colonel there. Also, it's been used out in Bosnia by them before and also us on many tours. Their only flaw seems to be the blasted antennae which are susceptible and vulnerable to the elements of changing weather plus just wind damage and rough use and handling."

Looking at Colonel Price as he nodded his agreement with Chance, Mac said, "Just have to tell our lot to be a damned sight less heavy handed then, heh?" adding, "Is there anything else you want to add at this time Chance?"

"Only the obviously important one that I highlighted of these Clansmen family of signal radios, with the exception of the 349 and 350. It is that they have the ability to act as automatic relays, re-broadcasting received signals. This way, all your command messages can quite literally be passed down the line to forward units over ranges that would have been quite impossible had they even been individual sets. This in itself, Sir, was our major factor of choice in picking them!"

"Communication is critical Chance. We will get your Crypto Gun brought over, but in the coming weeks, I want you familiarizing all who will be using these Clansmen radios of any sort, in their actual use. From commanders down to the radio operators, especially the radio operators. Give them all crash courses if you have to but get them all on the same wave length, no pun intended!"

"Yessir."

"If there is anything else you need in the way of equipment, anything at all, see Major Biggle or Major Galloway and have them requisition it immediately. No haggling, have them do it immediately, or see me!"

"The only thing I can possibly think that we would need besides this Crypto Gun and batteries is spare parts Mac," said Col. Price, "What do you think?"

"Good idea. Make sure we have enough available, okay Chance?"

"Yessir!"

"And Chance?"

"Sir?"

"Well done, carry on."

After Maj. Rance left the room David said, "I'm beginning to like that young man more and more, he definitely grows on you!"

"You're right there, David. Now, where were we?"

"You mean who's next on our list don't you?" he laughed, looking at Marc.

In the next few days things got really busy around the encampment and Mac got down to some serious briefings with his two senior officers. Then one evening, he called them to a meeting in his designated command tent come office. Colonel Price, the 2IC and designated intelligence officer, had recently been going over a scale model of their possible first offensive, Mount Igman.

"Leave that for a minute if you would please David, and come over here to my desk and help me analyze our integrity and battle readiness with Marc."

"Well we know communications is on line Mac," he stated while walking over.

"Yes, but what about the rest, you know, the Mechanized Infantry Battalions and Logistics and Air Cavalry and the Armour and Artillery Battalions? Where exactly are they all at and are they up to speed?"

"Fair question. Let's call the Battalion Commanders in here and have them bring us up to scratch on it all then."

"That's what Marc just told me."

"So, what's holding you up?"

"Too long. I have a better idea. I want us to bring everyone up to scratch at the same time! We just don't need to waste time on this. I want an OrBat done and equipment assessment done too, as well basic specs compiled all ASAP. When it's ready, have the RSM get it out to all WOs and officers."

"I think the hardest task there lies with the RSM," said David.

"How so?"

"Tent City, no offices about here with the usual pigeon holes or in-trays, or even access to email. I think the RSM will have to get his Orderly Corporal and resurrect that old reliable format from the history archives—the Regimental Runner."

"Whatever works," Mac smiled back, "But just do it ASAP though, David, we need this in place urgently. This way it can also be passed on when the remainder come to join the Battalions. Can you get some officers together to do an overnight job with Marc's help, of course, and prepare this?"

"Yes, sure."

"Good, can you schedule a meeting for 0930hrs after roll call then?"

"The impossible we do at once, miracles take a little longer!" David quoted cheekily, "But we'll get it done."

The following morning after roll call, the entire Brigade's officers complement and all WOs were seated in the huge mess tent.

"Gentlemen," began General Logan, "let me introduce the Sabre Brigade 2IC, Colonel Price, who is also now our Intelligence Officer. Also, let me introduce you to your new Field Commander, Colonel Lafluer. They have made the briefs and, more importantly, the OrBat and specs you will get shortly on this Brigade of ours." Then, just as abruptly as he started, said, "Colonel Price, the floor is yours."

"Thank you General. Gentlemen, I have been assigned the task of identifying the Brigade's present strengths and position for your knowledge and later for ready reference. The following might also be useful as you might not find it listed on your OrBat or specs: one Company from one of the above Battalions is or will be, our Mountain and Special Warfare Company. That is where all our specialists, snipers, etc are, along with members of the Path-finder Platoon.

"This entire Brigade, gentlemen, can also be transported on relatively short notice fully equipped, in just over 110 flights of C-141B or C-130 planes, or a mixture of military and com-mercial ones. The light infantry battalions of the US XVIII Airborne Corps Battalions, or the new British 16 Air Assault Brigade, are basically small and lightly equipped to be easily transported by air, for a role of low intensity combat. Our *only* similarity is that we can be easily transported by air, but our Mechanized Infantry Battalions were and are designed with hard core rugged all-terrain close and heavy combat in mind! We prefer the insertion, if we cannot parachute in, of Tactical Airland Operations (TALO), deplaning rapidly, to take the enemy completely by surprise. We are fortunate in this respect of having so many ex airborne troops with us, for they obvi-ously are experts in this type of insertion.

"If our initial soldiers from the Pathfinder Platoon from the Mountain and Special Warfare Company are *not* jumping in first, they will split and team up with the Recce and Scout Platoons in the Armoured and Artillery Battalion.

"All Battalions will get logistical support from our Logistical Battalion itself, namely made up of our Engineers, Signallers, Transport, Medics and MPs."

After shuffling some papers and conferring with the other senior officers up front with him, Col. Price then returned to face the assembled officers, "I would now like to pass you over to Colonel Lefleur, thank you!"

"Gentlemen," started Col. Lefleur, "as the Brigade Field Commander, and the one in charge on the ground, I will be tasked to direct you in the field of combat from two sources. I will be in constant contact with both those sources at all times. They are this Brigade's Commander, General Logan, and the Brigade 2IC and Intelligence Officer, Colonel Price. From my Sultan Command vehicle CVRT, or field HQ, I will be their link to what is happening, from the commencement of battle to the end consolidation.

"Let me start by telling you that the lessons of warfare that have been learned from past battles is that tanks and their guns are critical. But, just having a lot of tanks is not enough, you must have the right kinds of tanks, which have the right balance between firepower, armour, speed and mobility. Above all else, you must have an accurate and powerful gun and an accurate aiming system.

"Strategists and military planners in the past have argued that forces consisting only of large numbers of tanks would be decisive on the battlefield. They have stated that independent tank forces would dominate, that infantry and artillery support were not needed. They could never have been more wrong! We proved conclusively in the Gulf War, even in Bosnia on occasion, that infantry *must* have effective anti-tank weapons. You can never be sure your own tanks will be there and military history shows infantry morale will collapse rapidly if the infantryman is attacked by tanks and they do not have powerful and effective weapons to stop them.

"The other lesson of warfare is the importance of artillery. Artillery towed on trucks could be effective on the battlefield under certain circumstances (dug in) but is too often vulnerable and often cannot move or keep up with tanks and mechanized infantry in a fast moving combat role. Today, *all* artillery battalions in armoured and mechanized infantry are light, armoured and self-propelled. In this regard, we will use an assortment, but mostly the 155mm and 105mm Light Guns for our field artillery.

"It is also my duty to inform you gentlemen," continued Colonel Lafluer, "that *after* we take our objective . . ." then he *definitely* had to stop for the thunderous applause and enthusiastic whistling and cheers. Stopping and looking at General Logan and Colonel Price's happy faces, as well as the other officers up front with them, he tried again, "It is my duty to inform you all that *after* we have taken our objective, we will have one final piece to our Artillery arsenal to establish and defend it. One of the weapons we will have to do this with is the American Army's most advanced air defense weapon." Now the crowd hushed. "The Patriot surface-to-air missile system!" The cheers and whistles started up once again.

"This was also not in your specs, so I will give a brief overview for the uninitiated. A key element of the patriot missile system is the phased array radar it has. It combines, in a single radar set, the target directional search detecting and tracking functions. A patriot firing battery has an engagement control centre (ECC) and a number of quadruple missile launchers. As many as eight missile launchers can be controlled by a single ECC. Typically, up to five launchers are assigned to a patriot firing battery, or in this case, Company. A Patriot missile is propelled by a solid propellent rocket motor and reaches speeds of Mach 3 or better. It carries advanced high explosive-fragmentation warheads! The missile's range is approximately forty miles and its maximum engagement altitude is approximately 75,000 feet. The Patriot is obviously a highly effective surface-to-air missile which, again, was proven in the Gulf War!

"The Patriot will definitely provide us with a defensive capability against tactical ballistic missiles the Serbs or anyone else might have! There is a built-in self-defense system against nearby critical targets. These modifications are designated as Patriot anti-tactical ballistic missile capabilities (PAC). Tests conducted at White Sands missile range prior to the Gulf War confirmed that Patriot missiles can intercept and destroy tactical ballistic missiles in flight—which the Gulf War proved through taking out the Scuds! On that final note gentleman, I thank you and would now like to pass you over to the Phoenix himself, General Logan."

"Thank you everyone," General Logan said, standing in front quietly.

"You should all realize that Colonels Price and Lafluer stayed up nearly all night preparing the OrBat and specs, plus the briefs and overviews you all were handed, with stalwart aid given them from those Battalion Commanders already designated. I just want to add that I know that most of you are specialists of certain aspects of the various equipment listed in your handouts, so for the most part, some or all of what you get might be boring for you. I hope not. I hope that it gives you a better insight of our awesome capability as a military fighting Brigade.

"Real war is and can be a pretty grim and confusing affair gentlemen. Without the right kind of equipment or organization there will be added unexpected events and surprises. These Battalions that make up the mix of our Brigade make for a formidable force. Our mechanized fighting capability will enable our men to take a far larger role in any battle.

"Myself and Colonels Price and Lafluer needed to know exactly where we stood and what we had available to us so that we could better formulate our battle plan. If any of you present here have any constructive ideas to that end, don't be afraid to approach us with them. So far, I can tell you that no plan has yet been implemented, we are just looking at what lies ahead and mulling our options, so to speak. This way, we should be able to make sure those who will be joining us are with the plan. It's just as much up to you all now to make sure the OrBat and specs get passed along to appropriate Battalions to ensure conformity. I hope you all now have a far better insight with it being presented to you this way. Thank you, and that is all!"

With the end of the debriefing and General Logan's speech they started to file out. Small groups formed and discussed amongst themselves once again what it was they had all heard. With the main group now gone, Col. Price turned to Gen. Logan saying, "Well, that seemed to go over well."

"Yes, I'm quite pleased. Now what were you saying on the way in about equipment to train the men?"

"Yessir. The RSM and his other Senior Sgts were asking me as to where, when and how we can build ourselves an assault course?"

"Let them figure it out Colonel Price."

"How Sir?"

"Colonel Price, there's a lot of natural resources out there in the hills in the way of logs that they can have the men go fetch, not to mention enough bricks and mortar and lumber that will be arriving shortly. Anything else they need, they can just go and find Major Galloway and make their requests. I hope that has made the matter clear?"

"Very much so Sir!" said a friendly Col. Price, looking at the others who were nodding their approval.

ORBAT

The Sabre Brigade totals 27,000 men, comprising 982 officers and 26,018 enlisted ranks.

Its size should be equal to any force currently used by NATO or the UN in any Theatre of Operations. As an example, SFOR's total personnel numbered nearly 32,000.

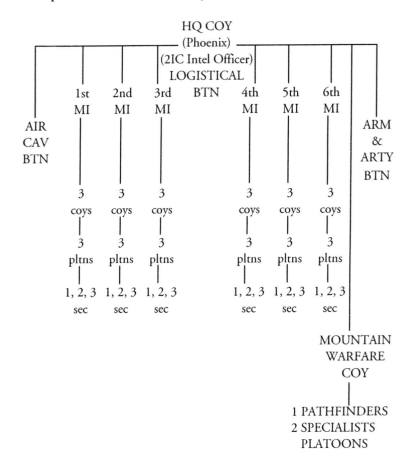

Examples: 1 Section, 1 Rifle Platoon, A Coy, 1st MI Btn, SB.
3 Section, 2 Mortar Platoon, B Coy, 5th MI Btn, SB.
*Contingencies are always in place to improvise and all Battalion Companies have at least 1 "designated" Recce Platoon of their own.

EQUIPMENT & SPECS

Logistics:
Engineers, Signals, Medics, MPs, Storemen. Will be detached in the field to designated battalions, with ALL necessary equipment and supplies. The role of the Combat Engineer specifically, is absolutely vital to battalion success in areas of: bridging, demolitions, EOD and mine-fields. The Infantryman can fight—but we must never forget we need the support arms to keep us supplied, mobile and effective.

Infantry:
Personal weapons. 9 mm Browning automatics, Heckler & Kosch MK5s.
M16A2 Rifle: exceptions; Snipers and Marksmen.
M242SAW (5 mm rounds, same as for: M16A2, SA80) 200 round belts.
LMG-C9 Light Machine Gun, GPMGs.

Mortar Platoon:
M203 Grenade Launchers.
MK19 auto 40 mm Grenade Launchers.
60 and 81 mm Mortars.

Weapons Det:
M47 Dragon anti-tank, Milan anti-tank.
TOW anti-tank Missile Launchers (*other than mounted, 27 assigned to HQ Coy—from there, 1 assigned to every Battalion Coy).

Mechanized Infantry (MI) Vehicles:
Your standard APC—LAV25s (Light Armoured Vehicles).
Bradley Infantry Fighting Vehicle, known as the M2.
*There ARE different versions, The Sabre Brigade will use them.
Lavs are light enough to be 'Air Lifted' or air portable. Our Airborne troops can attest to that. They can carry a fully loaded LAV or APC weighing 16 ton slung underneath a helicopter, up to a distance of 100 miles. They can then be landed, manned and ready for action in less than 60 seconds! This will be critical and tested many times over, as we will have to rotate battle weary troops for fresh legs.

These vehicles have crews and can carry a squad of men in their bellies also. Their own armour WILL stop .30 cal and .50 cal bullets, as well as fragments from 155mm Artillery at "miss" distance but a direct hit or near miss is capable of taking them out. They must therefore rely on superior tactics stressing speed, surprise, concealment and then their own accurate firepower.

They are armed "to the teeth" with 25 mm Cannons, with high velocity full trajectory, direct fire capability. Any LAV, APC or Scout vehicle armed force like our Sabre Brigade will also need high angle fire support weapons assigned and moving with these Mechanized Infantry Battalions so mortars can and will in this instance be mounted. The standard 25 mm Cannon will deal effectively with anything that moves on the battlefields excepting, of course, their main battle tanks. Some versions therefore, will be equipped with the TOW 2 Missile Launcher having the BGM—81—TOW heavy anti-tank missiles. This will even the playing fields some, for crew and missiles are protected by armour on these LAV versions, which make them a very effective weapon against tanks.

To back up our Mechanized Infantry Battalions, we will use the CRVT Scimitars. They have 30 mm Rardon Cannon that fire HE and APDS rounds. They will belong to the Armoured Recce and Scout Platoons, as will some of the more modern Grizzly/ Bison/ Coyote FAVs and LAVs. They all have mobility, speed and fire power and will be an invaluable asset. Some question their effectiveness for this type of terrain. Well it's been said many times over but I'll repeat it—nothing REALLY gets tested, proven, pushed to it's limits or even improvised until times of war, so withhold judgement for now!

Last but not least, the ALVs. Armoured Logistical Vehicles. These workhorses will move: rations, ammunition, fuel, spare parts, in fact anything and everything up to the front lines and back in direct support of all Battalions.

This may seem like a bewildering array of vehicles, it may even seem complicated, but when you analyse and think it through they are not many and their individual specialties make for a lot of sense. Firepower, mobility and speed is the heart of this Brigade concept. There are over 240 of these vehicle assortments in the Mechanized Infantry Battalions, averaging over 12 for each Coy. They will not carry all the men in at one go, but in relay and re-supply plus as reserve, they will allow us all to be there in time to fight. They have proven "off road" agility, granted, some more than others, but they can and will do their jobs—move this Brigade, manoeuvre and fight with great agility. In all, quite the most for-midable of Mechanized Infantry Battalions.

Armoured & Artillery:
This will consist of M1 Tanks. M3 Cavalry Fighting Vehicles—specialized reconnaissance versions of the M2s. We have 50 M60A1 Tanks. Updated stringently to M600A3TTS configuration. This main difference is in their critical fire control system. These up-dated versions have the AN/VGS-2 Tank Thermal Sight (TTS), the AV/VVG-2 Laser Range Finder and M21 onboard ballistic computer. All this update stuff gives the M60A1 tank a much "higher" first round hit probability or accuracy, and an even better chance of hitting it's targets at longer range.

The tanks are 4 man crews armed with an M58 105 mm gun carrying 60 rounds of ammo mounted with the .30 cal and .50 cal machine guns. They weigh approx 58 tons combat loaded, a perfect lethal choice.

An armoured artillery battalion towed on tracks could be effective on a battlefield under certain set circumstances (dug in maybe—like the Serbs are now) but this is too often vulnerable from air and mobile attack and often this leaves you unable to move strategically or even keep pace with mobile tanks and mechanized infantry alone in a fast moving combat zone. Today, all artillery battalions, especially those currently in an Armoured or Mechanized Infantry Brigade (at least ALL Airborne Brigades) are designated "air portable" in that just like the LAVs, we can carry them slung underneath our big helicopters to key strategic points, as they are light, fast, self-propelled and as some bright spark pointed out—because we CAN and like to do this!

In this regard of Armoured Artillery, we will use an assortment mostly of 155 mm and 105 mm Light Guns for our field artillery needs, being supported by UN and NATO air strikes, if and when needed!

Air Cavalry:

Our main helicoptor is the Bell AH -IS Huey Cobras. While it is not as advanced or as fast as the 64A Apache, it is still one heck of an attack helicopter and definitely one to be reckoned with. Our own versions will be extensively modified however, as we will incorporate many state of the art improvements to enhance their capabilities. They have a speed of 140 mph give or take, even while carrying 8 TOW anti-tank missiles and armed with M197 3 Barrelled 20 mm Gatling Guns, which have 750 rounds of ammo. In addition they carry 2 GAU-13/A 30 mm gun pods, 2.75 inch rocket pod, AIM-9L Side winder missiles or AGM-92A Stinger Missiles for "air to air" combat, if necessary! Fitted with laser designators, they can carry 8 AGM-114A Hellfire anti-tank missiles too. They will also have fitted or installed, a C-Nite program. These C-Nite modifications give the Huey Cobras day or night attack capability. They will also have an imaging infrared FLIR system which allows them to operate at night, which they'll definitely also need.

To top it all off, they have an M1 tank thermal imaging sight, combined with a TOW2 system thermal tracker, benefits of which will prove itself in battle I'm told. As all this with the C-Nite as well, basically gives it the capability to acquire targets and fire missiles day or night, through smoke screens or thick smog. So to sum it up and round it out, our Air Cavalry Battalion will have 20 of these Huey Cobra attack helicopters. In addition, 10 OH-58 Kiowa Scouts for reconnaissance purposes. 30 CH-46E Transport Helicopters and 30 CH-53s and Chinooks. These last big work-horses have proven themselves time and again in SAR operations and will also be used to land our troops, LAVs, APCs and Artillery basically anywhere we require. They will predominantly be used extensively ferrying/transporting troops in relay, even behind enemy lines and into difficult areas of terrain we can't get to or reach by any other means, which I'm sure you know also means rapelling the troops down into sticky areas.

*For more detailed specs on equipment, make your enquiries to your own Battalion Commanders as per normal procedure.

PART 3

"I don't know if I'll ever get used to this new title they gave me of Sergeant Major," said Top Sgt. 'Gunny' Ridgeway to his new friends and comrades in arms, his French counterpart and the RSM who were near him.

"I too, mon ami," joked Sgt.Major Brassard, "But I am sure the men will still call you 'Gunny' no matter what title they give you."

"Just remember who's in bleedin' charge here!" quipped RSM Whittle, as the three of them were also involved in a discussion about their impending needs for building the physical training grounds for the Brigade. They had just been convinced by Sgt. Major Ridgeway to construct what was known as a Bear Pit, which was a standard on most US assault courses of their elite forces. It was a huge pit the men jumped into and also ran across and climbed out of, or used as a sort of physical arena which only one man came out! A military version of the Ultimate Fighting matches. They had conceded mostly because of the ease with which it could be constructed. With this now agreed upon and put to rest, they started up once again on just how to proceed with the other plans.

"So, we know *where* we are to get our supplies from, but how do we go about it?"

"Easy! Just watch and learn, me 'ol son!" said the RSM.

Walking outside their tent, followed by the other two, he stood there until he spotted what used to be one of his own British Corporals passing by.

"Hey you. Yes you! Come on over 'ere now, you 'orrible little man!"

At the voice of thunder booming out at him, ex Cpl. Evans arrived there expeditiously (in record time) with the usual amount of trepidation and sprinkling of stunned anticipation such demands deserved. Most RSMs were renowned and famous in the British Army for their inconsistencies, because from one minute to the next, you didn't know if they were going to give you a supreme bollocking for being *exactly* nine seconds late, or ask you what you thought of their aftershave! Trying to figure out the logic and thought processes that lurked within the mind of an RSM or what he might say to you next was, for most Infantrymen, on a par with solving difficult equations on Quantum Mechanics—near impossible!

The RSM wasted no time. "Report back to me 'ere on the double with eight other bodies, if you ever want them stripes back soldier."

Ex Cpl. Evans ran off then, but not forgetting to shout back over his shoulder, "Yes RSM."

The RSM shouted after his disappearing body, "You 'ave exactly five minutes!"

Sgt.Majors Brassard and Ridgeway just stood grinning. The RSM turned and said, "Hopefully, before he realises he no longer has them stripes, he will order the allotted men in haste, or threaten them with their lives if they don't comply. Now let me see you 'orrible pair do the same from your own contingents."

Soon all the necessary manpower they had requested was assembled, totalling a group of some near twenty-five soldiers, excluding themselves. The group of soldiers stood waiting for who-knows-what, but didn't have long to wait as the RSM eventually spoke and sated their curiosity.

"I want you men to get over to Stores, *wherever* it is located right about now. Go directly up to RQMS White and return 'ere with some rope an' an axe each, even a saw or two, ready for cutting lumber."

"Can we get chainsaws then Sir?" volunteered a bright American Marine.

"That's a good idea soldier, what's your name?"

Beaming, the soldier said, "Davidson Sir!"

"Of course you can Davidson, if they have them available."

Moving close to ear shot so nobody else could hear him, Sgt. Major Brassard said, "I thought you said chainsaws would be too heavy and we shouldn't take them?"

The RSM whispered in turn, "Because I knew someone would volunteer the saws stupid, this way they don't mind as much and therefore they will just grumble about the other soldier's big mouth, not our orders!"

Three miles into their march and run into the hills, someone spoke up, "Whose bright idea was it to bring these 'ere chainsaws then?"

The RSM, turning to exchange smiles with his guilty compatriots in arms, bellowed, "Cut out the grumbling!"

. . . Wiping away the sweat from their labours in the afternoon sun, a soldier looked up and queried, "How many more logs do we cut, Sgt.Major?"

"Nearly done. Just finish up this pile and don't forget to cut them to exact length as we requested." Sgt.Major Brassard also came walking over to the RSM for what seemed like an answer himself. The RSM must have sensed the question, for as he closed up to him, he immediately whispered, "Give them another half hour and that should just about do it."

"What are we going to do with these short logs you had us cut up and trim RSM, is it what I think it's for?" asked trooper Evans grinning.

Smiling down at the British Para, the RSM said, "Evans, this is going to be old 'ome week for you and the lads. I have the intention of introducing the rest of the Brigade to some of the finer tricks of your P Company!"

"Oh no!" groaned one of Evans' orthodontically challenged mates.

"Oh yes!" laughed the RSM.

"So I guess we're cutting these logs for the log runs then RSM?"

"And for the assault course Evans."

Smiling now that he had accepted his fate but still curious, Evans asked in his strong Welsh accent, "What about a tranasium then Sir, are we getting one of those too?"

"Ah yes, a tranasium! Well just as soon as you and your lads get finished up 'ere, we'll get you to set one up for us 'ere close to that clearing in those trees!"

As he walked away he could hear the other men asking Evans, "What the fuck's a tranasium Taffy?"

"What the hell is a tranasium anyway?" asked Sgt.Major Ridgeway.

"Well, one version is some very high scaffolding with a platform on top at least fifty feet off the ground with a scramble net running up one side to climb up to the top on. On the other side you weave in and out making your way up and down. Once on top though, there is another height, oh about ten more feet above the ground, called shuffle bars. There are also some of the scaffolding clamps or whatever placed in the middle of these on the rails to make you lift your feet 'up and over' them. If you fall off, it's only a short drop to the platform, but it's the height off the ground of the whole contraption that always gets them."

As the Sgt. Major looked on in disbelief, the RSM said, "It is *very* effective for testing heights or seeing who has no stomach for them and getting over those fears."

"To say the least!"

"We'll obviously have to get the Engineers up here to do that or at least direct the others," said the RSM. He continued in nearly the same breath, "Another type.."

"Wowa, whadda yah mean another type?"

Grinning broadly the RSM continued, "This is what I was talking about to Evans. It is just some ladders that are mounted to but up and running through the trees! They are going up, down and around at different angles about thirty feet or more off the ground—for about a half mile at least—with a platform and net and rope at the end to swing and fall into. If you miss? Plonk! Right into a bloody cesspool!"

"I heard about that, can't wait," he said sarcastically as the extremely fit Legionnaire, Sgt.Major Brassard just laughed and said, "Mon ami, did I not tell you we would 'ave us some fun here?!"

"Sick bastards!" muttered Gunny as they continued laughing.

When they eventually got back to camp after a slow jog the

RSM said, "Evans and you other ex Corporals, I want you here with the same men bright and early tomorrow at 0700hrs sharp. We have to get some vehicles up there as close as we can to get today's work loaded and brought down. If anyone else tasks you for duties, tell them that you already have some work assigned to you for this RSM's detail. That's it for today men. Dismissed!"

The men fell out and went back to their tents tired and dripping with sweat.

Gunny said, "If you no longer need me I have some other duties I need to attend to as well."

"You're free for now Gunny. See you both later, I have to look into some toggle ropes anyways."

"Some what?"

Laughing once more the RSM said, "You'll both see later!"

Three days later all the logs were down from the hillside. With all the carpenters and bricklayers Maj. Biggles could spare, the bear pit and assault course walls, as well as other obstacles, were on their way to being built. They even had a little tractor of sorts with a rear digger scooping a ditch out for the culverts for the tunnels on the assault course area, so it was well on its way to completion. Maj. Biggles had also assigned the task of building the scaffolding tranasium to other Engineers as was also requested. The RSM had given added instructions to the assault course construction team that it was to be longer and further to run than the three miles or so of the Royal Marine Commandos' assault course at Lympstone in Plymouth. The RSM also gave instructions that it was to have even more obstacles than the Guards' training course in Pirbright, just outside of Aldershot, not forgetting the American and French Foreign Legion obstacle course specialties thrown in for good measure. In fact, he was quite pleased with its progress for a few days later it was taking shape handsomely and well ahead of schedule as far as the RSM was concerned. He had even talked with General Logan and been sent to Maj. Galloway to see about getting the wooden ladders for the different version of the tranasium.

"How much longer for this assault course RSM?" asked General Logan one day.

"Be ready to use in a matter of days now Sir. Just have to wait for the cement in the brick walls to set and harden."

"Any ideas on getting this Brigade exercised in the meantime?"

Grinning from ear to ear the RSM said, "Well Sir, I just happen to have these 'ere ropes and logs . . . "

"How does this damn blasted toggle go on again RSM?" queried Maj. Stacey.

Already getting the experienced British contingent to go around the assembled Brigade showing them exactly how to attach their toggles to their logs, he called out to the nearest man.

"Jonesy, would you come over 'ere and show the Major and his log crew of four how to attach their toggles correctly please?"

"Yessir," was the crisp reply as Jonesy quickly ran over and set to placing their toggle ropes for them. When the entire present Brigade of HQ Coy seemed or appeared ready to the RSM, he shouted very loudly in his booming voice, "Brigade, lift your logs!"

Amid the noise of the logs being lifted, a chorus of curses started emanating from the men of the Brigade.

"Oh, sacre bleu!"

"Lift your end, goddammit!"

"Fucking 'ell, that one hurt!"

"Watch it you dickhead!"

As the groans and grumbles continued but settled down, the experienced British troops were in their own element here and loving every minute of it. They were also helping out by giving them the necessary info to do it properly.

"Pull out on the toggle ropes if you can, that way you keep the log away from you as you run!" above the chorus of more "Ouches" and "Hey man, be careful there."

The RSM smiled contently, knowing they were ready! He shouted out, "Follow my lead!" and immediately set off running with his own log and partners who consisted of Sgt. Majors Brassard and Ridgeway and Staff Sgt. MacKay.

The curses from all the assorted groups in the outgoing uphill five miles of log run was a mixture of unpleasantries associated to the log, against the log, and about the log! The Brigade was told to remain in their respective contingents with the British leading, followed by the French and then the Americans. There was never any special order to these formations, it was always just the way they all fell in on parade and set out. As they reached the turning point for the return leg the RSM called for the allotted five minute break which was also his signal to switch sides! Men of the Brigade HQ Coy's different contingents fell to the roadside holding and rubbing aching arms and rope burns on the wrists from the ways they held their toggle ropes, the moaning and groaning was heard everywhere!

"Don't you think this is just a little barbaric RSM?" pleaded the aching and newly promoted Maj. Rance, as the RSM walked by.

The RSM just grinned, especially at all the smiling Brit Paras, as he continued on and went about the men enquiring of them, but completely unfazed by their comments about brutality. Looking unhurried, after taking a first swig from his own water bottle, he eagerly cried out, "Come on you 'orrible sorry lot! I thought you were the best there is?" To which the pride of men who felt insulted caused them, beginning with the British, to rise from their resting places and get adjusted for the return leg.

"That was an awfully quick break wasn't it RSM?" asked Col. Price.

"We're about right on schedule Sir!"

With moans and groans from even the General down to the lowest rank they all fell in regardless, trying to numb their minds to the repetition of it all. The only exception seemed to be that of the RSM and his fellow log partners who were either a lot fitter than the rest of them or they were doing an excellent job of covering up their own aches and pains! With everyone assembled and

Sgt. Major Brassard calling for all to make sure they had changed over hand grips, RSM Whittle shouted, "Okay men, here we go again, just follow our lead!"

The return leg was even more difficult with men starting to argue and curse each other as the logs they carried incorrectly would bounce against knees and the like! The men were also making fun of each other. The British felt that this being one of their specialty exercises, they had to set an example and prove to the others how easy it was by making fun of the Americans. The French soon joined in, resenting being left out of this good-natured ribbing. Not a mile from camp and resenting the ribbing, the American contingent were getting snarly when surprisingly, one of the French log teams just suddenly broke rank and bolted past the RSMs, heading for and trying to be first back!

The RSM's yells were lost amid the French cheers. Seeing this, the American contingent at the rear of the column behind the French looked to their stronger team as they urged and yelled at them to run and try to catch the French. The Americans gave chase as one of the British contingent's captain's shouted out, "Sergeant Steele?"

Running as he should with his own team he shouted back, "Yessir?"

The voice that replied was full of humour and the spirit of the moment when it bellowed, "Sgt. Steele, what the bloody hell are you waiting for—go catch them!"

Sgt. Steele's purely British paratrooper team started their chase and ran past all those teams ahead of them in the formation, now they too were off in their pursuit of the other two log teams that were racing away. The roar from the British contingent and other ranks was deafening, for now they all knew they had a race!

Gen. Logan was looking all around at his officers in anger. He felt strongly this would isolate rather than bring his men together. In lieu of the situation though, Mac resigned himself to the fact he saw this was coming anyway and in its own way was inevitable.

Realizing this, he also knew he couldn't stop it and that he could not now deny the thrill of the race to his soldiers.

To the race itself though, a half mile from camp the American team finally caught up to the smaller French one to the great cheers and hollering from the rear of the rest of the Battalion—especially since they had come from the farthest distance. They both now ran neck and neck, French and American together, with the British gaining on them. About a quarter mile from camp the American squad began to break away from the French team amid more roars of encouragement—with the British still chasing them, ignoring the pains and labouring lungs, refusing to lie down and quit. Less than 400 metres from camp now, the British log team moved past the French one and drew level with the Americans— the race for the unofficial finish line was now a sprint!

It was the British who surged ahead in the last fifty metres— to the deafening cheers from the rest of the Brigade.

As the main group of the Brigade arrived back at camp the British contingent were hoisting and cheering Sgt. Steele and the rest of his team to the amazed and stunned looks of those defeated soldiers in the race. Amid the louder cheers of the British, as they dropped their logs and jumped around in joy, Mac went directly over and said, "Well done Sergeant!"

Pushing through the jubilant throng of soldiers while looking around, Mac shouted for his officers to come to him, and taking them all aside he said, "That was a bone-headed stupid thing. I want to find ways to bring these men together not drive them apart!"

"Sorry Sir, I just thought it would help the men's morale," spoke up some French officer.

"Just let's not see it happen again, alright?"

"Yessir!" they all said and as soon as they were dismissed, even the British officers ran immediately over to Sgt. Steele to congratulate him. Unable to contain his own smile from the excitement of the race, Mac walked away with a proudly beaming and smiling Col. Price looking on.

He's going to be insufferable, Mac said to himself knowingly.

After the British soldiers had all finished slapping Ben and his men on their backs and gone their separate ways, an American officer, Maj. Stacey, approached Ben to say, "Well done, Sergeant. Last time I met you we were on that 'Operation Scavenger Hunt' out there in Iraq, remember?"

Looking up, Ben said grinning from ear to ear, "Hello there Major. Yes, I remember. The last time I saw you, you were also a Captain!"

As the Major stood there grinning with his hands on his hips he moved forward to start shaking hands with Ben and said, "Looks like we both got ourselves promoted, heh? So you'll have to meet me later Sergeant and fill me in on what you've been up to since we last met, deal?"

"I will consider that a pleasure, Major!"

"Oh, Sgt. Steele, did you know that Gunny was along on this shindig? They even promoted him to the rank of Sgt.Major!" he laughed heartily.

"Yes, I know. He's been nagging me something mercilessly from the moment he set eyes on me!"

"Thanks for the news, now I really feel at home!" Maj. Stacey said, adding, "One last thing before you leave Sgt?"

"What's that Sir?"

"It's good to have you here on our side!"

"Thank you Sir," grinned Ben, "likewise."

Later in his tent along with the old Gunny, they were sat around sharing a bottle and talking and swapping stories.

"Since the Americans found out today that you're also a native Canadian Ben, they feel it was okay today that you won the log race. They're now saying it was a 'North American' anyway who won—and all that!"

As they burst out laughing, it was Maj. Stacey who then changed the topic to something more personal and asked, "So how long has it been now Ben since we were in the Gulf together?"

"I'd have to say it's at least seven to eight years Sir!"

"At least!" said Gunny, raising his glass of Scotch.

"Shit, that long?"

They talked for some hours, "Well, you're kind of quiet there Ben, how come?"

" 'Cos he's still pining his heart out over some General's daughter I've been told."

"Not really Gunny, I was actually wondering about how strange it is for us all to meet up here like this."

"Considering that attack on the El Tariq viaduct, I never thought for a moment we would see each other again during or after that unless we were on detached duty or other," offered the Major.

"That sure was some battle though, heh?" laughed Gunny. "Do you both remember how that went down? You and the rest of your SAS headbangers, what a crazy scary mother of a bunch!"

Finally laughing at the good-natured jest about his former unit, Ben came back, "It was pretty black that night though, heh?"

"I'd say so. Zero hour 'til all hell breaks loose and we unleash the dogs of war you called it? Wow, were you ever right!"

"How did you read it went down then Ben, seeing we were not there back at Hereford for your famous debriefing?"

"Well Sir, when you gave the signal to charge which started that firefight, we just up and went down those slopes a-screaming and firing, shooting at the night and at anything that moved! I remember that we threw out our hand grenades as we also ran with bodies flying through the air and screams of agony from the shrapnel and Iraqi soldiers being shot, it was deafening. It seemed we did hit them at just about the right time too, for we had an open hand before they realized we were upon them. It was too late for them to regroup for as the explosive charges we lay started exploding in clouds of fire and thunder, they all stood about stunned, then we turned and came charging back, mopping up! I never saw so many dead bodies in one place or battle. Not outside of the war in Bosnia anyway! Took us no more than a few minutes but our combined teams of twenty-four men had to have taken out at least 450 of the Iraqi Red Guard that night, besides destroying their radar and satellite installation. Which reminds me, I also remember that lone sniper taking a bead on you and *me* taking it in the leg as I came across your path to get a better shot at him—never told you Major but it fucking well hurt—you owe me one!"

They all laughed then.

"That I do, Ben, but you also got me the Silver Star for helping me live through it to get back, for which I am also forever grateful."

"Not to mention my Bronze Star also!" grinned Gunny.

"I think it was your spotting of that mobile scud launcher we managed to attack and overpower to bring back successfully. Now that sure put a shock on their faces, heh?"

"Don't forget those scared officers of Saddam's Red Guard we found cowering in that gully too!"

So by drinking, laughing and talking it over a couple more hours, they were able to deepen their special bond they held for each other, from having shared combat experiences and more importantly, surviving them! Eventually the conversation drifted back to a personal one with them asking Ben what all this crap was about him losing it over some General's daughter anyway.

"It's a long story—she was and *is* special though!" he appeared to say sadly, to which they weren't sure was a reaction from the vast amount of alcohol or true love.

"Heard some dick officer also made it difficult for you?"

"Yes, well present company excepted, they are not my favourite breed right now!"

Looking serious at him, Maj. Stacey said, "Ben, I'm real sorry to hear it but if you ever want to point the bastard out I'd be happy to punch his lights out for you."

"Nice try you two, but I can take care of it myself thanks!"

"Just the same? . . . " they began.

B.A.F.A.
CANADA

"Ad Unum Omnes"

British Airborne Forces Association, Canada

16 · 05 · 03

Hi Mike,

Sorry for the delay !!
If you don't like the read, I hear it makes a great doorstop !! :)

Cheers, Derik

"It's okay, really. I'll tell you about it another day, okay?"

"Okay!" they said drunkenly.

"I understand you and Sgt. Major Ridgeway had an old-fashioned get together with Sgt. Steele yesterday Major," said Mac to Maj. Stacey while waiting for breakfast.

"Saved my life in the Gulf Sir, never had a chance to say thank you!"

"I understand Major, but don't think I'll let you get away from your duties with a sore head?"

"Yessir!" groaned the Major

"Major, one more thing!"

"Sir?"

"Tell me about it sometime, the Gulf thing?"

Smiling for the first time Maj. Stacey said, "No problem Sir!"

During breakfast Mac looked to Col. Lefleur and said "After breakfast Colonel, let's unleash the prowess of Sgt. Major Brassard on these men and show these soldiers the power of the French art of Savate and Karate and unarmed combat combined, heh?"

Smiling, Col. Lefleur said, "It will be a pleasure for the French, Sir!"

"What's that nonsense about?" asked Col. Price.

"An opportunity for the French to regroup and pick up some badly needed bragging points David," said Mac.

True to his word, that day Mac had the entire Brigade out on parade ready for unarmed combat training. Besides looking for experts for future work assignments, this was also an excellent opportunity to train the Brigade under the very skilful abilities of Sgt. Major Brassard of the French contingent and particularly the French Foreign Legion. Contrary to popular belief, men nowadays did not join the Foreign Legion because they were running away from some crime, but did so because they were an elite, well trained and disciplined force.

Sgt. Major Brassard was a veteran of the Legion for some

fifteen years now who joined as a young man from Lyon and transferred into the English speaking unit 2eRep to improve his own
English speaking skills. He was a decorated soldier who had risen
through the ranks having seen and been in action in Somalia,
Angola, Afghanistan and the Gulf War. He was holder of the Croix
De Gurre, France's highest military honour. He was also one of
their favourite sons. An expert in a variety of martial arts. Today,
Sgt. Major Brassard was going to start the Brigade out and let
them know some of his secrets. Making the entire Brigade pick a
partner and spread out, enlisted men and officers alike, Sgt. Major
Brassard went to each contingent and systematically brought out
their biggest and toughest-looking men or officers. He then systematically started throwing, flipping, grabbing, punching, trip-
ping, hurling them all through the air and back over heels all with
no preference or bias!

There really wasn't time for these soldiers to learn a complete
self-defence course or system that took years to master, but the
blows and throws that were being taught and drilled that morning were deemed necessary for those "life or death" situations they
would surely face at some future date. To practice them now until
they became as natural and instinctive as possible was imperative
if it could help save any one of them on the future battlefields. The
object was naturally to demonstrate what he was doing and then
have the Brigade follow or copy his moves. Sgt. Major Brassard
brought out the rest of the Brigade's soldiers with a high level of
skill in the martial arts. He had them also then go around with
him to watch how the rest of the Brigade performed his manoeuvres,
showing or correcting them individually.

It was easy for Sgt.Major Brassard to spot potential talent or
experienced men and part of his duty was to identify these men
and categorize them all according to ability. This he was also doing along with the aid of his experienced helpers. Sgt. Major Brassard could not resist going up to the burly Sgt. Major Ridgeway
and his partner to say, "Mon Ami, if you throw a punch like that
this will happen—as he unceremoniously dumped him onto the

ground! The French contingent liked this particular moment and cheered loudly. Understanding the reason and purpose for it all, Ridgeway was not upset; rather, he just stood in amazement with everyone else scratching his head asking, "How does he do that?" Sgt. Steele was one of the experts assigned to help Sgt. Major Brassard this day and as he passed Col. Lefleur and Maj. Stacey, who was bobbing and weaving making fun of his opponent he just said, "I have to advise you Major, the Colonel here is nearly as expert as Sgt. Major Brassard, so I would advise you to not make fun of him!" As Maj. Stacey turned to look at Sgt. Steele, Col. Lefleur just came up under his outstretched arm, hooked and then unceremoniously flipped him over onto his ass. Looking back at Sgt. Steele from the ground he glared at him while seeing the beaming face of Col Lefleur above! "Thanks for the warning!" the Major shouted out to Sgt. Steele as he passed.

For some the morning seemed to last forever, while for others it came and went too fast. Eventually though it was over with and before they all departed for their various tents and other duties, Mac shouted out for Sgt. Major Brassard.

"Sgt. Major, as you may be anticipating and aware of, I do have to appoint someone to eventually direct the physical training of this Brigade." He continued smiling, "I wanted to tell you this personally, going over records and from what I have learned from almost all of my officers, it does seem obvious to us all that you're the most qualified person in this Brigade or anywhere, it would seem, to head it up! Therefore, I am pleased to inform you that you will be the one responsible for its physical training until I can at least appoint an appropriate officer to direct your new wing. Even then, you will still very much stay involved, as your skills are indispensable." Not waiting for a reply Mac continued, "So I want you personally to get whatever manpower you require from the ranks to head it up and assist you, understood?"

"Yessir!" said Sgt. Major Brassard overjoyed with his new position, "Sir, a request?"

"Okay," said Mac, a little more curious rather than expectant, for he learned by now from the men in this Brigade to stay prepared only for the unexpected.

"I would like to ask for and start with Sgt. Steele if you do not have any other purpose or duty already to assign to him?"

"I wasn't sure but I thought that might be it," Mac smiled. "Alright Sgt. Major, I'll let you ask him for yourself. But also make up a list of all the others you need, then give it to the RSM for me."

"Thank you Sir!"

Walking over to Sgt. Steele to make his request, Sgt. Major Brassard was stopped and complimented by a large group of the men for his lesson of that same morning. Caught up in this congratulatory group he then had to shout out to Sgt. Steele before he walked out of hearing distance. The sergeant stopped to wait for him, wondering what he wanted. He was not surprised to hear his request.

"Sgt. Steele, I would be pleased if you would join me on the Brigade's new physical training staff, mon ami?"

"Love to Sgt. Major, at least it will get me out of whatever other duties will be flying around here, eh?"

"Seriously Sgt., I need, or I should say, was allowed, a staff of twelve. Eventually anyway, not counting yourself."

"Have you made any other choices then?"

"As a matter of fact I have a list of those French members that I know would be suitable, but I was hoping that maybe yourself could choose the British staff we will need, you will know them better anyway, then we will make time to choose some of our American brothers, or Gunny will get upset at us for sure," he smiled.

With a smile on his own face Ben added, "One thing Sgt. Major, can I ask you why you chose me"?

"Well mon ami, besides seeing for myself how well you performed on the unarmed combat this morning, I was given the 'inside' on you, as Americans like to say, from our friend Gunny of course, plus the RSM. Let us also say that I sort of expected and wanted to be offered this position, so I made enquiries, your name came out on top most every time!"

"Well thanks for your honesty Sgt. Major. It's my pleasure, I really do look forward to it and will give you my best effort!"

"Thank you Sgt. If you take this list, I will go and try to start filling in the blanks with the others and find the rest of our staff we will need."

As they parted company Sgt. Major Brassard was approached by the RSM, who congratulated him on getting the new position, one he had previously been aware of and knew was going to him sooner than later.

"Well done Marcel. I understand they finally gave it to you then mate?"

"Yes mon ami, but from enquiries and conversations I have had since myself, I understand that you had a few words yourself with our good General about me?"

Waving away his thanks the RSM said, "Nonsense, it was obvious you were the logical choice! Anyway, no other man in the Brigade comes even close to your skills or abilities with the exception of Sgt. Steele, of course, but then even he himself would be smart enough to defer to you I am sure!" The RSM continued, "Well, have you asked him yet?"

"Just now mon ami, and he accepted."

"That's bloody marvelous. By the way, I have another piece of good news for you, you'll be glad to know that both the tranasiums, bear pit and the assault course are built to exact specifications that we discussed. Starting tomorrow they are ready for your use!"

Smiling at the RSM he added, "I think this Brigade is going to be pretty okay now mon ami!"

For the next few weeks the Brigade's daily routine included a physical dose of either the log runs or assault course or the newly built Ranger bear pit to test their physical prowess, with *all* ranks participating, no exceptions. Even those who had found it difficult in the first few days were now able to complete them, which was testament to Sgt. Major Brassard and his staff who encouraged, cajoled or used any and all means necessary to see that they all arrived back or completed it, as they did not want to see any drop-outs. The career paras and combat infantry soldiers seemed best trained and suited to these rugged and demanding exercise routines, it was after all, their bread and butter. The exceptions who found it difficult seemed to be the logistical types of Major Rance and the like, having never participated in quite this level of physical endurance training in their careers before. To their due though, they were hanging in!

The camp itself was also finally beginning to rise up and take shape. For the first eight weeks the whole encampment seemed to be just like a beehive, alive and buzzing with noise and hustle and bustle of construction. The huge mobile concrete mixer vehicles were a constant routine of dust, wheels and roaring engines that were forever coming and going day and night under huge floodlights. There was never any let-up nor could there be, for they had definite deadlines to meet. Then one day, as suddenly as they had all initially arrived and started their work, they stopped. This could only mean one thing—the concrete pads had all but been completed! Also, the added silence these vehicles left behind seemed to give another stir to the camp as it would seem the soldiers and men in the encampment were more than a little ready and anxious to finally leave Tent City.

The Main Stores Warehouse had already been constructed and so had the Infirmary and Medical Centre and the TT&C, and the Engineers and Logistical types were now involved in the final stages of completing HQ. This also meant now that only the easy tasks, so to speak, remained which was to complete the rest of the Brigade's camp. This consisted of the individual battalion stores, mess and dining halls and finally, the mens' barracks and living quarters. The whole encampment just seemed to flow into a different level of existence, being alive now with activity. People, jeeps and other vehicles and forklifts were forever, it seemed, scurrying in all directions carrying, driving or delivering stores and equipment up to the front entrance of each and every completed building.

On opening day over at HQ, Mac, his two Colonels, Price and Lafluer, the RSM, the other officers and the enlisted soldiers who would make up the permanent HQ Staff when the rest of the Brigade started to arrive, were, to say the least, ecstatic. They went happily and merrily about this routine of carrying in their supplies and equipment that the good Maj. Galloway had so expertly delivered on time. No detail seemed to be left out, from computers to pen and paper. It was an absolute brilliant job of logistical skill. Mac even had his bunk and items transferred over from his tent and put into the back room of his office which they had built especially for that purpose until the officers' mess and quarters themselves could be built. Everything was going to schedule, as planned.

"Good morning Sir," said Maj. Stacey coming to attention in Mac's new office, "Nice office Sir."

Looking around himself and smiling now, he replied, "Yes, it is isn't it?" then continued, "Well Major, I certainly liked the way you and your improvised staff have conducted the small arms weapons training for the Brigade these past four to six weeks. I might add, it just confirms my own opinion that we Americans are the finest marksmen out there. Which has me wondering, how would you like to head up our sniper team training and selections, as well as armaments and small arms depot? Until we're up to strength and probably a more permanent replacement is secured?"

"Sniper teams Sir?"

"Plus the other stuff, but yes." Calling him by his given name for the first time now, Mac went on. "Luke, a good sniper should be able to take out a man at 800m with a first round every time on average. Then he should be able to put down harassing fire from any range up to a good 1000m. Those skills sometimes get forgotten and put on the back-burner, but then when you do need snipers, you usually find you are low on them or even have no qualified personnel at all. I don't want that happening here, we can't afford or allow that to happen under any circumstance."

"Okay Sir, of course I'll do it, but it's also important to me that I can still go with the Brigade if and when any intervention or battle assignment is given to us. I don't want to get left behind if it's possible."

"Well, you'll be happy to know Luke, and you can even pass this information along by the way, that part of every soldier's duty in this Brigade is that 'if and when' it is called upon to react to any given battle situation or armed confrontation, I would like to see that just about *all* my officers and men do attend, so no one is exempt from that duty here, if I can help it."

"That's pretty much what I wanted to hear Sir. Just wanted to do my duty and be alongside my men, if and when called upon!"

"I understand, Luke. Now, about that position I just offered you?"

"Yessir!" smiled Maj. Stacey.

"You will take over that tasking immediately."

"Yessir. But can I also enquire, does this still mean that I will eventually get assigned as an officer in charge of a Mechanized Battalion or not?"

"That's a given," said Mac.

"Just one more thing then Sir?"

"What's that?"

"What will you do about the camp guard and security that my men and I have pretty much controlled and been doing since we got here?"

"For now it will continue but only until the final formation of those who follow. When it happens, Major Buxton-Smith and one other will be taking over those duties, probably on a more permanent basis."

"One last thing Sir?"

"What's that?" sighed Mac wearily but friendly-like.

"The uniform issue, Sir. The men have been badgering

me and have asked me to enquire as to whether or not you have settled on a design for our insignia and flag standard and such that they have already given to you through the RSM."

"Yes, I've been giving it some thought. I think maybe I'll leave it in the hands of the RSM for a while longer. He appears to have done his homework and has some interesting designs and ideas, or at least the whole Brigade does."

"When will he know by then Sir?"

"Everyone eager to know that much, heh? Can't say I blame them I suppose. Okay Luke, tell them that I will decide on the final choices the RSM gives me before the month's end, two weeks before this present contingent of the Brigade's strength gets to pass-out."

"Thank you Sir."

"Thank you for your fine work Luke," said Mac. He returned to formality with, "You're dismissed Major."

Grateful for his assigned duties and this little insight and prior information, Maj. Stacey came to attention, saluted, then turned and quietly left Mac's office.

"Take a butchers at these designs then Gunny," said the RSM, with whom he shared a tent, along with Sgt. Major Brassard and QM White.

"Heh, that's pretty clever Tom, what do you reckon Marcel?"

"Hey, what am I, chopped liver?" spoke up the QM.

"Sorry Chalky," laughed the RSM, " 'Ere, what do you think too mate?"

"I think it's flashy. But then why not, it's not just us reserved British who will be wearing it after all, have to think of the Yanks and the French, heh?" he laughed robustly.

By now all fully understanding most of the quarks and idiosyncrasies to each other and their particular brand of humour, Sgt. Major Brassard didn't take it personal at all. "What is the purpose behind the arrowhead though?" queried Marcel. "I mean, the insignia is meant to last forever and represent the Brigade, I don't understand."

"It's symbolic," retorted Gunny. "You see, the very first of all American Special Forces known as the First Special Service Force under Colonel Fredericks, that was originally formed right here on these very grounds, were basically the standard for all Elite units, more or less, and that shape was their insignia!"

"I especially like the arrowhead design being the same blue colour as our United Nations berets that we'll be wearing. I like how the shoulder flashes have the word S.A.B.R.E. down the length of it with the words UNITED NATIONS round the top point on either side, and the word BRIGADE round the bottom."

"Yes, it does have a very distinctive flair and look to it, heh Marcel?" said Chalky.

"You mean 'Savoir Faire' don't you mon ami?" laughed Marcel.

"My my, he has done his homework, heh?" said Chalky.

"Yes, I like it mon ami," said Marcel.

"I second that."

"Well, I'm glad that's settled then," said the RSM continuing, "For the cap badge, we have kept the symbol of peace of the UN in the white laurel leaves, but inside this, instead of a globe, we have put in a phoenix, created in another blue to stand out against the beret. We wanted and needed it different from the present cap badge insignia of other UN assigned troops. We all thought that a Phoenix rising from the ashes surrounded by the laurel leaves would do just nicely, seeing that is what we have literally done with this camp and in our Brigade."

"Not bad," they all seemed to echo.

The RSM continued talking, "I will put the request to the General that all enlisted personnel who have their jump wings wear them on the left of their tunics, unless they can be worn on the right sleeve like the British. Also, above the left breast pocket, it is an idea that we wear a Sabre. That is designed in an enclosed surround, sort of like they do with the US Combat Infantry Badge, only ours will be a Sabre as opposed to a rifle."

"I like that idea too, but why the Sabre?"

"Yeah," said the other two.

"Well see, the General, in his information told me that we were classified back there in New York as a *Strategic Action Battle Ready Entity*. Also seeing that our very own British SAS Regiment of which you have all heard and know about, not to mention the fact that we even have a few ex members here with us, they also serve in what are called Sabre Squadrons. Putting two and two together I came up with a design emblem that would represent a form of insignia that would be awarded to *all* graduates of our training program and final induction into the Brigade itself."

"So now that's taken care of, what else is left?"

"Rank and Epaulet insignia for the officers will be British while for the enlisted ranks, due to the fact we will be keeping the ranks of RSM and RQMS and Sgt.Major, and Staff Sergeant and Colour Sergeant, the majority of it will all be British. But a slightly scaled-down version. As for everyone's collar insignia, I figured on using a smaller version of the cap badge, the Phoenix in a wreath thing."

"Just wonderful mon ami, now we really will be specialized," said Marcel.

"Yes, so when will we be getting this uniform and insignia? I mean, being in charge over at Stores it will be up to me to issue it all most likely."

"Oh I'm sure of that," said the RSM, "but remember, the General himself will have to approve its design—and give us our motto."

"Motto?" they all said in unison.

"Every Regiment or Corps has a motto, mates," said the RSM. "I can't give away ours just yet, but I think you will all agree to the very last man that the Phoenix has a good grasp of our Brigade when you read it."

"Come on Tom, we're your bloody mates for crying out loud," said Chalky.

Taking them into his confidence then, the RSM explained about the motto.

"It reads, Si Vis Pacem, Para Bellum," said the RSM.

"What does it mean mon ami?" said Marcel.

"It means IF YOU WISH FOR PEACE—PREPARE FOR WAR."

"Bloody hell," was all that was muttered softly from one of the awed group.

"My sentiments exactly. For the most part, I'd say our Phoenix has done his homework and now just needs to give us his final confirmation of our choices."

After congratulating the RSM on a job well done as well, they all decided to call it a day and make an early night of it, as they were all putting in very long days and were getting a little weary.

In the silence of the tent riding on the chill of an evening breeze, the only other noise was a hushed voice that broke the quiet. "What do you say to the idea that to earn the Sabre, besides doing the physical and small arms testing, we all have to 'jump' with our new Brigade?"

Before anyone else could answer, the RSM spoke up, "Actually Gunny, a lot of the lads have mentioned that very same point and I have already included it in my recommendations to the General."

"Well, I guess now that we've dressed the entire Brigade we can get some shut-eye around 'ere?" understated Chalky as boots and books and whatever else that could be thrown came flying over to Chalky's cot in fun, while mock yells of laughter and hurt filled the night air.

The Brigade HQ Coy were assembled for their morning log run. The RSM approached Sgt. Major Brassard and Sgt. Steele and said smiling, "Gentlemen, the tranasium is ready."

Smiling himself now, Sgt. Steele replied, "Well Sir, would you like us to introduce Brigade HQ to its unique qualities?"

In total understatement and laughter, the RSM replied, "Go for it son!"

"Officers and men of this Brigade," shouted Sgt. Major Brassard to the assembled troops, "we are going for our usual morning run, after which we will introduce one and all to our long awaited tranasium!" After the hollering, whistles and yells died down he continued, "I remind you, this can be safe if you treat it serious and keep your wits about you, otherwise you can have some very nasty falls and tumbles!" After a brief pause he shouted, "Let's go!"

They jogged and arrived at their destination up in the mountain foothills that were above the camp. In the tree line they all fell in singly behind the RSM as ordered. The Colonel and the Officers watched as they climbed the platform to where the first ladder started and just stared in awe as the RSM suddenly began to run along the ladder rungs through the trees, suspended thirty feet or so above the ground!

After the men, Brigade Officers tentatively followed. Sgt. Steele started shouting encouragement to the "faint at heart" yelling, "Come on look lively, the bloody Girl Guides can do better than this, it isn't that difficult!" Amid the usual groans of, "Like to see 'im do better!" What the brigade did not realize was that for the past two days, Sgt. Major Brassard had made the entire Physical Training Wing of the Brigade go over and over the entire course first, to test for safety!

The tranasium ran for approximately a half mile through the trees changing its direction and angle and height and drop. Just to make the British feel at home and to keep everyone on their toes, they had deliberately removed a few rungs here and there! There was the odd fall and slip "between the rungs" testified by the screams of men landing on their balls with the good natured yells of, "Get the hell up, I can't stop, I'm gonna hit you you bastard, aghh!"

There was one nasty fall already being tended by a medic below, but the majority of Brigade HQ seemed to make their way to the end platform okay, then it was the one final leap to the rope and backward leap into the net—hoping you could hit or grab it to prevent yourself from landing on the wooden cross-beam or into the cesspool below. The familiar "splash" and "plonks" were music to everyone's ears. There were plenty who failed this aspect of it, much to the delight of their comrades. There is a universal and wickedly sinful delight all soldiers seem to take in seeing their fellow friends splosh into a pool of muddy, murky questionable water!

When the entire Brigade HQ had completed the first tranasium they went onto the next. The net that breached the height of the scaffolding tower was soon full of clambering bodies and once on top, the next stage was climbing up and shuffling along the parallel bars and surreptitiously lifting the feet. They all made it across and down the other side. Sgt. Major Brassard and his staff then directed them over to another final surprise.

Further into the woods they had cleared an area where they had built another high-towered platform with a death-slide coming down from it. "This is our treat for all you lucky men for completing the tranasium," bellowed out Sgt. Major Brassard.

"RSM, would you like to be the first?" Amid the cheers and roars from his fellow men, the RSM climbed the high tower, gripped onto the handles of the roller-pulley either side of the wire rope being proffered by one of the staff stationed there and leaped off the platform to slide down a 400 metre wire cable amid the cheers of his men below.

"Who's next?" a voice with a distinct French accent bellowed from above. After another half-hour of getting the rest of Brigade HQ down the death-slide, they all assembled for the slow jog back to their camp.

Back at Tent City, Sgt. Steele was just laying back on his cot with his headphones on listening to country music on his Sony walkman. He was more preoccupied though, with reading over silently the address of a letter he had recently received, doing so for about the umpteenth time. He just kept slowly turning it over and over in his hands and sniffing and smelling the lightly scented perfumed paper like it was an intoxicating drug getting him high—and to Sgt. Steele that's exactly what it was! He checked the postmark once more and marvelled at the ability of the army postal service to catch up and locate you, no matter where. He finally tore the top edge of it and let the soft blue page slip from the envelope. He held it once more just staring and finally decided that he could no longer put off its reading and so he began.

My darling Ben, I suppose I should first ask how you are, for I wonder about that everyday. My life has been miserable since you left and I miss you terribly. You should know you took my heart with you for I should never love another while you are living . . . I constantly relive the first time you walked into our lives larger than life! I can't imagine what chain of events brought you to where you're at, but I do regret my part or rather, my lack of courage in defending you further. Please find it in your heart to forgive me. I will love you forever and will forever miss you! If you ever need me, I'll always be here waiting for you!

I love you my darling

Jane

Ben just softly closed the letter. He took off his headphones, stood, and walked out into the cool Montana evening air and with his thoughts, walked over toward the assault course and square. Letter grasped tightly in his hand, he softly said to himself, "My poor Jane, there you go again blaming yourself."

Out for an evening stroll himself under this big sky, the RSM spotted Ben in the setting dusk and quietly approached him. Instantly spotting the anguish on his face and then seeing the letter grasped in his hands the RSM tactfully said, "Would you rather I left you alone Ben?"

Whether it was just the friendly fatherly nature of the RSM or the right moment of unloading his burden as a parishioner would in confession, he started to just pour out his woes to the RSM. Explaining his tasked position with General Crenshaw, what had innocently developed with his daughter and transpired, then the circumstances culminating so close to his ultimate departure from the Mews. Then back to Hereford and the Regiment and his quick turn around to here.

In consolation, the RSM tried to explain that there were other men who were married within the Brigade, including himself, who had left loved ones behind and until they built married quarters, which was last on the list, they too would just have to deal with these family separations and emotions! The RSM knew this to be a pretty flimsy console, but under the circumstances it was the best he could manage, so with no more words to say, the RSM patted Ben's shoulder and the two men walked away from the assault course in the setting sunset back to Tent City.

As the officers left the mess tent, Mac stayed behind mulling over his cup of coffee. As the orderly offered him another cup to which he looked up and gratefully accepted, his mind was lost somewhere between here and United Nations HQ in New York City. He also found himself thinking of Maggie. He read the telegram from General Frank D. Clarke once more.

RETURN HERE AT ONCE STOP IMPORTANT
NEWS STOP BRING YOUR OWN COURIER STOP

Mac had called David to his office. There was a knock, then the Colonel entered. "You called me Sir?"

"Yes. Fact is, I have to return to New York on the next available flight, our boss wants to see me."

"Oh my."

"Exactly!"

"Any idea why then?"

"My hunch David, is political fall-out again over this Brigade formation, or upgraded news regarding Bosnia. I think it's trouble brewing for sure. Politics and such, either way I have to leave, which was my reason for calling you, to let you know I am leaving the Brigade in your capable hands!"

"Don't worry Mac, I'll make sure it keeps rolling."

"I'm sure you will David, but listen, I want that Sgt. Steele to come along. I know he's assigned as one of Sgt. Major Brassard's P.T.I. Staff right now, but I need someone familiar with Hereford who has a sharp mind and eyes and I need his skills doing double duty as a courier bodyguard. He's familiar with all of that. Anyway, have him issued with his new uniform immediately as we're both going as representatives of *this* Brigade, are we not?"

"Yes, and I'm sure Sgt. Steele is an excellent choice Sir, not to mention the fact that the men will be excited to see an advance unveiling of their own uniform!"

. . . As Ben was dressing, to the watchful eyes of his tent companions *and* the entire Brigade HQ, it seemed, who were peering in through the hatch flaps, he finally buttoned up his tunic as the RSM inspected him. Leaning close to his ear, the RSM whispered for only Ben to hear, "Take a walk through Tent City, will you lad, for the lads to see what they have to be proud of?"

"Consider it done Sir!" spoke Ben proudly. As he walked through the compound complete in his new uniform including valour and campaign medals topped by the Brigade Sabre (a premature move, but acceptable under the circumstances) bedecked with full insignia including a light blue lanyard, Ben walked through Tent City to the awes, whistles and compliments of the Brigade.

For the very first time it seemed to bring them all together as one like never before especially in lieu of the fact most of them knew of the Sgt.'s reason for being so dressed and for once, to a man, they held that worried look as if they might be disbanded or something drastic. It was obvious that the General's departure was a mystery, but their instincts gave them these feelings, and a soldier's instincts were usually right!

As both Gen. Logan and Sgt. Steele sat side by side in the jumbo jet flight from Denver to La Guardia airport, they slid into a low hushed conversation about Ben's military background.

"I'm not exactly sure why you chose me to tag along with you Sir, but I'll do whatever I can to assist you."

"I know that Sergeant, so I'll tell you now. Most of your job will be to continue on to Hereford once we sort out in New York, as we need you to bring us an item back from there—plus you should know your way around there, it being your old unit and all."

"That I do Sir," smiled Ben, now looking forward to the trip back and a visit with his old mates with the 22 SAS.

"But there's another reason and part to this trip I have been hiding from everyone else," he said with a twinkle of the eye. "You seem to know our boss' counterpart over there in England? Some Staff General by the name of Brigadier General Thomas Crenshaw I believe."

Startled but keeping his composure, Ben said, "Yessir, I was his Executive Protection detail, bodyguard and all-round chauffeur for him and his family. Left just prior to my RTU to the Regiment and then posting to this Brigade. But tell me, how did you know the connection?"

"Relax Sergeant, I've read the file and contrary to all I have read, I have heard from certain men and officers of the Brigade, and I can assure you that there isn't any doubt in my mind or theirs, that you were victimized by the efforts of a jealous officer and if I ever get to meet him I'll be sure to give him my best, with your regards, as they say!"

"Thanks for the vote of confidence Sir!" smiled a now relaxed Ben, "but under the circumstances, do you think I was the wisest choice to attend here with you?"

"Simple Sergeant, if I need a read on this General, who in my Brigade knows him better than you?"

Laughing now, Ben said, "Of course!"

As they entered the familiar oak panelled office of General F.D. Clarke at the UN Building, at least for Mac, Maggie was there to greet them and say, "They're already in there General waiting for you."

"Take care of the Sergeant here then, will you Maggie?" he smiled back over his shoulder as he had his hand on the handle to the inner office door.

"Be my pleasure. By the way, nice uniform!"

As Mac entered, General Clarke smiled and rose to greet him along with his British guest Brigadier General T. Crenshaw.

"Well Mac, I guess you're itching to know why we called you here to say the least, heh?"

"That's about as easy a guess you'll ever get out of me."

"Well Mac, the British and French are a little concerned as to how their men are being trained for future deployment into battle and are anxious to see their development, your Brigade location and facilities that have been afforded them."

"The men are doing well in their training and our location is growing and expanding every day courtesy of the Engineers and other specialists. Our facilities are going up daily and they are also expanding. Our heavy equipment of fighting machines and artillery pieces are arriving steadily by train. Our only hold-up seems to be in the munitions and small arms, regular transport, both attack and mobile, and all that high-tec sensitive satellite stuff and telecommunications."

"Can these all be sorted soon?"

"Yessir, given reasonable expectations."

"How soon do you expect to be up to full strength?" spoke General Crenshaw for the first time.

"Just a couple more months, Sir, the core Staff are in place for HQ, camp security, stores, hospital, armaments, telecommunications and battalions, plus a few other logistical elements like catering, transport, etc. need sorting."

"Then by your own report, it's just a matter of logistics and manpower that's holding up your progress?" queried General Crenshaw.

"Pretty much so, General. We have the best and most highly trained combat engineers right now assisting in the design and development of the camp."

"I hear the men are billeted right now in what you would describe as a Tent City. How long do you expect they can live and function under those conditions?"

"Well Sir, putting it bluntly, during the Second World War men lived under those conditions and then went into battle to places like Normandy and Arnhem long before any of us ever tried it. Regardless, ours is just for a few more weeks before our permanent living quarters are built."

"Very well said. Now your training, that's also well under hand?"

"Yessir!"

"So, what do you suggest or expect the final rating of your Brigade to be?"

"We have the very best professionals your country and others could spare Sir. They are more than qualified to wear this uniform."

"Yes, that is an extremely fancy looking uniform you have designed there, but can your men live up to it?"

"They're top rate Sir, the very best fighting soldiers. Yes, I think I can safely say they can!"

"And the men, how are their uniforms designed, similar?"

"You can judge for yourself General, if you'll wait on just a moment."

Getting up and walking to the door, to their surprise he just leant his head out and gestured with a wink and nod upward for Ben. As he entered the office, the clap and look of appreciation from General Clarke was stark in contrast and quite the opposite reaction of General Crenshaw. Upon noticing who was in the uniform, he let his guard down unfamiliarly and asked, astonished but friendly, "How is this meant to be, Sergeant . . . ?" obviously wanting answers.

Immediately Mac spoke, "Well Sir, he'll be on a detail travelling back to the UK with you heading to Hereford, but mostly due to just the simple fact that I knew that the Sgt. here had served on your staff and I also could think of no-one better qualified to answer your questions, if you have any regarding the men. You know, hear it from the horse's mouth."

"Yes well, that's all right then," he muttered.

After establishing the need for Sgt. Steele and lengthy explanations of the Crypto Gun were debated around and the need for the courier detail fully understood, the important stuff also over and out the way, the conversation returned to the uniform.

"Who designed these uniforms anyway, you or one of your officers?"

"The men themselves Sir, under the care and direction of RSM Whittle."

"Is he a big red-haired ex-guardsman?" asked General Crenshaw getting his composure back quickly from the surprise of seeing Sgt. Steele.

"Yes he is Sir, do you know him?"

"Yes, sort of, presented him his Military Medal for Tumbledown Mountain."

"Tumble . . . ?" began Gen. Clarke.

"In the Falklands War Sir," interjected Ben.

"Ah yes."

"Why let the men design the uniform though, isn't that a job better suited to the officers?"

Speaking confidently now, Mac added wisely, "The fact of it is Sir, I thought that if the men themselves had most of the say in its design, including the input of my officers, I may add, I felt that they would bond better and feel more proud and agreeable in wearing it, 'Their Own' so to speak, as we know only too well how proud they were, and still are, of the units they have left behind."

Smiling now, and taking a long hard look at Ben, the General said, "Good decision, one I would have made myself and on Sergeant Steele here, it looks impressive indeed. Yes, I quite like it."

"Thank you Sir."

Then, dismissing Sgt. Steele to the outer office with Maggie, the three officers opened their folders and got down to business. As they sat there around the oak desk exchanging paper files and reading and just talking for the better part of an hour or so while drinking Maggie's coffee, General Crenshaw said, "I have to leave you both now, as I have another appointment at the British Embassy, but, by the way, if you no longer want or need the presence of Sergeant Steele here, I would appreciate him accompanying me, sort of catch up on old business?"

Calling Sgt. Steele back into the office and telling him of the General's request while looking at him closely for any doubts and receiving none, Mac replied, "Of course not, if that's agreeable to you then Sergeant?"

"Not a problem Sir, I would like the opportunity to speak with the General!"

They never spoke a word to each other from the moment they left the office together, entered the elevator together, and entered the staff car together. Finally though, the General broke the silence.

"Never expected to see you again Sergeant, but you never can tell with these SAS types heh?" he said smiling.

"Understandable Sir, I never expected to see you either, so soon that is."

"Regarding the incident at the Mews and at the Legion Hall with that Guard's Captain prior to your departure, it did eventually resolve itself with a little word here and there."

"How so Sir, I thought all that was over and done with?"

"The truth of the matter is Sergeant, that after your departure the Captain lied some more and pushed the issue to a higher level, which I gather resulted in your immediate posting to this Brigade. Something of which I obviously knew nothing about until it was too late," then turning to him slowly he proffered his hand and said, "Sorry Ben, never expected this to happen."

"Sir," said Ben smiling, "I'm kinda pleased the way it turned out. The Captain did me a favour and he doesn't even know it. I like it here, the compliment, like what we're doing, even happier now to know you're onboard!"

The General squinted and eyed him closely and decided he was telling it straight, then said, "Well, I suggest we put that chapter behind us, heh?"

Smiling broadly Ben said, "Sir, I already have!"

The two men leaned back and let out their respective sighs.

The General added, "By the way Ben, that Lieutenant of mine who so fondly cares about your welfare would appreciate to hear from you!"

Knowing this must have taken the General a long time to come to terms with, Ben looked at the General for an answer to which he received through a smiling nod and the following statement, "Hell Boy I came through the ranks, I wasn't born an Officer or General you know!"

"Mrs. Crenshaw?" enquired Ben.

"As delighted at the prospect as any of us!" he chided.

For the first time in his life Ben was well and truly out of sorts.

On reaching the British Embassy, General Crenshaw directed the driver of the vehicle to continue on and drop Ben off at his hotel where he was staying with General Logan. With a parting smile, he gave words that he would see him in the morning.

The trip back to the hotel was just a blank ride and while finally settling into his New York City hotel room, Ben laid back exhausted on his bed, remembering all these events in his life this past year. Then, in a sort of panic-reflex, he hurriedly reached into his tunic to touch the pale blue air mail letter that rested there. It seemed a reassuring touch as he relaxed and let his mind wander slowly back. Ben took out his letter one more time and began to read it over again to himself mouthing the words Jane wrote, trying desperately to remember her voice, see her face, then closing his eyes, there in the secret enclaves of his mind just like he had imagined a thousand times before, she came . . .

PART 4

The next morning Ben met General Logan in the hotel lobby. The General enquired of him, "So, how was your little ride with that British Staff General Crenshaw of yours?"

"It was fine Sir, the same old General!"

Mac asked in follow-up, "What's your make on him Sergeant, do you think he's on our side in all of this?"

"Well Sir, I don't know exactly what's going on at your level of discussion but if I have to make a guess, I'd say that the General is, how do you Yanks say it, Gung Ho?"

"I hope your read of him is right, for the fact is, there is a massive political push on to sink this new Brigade of ours. We're going to need every friend we can find in high places to keep our little show on the road."

"What exactly is the sit rep then Colonel?"

"Well, putting it bluntly, I think the politicians over at the UN Security Council there, with their counterparts in NATO, are afraid we might never get into Bosnia as a Brigade. If we can't get the Brits and French to turn the screws a little harder on them, we just might lose out. Part of the reason I brought you along with me was so that I could get you to give me an 'insightful read' on this General of yours. After all, you're meant to know him better than anyone on my Staff."

"Well, I can tell you this much General, he's considered a 'real thinker'. They didn't put him in Intelligence for nothing. Do you want me to have a straight-up talk with him though, just out and out ask him what his feelings are on the whole situation?"

"I'd rather do that myself, but if you can tell me first what sort of man you know this General to be, it would benefit me greatly."

"Well, no disrespect intended Sir, but he's a lot like yourself. A straight-up brave son-of-a-bitch who would lead his men into the gates of hell if he had to. What you see is pretty much what you get, just don't let that British accent of his or pompous tone deceive you, he's every bit a hard-assed soldier."

"Well thank you for your frankness, and your compliment I hope? Tell me Sergeant, if I'm not intruding too much on private ground, did you get to resolve that situation you have with his daughter?"

Taking a deep breath, Ben said grinning, "He gave me his blessing."

Mac slapped him on the back saying, "That's excellent news, a man can spend just too many lonely nights defending his country. Nothing wrong with having a good lady to come home to, take that for what it's worth from a confirmed military bachelor!"

Ben added mischievously, "Not if that Maggie has her way!"

"What are you saying?" babbled Mac, pleasantly surprised.

"Just that she's burning a torch for you General."

"Maggie heh?"

"Yep!"

"Good morning to you General, and you too Sergeant. General Clarke and that British General, Crenshaw, are already in the office. Can I get you a cup of coffee?" interrupted Maggie, as the two of them entered her domain.

"Please," said Mac winking at Ben. Then he deliberately leant over Maggie's desk to look right into her eyes, "When I'm finished here myself, can I take you to lunch Maggie? We need to talk."

Looking flushed but excited, Maggie just barely managed, "My pleasure!"

"Keep Maggie company for me will you Sergeant, and don't forget to keep telling her what a catch I am, okay?"

"Will do General."

"Oh, just one more thing, I meant to ask you this earlier. Speaking unofficially for the British contingent in our Sabre Brigade, how do they feel about us? Any urges to return to their parent units?"

"You couldn't be further from the truth on that one Sir, the men are all yours, that includes the American and French, to a man!"

Beaming broadly Mac nodded, "Thanks Sergeant, I needed to hear that." Then turning abruptly, he entered the inner office.

Looking at Ben now Maggie said, "What did you go and say about me?"

"Only that the Colonel is getting too old to remain a bachelor Maggie," as he winked at her.

Blushing demurely Maggie asked sweetly, "How do you like your coffee?"

Calling Sgt. Steele into the General's inner office Mac said, "Sergeant Steele, General Crenshaw here will be returning to England tomorrow and reporting to Whitehall, we would like you to accompany him. Courier some documents back for us, from him and his superiors, as well as fetch this Crypto Gun of course.

"I don't understand Sir, can't all that be faxed or something now?"

"That's just the problem, not without this Crypto Gun to encrypt it all. Besides, there are too many leaks that way, you know that. I much prefer the old fashioned method myself too, but at least you were trained by the world's best in the business of couriering were you not? Just saves us the added task of deciding on someone else as your alternate. What do you say?"

"If you're all for it, it's a duty I would like to perform Sir," adding, "How long is the trip for?"

"Should be about a week in total. What with all the top secret meetings, driving and visits the General has to make. He will gather all the documents together and have you bring them back to us all in one shot. While he does that you collect this Crypto Gun and bring it all back together, simple really."

"Yes, no problems Sir, but what about accommodations, where will I be staying?"

Turning to look and reply directly himself, General Crenshaw added, "With me as my guest, unless you have an alternative choice in mind Sergeant?"

"No Sir!" he grinned.

Mac left them in the office just long enough to pop out and ask Maggie to add Sgt. Steele onto the General's flight, by hook or by crook. While Maggie went about their flight arrangements, Mac gave Ben his last minute instructions. "Enjoy your visit by all means Sergeant, but don't forget the purpose behind it, you have to return with that diplomatic bag ASAP if you understand the meaning of urgency."

"Don't worry Sir, I won't let you down, and thanks!"

Patting him on the back Mac said, "Well, at least this is my opportunity to get to know Maggie too, heh?"

"She's a nice lady Sir, I know you'll be very happy together."

"Humm!" grinned the Colonel.

"Flight arrangements all taken care of," added a confident Maggie.

"Well Sergeant, I guess all that's required of us is to stop by your hotel and pick up your bags. By the way, keep the uniform on, I'd like to see you impress everyone with it."

"Yes, show the British what a great Brigade you've joined by all means," added General Clarke.

They all stood there in Maggie's outer office shaking hands goodbye. Soon, General Crenshaw and Sgt. Steele walked out and down the hallway. Turning the corner, the General looked at Ben, "Couldn't resist the opportunity Ben, besides, we'll all be happy to have you back home, including me!"

"Thanks General, I really mean it, thanks for everything."

"Yes well, let's get on our bikes and make sure we catch that flight in time before we look like a pair of silly buggers, shall we?"

'That's a go General," replied Ben, as they both raced down the hall.

The flight out of New York went without a hitch and approximately five hours later they were disembarking at London's Heathrow Airport. The Sgt. Major was waiting for them at the terminal gates. He gave Ben a nice friendly hug when he came near, then shook his hand energetically.

"Don't worry me 'ol son, it's only me the General informed of your little tag-along. Oh, and Jane just happened to arrive home for the weekend an hour before I left!" the old scoundrel added with a wink.

"Hello General Sir, good to see you!"

"Yes, well give me a hand with some of these bags and we'll probably find you speaking a different tune!" Bags in hand, the three of them left Heathrow Airport main terminal. The General and Ben waited outside for a few minutes while the Sgt. Major brought the Bentley around.

"Where to first?" asked the Sgt.Major.

"Unfortunately a quick detour into London is first on the list. We're close by, plus I have to get this ball rolling. But stop by the offices at Whitehall first, will you Sgt. Major, we have to have a chat with some of our friends and peers. Then maybe yourself and Ben here can find yourselves a pint and bite to eat and get acquainted while I'm gone."

"Sounds like a smashing plan Sir."

Pulling the Bentley up to the curb of the steps at Whitehall, right outside the Department of the Army buildings, the Sgt. Major dropped off General Crenshaw with the instructions to be back within an hour and a half. They drove off but soon stopped at a favourite pub of the Sgt. Major's in the army garrison area. Parking the Bentley in the rear lot, they went inside. The regular lunch crowd had already left so it was easy to find a relatively quiet table in some corner of the pub. The Sgt. Major left for a brief minute to place his order at the bar. A barmaid soon returned to their table with a ploughman's lunch each and two pints of its best bitter.

"If you don't mind me asking dearie," said the barmaid, "but I seez them come in 'ere from all the surrounding barracks, I do, and for the life o' me, I ne'er seen a blimmin uniform of the likes o' that, what kind o' military uniform is it, pray tell?"

Ben looked up at her grinning, "It's part of the United Nations!"

"Really?" she said, standing there with hands on hips.

"Really!" Ben laughed with her.

"It is pretty though," adding, "well love, I'll let you alone and eat."

"Thanks for the food."

Looking at each other the Sgt. Major and Ben could only grin, then went about reacquainting themselves. Later, they stopped to pick up the General at his prearranged spot, speeding off on the drive back to the Mews and to Basingstoke.

The summer was over now here in England. The cold of autumn was easily upon them. Ben looked out of the window of the Bentley as it drove up the familiar driveway to the mews and felt warm and content looking at the sunburnt mat of oak leaves lining its path. As the wheels crunched the gravel below as silently as it could, they drove slowly up and around, parking the vehicle at the main entrance. The Sgt. Major helped the General get their bags out the trunk as he urged Ben to stand aside in case someone spotted him and ruined their surprise.

Mrs. Crenshaw met them at the door. After her warm greeting kiss and hug for her husband, shouted, "Children, your father's home!"

They came a-running. At least little Amy and Tom yelling, "Yippee, it's daddy!"

Leaning over his wife, the General whispered into her ear, then made her look back as he held a finger to his lips. Her gasp of surprise on seeing Ben was genuine and warm. Quickly moving to give him a greeting hug, she stood aside as the General said, "I don't suppose we could get Jane to fetch this bag I have forgotten standing here by the front door do you?"

Smiling confidently, Mrs. Crenshaw added, "Just you watch!"

The Sgt. Major went through the main door leaving Ben standing there alone. He didn't have too long to wait though, for he heard the arrival of oncoming footsteps. Jane turned the corner nonchalantly into the hall foyer, then stopped abruptly in her tracks. She let out a gasp, clutching her face in her hands.

"Hello Jane," Ben said awkwardly.

Moving her arms uselessly, then bringing her hands up to hug herself, she looked a little ashen. Jane asked, "Is it really you Ben?"

"Yes, it's really me!" he grinned. She came a-running then and threw herself into his arms. She clung on and hugged him with all her strength, until even Ben felt the tightness take him by surprise. As she relaxed some, looking at him with moist eyes she implored, "My darling, you'll never know how I've missed you. Please, just tell me you love me back and that this is not a dream?"

Holding her confidently now, Ben picked her up easily and said boldly, "I love you with my very life and soul Jane Crenshaw," adding for her benefit, "this is also not a dream." Then they kissed again. Locked in embrace as the Sgt. Major and aunt May and all the rest of the Crenshaw family came up behind them and said happily, "Come on Jane, we all want to see Ben as well!"

So, with Jane holding onto his arm with both her hands and looking up into his face with tears of love and joy she said, "Well, what say we join them in the kitchen?"

"Let's go then," he laughed quietly, adding silently so only she could hear his whisper, "Until later."

Kissing him on the cheek, she whispered back blushingly, "I can't wait!"

Aunt May readied Ben's old room for him, saying to him as she came out onto the landing where he had carried his bag up, "She spent many a night in here crying for you Ben, many a night, so don't go hurting her. I don't think the poor thing could handle the heartbreak, she was a nervous wreck and just let herself go for the longest time when you left us. She never got over it, or you it seems!"

"It's okay aunt May," he reassured, "I promise I won't let her or anyone else down, okay?"

Tapping him gently on the cheek, then pausing to give him a light peck there, aunt May said kindly, "I know you won't dearie, just letting you know how much that young lady down there has pined for you is all. Now what do you say we go back down and join 'em?"

"For sure!"

The young Crenshaw children were long away to bed and when aunt May and Ben entered the kitchen, Mrs. Crenshaw chimed in, "My husband has been holding us all enthralled with the details of this new Brigade you seem to have joined Ben, you must feel very proud!"

"Yes I am Ma'am."

"Is it going to be very dangerous?" she added, then looking at Jane as if to say, *there, I asked the question for you!*

Looking first at the men, then the women, he answered, "I don't believe so, no, from what I know anyway. The fact is, I think it would take a lot of political pull to just see us get involved in any military engagement. But when that's all said and done, that is the nature of the business we're in, isn't it?"

"Too bloody dangerous for my liking!" spoke up Mrs. Crenshaw, "I'm sorry, but that's the way I feel!"

"Then I'll take extra good care of myself to keep you all happy. Come on you lot, don't go getting morose on me, it isn't that bad, and if it was, just remember the old saying, 'nothing very bad lasts for very long'!"

Trying to lighten the drama of the situation, the Sgt. Major added, "Yes, and just look at this fine peacock uniform they gave him!"

After they had all finished laughing at that remark, Jane spoke. "It is a very striking uniform," she said coyly.

Then they all burst out laughing again.

Eventually the General spoke out for all, "Let's us older lot just get lost and get off to our beds and leave these young two here alone, I think they would rather we did that sooner than later, heh?"

Saying their good-nights and listening to their footsteps grow fainter with each passing second, Jane and Ben were finally alone at last. They had another coffee and for awhile just caught up on past and current events themselves when suddenly Jane reached for his hand and said matter of factly, "Let's go to your room."

"What about the other folks?"

"Well I'm a big girl now Ben. At my age, I do think I have earned the right and privilege of deciding who and when I make love to someone. Besides, if they haven't figured it all out by now or expected this, then daddy should have never brought you home, should he?" she said with her eyes twinkling mischievously.

Scooping her up in his strong arms, smiling at her lovingly, Ben said, "Watch your head on the walls as we go up the stairs!"

Burying her head in his muscular chest while clinging to his arms, Jane felt the urgency and pending excitement of love return to her. That feeling she felt earlier when she first saw him. The one she had imagined and dreamed of a thousand times over! Closing the door behind himself now, Ben lay Jane gently on the bed while he sat down beside her to remove his boots. He pushed them beneath the bed itself. Rising and keeping his back to Jane, he walked across the room to disrobe.

Sitting on the bed, Jane started the same. Complete, she quietly slipped between the sheets, but she kept her eyes glued onto Ben. Turning to face the bed once more, he walked across the room in only his birthday suit and turned on the night-lamp while he crossed the room to put out the main light switch. Her eyes watched his naked movements as he moved to bed and slipped quietly in next to Jane's hot body. They both turned to face each other and she reached for his head clasping it in both her hands while he reached behind her arched back with one arm to support her and gently touched her breasts with the other, cupping one of them into his hand and squeezing it lightly. She came to him then, kissing his mouth passionately and reaching and searching for his tongue with her own. Frantically but gently, she reached for his hand and guided it down to the triangle of hair that lay between her legs and spoke for the very first time. "Make love to me darling, I've waited so long for this, for you to love me and make me feel like a real woman!"

"I love you Jane!" he blurted out, as he moved on top of her, with passions fully aroused for both of them.

At about 10 o'clock the following morning, there was a polite knock at the bedroom door. Laying there cozy and relaxed, just soon roused from sleep herself, Jane said lazily, "Come in aunt May!"

Entering with her best friendly smile aunt May asked, "How did you know it was me?"

"Because you're the only one who knocks around here!"

"Humm, well I just wanted to see if you love birds were into some nourishing food, especially after last night!" she added rather cheekily, "How is he?"

"The poor darling is sleeping like a child, I think I wore him out aunt May!"

"Yes, they do have a tendency to sleep like that after, better get used to it girl!" she admonished playfully.

"Is everyone else up aunt May?"

"They're all out the house. Went into London with your dad for the day. But do they know you're sleeping here is your real question right?" and receiving a smiling nod, aunt May continued, "I'll hazard a guess that they jolly well do!" she laughed heartily.

Then sheepishly and demurely, snuggling back into the blankets and the warmth of Ben, Jane said, "Make us both some bacon and eggs, will you aunt May? I'll see what I can do about rising Rip Van Winkle here!" she giggled.

Closing the door behind her, aunt May threw over her shoulder first, "I'll believe that one when I see you both down there!"

As he stirred awake from her prodding, Ben caught the smell of soft delicate perfume on Jane's body which was like an intoxicating stimulant, and grabbed her and pulled her close. Snuggling and giggling, they playfully wriggled around until their passions overtook them once more!

Later, lying back exhausted and sated, they both decided to rise. Propped on his pillow, it was Ben's turn to marvel and stare at the nakedness of Jane. Turning to give him a farewell pose Jane said, "See you downstairs in twenty minutes loverboy!" Then she was gone. Jane was down in the kitchen talking to aunt May as their late breakfast was being cooked for them both.

"Morning cheerful!" he said as he entered the room. Coming over to kiss him, Jane said, "Umm, you smell good too."

"Knock it off now you two or I'll make you cook your own blinking breakfasts," scolded Aunt May, as she joined in with her playful banter.

"Ah, you love us too dearly to do that to two starving waifs!"

"Don't count your chickens . . . " aunt May let trail off, laughing.

Sitting there eating and talking while aunt May was just having her morning cup o' tea, he wasn't sure how it all started, but the conversation came round to engagements.

"Tell me what you just said again, just in case I misunderstood?" urged Jane.

"It's simple really," said Ben as he reached over to touch Jane gently, "Look Jane, I meant what I just said."

Receiving a reassuring nod from aunt May and amid her happy sniffles Jane urged him on, "Tell me again, or pinch me. Did you say what I thought you just said?"

"Yes!"

She cried out then, blinking a tear away as he passed her the ring.

"If you don't like it you can change it, but I feel I have to make an honest woman out of you, but if you really don't want to . . . ?" he went on, adding, "Jane, I believe I once told you, but I'll say it again, I happen to have some property in Canada that was left to me, we can use that as a start!" Quietly adding more, "Do you think you could handle that?"

Jane said slowly, "Don't joke with me on this Ben, it's too important an issue!"

"I'm not joking, look, it's some prime property Jane."

"That's NOT what I meant!"

"I know, I was kidding, but I meant it, will you marry me?"

Startled now, she just looked at him, then began getting excited, realizing what he had just asked her. She looked at aunt May who was all agog.

"For some reason Jane, I'm sorta attached to you and this family," he understated. Jane then came up running from around the table and jumped onto him hugging and kissing him, he cuddled her close while even aunt May came around to hug them both. Moments later, after all the sobbing and the tears were dried, he said to Jane, "Let me tell your parents?"

"No, I'll tell them, when they get home."

"How was London Sir?" Ben asked of the General and Mrs. Crenshaw.

"Frantic! Had a lot of running around to do also, on some private banking matters with Mrs. Crenshaw, plus the only places I could find any of the Staff officers was over at their private club in Mayfair. Still, we did make some headway, heh Sgt. Major?"

"That we did Sir, that we did!"

"Now, what's all this about Jane being in my study waiting to talk to her mother and I?"

"That's the message she gave me to pass on to you both the minute you were to get home, her exact words," added aunt May.

"Well dear, let's not keep the poor girl waiting, it must be important stuff if Jane's waiting on us!" said Mrs Crenshaw.

As the Crenshaws returned from the General's study and entered the kitchen, they had that stunned look of incredulity on their faces, as well as something else. Was it happiness?

"Could we have some strong coffee aunt May? Better still, will you fetch the whiskey bottle Sgt. Major, I feel an urge for a stiff drink and some celebrating!"

Jane soon followed and stopped in the doorway to lean against the post and lingered long enough to give aunt May a smile and blow a kiss to Ben. Then she fully entered the room and sat down on Ben's lap across the table from her parents and said, "I may as well completely shock you, look at the ring I received from Ben, it's an engagement ring, I do hope you both approve?"

"Will someone kindly tell me what the bleedin' 'eck is going on?" blurted the Sgt.Major.

Then, with all the rest laughing in relief, the General good-naturedly said, "Shut up and have a stiff drink with us, that good lady of yours will fill you in on all the juicy details later!"

With things finally settled between Ben and Jane, the General was fully able to devote his time and energies to getting the necessary willpower and approval from his peers. Meeting those military and political connections, while using his own determination to back the venture of the Sabre Brigade to its full formation, or possible deployment if ever needed, the General and Sgt. Major returned to Basingstoke and the Mews, leaving Ben just one last night with Jane before his own departure to New York and General Logan and The Sabre Brigade, UN.

The final evening spent together at the Mews was a memorable one and they all celebrated the presence but impending departure of Ben in fine style. Even taking time out to visit the Rose and Crown for a quiet and eventful free evening this time round, for an enjoyable few pints of good 'ol British ale.

Later that evening and alone once more, Jane ensured that Ben would not leave her without enjoying the pleasures of her body one final time! Once again, her raw and glorious beauty enthralled him. He caressed her breasts and with the heat of the moment they fully embraced each other and proceeded with their passionate love like their very lives depended on it. It seemed to last for hours until they drifted asleep, satisfied and sated once again beyond belief!

They rose early and with all in their nightgowns they said their tearful farewells to Ben, hugging and kissing him and shaking his hand urging him to phone them as soon as possible. As Jane started her car in the early morning mist of a fine British autumn day, they eventually but slowly drove off down the driveway on their way to Heathrow Airport. Once there the impending departure was one charged with emotion for the two. Jane had elected to leave him sooner, rather than to see him leave through the gates and down the gangway to the boarding area. It was a bittersweet departure for sure, but what Ben was not aware of, was the lone strong figure of Jane leaning against the window pane, crying silently as she hugged herself and watched his flight soar off into the cloudy morning sky.

He landed in New York's La Guardia airport and it was business as usual for Sgt. Steele as he was all the professional soldier once again. There was no military escort awaiting him so he hailed a cab going straight to the United Nations Plaza Building to deliver his diplomatic bag and papers to Generals Clarke and Logan. He was fortunate to find them both there in consultation. There were warm greetings for Ben from Maggie who seemed to have a special glow about her these days also.

"Well done son, can't tell you how much this means to us all!"

"How is that English Rose of yours doing, was she glad to see you?"

"An understatement Sir, we ended up getting engaged!"

"Well that makes two of you!" boomed General Clark in his deep voice, standing unnoticed in the doorway. "The General here is determined to take Maggie away from me and leave me stranded. Do you have any idea how long it took me to train that girl?" he said in jest.

"You mean you just don't want to go through the growing pains of having to have some other nice young thing train you, you old crotchety bastard! Anyway you can relax, it will be some time before Maggie lets me take her off your hands!"

"Well, that's a relief," sighed the General. "So son, what news have you brought us in that goody bag then heh—besides that Crypto Gun gizmo?"

"The kind you've been hoping for I believe Sirs."

As Gen. Logan checked over the Crypto Gun, securing it back in its container for Maj. Rance's later possession, Gen. Clarke picked up the papers to read. After spending a few more minutes quietly reading to himself, General Clarke leant back in his chair and whistled softly.

"What is it Sir?" asked Mac.

"It's a compromise Mac. The British over in Whitehall feel strongly we can only proceed if we get the Canadians involved. They have strong feelings about leaving them out of this one. They're not too concerned about future numbers from them, they just want them onboard. The fact they are the world's ambassadors as peacekeepers carries a lot of weight with them, especially with the politicos over there in NATO and SHAPE and here too with the Security Council. They will however bring the same initial numbers as the rest of you, approximately 100 men. They are to be sent to your Sabre Brigade with all due haste. They are sending men from the JTF, RCR's, PPCLI and R 22e R. These are all good Regiments Mac, any questions?"

"None!" he said with conviction. "I served with the Canadians in Bosnia as well as Somalia. I was sorry to see the politicians in Canada disband a very good Airborne Regt. of over 1,000 men for the sake of half a dozen bad apples, then drag good names through the mud for four years or more totally demoralizing and paralysing their entire military, then having the gall to say *morale* was their problem?! All armies need elite fighting units to aspire to, to try and join and be proud of. Airborne tasking and training does that and more!"

"I agree Mac, all of us in the know agree, it was overkill! So, the Canucks are onboard heh?" he grinned in understatement.

"I'll confirm through usual channels then," he said flatly as though the issue was resolved and taken care of, and it was. A half hour later after reading over everything completely, they agreed unanimously that Sgt. Steele had been right, they now had all the pieces in place they needed to get their show back on the road.

"Care to join us in a little celebratory drink here Sergeant, seeing as we couldn't have done it without you?"

"Don't mind if I do Sir," he accepted agreeably.

"I think I'll just put in that call to Colonel Price now and let him and the rest of the Brigade relax also."

"Excellent idea Mac," said the General as he poured their drinks.

When they finally got back to barracks in Helena, Montana there was a stir and air of excitement. The nearly two-week absence for the General and Sgt. Steele had seen a lot of changes. For one, the camp was being built at an incredible rate and the Officers and enlisted men had the opportunity to move out of Tent City and into Buildings.

"Where is everyone?" enquired the General to their driver, noticing a marked absence of bodies.

"Over in the mess hall—awaiting your arrival Sir!"

"What do you say, Sergeant Steele, want to go over with me and see what's going on?"

"Be a good idea I think Sir."

It was dark when they entered the hall except for a small light, but as they fully entered the room, the lights came on and every man of the Brigade it seemed was there, with glass in hand, standing all around holding a drink. RSM Whittle was holding out two glasses with a smile to General Logan and Sgt. Steele, which they took with a little surprise, while Colonel Price spoke.

"Gentlemen, just like in the movies with the first Devil's Brigade, we too have just had our growing pains and come from the brink of elimination, but where as that Colonel Fredericks was the Devil himself, let's lift our glasses to the man who brought us out of the ashes—to General Logan!" he shouted, and as they raised their glasses he added, "To the Phoenix!"

"To the Phoenix!" the men of Sabre Brigade chanted in unison.

As the officers surrounded General Logan for additional news of their situation, RSM Whittle gave Ben a look of anticipation with raised eyebrows that signalled that he wanted to know also how it all went—including the situation with Jane.

Nodding his head slowly to let the RSM know that everything was sorted, the RSM gave a huge roar and chuckle and said to Ben, "Come 'ere so I can hug yah, you ugly little man!" as all the others burst into laughter. He didn't give away too many of the details, just made them aware of the simple fact that while they were stuck here in no-man's land, he was screwing his brains out with a beautiful woman while being waited on hand and foot! The men fully enjoyed being teased in this manner, saying things like, "Lying bugger" and "Lucky you Mon Ami!" After the festivities were over, all the sergeants took Ben over to his new accommodations and where his belongings had recently been moved to. He had a single room to himself.

Sgt. Major Brassard came up and spoke, "Tomorrow bright and early mon ami, we have to start getting prepared for our parachute jumps as a Brigade, there is much to do to prepare!"

"I'll be ready Sgt. Major, thanks," he said before entering his room and falling exhausted and a little drunk onto his bed, just dropping his bags onto the floor where they lay.

The following day the entire Brigade of these initial members known for the present as HQ Coy were out on parade. Standing out at the front of the parade, a little removed from RSM Whittle and the rest of his officers, the General addressed his Brigade.

"Men, we have this one final parachute jump to do as a Brigade and march back into camp as fully fledged members, then we can have our pass-out parade in front of all the top brass in the world in our bright new uniforms!" Awaiting the cheers to die down he continued, "Then the real work begins! We await the arrival of more new recruits starting next week and we, the originals, will be expected to train them and bring them up to our own level of superior skill in a very short time.

"Some, probably even most of you, will not be involved with the training in the physical sense, as your skills will be needed elsewhere where they really lie, and that is putting your knowledge to good use keeping this Brigade functioning as a finely tuned machine!" Pausing, and looking on proudly at his assembled men, he continued, "Well, let's not dawdle, do as the RSM and Sgt.

Major Brassard and Sgt. Major Ridgeway ask of you, let's get going to those transports and get this jump done, what do you say?"

Amid the cheers and whistles, General Logan turned to RSM Whittle and asked him to take over the parade.

"As you were, you 'orrible lot!" boomed the RSM in his rich deep voice, "I want all the Sergeants to march your troops off the parade square in columns of three and fall them out into the awaiting trucks. Make sure everyone does a quick kit check before we leave." Once this was achieved, they made their way onto the trucks heading out for McCord AFB across the state line into Washington State, heading for Fort Lewis and the Airborne Ranger Detachment.

"We will be jumping onto the Mt. Rainier DZ in the Yakamo training area," added the RSM.

As they arrived, they waited in the hangars and out on the runway checking and rechecking equipment ensuring their equipment containers were correctly attached to the harness by the webbing strap. They checked their weapons too for something else to do. Taking them apart and going over the working mechanisms and moving parts with a dry cloth, then re-oiling them like they were always taught when cleaning their rifles, was an effective and useful way for soldiers to relax.

Their transport planes, the US equivalent of the British Hercules C130s, were all parked a short distance from the hangar. The loading, well in progress, was being supervised by the ground crew. As they waited patiently in the "hurry up and wait" mode, all sat quietly in little groups around on the runway, amongst their gear and packs, while others waited inside the hangar. As the buzz word came to ready-up, soldiers could be seen leaving the hangars and picking up those already outside. They began making their way across the runway, as the loading from the rear of the large transport planes was done and up went the ramps!

The parallel flight path of the six big transports in the sky was a pretty sight. Inside them though, the drone of the large planes' engines were a rhythmic background that was in its surprisingly own way, a reassuring comfort. They seemed to be airborne for about little more than thirty minutes before the ever watchful eyes of the forward looking Loadmaster and their movement indicated they were nearly there.

As the "wedge" containers went out over the rear ramp and their white canopies opened with static lines hitched, they all anxiously awaited the US Jumpmasters who were controlling all the paratroopers leaving the aircraft. Their drills were much quicker than the British for the aircraft safety checks are minimal as all checks are conducted on the ground prior to enplaning. They also drop much lighter as equipment is fitted. The commands finally came amongst the roar of the engines.

"Outboard personnel stand up, hook up!"

"Inboard personnel, stand up, hook up!"

"Check equipment!"

"Sound off for equipment check!"

"No.1 on the left door, No.1 on the right door, report!"

"ALL OKAY JUMPMASTER."

"ALL OKAY JUMPMASTER."

"Stand by!"

"Go!"

Each stick moved down the plane now, being dispatched expeditiously from both doors simultaneously. One by one they could be seen tumbling out of the huge Hercules transports as the static lines of previous jumpers were gathered to the left, ultimately snapping their parachutes free! They were jumping from 800 feet and would be on the ground in less than forty seconds! They were all using the US T-10 C parachutes. Checking canopy, then sky, then releasing equipment, with drift assessed they spilled air to steer away from one another ready to land with arms in close, knees and feet together.

The pathfinders had left previously being the first to land. Their role was always lead the way first, to recce and scout and to mark the DZ and be ready for action! They would report and radio, or use a satellite link to Brigade HQ while awaiting the main drop. The rest of the Brigade came to join them, hurtling and dropping from the sky. Soon the familiar and distinct cry of Colonel Price's British hunting horn let out an eerie chilling cry into the air and fast approaching sunset. General Logan thought aloud, "Damn, but that's a blood curdling shriek, even out here in the wilds of the mountains!"

They all were landing and falling from the sky above and all around. Pulling and gathering in their chutes, exiting harnesses and quickly putting on Bergans and checking weapons, they closed in. Smiling faces greeted one another as they finally felt bonded and as a whole! It was amazing the effect the thrill of a parachute jump can have on the morale of an elite airborne unit—especially as they all knew that in this modern age, the use and demand for airborne jumping units was a thing that was being labelled as something of the past. To the troops themselves though, jumping from these planes in their parachutes was a skill and they had hoped the professionalism would remain with *all* forces, for it was, in a very large part, a major reason that had brought them into these units specifically.

The men moved quickly and meshed into their roles and positions with an expedient and startling speed, giving credence to the fact that these were indeed some of the world's finest elite troops assembled here. Soon they were all together, ready for their final march back to their camp and into the gates and annuls of elite airborne history! The march back to camp was an easy twenty mile yomp as the British Royal Marines kept saying to anyone who cared to hear, while the British Paras just compared it to another "tab" not worthy of the Fan Dance. On reaching the gates this time though, there were no surprises and the Brigade settled back into their respective ranks and roles. The proud General, followed closely by RSM Whittle, led the brigade through the gates of the as yet unnamed camp of the Sabre Brigade.

Soldiers assembled proudly for their impending Pass-Out Parade in front of the top brass of all their assembled native countries. They stood and watched and cheered as they saw RSM Whittle remove a flag with the United Nations crest in the upper left hand corner, whilst dead centre was the emblem of their Phoenix! THIS was their Brigade Colours now and they looked for the motto, feeling proud of the moment. The RSM handed the flag to Sgt. Major Ridgeway and stated proudly, "Here Gunny, no one deserves the honour amongst us anymore than the other, and you are the one on home soil . . . !"

Taking the proffered flag, Gunny joined those other men of their Brigade who had been so honoured to carry the standards of their native countries, alongside the UN standard, for this final pass-out parade. The band played and the 300+ men of SABRE Brigade United Nations marched onto the square, minus some of their Officers who had no choice but to be in the reviewing stands. They marched proudly and came to attention before the dais where the Secretary General of the United Nations himself stood, and from the podium he began talking in his deep monotone voice.

"Men of SABRE Brigade, yours is the highest honour and duty to perform! To try and put the needs of the free world even before the need of your own countries. It will take great leadership and great men to perform this task, and you, the first of many, will have this task and duty to instil in those many who will follow you. The day may also come sooner than some may expect when the professional skills you all have in common with each other as highly trained soldiers will be put to the ultimate task and sacrifice. Be proud, for your countries surely are and so am I. May your Gods look kindly on you, thank you!"

After the brief ceremony of dedicating their flag and their allegiance to the United Nations, the band resumed playing. They marched off the square being led by the four Scottish Highland Pipers. The occasion was pompous and full of glory and for most soldiers who detested such patriotic showings of pomp and glamour, this was one of those rare moments they all seemed to enjoy getting dressed and being on parade for, drill bashing. It was a moment to revel in, as a presentation of Brigade Colours was not something that happened every day.

Coming off the square they fell out of formation, singing and chanting and holding and patting and slapping each other on the back. Getting out their cameras and posing for quick photo opportunities with new and old friends alike, a few bottles began to appear, soon they were all drinking and cheering over in their respective billets. A two week furlough was in order for any and all men of the Brigade now, with plane tickets to their respective homelands if desired.

Few of the officers of the Brigade were assigned any leave, as there were just too many logistical matters to attend to that needed an officer's approval.

Gunny asked the RSM if he would do him the honour of accompanying him home in time for Thanksgiving.

"I'd love to Gunny, but Mrs. Whittle would be a mite upset I'd hazard. Maybe when they get us set up 'ere with married quarters we can 'ave you over to dinner, how's that?"

"How about you then, Marcel?"

"Mon Ami, like most men of the Legion, I am unattached and would consider it a pleasure to have the honour of meeting with your family and visiting this country of yours!"

"I promise you some good old down home country cooking that's going to make your mouth water my friend!" shouted Gunny.

"Never mind the food, it is the women I need mon ami!"

"That won't be hard too come by, strutting in that uniform my peacock friend!"

As the celebrations continued in different parts of the camp, vehicles were also taking departing men on leave to bus depots, train stations and the airport. Only a small skeleton staff had volunteered to remain and thus await their turn for another date and time.

The returning men of the Brigade who had been away on leave had found with their return that their own positions had been evaluated at long last. With some promotions and transfers from all three original detachments, mixing the men at last and transferring them into the different Battalions and Companies, they now only needed to await the next influx and newest members of the Brigade.

While the men had been gone the continuation of the building of the camp under the command and direction of Maj. Biggle of the Army Engineers was coming under completion. The only task remaining really was for his own specialists to hand over the keys in the literary sense and show the men of the Brigade the inner functions of some key equipment. Before Maj. Biggle could leave himself though he had to report for some unknown reason personally with some of his selected staff to the General of the Brigade on his return himself from New York. So with the men returned and the camp back up and running, Biggle made what he thought would be his final visit to General Logan, fully expecting the General to shake his hand or something and to wish him a fond farewell for what he considered was a job well done.

When his presence was announced by the Orderly Corporal over at HQ, he came out of his office personally to greet the Maj., saying, "Welcome Major Biggle, please step into the office. Can I have the orderly fetch you a cup of coffee?"

With pleasantries aside then, the two men returned to the Phoenix's Lair, as the men now fondly liked to call his office!

"Major Biggle, I'll be direct and to the point. Major Galloway has kept me informed on the monumental task you and your men have performed here even if I was not able to meet with you personally to convey my thanks."

"No need Sir, just doing my duty is all," said the modest Major Biggle.

"Well frankly, some of us here feel that you went a little bit beyond the call of duty and find also that we, myself included, get along very well with you. So I'm asking you outright Major, would yourself and some of your key personnel care to join the logistical wing of this Brigade and keep it running for us?"

Quite shocked, the Maj. just sat there and repeated, "This is not what I expected at all, not at all Sir!"

Laughing now, Mac continued, "Look at it this way Major, someone has to replace Major Galloway from his duties sooner than later. I need him in an infantry role to take over one of the new Mechanized Infantry Battalions that will be formed all too soon, so what do you say?"

"Well to be quite frank Sir, if you have that much faith in my abilities, I'd be a fool to refuse such an offer. Besides, I always sorta wanted to taste the lifestyle of an elite fighting unit and it appears that this one is quite special indeed!"

"Special is an understatement Major, there is no other unit like this on the face of the earth, as you will soon find out."

"So how many of my men did you have in mind to join me then, Sir?"

"That I will leave strictly up to you Major, but just remember, they better be excellent choices because at some time or another, like yourself, they will have to undergo rigorous and what will seem like tortuous training to make the grade. So, are you in?"

"Thank you for this opportunity, yes I'm in Sir!" said a jubilant Maj. Biggle, rising from his chair to reach across the General's desk to shake his hand.

"Just check with clerks out in the office under the command of RSM Whittle to confirm your transfers and we'll get you placed and over to stores to draw your new uniforms and equipment that you'll need. Welcome aboard Major. I'll see you later in the mess!"

Maj. Biggle stood and saluted and then left the Phoenix's Lair and reported to the RSM to get the transfers of himself and selected men made official. He took his further instruction and direction from there.

There was a knock on the door to the General's office just as he was getting ready to call it a day and retire.

"Come in."

"Hello Sir," said Maj. Rance, "Sorry to bother you, but we just received a top priority signal from New York, felt that you should see it!"

"Hand it here, Chance," said Mac tiredly.

Looking at the message, he read the familiar code of General Clarke and it never ceased to make him smile. Papa Bear?—really! Reading the message further, he stirred in his seat. *General Blavic with that butcher of his, Aleksander 'The Gorilla' Marilla, had been shelling Sarejevo again and the international community is asking what we intend to do about it?!*

Mac seemed to be suddenly rejuvenated and came to life immediately.

"Good news I hope Sir?"

"Seems like things are beginning to move a little in this chess game of wait and see, Chance," adding, "This paging system still needs wiring in I'm afraid, so could you kindly step outside the office and have my Orderly Corporal paged or brought in here on the double, I have some work for him to do!"

Chance needed no further asking, he left instantly.

"Corporal Jones, would you please come with me to the General's office now please," was all Chance said before he turned and went back himself, assuming the Orderly Corporal would come as asked.

"Right away Sir."

"Corporal Jones, contact the guard for me and have Colonels' Price and Lafluer brought here ASAP. Better get the RSM too!"

"Yes Sir!"

"Chance, was there any other part to this signal?"

"No Sir."

Reaching for the phone, the General dialed and waited. Moments later the familiar tone of a ringing phone replied.

"Hello Mac," spoke General Clarke, "I guess you just received the signal from the UN?"

"Just awhile ago General, what's it all about?"

"Standard procedure, but I'd like you to come here to New York once again, and bring that English Sergeant, what's his name?"

"Steele Sir!"

"Yes that's it, bring him with you, I may need him to courier some material over to that English counterpart of mine once again."

"How soon Sir?"

"Now," was the last word he heard, after that was the click of the phone and the dial tone!

Having them in his office, Colonels Price and Lafluer, plus the RSM, Mac began to explain what he felt was going down.

"It seems gentlemen, that things in Bosnia are heating up and getting a little sticky. The Serbs have the Croats well contained up in the North and Southeast while only the new Bosnian Army in Sarejevo with the few remaining peacekeepers of SFOR being left with any real means to defend, that only being in a defensive/ passive role, too. The remnants of SFOR are sending out what patrols they can to gather as much intel as possible for us, but they are quite restricted, the Serbs have their own heavy patrols out. They fear Serbian forces may soon threaten and make a play for Sarejevo."

"Why, that would be madness!" understated Colonel Lafluer.

"Well Marc, it would be, but it may just be the place that we get sent into to defend and chase out the aggressor!"

Ben arrived just as the conversation had taken on a less "official" capacity and was ushered into the General's office to join them in time to hear the RSM say, "Bloody 'ell General, we're all behind you Sir!"

"Unfortunately RSM, the decision is not mine to make. I just get to decide on whatever action this Brigade is given!"

"All them men are willing to fight for you Sir, I think that is what the RSM is saying," added Ben.

"I know that Sergeant, damned if I don't know that, only I don't look forward to war as fervently as some of the men do I'm afraid. Writing those letters to those left behind is not a pleasant task, done it all too often," adding, "still, that's our business." "Anyhow, we Sergeant Steele, you and I, have been requested to return to New York. The General wants you to courier to General Crenshaw once more. Are you up for it or do you want me to send a replacement?"

"I'm up for it Sir," said Ben to their smiling knowing glances.

"It may just be a false alarm like a dummy run. I have no idea how long your turn-around will be Sergeant, but make the most of it. Now if you'll excuse me and just wait in the RSM's office, I have some business I have to take care of with these Colonels."

When the RSM and Sgt. Steele left the office, Mac looked at Colonels Price and Lafluer saying, "Pull up a seat, I'll outline as best I can to you the ready details we have briefly gone over before, regarding putting this Brigade on alert!"

Back in New York's UN Building, more specifically General Clarke's office, Maggie was nervous, pleased and excited to see Mac again. She came into his arms with a hug immediately, unfazed by who was watching.

"I missed you darling!" she whispered into his ear.

"And I missed you too Maggie," he replied as he buried his face into her hair.

"Um hum," coughed the General as he entered the outer reception area, "I always thought you two were a matched pair, took you both long enough to find out too. Now, if I can borrow him for awhile Maggie?"

"Oh you just go right ahead, we'll get together later," she promised.

As the two officers entered the General's inner sanctuary, Maggie turned to Ben and said, "Nice to see you again Sergeant, how's that English Lieutenant of yours doing?"

"Just fine Ma'am, who knows, maybe you'll get to see her one day."

"How's that?" enquired Maggie.

"Well, seems she has been assigned to her father's staff," he beamed, as if letting her into a great secret, and he was of sorts.

"Well now, that's a meeting I'm really looking forward to! Now, how did you like your coffee?"

Ben was given his last minute instructions and diplomatic pouch by General Clarke as he looked at him and said, "You know why I requested you don't you son?"

"Because I know the British General, Sir?"

"No you fool, because I'm a dang blasted softie! I know you have a thing going with his daughter, the old war-horse told me himself!"

"Now that's a surprise," he grinned.

"Enjoy the perk son while you can, but just remember for hell's sake, there's some serious implications involved with this sensitive material you're handling, so take good care of it, heh?"

"That's a given General!"

"I know it is son, just like to ensure I ask, and say hi to the General and his family for me, beginning to like that son-of-a-bitch!"

"Will do Sir . . . Oh, just one minor detail, Sir?" added Ben.

"What's that Sergeant?"

"Who's picking me up at the other end, MPs, or am I on my own?"

"Oh, I understand that one of the General's staff will be meeting you."

"Any idea who?"

"None at all."

"Must be the Sgt.Major," muttered Ben.

"Man, is he in for a surprise when he arrives in London. He doesn't know it, but the General's daughter herself is picking him up," laughed General Clarke.

"Why didn't you tell him?" chided Maggie.

"What, and spoil all their fun?" he laughed out boisterously.

Ben walked through the terminal at London's Heathrow. So busy looking for the Sgt.Major he was more than a little shocked when he saw Jane running and leaping into his arms. After hugging and kissing desperately, they just leaned back and observed one another.

"Surprised to see me?"

"That's an understatement Jane!"

"Any chance of taking you to lunch?"

"Sorry, Top Priority here."

"I sort of figured, but I had hoped, you know?"

"I know," he smiled, caringly adding, "besides though, if I grab a sandwich and a coffee here to go, I can have you all to myself on the drive to the Mews. We are going to the Mews aren't we?"

"Of course!" and leaning close to his ear whispered, "and just you wait to see what little number I bought for your pleasure later!"

Ben kissed her quickly but passionately, "Show me the way home Ma'am!"

Everyone at the Mews was excited to have Ben back home, for it *was* his home as much as theirs now, very much in the sense that they welcomed him and treated him as one of their own. Tom and Amy were excited as ever and kept holding his hand saying things like, "Come see this!" or, "Can I sit on your lap now Ben?"

After hugs from the ladies in Mrs. Crenshaw and aunt May, and even the Sgt. Major and the General, he really and truly felt like he had come back home.

Later in the General's study the General looked up at him, "Ben, unfortunately this material has to go back to New York almost immediately. I suspect that you have no better than an overnight stay here. Make the most of it and enjoy but don't upset them by saying anything unnecessary until you have to leave. That's an order!"

"I understand Sir. What about Jane?"

"Okay, I'll leave that call up to your own discretion."

Later after a marvellously wonderful British dinner of roast beef and Yorkshire pudding like only aunt May could make with her brilliant gravy that made you drool for more helpings, Ben and Jane went for an afternoon walk around the estate.

Walking around the assault course field in the back pasture now overgrown, Jane said, "Remember how you shouted so cruelly to me to make me understand the inner intricacies of P Company here so I could pass?" she laughed.

"How far was I off, heh?" he retorted.

He watched her play and dance around when she said, "You were unbelievably correct my darling!" still twirling and dancing. "You make me feel like a little girl every time I see you, one who wants you, right now, right here on this bloody grass!"

Later, as she lay there in his arms she laughed, "I always fantasized about doing it here, in this field with you," and leaned to kiss him once again.

"Anything to make you happy!" he said cheekily.

Poking him in the ribs she uttered, "Now how about showing *me* some stamina then soldier. What's that? No more bloody energy?"

She giggled like a schoolgirl pretending playfully to avoid him. He took her into his arms and made love to her once again under the English oaks. As he stroked her hair there was a slight breeze through the branches of some lone trees, almost knowing when to start simultaneously with this couple, whistling gracefully while they lay there! Eventually, they walked hand in hand back to the Mews.

"You seem awfully quiet there Ben, what is it?"

"This courier assignment I was given, only short term, probably means I'll be sent back first thing in the morning Jane."

"Oh my!" she gasped, then being brave she just clasped his hand and said, "Well, we had bloody well better enjoy ourselves thoroughly tonight then, heh?"

Stopping, he sensed and knew immediately she was just putting on her brave act. He turned her grimacing and tearful face in toward him as she was biting her lower lip, to hold her close and say, "Jane, I love you, you know that don't you?"

"Yes, but I'm just getting a little bit lonely here waiting for you and not knowing, you know?"

Awkwardly he said, "I think I understand, look if I am making you feel guilty of having some fun, understand I don't want to be holding up your life . . . ?"

Looking at him angrily now she exploded before he could finish. "You fool, you just don't get it do you? It's YOU I'm lonely for, it's only you I want. I'm allowed to miss you aren't I?"

"Yes, I suppose you are Jane," he said rather foolishly.

"Good, then don't you ever try to say anything so stupid like that to me ever again, do you understand?"

Yes," he said feeling foolish and stupid. He wasn't given time to feel too bad about it though for Jane had already moved on. She came into his arms with longing and desire. Holding each other in a lingering warm embrace, they kissed in passion and fear of the moment, of lost time they would miss out on. It seemed Jane had no further idea of the impending magnitude of this mission, and he was grateful for that, or else she was as clever at hiding her fears as he seemed to be. Holding hands once more, they walked further, enjoying this little part of an English countryside together.

She came to him later that night in her silk negligee, making his blood catch fire and boil with anticipation of the desire and secrets her body held in store for him. It was a night of love like they had never had. Urgent, seductive, wild, passionate! Once again, the scent of her perfumed body and hair intoxicated and urged him on as it brought his steamy desires to levels he had only before imagined. Only these feelings and emotions were now real experiences. Ones that may have to last him for awhile yet. He tried to commit her body to memory and then forgot it as he lost himself in desires of the love she had to offer, in her glorious surrender to him . . .

The farewell at the Mews was sudden for them all and their tears were genuine and concerned. Jane was, for the very first time, worried and quite concerned for his welfare. There was also a fear and urgency to her caress, shown on her face and in her tearful shaking body. She could not bring herself to drive him to the airport this time and so the Sgt. Major had the duty.

After the quiet and intolerably long drive the Sgt. Major dropped him off saying simply, "Come on home to us Ben, I think we all need you now!"

"I will soon Sgt. Major, very soon now, don't you worry," and with that, disappeared into the airport's maze of passengers.

Arriving back in La Guardia Ben was met by a Marine escort this time and taken directly to General Clarke, at his familiar UN HQ. General Logan was not there though and neither was Maggie. Alone, General Clarke invited him into his inner office. He sat awhile, reading the news contained in the diplomatic pouch.

Looking up and not giving a thing away the General asked, "Tell me Sergeant, soldier to soldier, how good is that Brigade of yours?"

"Well Sir," coughed Ben, "It is probably as fine a unit as you will get anywhere!"

"Are they capable of going into combat at a moment's notice though?"

"Well sir, over 75% of the Brigade have had combat experience of one kind or another, at one time or another, so I would have to answer with an emphatic yes!"

"From what I understand, you're one of those 22 SAS specialists, cloak and dagger types?"

"Was Sir, now I'm a member of this Brigade, and proud to be Sir!"

"For a British Soldier, I understand you're highly decorated. For a country that hates to hand out medals to its enlisted men that must be quite a feat, how did you manage it?" he grinned.

Ben answered nonchalantly, "Wrong place at the right time?"

"Ha ha ha, I guess I had that one coming!"

The General then changed the subject, "Where have you seen action then son?"

"Well sir, I've patrolled the streets of Belfast and Londonderry and countryside of CrossMaglen as a Para and seen action out in the Gulf War and Bosnia, plus 'detached duties' and a whole lot of little other places and assignments in-between, if you know what I mean?"

"I know exactly what you mean son, so how come a hard ass soldier like yourself ended up in this outfit anyway?"

"That Sir is one long story!"

With eyes gleaming the General urged, "Well son, Maggie and Mac aren't here yet, so why don't you put on a pot of coffee for us and you can tell me all about it?"

"It's long and it'll probably bore you to death Sir . . . ?" he said looking for a way out.

"Nonsense," said the General relishing the story and rubbing his hands, "besides, I understand that beautiful daughter of General Crenshaw has a role to play in all this?"

Looking cagily at the crusty old General, Ben said, "Somehow, I bet you probably know more about my past life than you're letting on here Sir?"

Laughing now and settling into his chair the General replied, "Just you let me be the judge of that, now come on soldier, pull up a sandbag and start talking!"

When he had finished the General looked at him and slowly said, "That's the damn blasted most romantic story I ever did hear. Tell me son, are you going to get out of this man's army soon or stay on and break her heart?"

"This is what I do best Sir, this is what I like doing, I'm also very good at it!"

"That may be so son, but few women have the heart or the stomach for that matter, of enduring long stretches of waiting for their men to come home. I think yours has also suffered enough."

Looking on at the General incredulously, Ben proffered, "Are you telling me that I should now get out of the army Sir?"

"No, what I'm saying is that you should give it some thought son. You've paid your dues and given enough blood for your country, let someone else take over. Pretty soon you'll have to, unless you take a commission and you just don't strike me as the Officer type, no offence intended. I mean, I just can't see a career soldier like yourself making that switch, unless you do it soon."

Sitting back and taking in what the General was saying, Ben acknowledged how difficult his affair with Jane must really be. Then just out of the blue he blurted, "Tell me Sir, if I wanted to make that switch, to an Officer, do you think I could?"

"To an Officer?"

"Yessir!"

"Sergeant Steele, I believe you're one of those rare individuals in life one meets who can do anything they put their minds to!"

"Well, thanks for the kind words and advice Sir and the vote of confidence."

"No, thank you for sharing your very personal and private story with me Sergeant, it's good enough for a Harlequin romance if you ask me."

Laughing, Sgt. Steele said, "I never thought of it like that Sir."

"Listen Sergeant, if you need help in taking that next step or whatever, I'll be more than happy to provide or add to a reference, hate to keep two good people apart like that!"

"Thank you Sir, I'll keep it in mind."

Rising from his large oak desk, the General fidgeted uncomfortably with these pleasantries and quickly reverted back to his familiar role. "Mac and Maggie should be arriving shortly with some very important guests. I hate to make a second request of you Sergeant, but could you put a second pot of coffee on, only make it a full pot this time?"

"Not a problem Sir, mind you, I can't guarantee it'll be as good as Maggie's!"

"Talking of Maggie, I understand it was yourself who sort of embarrassed our General into asking her out."

"Just set the General onto what he already knew Sir."

"Yes, well if he runs off and marries her and takes her away before I'm ready, I'll be looking for your hide to skin!"

"Somehow General, I gather that you're happier than they are about it," Ben knew instinctively.

Just as the General was pointing a finger in jest at Ben, General Logan and his guests walked into the office with Maggie, not sure what they had stumbled in on.

"Did we come at a wrong time Sir?" asked an inquisitive Mac.

"Naw, just educating Sergeant Steele here on the acts of war!"

As everyone stood around with puzzled looks, not quite sure how to handle the General, the General himself winked at Ben and walked back into his office shouting, "Maggie, coffee when it's ready please!"

The meeting, or better described as a debate, was held in the General's sanctuary and lasted a good two to three hours. They were working on their third pot of coffee when Mac appeared and said to both Maggie and Ben, "It's winding down now, we'll be out of here within the hour!"

As the large door opened they shuffled out clutching briefcases and attache folders and immediately went to the rack looking for their coats and hats to their array of uniforms. The assembled guests were from the four branches of the American armed forces: Navy, Army, Air Force, Marines. Two were even British and French Air Force attaches from their respective embassies. As they were led out it seemed that a sigh of relief was heard from General Logan.

"Sergeant, you and I have a lot of travelling to do again, this time back to our camp to prepare for battle readiness . . . "

PART 5

The encampment of Sabre Brigade out there in the hills of Helena, Montana was still without a name. It seemed that the more popular desire being touted by the men was to call it Camp Fredericks which unofficially they were already doing. Mac had to admit he sort of liked the respect that his men held for the commander of The First Special Service Force and Devil's Brigade leader, Colonel Fredericks of World War II.

"We had a lot in common with each other Colonel," mused Mac out loud.

"What's that you say Sir?" asked Ben from the rear of the jeep.

"Just thinking aloud Sergeant," as their jeep was waved on through the main gate and guard room into the camp. The driver first dropped the General off outside the Officers' mess and then continued on to do the same for Sgt. Steele outside the Sergeants' mess and barracks. Thanking the driver, Ben gave him permission to return his jeep to the motor pool and call it a night. Entering the mess, he dropped his bags into his room and made his way back down into the Sergeant's mess bar.

He was greeted by the RSM and some of the other senior NCOs. The RSM said, "Steve, scrounge up a meal, and quickly for the Sgt. here, and bring him a pint too, on me!"

"Will do Sir," the mess barman shouted back.

Ben was led to a table being occupied by the RSM and a few of the others.

"Okay Ben, let's have it, you weren't taken on a joy ride to New York for nothing. What's the scoop, what's going down?"

"Well Tom, I really don't know the whole story, but what I do know is that we have to shortly go into battle readiness, and my gut instincts tell me we're really going into Bosnia this time!"

"Hot damn!" said Gunny as excited as a schoolboy.

"Yes!!" said another, pumping his fist by his side.

As the RSM looked into the tanned face and deep brown eyes of Ben, he just grinned and said, "Going into Bosnia, heh?"

Grinning back, Ben said simply, " 'Fraid so!"

"Interesting," said the RSM, then in afterthought added, "well at least Mrs. Whittle will be happy!"

"How's that?" said Marcel.

"Leave, me boy, they always give you leave before a pending engagement if they can!"

There is this myth about soldiers that they hate war. Well they may hate it while they're in the thick of it, or forever afterwards, but the truth of the matter was that this is what they trained and lived for, the heat of the battle! The warrior spirit and code and the chance to test their skills against the enemy or foe. Very few failed to meet the grade when it came!

"Well," said the RSM once more, "I guess we may as well sit back then and wait for the General's briefing that we're bound to be getting shortly," then added in spontaneity, "barman, put a barrel on, on my tab!"

Cheers went up and men rushed to the bar for their free pints of ale. The RSM looked at Ben, "Are you sure Ben? Bosnia?"

"Pretty sure."

After returning to the Officers' Mess, Mac stopped long enough to let the Mess Officer know he wanted a six a.m. wake-up call, then retired to his quarters to fall onto his bed exhausted. When the knock on his door came in what seemed like just a short while, the orderly entered in his usual fashion. He realized the General had fallen asleep fully clothed. Thanking his orderly for the coffee and directing him to place it on the table, when he left the room Mac stripped down and took a quick shower and shave and redressed before returning to his now lukewarm coffee.

During breakfast in the new palatial Officers' Mess dining room, Mac sought out Colonels Price and Lafluer. He indicated to them that he wanted to see them immediately after breakfast and morning parade were over. They seemed worried and agitated that the General just sat there opposite them quietly thinking.

In his office he was asked, "Is there anything specific you wanted to tell us about your trip to UN HQ?"

"Yes guys, there is. I don't know any other way to tell you this, but it seems in all likelihood we're heading into war!"

Half rising from their seats, then sitting back down, Mac decided to leave them with their quiet thoughts for a moment.

"Thank you for letting us be seated for this news," grinned Marc.

"Yes, it comes as a bit of a shocker, even when you sort of expect and prepare for it heh?"

"I'll say old chap," uttered David. "Tell me, when was this decision made?"

"Just last evening!"

"How many of the Brigade have been informed Mac. Is Sergeant Steele aware?"

"No! That much is sure, why?"

"Just that there's already a rumour running through the ranks like wildfire and I guessed he was the logical source."

"Just open speculation and intuition of the enlisted men David."

"So what's first on a 'need to know' basis?"

"Well, how about the fact some Canadians are now joining us in the Brigade very soon. Their numbers will not be as large as our own but the initial bunch will equal what we have here already. They're on their way as I speak, so make arrangements."

"Canadians heh?" David mused, "That's really good news Mac, they have some outstanding leadership and are right up there as having one of the toughest and best officer training programs you'll find anywhere. These Canucks can more than hold their own against anybody! I have also been over the numbers and I know we'll be short of Platoon Commanders so this is good news. Their training is as tough and excellent as the rest of us get, up there in Gagetown Sir, they'll fit in well."

"I agree, well, let's make them welcome and settled in smoothly."

"So, Canucks aside Mac, the big question is, when do we go in? We are nearly ready and up to strength. Progress and training has continued incessantly with improvements and additions in equipment and staff arriving constantly."

Time had slipped quietly by "week after week" so much so that nobody really noticed it at first, but the manpower had gradually built its strength and complement up to nearly the maximum required. The Sabre Brigade was now close to being officially up to par and their only need and purpose now was to continue their drills and training the remaining new influx while awaiting their call to arms.

"Do they plan on going in right now?" asked Marc.

"Not likely, if they try to do it right now they'll have to go back to a standard UN or NATO format, can't wait for us," spoke David.

"Not likely David, we speed up this show no matter what!"

"So what's the 'sit rep' out there then?"

Without hesitating Mac replied, "The Bosnian Serbs with more reinforcement of Serbian Serbs, in what can *only* be described as a total reversal of yesteryear. I just can't believe we're all actually back to square one. Fact is I know we are. Well anyway, I can only presume they'll make their move pretty damned soon then. Those combined Serb forces have forced not just the Croats but the Muslims as well out of the Krajina region creating mass refugees by the thousands. They are all strangled and boxed, held hostage and surrounded in little enclaves once again. There's a new twist this time though, Intel tells us they have this 'BZ' chemical agent they used in Srebrenica they must have stockpiled and hid and we're afraid they just might use it here soon. That threat alone can only mean we have to move soon to not only stop them using it in the spread of Serbian ethnic cleansing, but to also save the city of Sarajevo from their clutches."

"They're finally making a move on Sarajevo itself?"

"Not yet, but we believe it's coming soon!"

"That's it then," David matter of factly said, "when do we mobilize the Brigade?"

"Just as soon as I've held a briefing for all the officers, then one for the men."

"Do you think it's wise to tell the men just yet?"

"They will have to know, but maybe you're right. We'll give them all as much leave as we possibly can, but putting them all on notice of standby and alert for any ready re-call. Then we'll tell them. When they're all back at camp all further leaves or movements will be cancelled, then we go into accelerated training mode."

"Makes sense to me Mac, always decent to give the men a chance to see their loved ones especially when you're sending them into battle and you anticipate that some may not be returning."

"Exactly!"

"Just one thing," said Mac, before they left his Office.

"What's that Mac?"

"Remind your men to write their final letters and leave them behind, just in case."

"Yes, of course," they said sombrely.

After the morning parade and the arrival of the Canadians who received the usual good raucous welcome, Mac informed the only non-officer in his little group, the RSM, of the impending meeting he was to give that morning, requesting of him that his presence on the door be the only visible security, to keep curiosity to a minimum and to keep prying ears away. So later, with the RSM standing at the entranceway and greeting the officers as they filed into the Operations Briefing Hall, as the last officer entered, the RSM closed the two doors behind himself, as the General himself winked. The RSM seated himself, positioned as close to the doors as possible of course.

The excitement, anticipation and anxiousness for the General's speech was obvious. Most of the officers assembled there had themselves been privy to and heard the rumours sweeping through the camp before setting foot in this room. It was a little smoky and jam-packed with every available officer of the Brigade in camp there that morning. In showing no sense of drama, even though the tension and excitement in the room was electrifying and so visibly thick you could cut it with a knife, Mac, being the last to enter, strode to the front of the room and seated himself at the table between Colonel Price and Colonel Lafluer. General Logan walked to the podium.

"Gentlemen, your final coughs and clearing of the throats please."

When only the silence remained he began in on his soon-to-be-famous speech by saying simply, "Gentlemen, good morning to you all. First, let us welcome our Canadian cousins aboard."

After the cheers and welcome died down, he went straight to the quick.

"The place and location is Bosnia." He waited for that buzz to die down before adding, "Now let me explain . . .

"Let me give you a brief history lesson. For those of you with history degrees in political science please bear with me. I know most of you all know and have been watching with great interest these past years, if you haven't already been serving there, news about a place there on the map now called Bosnia and Herzegovinia. Few people in the world even knew it existed, let alone where it was on a map, just a few years ago.

"Let me start here. The civil war in Bosnia itself began in April of 1992 with an aggressive JNA paramilitary campaign into Croatia with active assistance from a vastly superior equipped force from the Serbian part of Yugoslavia, when Bosnia declared independence. The Serbs were fearful of Belgrade and distrustful of the Muslim leaders in Sarejevo. Outraged passions made them try to secede and set up their own Serbian Bosnia. When they began the horror and atrocities of ethnic cleansing and this systematic genocide attributed to them, it immediately labelled the Serbs as the villains of the peace as they went about trying to consolidate positions and territory everywhere else.

"Then 'as and when' the JNA eventually 'officially' withdrew, very large stockpiles of weapons and all sorts of military equipment were strategically left behind. More importantly, the Bosnian and JNA Serb soldiers were also able to remain behind as well, subversively, to continue to fight for the Serbian cause in Bosnia. Mostly in select regional paramilitary groups with romantic colourful names like the Wolves, Chetniks and Policija to name a few. We know now too that most of the entire East Bosnia region came under eventual Serb control as thousands of the non-Serbs fled their regions or were put in the detention camps if they weren't brutalized, raped or killed.

"In one response, in July 1992, NATO established a joint naval operation to patrol the Adriatic, enforcing one of the first UN economic sanctions. Later that year, the UN established a 'no fly' zone in air space over Bosnia. In 1993 NATO also agreed to enforce it. In early 1993, the US led an air-drop of food aid to the surrounded enclave of Srebrenica. The French Commander of UNPROFOR at the time, forced his way in. Not a single Serb shell fell while he was there, he tried to allay the peoples' worst fears by saying to them bravely, 'You are now under the protection of the UN Forces, I will never abandon you!' That's one helluva soldier in my book.

"As the Serbs renewed attacks, the UN Security Council passed Resolution 819 declaring Srebrenica a safe area. The first contingent of UNPROFOR peacekeepers that went into Srebrenica were Canadian. I can tell you all here proudly by the way, that some in that contingent of Canadians are also here today, just joining this Brigade. Bring them 'up to speed' and make them welcome, they are now one of you!"

"To continue. In June 1993 NATO announced it would give close air support to all peacekeepers to enforce their intentions and to back them up. The world knows the Peacekeeping Mission went through hell and destruction and the mass genocides committed by the Serbs (though not just a Serb tool, as it was used very effectively by the Croatians in the Kryjina too, and Muslims elsewhere) were blamed on a US led arms embargo, which in turn was backed by Member States of the United Nations Security Council. In August that year NATO threatened to start those air strikes in the event any more UN safe areas came under attack. This included Sarejevo which was under siege at the time and was designed to break that strangulation hold the Serbs had on them.

"Renewed Serb attacks on all the safe areas made NATO establish their own 'heavy-weapons-free' zones around the areas of not just Sarejevo, but also places like Goradze. At this time the Dutch UNPROFOR Battalion, Dutchbat, a small light force of about 450, were not equipped with adequate arms and because of this lack of fire power were severely hampered in their efforts to be effective. The NATO planes therefore finally kept their word, after I don't know how many threats to do so, but eventually engaged in close air support of them and air strikes on several requests, via the UN. The arrangement that NATO and UN Commanders had to 'mutually agree' before any air attacks could go in, created an obvious limited effectiveness, a situation forever more to be known as the infamous 'Dual Key.'

"The European nations, who so far in this ugly mess had the only combat troops on the ground, were angry once again with the Americans trying to dictate policy, but with no troops of their own present on the ground. That initial window of opportunity to dissolve and combat the Bosnian Serb aggression backed by Serbia itself had long disappeared and the allies were thus back to square one all over again. A depressing stalemate. On top it all, the monumental task left to them of identifying borders was near impossible but the United Nation peacekeepers did an unbelievable task of identifying them, using the global positioning systems, GPS, a relatively new and invaluable tool. Other than this though, and the food convoys they managed, UN power and control was forever constantly being challenged, undermined, and tested many times over. Any person in this room who has served there can attest to that fact.

"Those UN troops who were still on the ground during all this were shackled and hampered by a form of weak leadership with no clear policy, thus indecision and confusion reigned. Something I am sad to admit has made us ineffective at times. We were unable to use our own weapons to back up our own policies and positions which those Serbs and on occasion even Croat or Muslim, knew all too well, so the gun battles, conflicts and atrocities continued. In all, it reduced the UNPROFOR troops of the UN to unintentional bystanders of the slaughter whether they liked it or not! Then as those final UN-brokered safe areas fell, like Goradze and Zepa, right after the Multi-National US led bombing flights, it led to the Dutch, Canadian and the other peace-keeping nationals being taken hostage. Chained to strategic targets for propaganda use for all the world to see on their TVs—it seemingly appeared only done to test the patience and resolve of the UNPROFOR Command for what seemed like the millionth time.

"About that time the United States Senate voted overwhelmingly against US policy as being just compromises of war. In mid 1994, at the request of the UN, NATO began its own contingency plan which called for the complete withdrawal of all UNPROFOR troops, known as OPLAN 40104.

"In July of 1995, as the Vojska Republik Srpske (BSA), which is the Army of the Serb Republik, although not recognized by the international community, then started an offensive to effectively eliminate the three Bosnian enclaves of Srebrenica, Zepa and Goradze. In doing this offensive, soon over a dozen UNPROFOR checkpoints were systematically overrun while even more of the Dutchbat troops, along with some Canadians, were taken prisoner. This act sent the US, its Allies, and even the Russians, to conference in London to simplify procedures for all future air strikes in order to prevent more Dual Keys—which afforded a definite lack of protection for the ground troops, as Air Command failed to act quickly to protect them, contrary to orders of engagement.

"In Aug. 1995 the Serbs attacked the safe area of Sarejevo itself, rejecting UN and NATO conditions for heavy-weapons withdrawals. This brought down NATO's largest air and artillery campaign of the entire civil war. For the first time the Serbs actually considered the possibility of defeat which made them talk about peace seriously.

"On Oct. 5, 1995 a cease-fire agreement was initialled in Dayton and on Dec. 14, 1995, the Bosnia and Herzegovinia Peace Agreement was then signed in Paris, to evermore be known as the

Dayton-Paris Peace Agreement. This led to the withdrawal of the UNPROFOR, and after four years, the civil war in Bosnia was over!

"On Dec. 16, 1995 the Americans entered the former war zone for the first time. NAC sent in a NATO-led multinational Implementation Force (IFOR). It was the largest military operation ever undertaken by NATO under the approval of the United Nations Security Council Resolution 1031. Their mission? To institute all military aspects of Annex 1A of the Peace Agreement. They were tasked to separate two of the warring Entities (Serb and Croat) transfer areas and territory, move their troops and heavy weapons into approved sites, patrol the 1400 KM 'Inter-Entity' Boundary Line. A monumental task, especially as all knew, it commenced in the middle of a Balkan winter, not an easy way to start.

"NATO initially devised a plan to divide Bosnia into three main sectors with each one being controlled by the Major Allies. The British had the Northwest of Bosnia, their HQ being in Gornji Vakuf. They also had help from the Canadians, Belgians and Dutch to patrol this area. The French had Southern Bosnia with their HQ being Sarejevo itself. The US with help from Russia, had Northeastern Bosnia, and their HQ was in Tuzla. They were also responsible for what was known as the Posavina Corridor, a very narrow strip of land up on the border previously under Serb control, which they did not want to relinquish and Bosnia wanted to keep control of. It was an area that gave whoever held it direct access to the Sava River which was a crucial asset they both wanted control over.

"NATO were also to assist the International Criminal Tribunal for the former Yugoslavia (ICTY). Also, an International Police Task Force (UNIPTF) was implemented to monitor Law Enforcement activities to advise and to train. Over the next year the transitional parties put into place a program designed to bring Bosnia and Herzegovinia back into a peaceful stable environment. Conferences were held and policies were made. After a peaceful election the next phase of the peace process was put into place as the

United Nations Security Council under Resolution 1088 sent in a reduced military presence of approx. 32,000 troops. This was done as the IFOR mandate expired and the multinational Stabilisation Force (SFOR) began.

"In Operation Joint Endeavour, IFOR was tasked to implement the peace. SFOR, in Operation Joint Guard, was tasked to stabilize the peace. SFOR were also tasked to implement the military aspects of the Peace Agreement as legal successors to IFOR as dictated under Chapter VII of the UN Charter on Peace Enforcement.

"As Operation Joint Guard ended, Operation Joint Force began in 1998. It was in place until Kosovo came up. Most of you fortunately have seen peacekeeping service in Bosnia either under the UN or NATO. You are all aware that SFOR had a unified NATO-led Command in place under political direction of the UN and NAC under Annex 1A.

"The overall military authority for Bosnia is still in the hands of NATO's Supreme Allied Commander Europe (SACEUR). Contributing non-NATO forces are represented by liaison Officers at SHAPE. This is all done politically through the NAC+N combination. The participation of Russia is still being evaluated, as their own interests are biased toward Serbia. You all should know that AFSOUTH (Kosovo) put into place in the following succession: Operation Eagle Eye, Operation Determined Guarantor and Operation Determined Force. We sent in over 40,000 troops of the NATO Rapid-Reaction Force backed by over 20,000 from Bosnia. That was our mistake gentlemen. We are now mired and bogged down in the Kosovo civil war. This leaves less than 10,000 total troops in Bosnia now, spread out in a defensive role from Sarejevo and other isolated enclaves all over Bosnia right now. So we are at war, or will be shortly, with the Serbs in Bosnia."

He paused to let the rustle and murmurs die down to a quiet hush.

"The main cities, towns, and enclaves are all back in Serb control. That should anger you, as it surely does me! I don't like my hard efforts with my comrades all these years being rolled back.

Anyway, the Serbs moved swiftly to consolidate, having amassed huge numbers in key strategic former strongholds. Refugees in the hundreds of thousands are once again spilling all over hell's half acre. You should also know that we have been allowed to pass along this following, but very sensitive Intel. Being mostly from elite units here, you may all have firsthand or better knowledge of what I am about to say than I do myself."

As the laughs died down he continued.

"We now know that the Bosnian Army, being mostly Muslims, have now brought in their own military observers from Iran, in areas like Fojnica. We have therefore had our hand forced and sent in our own respective covert operatives to monitor and evaluate that situation for us. Their reports have come back showing us they are not a threat 'for now' and neither in our path, but the importance of this delicate and touchy information lies in the fact they could be an extra element we just don't need right now. So we do need to watch out for and avoid any contact with them if we can. We really cannot afford their interference at any cost when we go in, for all the obvious reasons.

"Lastly, you all know the stories of the 'BZ' chemical agents by now. These stockpiles are supposed to be controlled by Aleksander 'The Gorilla' Marilla, the monster from the Krajina region. He has conducted attacks on many of the enclaves from the early days, including in the past, Srebrenica. He has never been detained, caught, or punished for his war crimes and he is here now and is a major player.

"We're in a race against time, gentlemen. We need to act swiftly and deadly. It is simply the only way. The fact that Sarajevo was the historic place of 'The Shot That Was Heard Around The World' had some bearing on the fears of repeating history, and thus starting of another major war. Well it's too late to worry about that as it is here upon us. Unfortunately, without strong leadership to move it in another direction, events like this dictate themselves and sooner than later, have a nasty habit of coming full circle to bite you on your ass! The politicians came to realize this all too late once again. Wars are better fought and decided by Generals, NOT politicians!"

His final comments brought a subdued hush. He had spoken on for some length and he knew they were restless. Taking a breather and letting this all sink in, he then continued, "So gentlemen, my senior officers and I will be evaluating the situation and the task that is set before us. Let us all step back and take a look to evaluate the bigger picture. What do we learn from it? As to what has happened in the past up to now, and what do we learn as to what is going to happen to us in the immediate future?"

Then, true to the RSM's predictions, it came.

"We have to plan, gentlemen, and be ever vigilant and prepared. If any of you, anyone at all, has any bright ideas, please pass them on. Our potential enemy has been dug in on that mountain that overlooks Sarajevo, Mt. Igman, for some months now, as he also was once before, nearly seven years ago. The big difference is, he's been there before and he must now know what it is going to take to keep it. If anyone here thinks that there won't be some brutal and ugly hand-to-hand combat ahead for us all, then they had better take another long hard look! This is not a walk in the park, we will be outnumbered by four to one odds at the very least, against a bitter, determined, battle-hardened enemy. Let's not underestimate our foe and let's not forget this past history. Let's go in prepared!

"Gentlemen, as of right now, you can issue as much emergency leave to your married men and any others you can spare, with the standard and necessary request of knowing their movements. They may need to be recalled within twenty-four hours notice, but as for the remainder of the Brigade, you're all put on forty-eight hour standby effective immediately. Before there is any leave handed out, have your key men issued with any required and ready equipment and have them ready for full battle order. I want *all* your Battalions kitted out for war! For now, that is all, thank you!"

General Logan's Brigade officer compliment had been given some pretty heavy stuff to digest and they all walked silently out now, most deep in their own thoughts . . .

On the other side of the camp in the Sgt.'s mess, Ben was talking to an operator on the phone in the lobby saying, "Yes that's right, Basingstoke England," as his peers laughed at him in passing, due to his duty of having to remain behind with the skeleton crew. The RSM stopped long enough to say with his big smile, "Look you 'ol wanker, want me to pop round and give her your best?"

"Thanks, but you just concentrate your energies on Mrs. Whittle and the kids, you've been away awhile there Tom!"

"She'll probably have my guts for garters for not writing enough, still it'll be nice to see the 'ol girl again. Very well, take care then you plonker!" laughed the RSM as he slung his kit bag and headed out the door.

"Yes operator, that number again is, Basingstoke 2 4. . . . " he was past exasperated, but at last he finally got through.

"7 the Mews, can I 'elp you?" came back a familiar female voice.

"Hello aunt May," he laughed, "How's everything back there in good 'ol Blighty?"

"Just smashing dearie! Where are you calling from?"

"From the base aunt May, I wasn't one of the lucky ones. I get to hold the fort here on the rear guard!"

"Oh my," and after a pause aunt May added, "There's lots of people here who love you still and will want to talk to you or have a few words, tell you what, I'll get Jane for you first before the others know, is that alright?"

"Thanks aunt May!" he chuckled.

"Hello?" a sweet and loving voice asked.

"Hello Jane, it's me!"

"Oh my gosh," she exclaimed, then quickly, "Where are you?"

"As I told aunt May, I'm stuck back here holding the fort!"

"They're just equalling it all out, getting you back for all those earlier trips that you made here, gosh but I miss you and love you!"

"I love you too Jane!"

"Ben, does this mean what I think it means?" she asked anxiously.

"Naw," he lied, "Probably just another drill!"

"You're lying to me aren't you, just trying to make me feel better?"

"Yep!"

After a long pause and what he thought were sobs and sniffles he said nervously, "Jane are you still there, Jane?"

"I'm still here darling, tell me again you miss and love me!"

"I miss and love you Jane, are you okay?"

"Just lonely for you in more ways than one," she said sexily.

"If you'll settle for dirty talk, that's the best I can do for you. And me, considering the circumstances," he laughed.

After talking privately for a further twenty minutes or so, Jane said, "I hate to give you up, but there are others here who would like a word with you, is that okay?"

"Perfectly," he lied.

After talking with all the children and the other women of the house, and including the crusty old Sgt. Major, the General finally came onto the phone.

"Hello there Ben!"

"Hello Sir, how are you?"

"Fine, just fine. Actually, I'm a little concerned about you. I'm in the know of course. Want me to let Jane in on the secret or not let her worry?"

"She'd probably guess or find a way to find out, especially now she's on your intelligence staff. Better tell her Sir, if you don't mind?"

"Not at all. I'll just find a quiet moment later to make her cry, if you know what I mean?"

"I do Sir. And general?"

"Yes?"

"Thank you Sir, from the bottom of my heart!"

After talking with the General for a little while longer, the General closed by saying, "Do be careful there Ben, that's an order!"

"Thank you Sir, I will!"

After a few more words with Jane Ben said his loving farewell and lingered and just sat for a short while with only the low drone of a dial tone.

Things started to happen fast now for the Brigade. Major Stacey was given a standing order by General Logan to consult with the RSM who had just recently returned from leave. They were to arrange and select four roving scout and reconnaissance patrols from the Brigade's Mountain and Special Warfare Company. When assembled, after a quick debriefing, the recce teams were to be dispatched with all due haste to their primary objective, Mt.Igman. They would be tasked to conduct covert recce patrols of the area on foot, to determine the current strengths and disposition of the Serb fortifications.

Cpt. Peltier, one of the experienced ex-Foreign Legion commanders, was given the task of Team Commander to lead these troops. Brassard and Steele together had been assigned to this advanced scouting and Pathfinder Company based on their past experience. A few days later, with Capt. Peltier, they were all in the General's office looking at a scale model of their objective. Col.s Price and Lafluer had also laid out tacmaps of Mount Igman and the aerial photographs taken by American Stealth bomber fly-overs. As well, they had computerized enhancements of satellite closeups. Looking at all the intel studiously, Ben couldn't help but notice a similarity between this location and that of Grouse Mountain that overlooked his native Vancouver, at least it seemed so to him.

It also seemed fitting to him that this strategic location, which the Serbs had used to dominate Bosnia from once before, having looked down on Sarajevo for those past long years like a haunting ghost, should now be their objective target and first priority in confronting Serb aggression now. While the Brigade sharpened and rattled their sabres for the confrontation they now knew would take place on this captured mountaintop, he suddenly felt relaxed for some reason.

It was a case of no longer having the uncertainty being there anymore, he reasoned, *for once you knew the objective, you always found it easier to come to grips with it.* He placed the feeling of "deja vu" to probably being that the terrain of sub-alpine meadows and stands of pine that formed the timberline would seem like stepping out onto familiar territory for him once again. Not that he wasn't familiar to all types of terrain in his previous training with the British Paras and 22 SAS he concluded!

From the accumulated intel they knew now that the Serb garrison was of some 120,000+ hardcore JNA and Bosnian Serbs all scattered on and around the mountaintop commanded by a hard core general by the name of Drago Blavic and his own protege and 2IC, Aleksander 'The Gorilla' Marilla. It being said of the latter that he had previously participated and was a major factor in the ethnic cleansing, hence his menacing nickname. Both men now held a deep hatred and contempt for the position and background of the previous SFOR NATO-led Alliance, also all Westerners in general. Their feelings were that they were all passifistic cowards afraid to engage in serious combat or pay the true price of victory, and in this belief they played them like fiddles!

They had long ago concluded that they were relatively safe from air attack if they didn't fire too many shells into the surrounded and besieged cities, especially Sarajevo, on a regular basis. Even if it was only being protected by the newly formed Bosnian Army and not nearly enough peacekeepers. General Blavic and the Gorilla had an impressive arsenal of firepower in ex-Yugoslavian weapons and Serbian Russian armaments. Mt. Igman was indeed a veritable bunkered tank fortress once again and there was no denying the stranglehold they now held in the area!

Hawked eyes narrowed and intent studiously pored over the scale model layout of the area, then gazed back to the tacmap. Ben said, "I don't know if anyone else has spotted or mentioned this to you yet Sir, but that other mountain that overlooks Sarejevo there, that Mt. Bjelasnica, it could pose an additional problem for the Brigade."

Everyone either turned or looked up immediately looking at Ben as Col.s Lafluer and Price seemed to say simultaneously in words to the same effect, "Go ahead there Sergeant, tell us what's on your mind."

"Well Sir, most of our air transport can land and secure the airports through TALO, that's not a problem as they're excellent for logistical depots and staging points for the assault on Mt. Igman as you've stated and shown, but what bothers me is that other mountain next to Mt. Igman there."

"How so?" Gen. Logan asked, sharing the same sentiments of all gathered there.

"Well Sir, just look and compare against their previous staging points. It's not Pale to the east that bothers me, it's that place Trnovo to the south. It's my contention at least, that we have to take this Mt. Bjelasnica as well as Mt. Igman if we're going to be able to stop them remounting any type of counter-offensive."

"Show me!" the General bellowed loudly, as the others gathered around.

"Here, look for yourself on the tacmap."

After they bent over the intel, giving it careful long hard stares and looks, it was Col. Price who stood up first to say, "Well now, he's right you know, it's just too much of a gamble not to take it!"

"Didn't that report we had say that no Serbs were there David?"

"No, what it said was, the Muslims were there in '93 but after the so-called Serb withdrawals, the Serbs later re-grouped and kicked the Muslims off the mountain tops. Now that they are back and even more heavily fortified if you can believe it, they have once more completely dominated and encircled Sarajevo, as pointed out previously."

"Yes, you're right of course," then after some pondering Mac looked at Capt. Peltier and said, "Captain Peltier, when some of your French troops were stationed on Mt. Igman with

UNPROFOR, then later with IFOR after the Serb fallbacks, did any of your lot get stationed on this Mt. Bjelasnica?"

"Yes, I believe some of them did Sir."

"Do you think any are still familiar with it?"

"Yessir."

"Good then, collect them after and get as much intel as possible. Do you also think you could mount a similar recce job on this Mt. Bjelasnica at the same time, same as we planned for Mt. Igman?"

"You mean you want my Mountain Company to recce both mountains Sir?"

'That's exactly what I mean Captain."

After some very careful thought and a little bit more looking at the scale model and tacmaps and assorted intel before him, Capt. Peltier stood and gave his final answer.

"Well, I obviously believe our men can do it Sir, but it just means a separate commander is needed for this other mountain which will also increase our chances of being spotted."

Looking around the room at the anxious and concerned faces, Mac spoke first.

"I'll take those chances Captain. I suggest you make your next-in-command for this mission Sgt. Major Brassard. Just tell me how many men you'll need for the smaller mountain now and who's in your squads. Better still Captain, can you tell me how many were in your planned squads in total for this clandestine recce to begin with?"

Coughing before speaking up in his very thick French accent once more, the Capt. replied, "Yes General, we are obviously not taking the whole of the Mountain and Special Warfare Company but we are taking four Scout and Reconnaissance patrols consisting of eight men per patrol."

"How much time then will we lose if Sgt. Major Brassard leads at least two of those patrols to recce out this other mountain?"

Capt. Peltier's brow furrowed as he thought deeply and quietly, making the necessary mental calculations, only then did he turn back to Gen. Logan and reply, "Three maybe even five days Sir."

Looking around the room the General said to all assembled there, "It looks like we have no other choice. Sergeant Steele is right of course, if we don't recce that blasted other mountain we could very easily leave ourselves open for a counter-offensive through the back door!"

Then, looking at Sgt. Major Brassard he said, "I'm sorry Sgt. Major but it looks like you have to tackle the other mountain. I'll leave you to sort the details out with Captain Peltier. Decide between yourselves just which men you each take."

Captain Peltier was not one for small talk or unnecessary lengthy waits and asked, "Thank you General, will that be all now for my men and I?"

"Yes, you're dismissed."

As the Capt. was leaving the room quickly with his men, the general shouted back at him over his shoulder, "Thank you Captain, and bring me the details of your plans later so that the Intelligence Officer and I can go over them!"

After all others had left the room too, leaving just the two colonels and the General, David looked across at Mac and spoke.

"I was first going to suggest we send them all in by HALO jump or HAHO jump from the tactical operations height of 25,000 feet, under cover of night, or even use the new technique of the 22 SAS which is LALO jumps. They're all qualified free-fall parachutists. But having second thoughts, the weather may be against us and those mountains are crawling with enemy Serbs. So I do think the best way for this Op is to send them out on a flight to Bosnia as 'pretend' regular UN troops, then let them disappear into the night."

Looking concerned and intently at the model of their objectives himself now as was Marc, Mac offered, "Yes David I agree, making a jump into that mess could be the end of them, better that they go there the long way and hike in, what do you say Marc?"

"I agree, yes."

Marc broke the serious silence that had ensued by asking, "I was also wondering, do you have any type of assault battle plan formulated yet, I'm still struggling myself here to identify and figure out how we'll actually take our objectives?"

"Well, there's no question now that we will have to liberate a few other places if we're to do the job for Sarajevo. Most of those places thankfully happen to be solidified through a maze of Serbian checkpoints. I like that because it probably means those places themselves are not too heavily defended.

"I can identify at least three towns, David. Dobrinja, Hadzici and Hrasnica, but these we concentrate on after. For now, we concentrate and worry about the two airports, The International and Butmir, which just leaves our two mountains, Igman and Bjelasnica, to sort out."

"I guess our only problem then is to identify what kind of armaments they have in place, where they're located, then decide how many of our own men we deploy and into which areas," commented David.

"Well, there's no question our major battle is going to be for this Mt. Igman, it's just too heavily fortified. So I'll guesstimate we'll need at least a minimum of half our Brigade strength to take it David, no matter how poorly it is armed, just because of the sheer numbers in men they have positioned there!"

"If Sarajevo is northeast on our tacmap," said Marc, "then when we do take our assigned objectives, what is there to protect Sarajevo from the north perimeter?"

"Good question. If we do our jobs it will be up to the regular UN peace-keepers coming in quickly on our tails. That will still be their job! We do the fighting, they take over after. With themselves on the ground once more it'll be up to them to patrol and put up a counter perimeter zone around that sector there and also Pale to our east, leaving our Brigade free to fight and protect them from the heights and to have control of the strategic positions, then we can consolidate them and facilitate a hand-over."

"Like I said earlier then, it's just a matter of finalizing our battle plans!"

"Yes and I want you to look over those suggestions from the RSM. I do believe he and yourself have prior experience in taking a fortified mountain top. For example, that Mt. Tumbledown or other from your Falklands campaign."

"I'm surprised, it seems nothing gets past you nowadays."

Grinning for the first time Mac said, "Where is the RSM anyway?"

"I do believe he's out there on bayonet practice with the mechanized infantry battalions screaming, 'Give 'em the cold steel lads— the dirty blighters don't like the cold steel stuck up 'em!'—Or something to that effect!"

The three of them then laughed together at the peculiarities and thoroughly British ways of their RSM.

"It's dialogue from an old British military comedy, Dad's Army!" said David.

Grinning, Mac said, "Yes well wherever, he is a character isn't he!?"

Laughing some more amongst themselves, David said, "Come on, let's call this a morning and go and get some lunch."

Over at the Officers Mess hall, Mac found Maj. Ed Stacey.

"Major, how are the Infantry practices going?"

"Well Sir, thanks to Gunny and the RSM I can safely say the men are now completely bullet proof. Oblivious to echoing cracks and ziffs of rifle fire as well as the thud of mortar explosions and let's not forget the benefit of 'cold steel'!"

"That's excellent Major. Now, after your lunch when you see them both again, can you spare them to come to my office for a little confab?"

"Whatever the General wants Sir!" said Maj. Stacey humorously.

Later that day back in the Phoenix's lair, the RSM and Sgt. Major Ridgeway said, "How can we help you Sir?"

"Well, you're both two of my most experienced soldiers and I wanted your input on this little expedition that is possibly upcoming for the Brigade, care to speak up on it?"

Smiling mischievously the RSM said, "Is that the little expedition we've been hearing so much rumour about Sir?"

Returning the smile, Mac replied, "The very same!"

"Well Sir, if you'll just invite us over to that small scale model, which I presume is the intended terrain, we'll take a butchers."

"He means a look see Sir!" said Gunny, not for the first time explaining the RSM's distinctly British, (for those who were not) very peculiar mannerisms and ways. After looking closely at it for some time the RSM said, "Right now Sir, I just don't know. But I'll be sure to ponder it and give it some recall, once took a mountain similar to this out in the Falklands."

"Yes I know RSM, that's why I called you in here with Sgt. Major Ridgeway. Now, before you two depart, is there anything else you can tell me that may be helpful?"

"Well Sir, without looking at our potential objectives, I can say right now that one factor that always gets overlooked or underprepared for in these matters is medical attention!"

"How's that RSM?"

"Well sir, there's always casualties and we better be prepared for an awful lot of them, as well as have the manpower to carry those blood-soaked stretchers. Our field medics will be treating our men for extensive bullet and shrapnel wounds I'd suspect!"

"Point well taken."

"One other matter Sir, if I may?"

"Go ahead."

"Sir, when will the Brigade be told officially about our intended objective?"

"Natives getting restless RSM?"

"Yes Sir!" he smiled.

"Okay, I'll confer with Price and Lafluer later. We'll try to schedule a rotation of each Battalion in the Operations Briefing Hall!"

"Thank you Sir for that advance confirmation!"

"Get out of here!" said Mac grinning, "Like you pair never knew!"

After the RSM and Sgt. Major left his office Mac yelled out for his Orderly Corporal. As soon as Jonesy entered he was asked immediately, "Will you please get Colonels Price and Lafluer back in here—and try to get me a sparky to wire up this intercom contraption before I lose my voice."

"Yessir," said Jonesy smiling broadly.

It had been two days now since Mac had spoken with Colonel Price about scheduling the different Battalions into the Operations Hall to give them their official instructions of their seemingly imminent and potential deployment now they were all back from leave.

Standing in place once again at the podium, up on stage in the large hall with the first of the Battalions, Mac prepared for the first of his many speeches that day . . . !

PART 6

"Men," began General Logan, "The destination seems to be Sarajevo, Bosnia!"

The commotion he anticipated erupted and he just waited for the silence once more.

"I believe it imperative that you all have a right to know why and what you will be fighting for. I know of no better way than giving you a little of the history of our given assignment and what its people have suffered. Certain details will give you the realism, importance and understanding of the task that actually lies ahead of us. Only then do I think you will have that courage and determination to liberate a people the world seems to have forgotten about once again—until now!

"The world is letting us know in no uncertain terms this time around that time is finally running out for Sarajevo and the imprisoned inhabitants of Bosnia. The Serbs' strangle-hold right now is brutal and oppressive. They have a tightened noose on Sarajevo even as I speak. Bombs and bullets once more rain down on these innocent people and terrify them, leaving only victims and the dead. These people have an inspired and persistent, even relentless will to carry on against harsh odds, a struggle these brave inhabitants must endure as they try desperately to remain alive. It is a sad situation magnified out of all proportion really, which makes those trying to persevere, question their own desires to live or even exist, only to ask tiredly, *why?*

"The cold brutality of it all, only reminds them once again too that years ago during the war, when under similar circumstances and when they had little or no water or electricity and the food convoys of the UN were constantly being turned back at Serbian checkpoints, they had to also resort to desperate measures to get needed supplies. Desperate times call for desperate acts, which in their need and search for supplies is killing them in large numbers. Sarajevo is surrounded and being held hostage and the hardship these people face each day is ugly and stark. It must be a real moral victory just to stay positive and alive under such harsh conditions. These cruel scenes are hellish thoughts to have to endure

or have replayed over in your minds and lives every waking moment of every single day. That's a nightmare I'd sure like to stop
happening to them. The people of Sarejevo feel forgotten, which
in turn makes them afraid as well as angry. With the rebuilt infra-
structure already ruined we are reminded of the past as they are
forced to 'run the gauntlet' of the airport road just to get to the
river for water once more. Some make it some don't! Previously
called 'Snipers Alley', that very area is an absolute slaughterhouse
and has a new name now, they call it 'Blood Alley.'

"The only analogy left to me to compare it to is that of the
blitzkrieg of Poland in Warsaw during World War II. The difference this time men, is Sarajevo has kept going in hope and on
blind faith, believing that the Western countries would still be
their saviour. The city of Sarajevo is now a ravaged, burnt, and
bombed-out carnage like that previous time in its history, some
seven years back, only this time it's even worse. The place is quickly
resembling the destruction that was left behind in Lebanon.

"Too much of this 'battle type' conditioning treatment, plus
necessity for basic needs is making the civilian residents oblivious
to their surroundings as safety and caution are thrown to the wind
in their search for water and food. The UN aid packages we do
manage to get in are few and far between now, as only the 'air
drops' remain open to them. Forced hunger and starvation continue as their besieged city is being systematically 'ethnically
cleansed' once again. Communities and homes are being shelled
upon constantly, within grenade and mortar range of the Serbian
front lines, all around the cities' perimeters. This is also happening
in all the other enclaves outside of Sarejevo too that haven't yet
been overrun or ransacked. The danger of shrapnel from fragmen-
tation bombs is an everyday threat from the artillery fire and shelling that they send in. The Bosnian Army's defence and so called
'diversionary units' are in reality just skirmishers who distract and
annoy the Serbs rather than sending in experienced units to attack
or repel them effectively.

"These people, men, feel the world has let them down, in

many ways it has! It is not just food that is failing to get past Serbian blockades now but badly needed medical supplies are not reaching the hospitals and the sick and the wounded are suffering too. This collapse and failure to act decisively in Bosnia is now considered unforgivable and the Western countries have regretted their mistake, hence our existence and tasking for final intervention. It may be impossible for us to rescue Bosnia right now but just as we rescued Berlin in World War II, or even more recently, Kuwait in the Gulf, it is our duty to rescue Sarajevo!"

Cheers and whistling erupted spontaneously from the men.

"There is a very real danger for us here, as every Western initiative before us has failed. The Vance-Owen plan. The Dayton-Paris Peace Agreement. All the Peacekeeping Missions of the UN and NATO. All those and this new recent failure. Where does it all end you may well ask. Well I will tell you. It ends right with us. We are that alternative reaction to aggression that the world has been clamouring and praying for. We will be the victors here men, have no doubts of that fact."

When the cheers erupted once again it was so loud it was a strain on his ear drums.

"The world is curious if Bosnia and Herzegovina will end with a bang or a whimper, to the sound of the bombs as they signal failure for NATO and the United Nations. The Serbs still encircle Sarajevo and when they pulled back and allowed the UN to put peacekeepers on Mt. Igman and Mt. Bjelasnica for the very first time, what they did in reality was exploit an opportunity! By doing so they were craftily replacing their tired and weary soldiers from Banja Luka in the north with fresh local soldiers who knew the terrain! Their Commanders knew back then that air strikes alone would not do it, that they could only be defeated in battle on the ground. Some two hundred and fifty French peacekeepers were in the territory of those two mountains back then, some are with us now. Luckily for us, with the help of this Intel and data, they have mapped all the occupied checkpoints and control roads in these areas, as well as strategic targets!"

Quiet ensued now as General Logan looked out on the gathered faces of his men sternly when he broke his own silence.

"So, now you know who our enemy is and what we are faced with here in order to remove him and liberate the people of Sarajevo which is, right now, a blockaded and encircled city. Hopefully all this background history and information will give you a better insight and grasp of the situation. Just remember, that liberation will be done through us taking key installations and other targeted areas such as the airports and these two mountains, followed by a few other key towns. Nothing ever goes exactly as planned or expected, but if we prepare ourselves well, we can do it men. It is left up to our skill, our might, our professionalism and our courage! Good luck and prepare yourselves. Listen to your Platoon Commanders as they brief you in your roles. You will be given your information and roles as soon as we move. You're all experienced and most of you have been in similar situations before, so rely on that experience. When it happens, you will be making history in this the very first action of The Sabre Brigade, United Nations! Just like that other Brigade, let us never give up ground and may we never lose!"

As a man, the entire Battalion grouped before him cheered and shouted, "For the Phoenix," or, "The Sabre Brigade!"

It was a rousing speech. One he would repeat over again throughout that day to other Battalions, being equally well received. Meanwhile, as the remainder of the Brigade readied for war, Capt. Peltier's four recce and scout troops had already been flown under guise of UN peacekeepers, arriving in Bosnia by C141B transport plane. They were going under their Canadian cover of observer replacements in one of the few enclaves not under total Serbian control. Their cover was ideal due to their strong American and French accents which would naturally prevent others from becoming suspicious. The rules never changed in such matters. Their contacts were to a minimum and were dealt with on a need-to-know basis. They were immediately transported to a front line Canadian encampment. There, they were billeted in a vacant transport bay, totally removed from the other regular Canadian troops stationed there.

Capt. Peltier had to meet with the Canadian officer in charge who gracefully yet professionally kept his own curiosity in check and asked no questions, but did brief them on the current situation as it now stood. The Canadian officer understood that they were not to be bothered and were here to do their own thing, no explanations required. Being a good, well-disciplined officer, he wished Capt. Peltier the best and departed.

The men of the M&SW Company recce and scout troop ate their meal only when the regular Canadian troops had finished, not wanting to have contact or engage in unnecessary conversation or to expand or lie about their presence any further than what was needed. After their meal they all congregated to the far end of the bay as they checked over equipment and went over their plans of engagement. Later, under cover of darkness, their four small clandestine patrols slipped out of the encampment as secretively as they arrived, then set out on foot to determine over the next five to seven days or so, the strengths and dispositions of the Serbian troops.

There was wind and some rain as they left and they found these conditions suitable and advantageous to their goal of gathering as much information on the enemy placements as possible, due to the fact harsh weather normally kept movement down. Most soldiers do not want to be "out-and-about" in such adverse weather conditions given a preference, especially if not equipped with suitable windproof or waterproof clothing. Later, having just climbed the lower elevation of Mt. Igman, the two patrols needed to split up.

"Do your men know their duties and directional co-ordinates to start the reconnaissance Sgt. Major?" asked Capt. Peltier.

"As well as can be hoped Sir, we've gone over this enough times."

With that understanding, they then parted company and the two patrols now went their separate ways. The Sgt. Major and his recce teams set off for Mt. Bjelasnica, the others kept on course for

Mt. Igman, but taking their different routes. Frequent driving squalls of snow and sleet with sudden changes in wind speed and direction hampered their progress for the very first time.

Carrying his knotted nylon para cord in his left pocket with its metered cords to keep count of distance, an old SAS trick, Sgt. Steele slipped off into the biting cold night with his men like ghosts. In weather like this the GPS's were a godsend as conventional map reading was more than difficult, it was near impossible.

The object of their recce was to establish a place to hide in total concealment away from enemy troops during the day, in places appropriately named "Hides" and to conduct their surveillance under cover of darkness. The night became their best friend.

Each night Ben did as all the other recce and scout troop commanders had been taught and trained to do and that was to open their small lightweight satellite kits and "splurge" their encoded messages back to Helena via their satellite links. Their encoded messages lasted less than fifteen seconds and due to the adverse weather conditions they hoped their signals were being picked up and received as the information they were sending back was vital. Aerial photography can only pick up so much intelligence. For an accurate account bodies had to do it the old fashioned way still, which is get in there on foot and check with your own eyes.

The days quickly passed as their task kept them busy and occupied but sooner or later they had to consider extracting themselves. The two Mt. Bjelasnica recce troops that had previously departed under the command of Sgt. Major Brassard were the first to return to their predetermined rendezvous on time which was an incredible feat in itself considering the adverse weather conditions. Sgt. Steele made it there shortly after with his own recce troop which now totalled three. Capt. Peltier himself was the missing troop. The foul weather conditions were creating fears of a near "white-out" condition developing and this brought fears of frostbite and environmental casualties.

Sgt. Major Brassard decided, as the senior man there, that a make-shift composite recce troop would now search for the missing troop immediately as he did not want to jeopardize the entire operation with them being caught, putting fears that they might already be, out of his mind.

"Look, before we extract ourselves from these mountains we have to determine Captain Peltier's disposition, we can't afford them to use their Sabres either, that would just give us all away." So the decision was made and the task had fallen on Sgt. Steele and a composite patrol to retrace and find the missing troops.

After some hours of by-passing already identified positions on their tacmaps, Sgt. Steele's make-shift troop with the combined skill and stealth that his men held, soon found Capt. Peltier's recce troop huddled in a make-shift "Hide" not three kilometres west of them.

Cold could be a serious problem, he knew. *What could go wrong? Muscles could cramp and tighten, then stiffen. Then there's exhaustion from the mere effort to stay warm and awake. They needed to act quick and not delay because of these factors.* He knew he would have to issue the order to the men to take the first opportunity and let them know they were here, that they had found them—but only after getting the pre-arranged signal to come in, he didn't want them walking into an enemy trap.

"Give the signal," Ben told Tiny. Only after the designated wait time when it came back did he tell his men they could approach their hide.

Ben grinned, "You plonkers get yourselves in a mess here on the borders?"

They were too cold for humour but one bright spark's brain cells were still warm as he retorted, "Not at all, waiting for our passports to be stamped!"

"Too much traffic and troop movement all of a sudden," said Capt. Peltier, "they were probably looking for better cover themselves. With this foul weather we didn't want to risk the chance of bumping into one of the Serbian patrols so we did the only possible thing left to us under the circumstances, we bedded down!"

"Understandable Sir," he said relieved, "But now we're here, let's show you the way home, heh?" he grinned.

Smiling back as gratefully as he could Capt. Peltier said, "Be my guest Sergeant," as his men were already gathering up their gear and getting their equipment back on.

"Take the point and lead us out of here Tiny," Ben said through chattering teeth, much relieved they were all now on their way out.

Some two hours later again, due to their discretionary tactics to manoeuvre and zig-zag away from Serbian checkpoints and other troop placements, the missing troop, with Ben himself leading now, came back to home base rendezvous. After some brief greetings Sgt. Major Brassard said, "This foul weather looks like it's not going to co-operate with us either Sir, so let me ask you, are you and your men capable of continuing off this mountain, we still have a ways to go?"

"We're definitely a little tired Sgt. Major but nobody wants to stay. We'll make it off okay, just lead the way!"

With those simple words and no indication of Serb presence, Sgt. Major Brassard led the four M&SWC recce and scout troops of Mt. Igman back to the Canadian base camp. Once back their first duty was to stow their gear and get their exhausted bodies into dry clothing. The next order of the day was to get some food and warm drink down their throats. Not long after but feeling much better now, Capt. Peltier asked the Canadian officer and base commander if he could use his radio operations equipment to get a radio link patched through to his headquarters. Once contact was established, above the crackle of the air-waves he heard the familiar voice of Maj. Rance come onto the line and say jovially, "The Phoenix is pleased. Everything received okay. Return home!"

Back in Montana in the Phoenix' lair, Gen. Logan sat there with Col.s Price and Lafluer like he had for many days and hours before, staring at their topographical maps and model of Mt.Igman and the surrounding area of Sarajevo and grinned, "I think the pieces of the puzzle are now in place!"

"I believe you're correct there Mac," said David, "I just hope we haven't overlooked anything, as there are no second chances as a rule in this business. Any blundering miscalculations will be paid for heavily here in this one I think."

"Well," observed Mac, "We have military targets defined now and complete arrangement with the allied NATO Air Force units for when we go into action. We also have a clearer understanding of how their chain of command operates."

"Yes, I think from our reconnaissance patrols we can now determine with some clarity that those initial troops from Banja Luca in the north which manned these mountains previously are indeed the very same troops now fighting so fiercely for the Krajina with the Croats once again."

"That can only confirm then that the re-inforcements for this battle zone will come like Sgt. Steele so correctly summarized— from Trnovo to our southeast."

"Exactly."

"I think that Belgium General had the United Nations troops do a masterful job of mapping out the possible strategic sites of Mt. Igman to begin with, even before the arrival of possibly the best general the British brought in, General Thorn."

"Yes, those maps plus information our scouts brought back from our own recces will be invaluable!"

Col. Price then asked, "So tell me again now we have all that, what's this new theory or style of attack you've designed?"

Mac started in slowly, "Remember the Zulu wars in South Africa in the Boar Wars? That famous pitched battle at Rourkes Ridge, or was it Drift?"

"Yes, I remember, we learnt it at Sandhurst when I was a cadet, Rourkes Drift."

"Yes well, this is shaped a little similar in principal, with the horns that is, based similar to that concept only instead of bringing the horns around to surround, we, with an extra added prong, strike out three ways. How do you like it so far?"

"Depends on what your concept of it is," said Col. Lafluer.

"It's called a Double Trident!"

His two colonels looked at him now and it was David who spoke first. "Well, I for one would like to know more about it Mac, especially as we haven't come up with anything so far. How far out does each prong of this Trident of yours extend for one, namely their range?"

"That's the beauty of it, there is no set limit. If we keep our heads down and stick to the parameters of our air-strike and artillery coverage corridors, we can thrust and extend as fast or slowly as we can, without jeopardising the future success of any of the other Battalions next to each other!"

"How will that work in principle?" asked Colonel Lafluer.

"Just come on over here, both of you, and I'll show you the complete principle and strategy of it all on the model."

Moving over to the large table that contained the model and seemed to take the entire space of his office now, Mac picked up some little flagged pins and said, "Here gentlemen, let me show you. . . . "

Entering the office the orderly corporal said, "Sir, I have an urgent message for you from our Tec Building via the UN."

"Bring it here Corporal."

"Do you want me to wait for any reply Sir?"

As the orderly Cpl. received a negative answer he closed the door quietly and left. Reading the UN message silently to himself Mac then handed it around, starting with David.

Inspired at the discussion that they had just had, Mac then said looking at David, "No need to call General Clarke, that old bear will be up waiting for us when we arrive."

"We?" he said surprised.

"Yes David, I think it's about time that you get to see the place that Sergeant Steele has had the privilege and luxury of seeing before you, and no complaining, you're coming this time— and that's final!" he laughed.

"I take it that's an order then?" David quipped.

"Absolutely, about time you had a taste of this jet lag syndrome as well."

After departing La Guardia airport in the Marine escort car the General and Colonel stopped long enough at their hotel only to drop off their bags. They then continued on to United Nations Plaza. Once there, Gen. Logan casually observed the Marines doing their work checking their IDs. He came to the same startling conclusion he always had watching them, which was the amazing efficiency at which these Marine guards, who at the different checkpoints, cleared and passed individuals to access certain areas of different security levels.

Their entrance surprised Maggie as he had not phoned ahead this time, but she did not let that prevent her from getting up from her desk to come round to greet him with a warm inviting kiss.

"Maggie, I would like to introduce you to my 2IC and current IO, Colonel David Price!"

Leaning against the shoulder of Mac, as well as holding onto his arm, Maggie said with her engaging smile, "Ah, I finally get to meet you, I've heard an awful lot about you Colonel."

"Only the good things I hope!?"

"You can relax Colonel, yes, only the good things!" laughed Maggie.

"Phew, that's a relief then," he joked back.

Then Maggie turned to Mac and jokingly punched him in the ribs saying, "So, whatever happened about phoning a girl and letting her know you're coming?"

"Sorry darling. It's just been a mad scramble to make the flight this time and all those other sorts of details . . ."

"I'll forgive you just because I get the opportunity to see you again!" then reached up and planted another kiss, this time on his cheek.

"Where's the General, Maggie?"

"Ah, for a moment there I thought you came especially to visit me. He's in there, surprised he's not come out, he must be engrossed in something."

As the two officers entered the inner office Gen. Clarke looked up from behind his large oak desk; he had been reading some files and bellowed out on seeing them, "Come in here son and bring your guest over and introduce me."

Smiling broadly Mac made the introductions, "We came here just as soon as we received your signal Sir!"

"Well brace yourselves, it looks as though we're going onto a seventy-two hour standby. This is finally going down!"

The two senior officers of the Sabre Brigade exchanged quick glances.

"So it's really happening, heh General?"

"Yes! The *why* of it is simple. The present Paris peace talks are stalled and considered irrevocable in lieu of the current break in the cease-fire and umpteenth attack on Sarajevo. This time they used mortars, killing at least thirty and injuring 70+ in the main market place. A blatant attack on the civilians, a place where they go for their groceries!"

"Yes, we heard it over the news Sir, we sort of expected some reaction."

"Some?! NATO and the UN are just absolutely exasperated and outraged this time. They can only get away with it so many times. So, the Secretary General himself told me to put you all on seventy-two hour standby notice, it goes into effect immediately gentlemen!"

"Can I use your phone then General?"

"What for son?"

"To call my Brigade. Let them know to cancel all leaves and recall any who are already out there."

"Good idea. I'll get Maggie to patch you through."

"What other action, if any, is the United Nations taking Sir?"

"The Security Council has approved and requested NATO to conduct air strikes."

"Is this measure an impulsive one Sir?"

"No son. It was considered carefully."

"When do you think it will happen then Sir?"

"Well, this is confidential, but as we speak the Allied planes should be in the air. They left Varno air base in Italy we've been using these past years. Plus from one of our carriers out in the Adriatic. As I said, they're in the air as we speak!"

"Do you know their targets Sir?" asked Col. Price.

"I believe it is to knock out the Serbian National Air Defence satellite system, then to clear the way for other strikes in the future."

"That will help us tremendously if we are sent in, and it looks to me like we are heading that way."

"That's why I wanted you here Mac, with your 2IC, to go over contingency and battle plans that you may have formulated, that I hope you've formulated, as I don't want you to leave it up to others to plan out, people who won't be part of any of the fighting. I've always felt Mac that the men who do the fighting are entitled to come forward with their own plans, after all, it is them that will also have to do the dying."

"Well Sir, we won't disappoint you, we do happen to have a plan," and turning to Col. Price, Mac added, "Don't we David?"

Nodding his agreement the two officers waited for the General to ask them for it and they weren't disappointed.

"I have to tell you Sir," said David impishly, "Mac's idea is not an original one."

"How's that?"

"Rourke's Drift Sir, he stole it from the Zulus."

"I did not!" Mac mocked in feigned indignation.

"It was a thoroughly original idea, I just needed a little direction is all!"

"Personally I don't care where the plan is from, I just expect it to work. Will it work Mac?"

"Well, you can judge for yourself Sir, we brought some intel and a tacmap along with us to lay out and explain the gory details to you."

After laying it all out on the other large table in the room, they proceeded to unravel the intricacies of his plan. With the tacmap laid out in front of him, he began.

"It was a difficult and agonizing decision to reach at first because I knew we only have the one chance which is vital to the total success for our Brigade."

"Understood. Now what have you named this operation?"

"We aptly named it 'Operation Poseiden's Thrust', Sir. I have to tell you, if it cannot force its way to its objective then a catastrophe of immense magnitude will be unavoidable."

"That's a pretty chilling and absolute statement Mac, all I want to know, need to know is, is it viable?"

"Well Sir, we've agonized and debated its merits these past few weeks and have come to the conclusion, if we make it a total surprise package, it's our best shot."

For the next hour or more they discussed its finer points and merits. "How does it break out again?" asked the General once more.

"Immediately after the airstrips are taken, recces go out to the three towns of Hadzici, Dobrinja and Hrasnica. Then the assaults on the check-points begin. As does the immediate advance by our mechanized Battalions, up to the mountains and high ground through our own *advanced* checkpoints, which by this time we will have re-taken from the Serbs."

"Artillery will have to move quickly to cover you too, no?"

"Not exactly Sir, you see we have light and portable artillery already. But by the time we have reached the mountain base our Allied Nato airstrikes should commence a devastating barrage that we can advance under cover, textbook tactics General."

"Those enemy tanks and artillery are embedded and will have

a superiority in numbers over you of more than ten to one in certain places, I sure don't like the sound of those odds."

"We may be inferior in numbers General," said David, "but I assure you, for most of our soldiers at least, they have all fought under such odds in the past. Our soldiers are first class Sir, they're the best combat soldiers the world has to offer right now, and if we can't do the job, you had better consider mass air-strikes."

The General poured over and pondered their tacmap and conceded points back and forth, recognizing advantages to the plan, convinced of air assault and covering bombing attacks being an air threat to be reckoned with, but worried if their land troops could operate effectively and what would happen if the air strikes didn't manage to inflict the expected damage and casualties to the Serbian Force. He felt the Armoured and Artillery Battalion, or vast components of it, had to be taken up front with them to be effective and supply them with the necessary cover in between the air strikes so they could continue to advance, thus preventing any opportunity of regrouping by the Serbs.

"Most men cower beneath an artillery bombardment Gentlemen," said the General adding, "it surely must be the most unpleasant experience on the face of this earth. It takes a skilled soldier to advance under fear of it reaching him, no mortal words can describe its thunderous noise, with flying earth and shuddering thuds!"

"I understand it Sir, but we'll just have to put our faith into the precision bombing of NATO Allied Air Command as well as our own artillery then."

"That's a considerable risk you're taking."

"Well General, that's the risk I knew I had to take on when you gave me this job!"

"I don't suppose you have time to reconsider any other type of plan, heh?"

"Sir," replied Mac, "this is the *only* plan we have. Certain Battalions of the Brigade have already practiced small parts of it, like the taking of the Serbian checkpoints, but when we return Colonel Price and I intend a full Brigade exercise to test its strengths and weaknesses."

Looking at them both almost fatherly now, the General smiled and said, "Due to the fact it's the only plan I've seen I'm willing to give it the opportunity it deserves, so get yourselves back to Montana with haste and try it out men!"

Mac looked at the General saying, "Thank you Sir, do you want us to leave this copy with you?" as he held up their tacmap.

Upon receiving an affirmative nod he continued on instinct, "What about coming down and observing the exercise Sir, get you away from this desk for awhile?"

"That's a hell of an idea Mac, maybe even invite that limey Crenshaw and some others, if that's alright with you?"

"You're all welcome Sir, it will give us an opportunity to prove our abilities and potential at the same time, once and for all, so there's no doubting Thomases!"

"Then it's done, we leave after dinner, but just one thing Mac, I'd bring Maggie for you but I need her here to hold down the fort for me while I play hooky!"

"I understand Sir, after dinner then . . ."

Back at Camp Fredericks as it was now officially called, some extra rooms were prepared for the visiting V.I.P.s of Gen. Clarke and his entourage.

"When did General Crenshaw tell you that he would be arriving Sir? Just so as we can make sure we have some transport over at the airport in Helena to pick them up?"

"I understand that he'll be arriving in a few more hours still with some staff aide," he said.

"Not a problem Sir," said the RSM as he followed them around, "We have plenty of rooms here in the mess for them now," then added, "will you be needing me for anything else Sir?"

"No, you can leave RSM and thanks for your help getting the men for these bags."

"Not at all Sir," said the RSM as he departed the mess.

"Well now, how about you and I take a brief respite General and retire to our bar for a few drinks with the men while we wait for General Crenshaw and whomever? The men are all anxious to greet you, Sir."

"Well, let's not have it said that General Clarke's a party pooper, heh?" he laughed, and with that, the entourage of officers made their way to the Officers Mess.

General Crenshaw arrived with his aide, his new IO being his very own daughter, Lt. Jane Crenshaw. Her striking beauty caused more than a ripple of excitement amongst the amassed officers of the Brigade who were already clambering and jockeying for a position to be nearest to her, all virile men and starved for female company like they were. On being introduced to Maj. Ed Stacey Jane just smiled and said, "I've heard a lot about you already Major."

He was surprised, "Then you have me at a great disadvantage Lieutenant, unless you care to divulge your source?"

Smiling confidently Jane said, "Maybe you've heard of a Sgt. Steele? I believe he's a member of this Brigade."

With those words a dozen or more heads turned as if in enlightenment, and now Maj. Stacey said kindly, "So you're the one who breaks the hearts of my men?"

Smiling back Jane replied in jest, "I try my best Major!"

In a gallant gesture Maj. Stacey said, "Then as long as you're a guest in this mess I'll consider it an honour if you'll allow me to protect your honour and reputation from all the dangerous low life here, to preserve you intact for the good Sgt.?" Then leaning closer, "You have nothing to fear, no one here would like their throat cut in the middle of the night for messing with the Sergeant's girl, so you're really quite safe!"

Returning the smile and gesture of friendship Jane replied blushingly, "I thank you and take you up on your offer Major, as long as you can arrange for me to see the Sergeant later, if you're a friend of his?"

"Didn't anyone tell you?" he blurted, then stopped.

"Tell me what?" she asked, suddenly concerned and frightened inside.

"I'm sorry to alarm you Lieutenant, that was a mistake, but I do think it's the General's place to inform you, so if you'll excuse me for a moment?"

Maj. Stacey found his Brigade General conferring with the other two and had a quick word in his ear pointing back in the direction of Lt. Crenshaw. Explaining the situation to these Generals, Mac approached the Lt., then spoke when close at hand.

"I understand Lieutenant that you were inquiring about Sergeant Steele?"

"Yes I was. Is he somewhere out there with the rest of the Brigade?" she asked, although sensing a sinking feeling in the pit of her stomach.

Looking at the two Generals now and receiving the go-ahead nod from them both, Mac told her, "I'm sorry that you have to find out this way right now Lt. Crenshaw, but Sgt. Steele is with other members of our very own Mountain and Special Warfare Company. He's in Bosnia doing advanced reconnaissance for us."

Trying to keep her composure but unable to prevent just a trickle of a tear from rolling down her cheek, as the male officers looked away compassionately, she tried to compose herself.

"If you can be kind enough to spare Major Stacey for awhile General, I'd like it very much now to return to my bags and room?"

"Perfectly Lieutenant. Maj. Stacey, will you oblige the Lieutenant?"

"Not a problem Sir," said the Major.

Taking her aside her father said, "Have no fear Jane, I'll do my damndest to find out what he's up to and how safe he is for you, okay?"

Kissing her father on the cheek and saying her evening farewell to the Generals, under her escort of Maj. Stacey, she retired to her room. Once inside it, she just let down her guard and the tears flooded out.

The following morning was a new day. Putting on a brave

face, Jane attended the special intelligence meeting with her father as the professional soldier she was. She gathered as much useful information as she could, at least information she felt would be useful to her father's cause. Col. Price, a typically English gentlemen, advised her that Sgt. Steele's party was gathering vital intelligence in strategic locations of artillery and heavy armour placements, as well as troop strengths of the Bosnian Serbs in their expected theatre of operations, at least predominantly on Mt. Igman and Mt. Bjelasnica.

"What is their ETA for getting back Sir?" she asked.

"Well, if all goes well, by the end of this week," he answered.

"Then I shall just have to leave him a message for his arrival, won't I Colonel?" she said as though she had some devious plan in mind.

The following day found the General's and entourage stationed in their observation post (OP) in the foothills of their camp in Montana. The entire Brigade had moved out into the mountains surrounding them to prepare for their exercise, ever vigilant and in constant radio contact. A part of the simulation exercise that was being tested for was speed and accuracy in case the situation in Bosnia changed quickly. The Brigade's presence of numbers were impressive as they went through their paces. They commenced their advanced training exercise, implementing and practicing the tactics that were planned out in earlier days.

There was a minimum of supervision. Done strictly to simulate real life conditions and to shake out the cobwebs, but for no other reason than to simulate as much reality as possible. While the testing of equipment and communications were essential under these practise conditions, so was bringing the uninitiated up to par. The Mechanized Infantry Battalions and Armoured and Artillery Battalion went through their live fire drills, as did the helicopters, loading and rappelling. Meanwhile, the logistical troops such as the Engineers practiced putting up their bridging units and laying and marking off mine fields plus clearing some while the rest of the Brigade concentrated on their assigned priorities. Every man had the opportunity to fire his weapon on exercise, whether it be a rifle, mortars, or anti-tank weapons at static targets.

The entire Brigade's Infantry drills for action combat were carried out over and over starting at the section level and working up through the chain of command into Platoon, Company and Battalion levels. It had to be stressed that these troops were not tackling anything new, as over 75% of the Brigade were combat veterans. Logistics were of vital concern, for without a constant source of delivery and re-supply of food, ammunition, and radio batteries, as well as the medical equipment and staff support, fighting could very easily come to a screeching, shuddering halt.

In the heat of the exercise, by the end of the day, tactics included the Advance to Target contacts, deliberate and concentrated attacks at Company and Battalion levels, with recces from the Mountain and Special Warfare Company doing roving attacks. There was no defence, just all out offensive operations, with possible and probable counter-offences. The most exciting thing to watch of the day was the multiple Mechanized Battalions Heliborne Infantry Assaults with the Huey Cobra and scout assault helicopters of the Air Assault Battalion accompanying their attack and reconnaissance positions.

The visiting dignitaries were also being flown all over the mock battlefield to observe for themselves how they could cripple any enemy with their technique. Then, with the exercise finally over, they and the troops returned to camp exhausted but eager, ready to carry out last minute preparations. The exercise had definitely bonded the men of the Brigade with a sense of purpose and readiness and determination. Their minds were concentrated and focused now on their objective, as they would continue with similar operations until news of their deployment to Bosnia.

Back at the camp Jane was getting ready to leave when she asked Maj. Stacey for a personal favour. She wanted somebody to escort her over to Sgt. Steele's quarters so she could personally leave a message and some things she had brought along for him. Maj. Stacey had no difficulty in granting her the request. He had the RSM personally escort her there.

"May I have a moment in there alone RSM?"

"Of course Ma'am, I'll just be down the hall here waiting for when you're ready to leave, just call me when it's time."

"Thank you RSM," she said kindly, and then using the master key offered her, Jane entered Ben's room. At first the very austere surroundings seemed too bare and she felt very sorry and melancholy, feeling that he would normally be here, living in solitary confinement almost like this. After sitting there awhile on the edge of his bed, she lay herself back and turned her face into his pillow, trying to breathe in any remnants of his scent. She actually could, as she felt closer and vindicated for doing so. When she turned back she was suddenly surprised to see the photo of herself plus one of her family with the Sgt. Major and aunt May in the framed photos next to his bed. Looking at them, she couldn't help but start to softly cry again, "Oh Ben, wherever you are, take care of yourself for me."

Just laying there in his room she felt an inner peace come over her and then she rose and laid her package she had brought for him directly onto his bed next to the window so he wouldn't miss it. Then on instinct she did one final thing, she removed her panties and laid them under his pillow with a quickly scribbled note before leaving the room.

"Thank you RSM, we can go now."

Returning to his men, Capt. Peltier informed them of the good news and success of their Operation, advising them to get some well earned sleep at last before they moved out in the morning. They passed by the Serbian checkpoints nervously, not wanting any contact or confrontation. Luckily, even though the Serbs glared at them, they took their military vehicles to be the only few regular UN troops remaining, but allowed them passage, especially when it was explained they were heading for the airport to leave. Soon they caught a regular Hercules C-130 transport flight back to Stateside.

On his arrival back at camp no-one had told Ben of the prior visit by Gen. Crenshaw with his fiance. So, jumping from the bus he went directly to his room expecting to quickly dump his bags and return to the mess. But as he opened the door he immediately caught the smell of a familiar perfume which filled his nostrils to a point that he thought his senses had gone amuck and that he was imagining things. When he was ready to commit himself, he spotted the package on his bed. *It's not my birthday*, he thought to himself, so walking closer for a better inspection, he read who it was from. Putting his bags down he now turned his eyes to the note sitting on his pillow. Moving the package aside, he quickly opened the note and read it.

> *My darling Ben,*
>
> *I had the good fortune to visit here with my father on official business. I can assure you I was never so disappointed in my life as to find you were NOT waiting here for me, only then to be told of your mission. I hope you don't mind the intrusion, but I had the RSM bring me to your quarters so I could drop off this package for you and just to see how you live, and maybe that way, in your private quarters, feel closer to you. I think somehow that the dear man understood. I just want you to know my Sgt., that I love you more than ever and pray for your safe return. Here are a few surprise items from us all from home I thought you could use, as well as one of aunt May's pies. Also, I took the opportunity to leave a little spur of the moment surprise from me, letting you know what you have just missed, under your pillow!*
>
> I count the days and hours until I see you again.
>
> My love always—Jane xoxoxoxo.

Putting down the note and pulling back his pillow to see what might be under there, he could only smile and grin, mumbling to himself, "Boy, what a loss!" This was just what he needed to snap out of the serious mode he had been in after their mission. How very close they had all come to losing it too. Laughing to himself in a new sense of happy feelings, he sat on the side of his bed and then opened his package like an excited schoolboy.

With the return of the four patrols of Mountain Company from Bosnia, the General wanted as many men as possible to hear their debriefings, and so had as many officers and men as possible crammed into the War Office (Operations Hall) to hear Capt. Peltier and his men give a description of their experience, code-named "Operation Scout."

When Capt. Peltier, Sgt. Major Brassard and Sgt. Steele himself had all had their say a standing ovation and rousing hand of applause was in order, for officially speaking, this was the Brigade's very first Operation in any theatre of combat, albeit a recce patrol, but nevertheless a first, as they were armed and prepared to fight!

PART 7

In the big build-up of the days that followed there was a lot of excitement as well as preparation and work to be done around the camp. On the big day there would be no emotional send-offs for these men of The Sabre Brigade. No family or girlfriends or bands playing to wish them well on their way. There was no hype or emotional drama to elevate or signal their departure in this particular way, they just readied to leave. The entire Brigade was transported by vehicles which was mostly their own, to the US Ranger base of Fort Lewis in Washington State in silent but mass convoy as they waited patiently and quietly to depart en masse as a complete and total Brigade. The entire Brigade, all 27,000+ men and equipment, would be flown to Bosnia in the huge transport planes deploying instantly into battle after disembarkation, then regrouping later.

They arrived at Fort Lewis on time with no hitch and for now as the crucial moments to load arrived, the men of the Brigade checked and re-checked their weapons and equipment out in front of the hangars under the stars. This Brigade movement would be done Battalion by Battalion, but the first departures and thus first arrivals, would be the troops of the Pathfinder units, all chosen voluntarily from the highest classifications and ratings. Pathfinders were from every Company, taking their lead from the members of the Mountain and Special Warfare Company.

First off would be the Rapid-Reaction Pathfinder units, also known as the shock troops, who were set to deplane under the guise of regular United Nations peacekeepers. Immediately upon arrival they would deploy instantly, doing so by setting out speedily and expeditiously, making first contacts by taking and securing the perimeter of both airports, the International and the one at Butmir. They were set to land here at them both soon. They were tasked in taking and securing their designated gunpoint and checkpoints and with putting up some of their own. Once secured, the remainder of the Brigade would be landing quickly behind.

Mobile scout and recce troops from these Pathfinders would also race ahead under the same "regular" UN disguise and re-take the Serbian checkpoints along the main roadways, doing so in a leap-frog effect and more importantly, creating a corridor for their following Battalions they knew would be coming along behind them with the same speed and urgency. Their initial role was every bit as crucial as theirs, for they needed to make it along this route that would lead them toward their prime objectives, Mt. Igman and its sister Mt. Bjelasnica.

Eventually the first of the huge transport planes started to land the Brigade in Bosnia-Herzegovina. They taxied along as the Brigade deplaned in their practiced and known TALO roles. The first waves of blue-helmeted Brigade soldiers, disguised as regular UN troops, deployed down the lowering back ramps before the planes had even halted. Others now too were already speeding off, racing across the landing strip into the night, in search of their own objectives. These troops in this initial assault had the important duty to retake control of the International and Butmir airports which they had just landed at. Theirs was a classic in-your-face raid very reminiscent of the Israeli raid on Entebbe years earlier.

Their need to reconnoitre was obsolete due to prior intelligence and reconnaissance having been done. Now they just needed to take out the gun stations, radio tower, perimeter guard and ammunition and aviation fuel dumps with as much haste as possible. Done with as little damage to the airports as possible too, as these would become their own tactical bases once they had been taken, a crucial asset needed for the steady flow of troops and supplies to follow them in.

A troop from the M&SW Coy was assigned the task of the International Airport while B troop was assigned Butmir, with back-up from pathfinders from other selected Coys who would remain in a defensive role until members of their own Coys arrived. The original pathfinders would then race off into the night to flank the Brigade movement along with the recce troops. On their landing and formation after driving out of the smaller and much less observed airport, due to them being taken as UN peace-keepers positioned there, two squads each circled back and raced off into the night to reach the runways. It was their role to establish that the VOR directional beacons for later arrivals were in place and in working order. The rest of the troop split up and circled into their selected assault groups now with the necessary support of light artillery and covering fire units taking position on the edges of the runway, selecting their targets.

Under almost perfect synchronization the two attacks commenced in unison with amazing timing. Simultaneous firing of green flares ordered that covering gunfire could commence. This sudden eruption of action kept the garrisons of the airport's Serbian contingent confused and occupied, while the rest of the raiding troop set about doing their part. Originally, the plan was for no radio contact until their objectives had been reached. Sighting of an oncoming group with mobile machine gun vehicles seen racing off in their direction, the troop commander used his initiative and broke the silence for an emergency warning. He felt justified that the element of surprise had already been attained, and now compromised by this charging bunch, he was concerned for the lives of his men, thus he felt warranted in his decision which later proved to be the right one.

Each airport perimeter was guarded by a Marine Tigercat SAM battery of the Serbian Marine anti-aircraft Regiment. As A troop approached their targets they were aided by the confusion of the artillery barrage, noise, illumination and even missiles. While their troops held demolition experts, they did not want to cause any airstrip destruction but keep it to a minimum so it could be patched in haste. They were there to attack, destroy, or capture the Serbian-controlled airstrips by engaging in a controlled but superior firefight. The combined men of A and B Coy soon had these airports under their control by 0622hrs, less than twenty-five minutes after they had commenced.

The hasty Serbian withdrawal and dispersal that was going on in a wild rush for freedom was allowed to continue unopposed as the less troops to worry over as prisoners the better. Their initial attack had been a brief but most spectacular success! There were only minor casualties to the men of the Brigade compared with heavy losses by the Serbian garrison that had been completely surprised and overwhelmed. More so, the two airports were now controlled by men of The Sabre Brigade.

The immediate and critical concern of all objectives once taken was the establishment of your own defences to protect against counter-attack. When all the OPs had been re-established as well as machine gun posts, roving foot and vehicular patrols were dispatched with a most welcome helping hand from the current detachment of Belgian and Canadian UN peacekeepers. These troops had been sufficiently well informed in advance to lie low giving The Sabre Brigade the opportunity to make these raids work, which was testimony to their own intel and prior reconnaissance. Now, with the excitement of the battle fresh, the adrenalin had to subside into the aftermath of silence.

The next wave of landing cargo planes, with follow up TALO Battalions of the Brigade on board, were now landing and deplaning as quickly as possible. The planes were parking out on the perimeter of the airstrips, out of trouble and away from the incoming planes' turbulence. As their planes landed in Bosnia the most critical phase of the operation had technically started, being the deployment of the Brigade to the mountain roadways at the foot of Mt. Igman and Mt. Bjelasnica. They were also lucky, for they were now shrouded in by a slow enveloping fog. This would be the only phase of the operation when the entire Brigade moved or travelled with no covering fire available to them other than flanking scouts and pathfinders. They just had to have faith that the earlier raiding parties of pathfinders from the M&SW Coy were able to take out the Serbs' checkpoints.

Maj. Rance's large communications unit assortment meanwhile were already being established as was Col. Price's Intelligence OPS, along with elements of the Logistical Battalion now taking over the available hangars at the airport. Maj. Rance had his satellites up and monitoring for any possible Serb movement, while Maj. Biggle's Logistics teams started almost immediately the movement and storage of supplies.

On the tank decks of the Armour battalion soldiers busied themselves on their vehicles, checking and securing scrimm netting and external equipment mounting, as well as ensuring their machine guns were operable. The point of no return was reached when, under cover of the incoming fog and its biting cold, the Brigade was committed to its operation as, incredibly, Col. Price's shrill hunting horn could be heard for miles in the still crisp air as he signalled to the lead vehicle to start off. Thus, in the shadows of fog and haze The Sabre Brigade convoy roared their vehicles' engines into life and finally moved out and away from the confines and protection of Butmir Airport.

Their luck held well under the cover of the fog, for as they moved out they were not spotted or attacked by enemy fire at all. Either this or their recce scout and pathfinders were on a killing spree. If only their luck could hold out a little while longer, they thought. It was soon apparent just how fortunate the Brigade was, for after travelling fifteen kilometres and passing the smiling and waving hands and faces of their own successful raiding troops now seen manning the last of the checkpoints, the mist lifted like the blanket it was just as The Brigade reached the foot of Mt. Igman, undetected.

"This luck is part of it all Colonel," Gen. Logan said to a smiling Col. Lafluer. "This is also where you take over Marc, I'll be staying in the rear echelons. You have my call sign, call me whenever in doubt. We've gone over the plan, you know it as well as either myself or David. We're already into our battle drills, so take them across the line of departure and go, get the job done for us!"

"Yessir!" shouted Marc. "You can bet I'm not going to sit here waiting for any reply from the Serbs. When that expected bombing run commences from the NATO Allied command bombers in

Aviano I will split this grouping of Brigade Battalions, here between these two mountains, each taking their own path to victory I hope!"

"Me too," shouted Mac, "You're on your own, good hunting!" as then his driver turned round and he sped off in his armoured car to establish his own Command Station.

During this little lull and waiting for the rest of The Sabre Brigade to get into formation, Col. Lafluer then called up his first two Coys of the A&A Battalion, moving them up into a fire position as a precautionary measure. Six field batteries of 105mm guns now took up their positions. Being air portable, they could and would be air-lifted out by the big helicopters later when needed further up into the battle Col. Lafluer knew all too well from experience would commence. Soon also, the low level air attacks would begin and the Brigade's Battalions would advance into battle under its cover which would lead them to make contact with the enemy—which would start the battles! He gave out his orders for his Battalions to advance and at what speed, the scouts in their fast scimitars flanking and going earlier. So far all was good. He knew full well his radio operator would use the correct radio procedure.

As their columns moved 3rd Battalion Commander Major Stacey was thinking hopefully that members of M&SW Coy, C Troop, being led by Capt. Peltier, Sgt. Major Brassard and Sgt. Steele, were *already* in behind them from an earlier HALO jump and were at this minute operating in this back area between Trnovo and Mt. Bjelasnica creating havoc. They had to be, for in the distances they could all hear the cracks of rifle fire and mortar and it was lighting up the sky to the east. The M&SW Coy's role, besides harassment being one of them, was to continue reporting the Serbian strengths and troop movements if any, and passing this on to Intelligence to prevent undefended counter-attacks from them, hence their role was a vital and pivotal one in the final puzzle.

Over in that area of the firefight in the distance behind these two mountains, what was happening was a rear guard position of the elite Serbian Guard unit digging in its heels. It seemed a lone Ski Chalet which was in a crucial position overlooking an open alpine meadow was now a radio tower relay link that had to be eliminated, and fast. An assault needed to be mounted and the Ski Chalet taken. It was in progress now and the results of which the rest of the Brigade were hearing.

At that precise moment, there at the foot of Mt. Igman, enemy salvoes of gunfire rained down on the Brigade as the Serbs finally opened fire with their heavy armour of tanks and artillery. The Brigade's artillery returned with their own opening salvoes of fire as Battery Commanders gave orders to fire at will. This was their cover, as they then anxiously waited for the Allied NATO air assault bombing that should be coming on in haste now. No sooner had the first salvo of gunfire commenced and stopped when the first wave of bombers could be heard "on their way in"—thank God!

It had been a long advancement in convoy for the main body of the Brigade to reach the foot of Mt. Igman here. As dawn broke the massed planes for the air bombing assault was seen flying in overhead ready to do their damage. Just before evening had fallen hours earlier in the late grey hours, the NATO Allied pilots had left their bases over in Aviano and also from a Carrier in the Adriatic Sea. Now, these pilots, with a professional endurance only rivalling the crisis they faced, came whooshing in with their glorious roaring planes and attacked with a vengeance that was almost apocalyptic!

As planned they arrived on time with their attack then taking place early in the morning so their incoming planes would be difficult to see against the sunrise. Part of their mission in a previous flight was to take out the National Air Defence Radar System controlled by Serbia. It was assumed that at least one of the bombing runs would take out the radar target with precision "smart" bombs. There were indications that ground radar did indeed spot them on their run in, their detection equipment concluded that fact, but the enemy radar went out as quickly as it came on, a sign that part of their mission was a success anyway, as one of their targets had been de-activated permanently!

In each of the planes' bomb bays, their payloads were a good ton or so overweight, but what was even more dangerous was the fact they had to fly a long distance with them and no alternative airfield available for emergency landings. With little or no practice other than relying on skill and training, these bombing crews faced a mission that also required the delicate precision destruction of a target such as the satellite system. Each wave of bombers, while more manoeuvrable at their cruising height of 10,000 feet, had to drop way below that ceiling to attack their targets and so were vulnerable to retaliatory anti-aircraft fire.

Once in flight and past a certain distance, there was no question of any flight leader signalling instructions to his planes, as strict radio silence was to be observed. Closing in on their targets the planes descended to under 500' to reduce the risk of radar detection, skimming the terrain, which is a very skilful but dangerous practice. Fifty miles from target the planes rose again to a higher ceiling of 5,000 feet for their bombing run. Turning on a heading of 130 degrees, heading straight onto their designated targets, all planes began their run-ins and commenced the dropping of their bombs. They were a few miles away as their bombs flew on and as they pulled up and away, they tensely awaited the retaliatory Serb ground-to-air missiles to come streaking in. Fortunately for them few actually did, but they easily sorted these.

Back on the ground not too far ahead of the Brigade the ground shuddered suddenly as it erupted with earth flying in big chunks and mounds everywhere. The Serbs had quite a handful to contend with from the bombing runs—which was the plan! It was an intense event to observe firsthand though, something you just could never adjust to comfortably, only trust in your instincts and believe they knew where their targets were. With what looked like starbursts of bright orange and white, it was a spectacular array of noise and colour that seemed to light up the sky and air, like fireworks on the fourth of July, Hallowe'en or an English bonfire night.

"Give the signal at once for the two battle groups and their battalions to split now and move out fast!" bellowed Col. Lafluer, "Do not stop under any circumstances, then advise all to be ready to react to the enemy fire as we've instructed, now let's advance to contacts and up to our objectives!" he screamed to his radio operator who once more busied himself relaying those commands.

During the commencement of all the firing the Brigade's own artillery had also joined in as the air bombing runs began, giving their own covering shelling bombardment as their own Mechanized Infantry Battalions moved out in haste as required. They knew they would get subsequent waves of air attacks to cover their advancing Brigade now, but they also knew that they would be under repeated enemy Serb shelling themselves and open to exposure without them. So the Armour and Artillery Battalion knew they had a lot to contend with in-between the bombing runs.

The pilots themselves also expected ground-to-air missiles to be launched at the NATO planes more so at the start of the campaign and as the Brigade advanced and came closer to the Serbs. If hit, no pilot could ever be prepared for the devastating impact of a missile on his plane, and few would survive them! When they ran out of bombs, some of the brave ones in their planes often disregarded safety and used their guns to attack the Serb fire positions. Until this day, the Serbs had held a free reign in bullying the Bosnians with murderous brutality, now General Drago Blavic, and his prodigy, Aleksander 'The Gorilla' Marilla, would face the wrath and fury of an advancing army with all the vengeance and fury the free world could muster!

The unexpected suddenness of The Sabre Brigade's invasion and attack on all the strategic targets rendered initial reinforcements and supplies incapable of responding to either side even if they had wanted to. General Blavic's 1st, 2nd, 3rd, 4th & 5th Infantry Regiments and his 9th, 10th & 12th Motorized Armoured Brigades were on Mt. Igman, the 6th, 7th & 8th Infantry Regiments and 8th & 11th Armoured Brigades on Mt. Bjelasnica. Each also backed up by the 2 Artillery Group with 3 Marine Battalions where the main thrust of his might embedded there.

Total Serbian military personnel on the two mountains stood well over 80,000+ officers and men. The vast array of hardened combat veterans were under the direct command of General Blavic, giving him a notorious power, plus he was not lacking in combat experience himself. His 2nd Infantry on Mt. Igman was reinforced also with a battalion of the Special Serbian Guard Units as was the 7th Regiment on Mt. Bjelasnica. Air defence was also provided by surface-to-air missiles plus three well placed batteries of Oerlikon twin 35mm anti-aircraft guns, of which two were on Mt. Igman and one on Mt. Bjelasnica.

The precision bombing runs of the Allied pilots were more than incredible, they were spectacular. Their co-ordinates had to be spot on, for if not, they would have wiped out the entire Sabre Brigade. Advancing under this covering of fire is second only in fear possibly to advancing directly into enemy fire. Doing both took brave men, and that's what the Brigade was doing this day.

Col. Lafluer ordered the separation now as he splintered off his two Battle Groups. Maj. Stacey was now in charge of the second group leading the 3rd and 4th Battalions plus components of the A&A Battalion and the Engineers from the Logistical Battalion. Col. Lafluer watched them leave as they took the initiative and sped off in another direction heading around the foot of Mt.Igman in a seemingly cool attitude, quite amazing considering the circumstances. The Colonel continued to watch intently as they now headed straight for Mt.Bjelasnica. Meanwhile the main body of Col. Lafleur's own convoy was still being given covering fire from the air and would so right up to and including the final taking of Mt.Igman. There would be obvious breaks in the waves of planes coming in soon now therefore he called for the soldiers from his own group of the A&A Battalion with their M1 armoured tanks and more artillery to continue to stand in for them and not let up.

Now separated, Major Stacey's Battle Group was now moving along the lower mountain road to the east of Sarejevo before they could cut back and head up the mountain highway to Mt. Bjelasnica, still in formation and spread out at the respectable and safe fire distance, but keeping a reasonable pace going. He knew by the next bend they would be out of reach of the Serb fire for a short while at least, and he intended to use this as a final stop to gather and re-group. This was Maj. Stacey's final opportunity before heading into the breech, to get the remainder of whatever fire power he had remaining in the rear echelon, then move them up to the front of their convoy for when they were met with certain retaliatory Serbian fire and shelling.

As parts of the artillery battery that were with him readied themselves to dig in, in case of surprise enemy fire, most of the M1 tanks had by now moved up to the front to lead the battle group. He wanted their firepower right in front. Major Stacey gave the order for the flanking armoured scout and recce vehicles to start the advance slowly, to see if they could tease the Serbs into firing. In true military fashion, the whole battle group then slowly hurried close behind as they waited for the next wave of bombers so they could move forward under its cover, thus conserving as much as possible, their own firepower until absolutely necessary. You could have the best tactics in the world but if you arrived for the party with no ammunition, you'd be about as useful as a spare prick at a wedding, as the saying went!

"Major Stacey," shouted one of his Captains, "some of the wheeled vehicles are bogging down in this slippery mud area. Any ideas Sir?"

Thinking fast, Major Stacey replied, "Yes, get yourself some of the tracked vehicles like the M1 tanks or the APCs, then get in behind them and shove them out!"

"Will do Sir—on it right away!"

"Make it fast Captain, we have no idea when the next wave of covering fire is due in, if it comes any second, we've got to get in under them and hustle it out of here."

As the men were stood on their vehicles giving the drivers advice on where to place themselves and push, this little scenario played itself out wherever these vehicles found themselves bogged down. Major Stacey's little plan was working, the wheeled vehicles were one by one coming up and out of the great deep mud divots that the weather conditions had created. They knew at the very outset that it would be difficult going and a true test for the wheeled vehicles in this terrain, which was obviously much more suited to the tracked ones, but the brain trust knew that if they stuck to the plan and kept the wheeled vehicles for the most part on the mountain road itself, they would manage. Besides, they felt if the Serbs could drive their vehicles up these roads as they did, so could they!

They also had the chains ready for use when they reached the higher elevations if bad weather conditions such as snow arrived, so they felt at least as prepared for that drastic contingency—until then they would continue on and persevere.

Having finally cleared the traffic jam created by the mud, the tracked vehicles had returned to their own places in the battle group just in the nick of time. As up in the sky another advancing wave of planes came bearing down once more and banked and veered off to commence their bombing runs again. As the planes came in swift and sure to give them the covering fire they had been waiting for, the Serbs also opened fire.

"Slow down just a little up front but keep it steady, keep the momentum going," the Major threw out in command for his radio op to relay.

Back at Colonel Lafleur's location at the foot of Mt.Igman, under the raining bombardment of shell fire coming from the Serb positions located there, The Sabre Brigade's own artillery fire was slow and haphazard to reply. There seemed to be some difficulty in co-ordinating it, for he knew instinctively it was too sporadic.

Where in hell were the FOOs and their target info, he wondered?

He called for some immediate input here from the artillery officers. They understood and took the initiative and once arcs of fire were allocated a controlled fire discipline and target recognition improved. Along with the covering waves of allied air power their combined fire power was punishing, it played havoc with the Serbs.

Back at Butmir airport the Brigade's logistical stores area (BLSA) was now established by Maj. Biggle and partially set up. The Major's teams were responsible already for moving re-supplies out, as storesmen were readying fuel and ammunition to head out to the Brigade's fighting battalions.

During these early stages of fighting that had been going on for some time now, the Brigade's aviation wing of the Air Assault Battalion had its own helicopters joining in the battle fray as they too continued to mix it up searching out Serb recce patrols and fighting them just as fiercely. All this, as well as pilots starting to ferry in masses of ground assault infantry troops in the big transports. Their wing were also busy dropping off supplies, ammunition, and gas slung on strapped pallets under their fuselages. These early stages were always critical in establishing the logistical pipelines. During the next few hours of battle, stores continued to be loaded and transported at a much more considerable and constant risk from the Serb artillery while they were at their strongest.

Back on the far side of Mt.Bjelasnica another battle was busy raging underway as the starbursts and tracer fire they were watching let them all know. Their battle had been noted and observed long before the commencement of their own flares had signaled the start of the attack on Mt. Igman some time ago. Later, much later, this battle would come to be known as the battle for the Trnovo Ski Chalet. C and D troop of the M&SW Coy was to prove there that their own fighting skills and training were far more superior to the best the Serbs had to offer, in their own Special Guard.

C troop of M&SW Coy were inserted just a few hours before the main Battle Group of The Sabre Brigade even reached Mt. Igman—by parachuting HALO into action behind enemy lines! The whole of the M&SW Coy now operated in their beefed-up and established 8-man assault teams. After their insertion and landing at night with little injury, they then set off on foot in their scouting recce groups looking to find and meet up with D troop who had come in by stealth from another direction overland. C troop had been four hours into advanced patrolling when one of the teams point members raised his rifle and gave the ever familiar but silent signal, notifying that he had spotted the enemy Serbs entrenched and occupying a Ski Chalet.

They had yet to clear this area and join Maj. Stacey and his smaller battle group comprised mostly of the two Battalions, the 3rd and 4th down on Mt. Bjelasnica. Having also just united with those of D troop, Capt. Peltier knew from his previous O group and battle preparations that C and D troop would have to proceed into action without the main body of any battalion support if they decided to take on any Serb units—as in this one. From his own vantage point and their combined troops' continued observation, the two troop commanders of C and D troop, Capts. Peltier and Riley were now able to ascertain that they had approached not just a Ski-Chalet but an actual Serbian radio relay station that was quite heavily entrenched and armed.

As they awaited team and section commanders of both troops to get to them, the troop commanders thought of using their own radios and calling in an air strike on the place. Thinking better of it they realized that if it failed it would damage the radio tower which they could well use or might need for future use themselves. A big factor in their decision was that they were also concerned that a direct air strike would alert any other units of the enemy in the immediate area to their presence. They didn't need to invite more to greet them. Not a good option if you didn't know what strength or numbers were out there first. They realized they had their hands full here with this one alone, so Capt. Peltier and the big black Ex Recon Marine of D troop Capt. Riley made their command decision to take it on and see if they could overpower and grasp control of it.

When their section and weapons det commanders arrived they all moved up and huddled down to observe the station and simultaneously hash out a plan for all the sections, which topped up, totalled about thirty-six men of C troop with an attached twelve man weapons det, and the same for D troop. At that specific time the plan they all agreed through the universal "Chinese Parliament" was to go in boldly with the element of surprise on their side, taking the enemy out. They had correctly determined it was obviously too important a target to pass up. They fully intended going in at first light but due to delays in some of the other teams getting there, they considered waiting just a while longer. The weather was still a little fogged in and with a little luck, if it started to rise before their attack, they may have a better chance of success. At least the element of surprise was on their side.

There were patches of snow on the ground from previous falls but as it wasn't quite cold enough for a good snowfall at this elevation and the ground was not completely covered as yet. About a kilometre from the chalet itself, from cover of their OP, their troops set off, closing in on the enemy. They found the ground hard, being semi-frozen and crisp, and that concerned them for they would certainly make too much noise and give themselves away therefore deciding if they moved in wider arcs and took the pace a little slower, even though it left more opportunity for their sighting to happen, it would still be the wisest move. They tried to maintain a brisk speed and momentum whilst still vigilantly looking for suitable fire positions and areas of affordable protection and cover in case of enemy fire. Luckily, most of the M&SW Coy members were skilled snipers in their own rights and so having an eye for blending into the landscape was second nature. Their professionalism and training also came into play as they skilfully ensured visual contact was maintained, while at the same time keeping distance between themselves. Thus, moving like this over the rough terrain, like wolves stalking their prey, they came up and onto the Alpine Meadow of the ski chalet.

Capt. Peltier brought his own men of C troop all the way up to the very edge and limits of their enemy location, constantly using the designated hand signals like the expert infantryman that he was. He was now ready and in position to control the firefight itself. He knew the drill—bring as much effective fire power onto your enemy to destroy him where he was. He knew he and his section commanders now needed to give fire control orders. Position for fire was important as was also getting cover from your mate. Each section commander must use his power of command now and get the attention of his section to carry out his fire commands.

They all had their orders now. Most were hardened combat veterans like himself but he knew that never changed things, as sending them in and possibly some of them to their own deaths was always the hardest part, at least for himself.

When Capt. Riley and D troop was also in position, Capt. Peltier, who had taken overall command on seniority and mutual consent, signalled to his section commanders.

"Engage the enemy!" he firmly shouted out loud—and his

reply came instantly as the commanders under his direction now shouted out their own orders.

"1 Section, 300m, the ski chalet, rapid fire!"

"2 Section, 300m, one o'clock, far right of ski chalet, rapid fire!"

"Enemy, eleven o'clock, far left of ski chalet, rapid fire!"

"Ten o'clock, by the trees, when they're in sight, await my order, fire!"

The commands and voices of the section commanders were everywhere while the weapons det commander's voice could faintly be heard calling out directions to his men to take out the identified Serbian Guard machine gun trenches. A piercing shrill whistle blast was then sounded with the accompanying sharp commands of Capt. Peltier, as both could be heard over the battle din, instructing his section commanders where he wanted them to proceed to next. The troop commander's aim was to consider all variables, factors and routes open to them to engage the enemy, then plan and control their movement even as the battle progressed, simultaneously adjusting to all the little nuances and pace of its flow, in conjunction with directing its forward movement. This all had to be done and orchestrated while still moving as the firefight progressed, never losing the initiative, or at least trying not to.

These men, Platoon Commanders, led by example and it was their efforts that ensured success in such attacks as these. Because of their place at the front in the thick of it, they held the highest casualty rate of officers amongst soldiers in battle.

The Sabre Brigade troops from the M&SW C and D Coy were now into the approach stages of their assault on the Serb controlled Ski-Chalet and radio tower, looking to get within grenade range, but all the while trying to keep the beleaguered Serbs as suppressed as they could muster. Now, all the weeks and months of the Fire & Manoeuvre Exercises and training drills they had practiced were put into serious and deadly use. They would soon be advancing into CQB territory and needed to be sharper than ever for it. The radios in D Troop were calling for sustained fire support from Capt. Peltier's own HQ team to try and keep the enemy pinned down, as the resistance was quite fierce. Maintaining fire and movement was critical now before they went into the next transition of battle drill. So many variables, yet it was just as important to keep your balance at all times, or at least be in control of your movements. Losing your footing now out of panic or loss of control would cost valuable seconds which in turn could spell life or death.

Taking them in, D Troop's own commander Capt. Riley had fallen from a withering concentration of machine-gun fire onto his team's advance toward a Serb machine-gun nest. His 2IC had adjusted and taken over his role and command. Elsewhere, one of the section commanders was also down, with his team member 2IC picking up the slack. This is how they trained and practiced so no momentum was ever lost. The hardest part was always to keep moving, knowing men were down. But that was for the medics. You did what you could, then if successful, came back to help them.

They had achieved their objective up to this stage, which was getting within grenade range! Bayonets had also been fixed. Magazines changed. This was a Platoon Leader's worst nightmare, his men running out of ammo on an assault or having a stoppage. These drills to rectify them also had to be called out loud and cleared fast so as partners could stop and take cover. Men's lives hung in the balance and you were no good as back-up or cover if you could do neither!

*Again, all down to training! And you thought it was all
a pile of shit having the staff running you around on cold wet
mornings and dark shivering nights on bleak desolate places
like the Brecons. Where the landscape was brutal, the weather so
angry, cold and foul, you'd never believe you'd actual live to
fight a battle in it—in something like this. Practising the drills
so they were second nature, the magazine changes being watched
and encouraged and bollocked by the staff, over and over and
over . . .*

Fragmentary orders were given. Team fire and movement was restricted at this stage of the firefight but the section commanders called for some smoke to be laid out, hoping the men remembered their regrouping if necessary—which would be only due to casualties. So here it finally was, the last assault line in their dash to capture or destroy their enemy! The section commanders had brought their teams to the very edge now of the enemy's location without yet getting in amongst them. They were in grenade-throwing distance now for sure, yet as they waited to get the final call to come to them to go "up and over" the relative safety and cover of previous held trench or rock or mound and then get stuck in amongst them all. They realized and knew from experience it couldn't be too long of a wait. In the organized chaos of bullets and mud Capt. Peltier tried to shut out of his own mind the smells of blood and acrid smoke that filled his nostrils, just staying totally focused on trying to keep his sections calm.

*God, whoever wanted to be a Platoon Commander, did he
actually volunteer for this job way back when?*

He tried to stop his voice from wavering—*why is my mouth so dry?*—He managed—and kept—his own verbal commands clear and controlled as he moved the teams into the final deadly stages of this Battle Drill.

He still had four good team sections left. He ordered the commanders of each section to divide their men into two fire teams and two assault teams, ensuring the M16 riflemen were in the fire teams while the assault teams had the sub-machine guns.

"1 section takes out the left side and its flanks. 2 section takes out the right side and flanks. 3 section, on my command, goes straight down the middle. 4 section, split and sweep round deep under all possible cover, coming in behind but also watching for any counter measures. We don't know what lies behind, so no need for me to tell you all to be careful. If compromised and dispersed, double back and join the flanking side assaults. No more talking, let's just go do it!"

> *With bullets whistling past and smoke and thunder in the air, while diving for cover he hoped they remembered their named Grenadiers and Trenchmen? The rules ran through his mind now in surreal distraction to what his body was conditioned to do from years of training, but seemingly in beat with his consistent measured breathing. Maintain visual contact with your sections. Done! Use aimed shots to begin, but do not forget to double-tap, dash, bound, close, remembering to change and roll from fire positions. If not the enemy will surely have you sighted. Done! Do not bunch up, try to stay 5-10 metres apart. Done! Section commanders and 2ICs must continue to advance the men to win the firefight. They were doing it, they were doing okay! Surprise is our ally. Good luck men, take it to them and bring that efficient and effective firepower to bear on this enemy. Make him surrender or destroy him in place! With a united purpose, they were re-grouping as necessary he noticed, in his numbing, hypnotic combat mode. I'm in too deep now. We all are. No time to ask how they are all doing. He thought and prayed.—Hail Mary Full of Grace . . .*

In action, Sgt. Steele was also a deadly efficient and competent professional and veteran who realized part of the reason he was still alive right now was due to training and more training. This could be observed when he gave his mags no second glance or look, just a reassuring tug—and he knew where the next ones were too, fully loaded! He took his orders from Capt. Peltier and then went to work doing what he had trained and dedicated his whole life to doing, first as a Para, then in the SAS, now here with The Sabre Brigade. He had put his own machine guns and mortars out in place at 45 degree cross-over arcs fanning out. Then he breathed in deeply and awaited the signal from Capt. Peltier to attack. On the whistle, he shouted out his own commands—loud, clear and with purpose.

"1 section Alpha Red, 200 metres, centre-axis, left side of Ski-Chalet, enemy machine gun, rapid fire!"

Amid the noise and whistle of bullets and mortar fire, a distance away, his 2IC gave a similar order. "1 section Bravo Red, 200 metres, 10 o'clock, enemy dug in trenches, 3 section moving wide left rapidly, cover their advance, rapid fire!"

As the firing and shouting commenced on all fronts the battle was once again engaged with all urgency in and around them, as the enemy were starting to respond to this advance amongst their own lines now. Ignoring the customary pounding in his chest and thumping in his ears he had known to expect from experience in other battles, but nevertheless could never quite prepare for still, Sgt. Steele and his troopers advanced by bounding ahead and rolling away whilst coming up for rapid firing and double-tapping on those Serbs instantly sighted. Constantly looking ahead for the enemy, he continued urging and coaxing—commanding his men onward.

"Cpl. Ruez, 150 metres, slightly right, watch and shoot, possible sniper."

"Gaza, cover 'n' roll, bound 'n' roll, machine guns move up. Bluey, centre-axis, left side still, fire at will!"

"Riflemen, keep moving up, keep distance with me now lads."

"1 section Alpha Red, 3 section Oscar Charlie, over," crackled the radio.

The radio operator replied, "1 section send. Over."

"4 section left, are clear and on their way. Reign in 1 section Bravo Red. Over."

"Affirmative, 1 section Bravo Red reign in", went back the response.

After a few moments, Sgt. Steele's 2IC received the message back with an additional, "Be advised, low level wire obstacles at 9 and 10 o'clock, over."

"Understood, over."

"Oscar Charlie out."

From a 150 metres out Sgt. Steele knew instinctively that the next phase of the battle and fighting would either progress in advance from there or bog down. He didn't want the latter or a longer prolonged firefight. Besides, he knew they did not have the manpower for a prolonged confrontation. He knew the Captain was directing this well. They must keep the momentum and the element of surprise and movement going, never allowing the Serbs time to re-group themselves or organize. So he shouted, signalled, and even whistled his own next intentions and commands, he wanted no doubts or hesitation about moving forward. Most of the men here were Paras anyway, so moving forward wouldn't be a problem. Just like them, he knew from the start they only got the dirtiest jobs with overwhelming odds, which was why they were all here—they were the best!

"1 section spread out, machine guns run and find the high ground if you can, we're closing in fast and deep now, just keep going lads," he panted, "move and fire at will, use your grenades for trenches, partner up for trench clearing—as you know the drills!"

He turned to his radio op Cpl. Ruez, "Stay close if you can mate, when you can," then hollered, "keep at it lads, we got 'em flustered!"

When the next stage came he shouted, "Follow me!" Then he lurched quickly up from the ground bounding ahead, shooting instinctively from the hip now—knowing they would follow.

Somewhere from 75—100 metres out his perception and world around him changed as it also became a surreal action for him. It seemed to go into slow motion, a silent event playing itself out for him. Looking around and ahead he could see facial features now on the enemy. He seemed oblivious to the pandemonium all around, as his concentration and senses were in this heightened state. He fired instinctively with uncanny accuracy on his enemy, seeing the tug on their bodies as the bullets ripped into them, biting into flesh. He felt a tug on his own sleeve and wondered briefly, *was I hit?*

Fifty metres out and closing, the sounds and sensations, then finally the pounding noise of the battle reverberating in his head came flooding back to him like an explosion as they were closing fast onto the Serb position and were at the final approach stage now for sure! Meanwhile, the orders came out of him automatically.

Were the orders necessary now? he thought. *Yes,* he told himself, *they would be heard deep in the subconscious mind of the men, more over, they would be listening for them—his men would rely on their comfort.* He knew instinctively now, too, that he needed to quickly give his final customary frag orders for his section team, using the pneumonic code. He moved fast forward in his mind now to what he already knew out of training and drill—*fix bayonets!*

"Fix bayonets—if you haven't already done so!" he yelled.

He was sure they had fixed them all prior to the attack going in. *What about the ammo? Were they loaded and ready?*

"Check and change magazines!" he yelled out yet another order.

He prayed his men listened and had made a final mag check before this run in—

"Assault positions!" he shouted, "Let's go!"

Hell, they were charging . . .

Just before they made their final dash and went in amongst them, Sgt. Steele knew his section continued to fire at will to contain the enemy. He listened for the designated Grenadier and Trenchman combinations they were also told in advance to be called out, ready to team up. Reassuring words now! As the Grenadier shouted out, "Grenade," his fellow team members went to cover, needing no drill book or prompting on that one! On the initial grenade detonation his order went in repeatedly, "CHARGE." Assault troops dashed and ran the Serb enemy positions then, firing and rolling at will, support troops covered, then the trench clearing began.

The first Serb came up out of his trench as members of The Sabre Brigade ran his position. The shock on his face was one of, "Oh shit, is this the end?" Instantly he was jabbed at and stabbed with a bayonet, then a soldier shot him, sending him flying backward to crumble at the entrance. "Partner," the soldier yelled, as another rifleman appeared and took up position instantly to one side of him as he threw in his next grenade! The rifleman then also shot at this enemy as they came running out. As bayonets ensued when they finally ran out of ammo, the fury and savagery of these soldiers' survival instincts in hand-to-hand combat took over. Amid all the blood-curdling screams and guts strewn into the open, bullets zipped and zinged about amidst all the smoke as the scream-ing and gurgling of splinter of bone and flesh being ripped and torn, then stabbed at unmercifully, continued . . .

The weapons dets of machine guns and mortars had effec-tively taken out four of the enemy machine gun nests as well as the corner OPs while also keeping their enemies' heads down and con-tained when it was crucial by their accuracy and HE rounds. Throughout all this, Capt. Peltier became conscious of the fact that the firing seemed to only be coming from the relative safety (for now) of the Ski-Chalet itself. All his men had either taken to covering position or were herding and guarding prisoners from the trenches who were surrendering en masse!

For their part in the final assault the 2IC fired his signalflare and, led by Sgt. Prosky, three sections from D Troop charged in. The assault teams fired their anti-tank weapons directly at the building now—two each from either side and opened up, firing their machine guns. This was also the cue for the assault teams to fire their grenade launchers and open fire with their rifles. Their firepower was quite accurate and lethal for such a small force and they attacked, yelling and screaming in text book fashion, bound-ing and rolling and double-tapping.

The enemy did not immediately come out of the ski chalet and instead seemed to be prepared for something. As the men of 3 section continued their assault charging closer, the enemy Serbs opened fire with all they had. But the men of 3 section continued their vicious and deadly assault until eventually the Serbian Guards recklessly came out shooting and firing as they ran at them in one final act of desperation!

All in all, the pre-planned assault went down very quickly as it was a case of a steady controlled advance under fire and cover, this was constantly in progress on all sides, by all the men of C and D troop. They had carried out their battle drills expertly but one was still left. You could hardly focus for all the smoke and fog so the enemy were hard to see as the two troops sought them out. They swept round the building as it neared and soon it was over except for clearing the position.

The radio cackled out, "Alpha Red, this is Oscar Charlie, enemy are surrendering, I say again, I see a white flag of surrender at the Ski-Chalet, they are surrendering, do you copy, over?"

"Affirmative Oscar Charlie, enemy surrendering. Over."

"Alpha Red, keep to ground cover, any prisoners? Over."

"Yes, unsure on exact amount as of yet. Over."

"Alpha Red, move your prisoners to rear, maintain your ground, Oscar Charlie out."

With the above relay of messages, Sgt. Steele knew the same signal would be going out to those in the other troop but his mind switched that off for the moment as he had other concerns. He signalled his 2IC and advised him to take command of the prisoners with his team, then remove them to a rear LUP. The radio crackled with life once more, "Alpha Red, cover our advance, we're going to accept their surrender, over."

"Acknowledged, over."

"Oscar Charlie out."

This was the hardest part for Sgt. Steele and some of his men. For every young British soldier knew of the legends of the Paras in Falklands War, now enshrined in place in its own Regimental history. He knew they would never forget the treachery and cowardice of the Argentinians. While those same British Paras were taking their surrender in battle, the Argentinians had a sudden change-of-face and murderously opened fire on their approaching captors. This was a fact of war that sometimes sadly happened and was something they were warned about and would *all* ever more be ready for—treachery of the highest calibre! Fortunately for this enemy, there were no such dirty tricks today and the Ski-Chalet surrendered with no further loss of lives!

By this time a body count had been taken. 128 Serbian Guards were dead, 163 wounded and another 82 had surrendered under the veracity of the assault! Teams were quickly put in place to search the Serbs for ammo, maps or other intelligence.

Regarding the men of the M&SW Coy, sixteen were dead and eighteen in total were wounded. Four deaths were messy head wounds who died instantly, ten were in the chest while two in the stomach and leg. The section medic assisted Sgt. Major Brassard as Cpl. Jones assisted with the other injured in their Troop. Of the wounded, shrapnel had entered the chest and leg of two of the men from grenades while a 7.62 armour-piercing machine gun round had just entered the back fleshy part of the thigh of an-other. While the lower leg shot of the other was the worst, for the round had shattered bone, damaged an artery, and left it quite a mess, they were all in quite a bit of pain and morphine was admin-istered where possible to ease the suffering.

Capt. Peltier quietly made his reports on ammunition and casualties. All that remained of the battle drills now was the final consolidation & to regroup the men in their new sections and troop. As the 2IC went into redistributing weapons and ammo, the casualties of both forces were being cared for by the medics and prepared for future casevac. The sectional teams then and only then, began to get re-organized into a classic all-around perimeter defence! A hasty but solid defence put into place for any possible counter-attack. Section commanders were then tasked to go around confirming individual positions, particularly those of the section machine guns and their arcs of fire. Only after these were in place did Capt. Peltier consider a search objective of the Ski-Chalet and Radio Tower. He called up two of the British and French Para Engineers to check for booby-traps and explosive charges.

The damaged remains of the Serb Guard relay-radio station was quickly and efficiently cleared and the injured casualties were transferred to the ski chalet which they, the Commanders of C and D Troop, decided they would defend as a staging point and use as a base now. As there was no way of transferring the injured back to their old OP because there was no way of getting the casualties moved out without further injury, the helicopters were their only way out—whenever they could come.

The Serbian Guard commander was killed instantly by a grenade according to his 2IC who was among the Serb survivors and spoke English. He also was the soldier they found the plans for some of the mine fields in amongst his clothing. These were tremendous bonuses and could save many lives and precious time in the battle or battles that lay ahead. He himself had been convinced that it was a full Battalion of American or French Marines that had attacked them, so devastating was their assault. He was quite shocked—and dismayed not only to be beaten, but to find out and see the small amount of men of C and D Troop who had done it as opposed to the amount of men he had!

The real value of defeating the enemy Serbs here wasn't so much the capture of the radio-relay tower or Ski-Chalet itself as much as it was being able to establish a presence, a rear-guard to prevent the Serbs from now passing this way to counter-attack the two mountains further on—at least not without a fight! The gathering of information from the prisoners was seen as a bonus. With this new intelligence information of Serb strengths and formations passed on by Clansman radio-relay immediately, to their Intelligence Officer Col. Price, Capt. Peltier called for an O group.

Capt. Peltier, who had sustained an injury himself to his leg and knew he would only delay them if he remained with them in their role, elected to stay behind and remain here at the locale of the Ski-Chalet and turn it into a fire base as well as a care station for the injured. He could also supervise most of D Troop who, besides taking most casualties, were those remaining behind in defence and with the prisoners until the casevac helicopters and reinforcements arrived! Then and only then did he task his own 2IC, the big Canadian officer but one of his more senior and experienced Weapon Det Commanders, Lt. Grey, to move out and scout and recce onward to Mt. Bjelasnica with the remainder of C Troop . . .

PART 8

Back at Mt.Igman it was now late afternoon. Standing by his armoured Mobile Sultan Command vehicle taking cover, Colonel Lafluer clearly had his work cut out for him. Mounting an assault that was all uphill now, until reaching clearings at higher ground was, nevertheless, a dangerous strategy and battle plan!

They radioed their present situation and position back to General Logan as well as Col. Price, monitoring it on *all* fronts. Col. Price stood over his model and Tacmaps reading co-ordinates that had obsessed him since they set up HQ in the Butmir hangar. He found enough time to give the Colonel and General a brief idea of what had transpired over at Trnovo Ski-Chalet.

At Mount Igman the General's battle plan still being used was the Double Trident, and it called for a bold and daring attitude, as well as the heliborne and armoured infantry battalions to forge ahead in spear-like thrusts upward, then to mount a straightforward frontal attack on reaching more stable, flatter ground that the higher elevations afforded! He would not waste precious resources to diversify an elaborate attack either "pincering" east or west. The only real military sense was this carefully laid out plan for the full Trident assaults!

As men crowded and checked and re-checked weapons before battle awaiting the battle drill assaults themselves, they were digging in where they could, just in case. Then the cry came over the radios, "Another incoming wave!"

The next wave of bombers came in from the south behind them, making a direct run at Mt.Igman, and as the planes screamed past overhead, down "Bomb Alley" as the troops had named their route, the planes were easily intercepting the ground-to-air missiles with relative ease it seemed. Their bombs were hitting every target, targets that had been previously identified and their job was made that much easier. After these planes dropped their loads they changed direction and veered low across the mountainside, dodging radar, if indeed there was radar anymore.

In any event, they were ferocious, mind-jarring assaults! Most of the bombs were an effective way of keeping Serbian heads down as the Brigade advanced, under little retaliation, when these bombs were dropping! As much as the Serb armour were high priority targets, the main objective was to provide covering bombardments for a slowly advancing Brigade. So as the Brigade Battalions advanced once again, ready to fight in earnest, clearing dug-in armour escarpments or clearing trenches of enemy Serbs—even hand-to-hand combat if necessary—and in some instances, it was and would be necessary—they made their advance!

The most difficult part of the advance strategy for Colonel Lafluer getting his men *up* Mt.Igman, was that he was having difficulty getting his troops into the assault positions they needed to be in to advance into battle. These dilemmas were never seen back at OP's HQ and specifically at the United Nations. With ever increasing pressure they all just wanted results.

Again, back at OP's HQ, Colonel Price was tasking the Logistical Battalion to have the huge workhorse helicopters of the American CH-53E's and Chinooks to transport ammunition and supplies over to Major Stacey at Mt. Bjelasnica who was in fierce fighting and receiving a lot of resistance!

The Commander of the Logistical Battalion, Major Biggle, was having a difficult time himself at Butmir, getting all his supplies off-loaded from the massive transports and his men were facing fatigue. Getting back-up teams in was also difficult, if not impossible! Plus the high explosives were ordered into a distant safe area as the ammunition seemed to get shipped out as fast as it arrived! It became evident that the most difficult problem and dilemma they faced were the critical problems of the jerry-cans. It seemed that in this war, as in every other war or conflict, there was always a shortage of these items. It appeared that refuelling in peacetime never seemed a difficulty, although in reality almost every battalion needed refuelling *where* it was, even if that meant 3000 feet up the side of Mt. Igman bogged down in mud! Few vehicles enjoyed the luxury of refuelling *away* from the front lines!

Back at the rear echelons of Mt. Igman, the main dressing station and Field Ambulance for the injured and casualties of war was erected. This is where the surgical operations would be carried out. Chances of survival were high, for the medics and surgeons would work swiftly and tirelessly under the most dangerous conditions, plus the medical officers were experienced and knew about battle casualties.

Meanwhile, further up the mountain the real test was about to begin! The vast majority of the men of the Brigade were about to fight for their very lives against overwhelming odds. A savage confrontation was about to start in the aftermath of the bombing runs of the NATO air strikes. Under the Command of Colonel Lafluer, who was fast building a reputation as a Field Commander who wanted to lead from the front, he called Major Galloway to bring the mortars and anti-tank companies to the front lines.

Colonel Lafluer was constantly followed by his radio operators. Major Galloway, acting as Colonel Lafleur's 2IC in the field of Mt. Igman, duplicated the small command staff. With the main OPs and HQ back at Butmir Airport where the very capable Colonel Price and his staff could handle all administrative loads of the Brigade—even as he was tasked with co-ordinating Major Biggle's Logistical Battalion with ammunition re-supply and casualty evacuation.

As the situation changed slightly for Colonel Lafluer he used the plan options to improvise, but keeping the over-all plan intact. He quickly "re-orged" and restructured certain groups as events demanded. He formed an 'Intelligence Gathering Unit' through the makeshift formation of some of the scout and recce infantry patrol units, quickly renamed the Spearhead Patrol. This makeshift company was vehicle mounted on the tracked M2s as well as operating in foot patrols. All information gathered now would be relayed back to himself, then to General Logan and Colonel Price at OPs. This way they all got a "butcher's look" as the RSM would say, and info could be sorted and collated, with him deleting out what he felt unnecessary.

Also for passing and relaying orders to the Battalion and Company commanders, through down to the troops, they worked on the principle that was implemented and known by the Brits as Chinese Parliaments. His commanders and he would talk through with the rifle and support companies as well as artillery and armour and air support, any and all options in the way their attacks should be done. This way, every man had a chance to air his view or opinion, pointing out certain difficulties or alternative ways to go ahead into action. Eventually, after debating the issue and after the 'O' group was disbanded, there should be no surprises, or at least they would be kept to a minimum.

Late that afternoon the main thrust of the Brigade's Double Trident heading up Mt. Igman had advanced along the roads and through some fierce but sporadic fighting to the open meadows on the outer edge at the Olympic Ridge. With the helicopters now available to rush the infantry troops in, as well as the potential advancement of the mechanized troops, the spearhead patrol company were doing their job putting in a heavy volume of automatic and anti-tank fire from the perimeters. This was making the Serbs stationed and bunkered down there think that they were under attack from a far larger force, thus deterring them from any massive counter fire as they hunkered their heads down. The other spearhead patrols reported in from their recces about the flat Olympic Ridge area. Their radios were saying it looked like the Serbs possibly had multiple battalion strength in numbers and were dug in in massive strength. From the time these reports came in, unknown to them, General Drago Blavic had sent in an extra Regiment to boost the area by another 1200 men and artillery, as it was a key position and the Serbs could not afford to lose it.

Before Colonel Lafluer gave any more orders to advance the Brigade any further, he got a radio link into General Logan in the rear HQ and Colonel Price at the OPs centre. Colonel Price confirmed that he was signalled with reports from the helicoptor scouts confirming the enemy positions were mostly straight ahead at the north end of the Olympic Ridge, facing them directly, with their sides having an open view, so technically, they now dominated the area. The spearhead patrols themselves had come under some heavy enemy fire but were saved when the returning scout helicopters with their missiles and machine guns came in straffing the Serb enplacements.

With this news General Logan gave him the okay to continue the advance of the Brigade, as the plan was designed to be a constant movement. After a set time on the battle field, units would literally leapfrog, bringing in fresh troops for battle-weary ones, moving others to the rear of the line to catch their breath and regroup. It was a form of reinforcement, just a variation on a theme.

So as Colonel Lafluer ordered his radio operator to give the signals the big heavy A&A Battalion moved forward now for the first time to establish a fire base overlooking the enemy flanks. The first contact with the enemy Serbs came when one of Colonel Lafleur's Battalion Commanders let the green flare indicate that the Brigade would continue the advance. Again as a first in this battle, this time totally under their own covering fire, not waiting for the air-waves to arrive to help.

Shells from both the Sabre Brigade and Serbs rained back and forth under the onslaught. The Serbs began to withdraw and their artillery and heavy armour shells were becoming more sporadic. This was done not through superior firepower for they were outnumbered, but the Sabre Brigade did have better equipment and more consistent bombardments, which told of better trained and skilled soldiers. Ground infantry were pouring into the area from the heliborne assaults now. Soon, the Serbs' right, and weakest flank, was over-run. A little later on the left flank, three of their positions on higher ground were also over-run and taken!

Colonel Lafluer advanced with A Coy of the first MecBtn. They came under instant machine gun fire from enemy Serb positions up on the timberline that had not been reached yet. Infantry immediately fired from the fire ports in the sides of the M2s and destroyed or quieted their antagonists. Ground Infantry were now running everywhere being lead by Platoon Leaders and their 2IC's and section commanders, a battle that continued on like this throughout the day in perpetuity. The Platoon Leaders were the heaviest casualties, as were the Sgt.'s. They did what was expected of them—led from the front by example, encouraging and urging their younger charges into the hell of battle. There were many fallen heroes lying over every other jagged rock, twisted in some grotesque position. In this, the cruellest example of man's inhumanity to his fellow man, comrades wept silently inside in their advancement, recognizing this face or that, knowing they could not stop their momentum other than to lay their friends gently back to a former dignity that had been taken so insidiously. In this bloody manner the Sabre Brigade advanced.

They left the price on every inch of ground they covered so arduously upward on Mt. Igman. Like they intended, and to a man, they never once retreated. B and C troops from the ground assault infantry then gave them the covering fire needed to reach a small jutting ledge and small promontory. Others surged around and advanced that way! Using this as cover, Colonel Lafluer told his men to dig in tight as they came under some heavy shelling once more, radioing to the spearhead patrols on the flanks to bring in some mortar and artillery fire if they had it and were able.

RSM Whittle and his crew had been charged with the task of taking care and control of prisoners. The numbers were building up fast and furious causing them more than enough problems, not just for transfer to the rear out of the battlezone seeing they were now "non-combatants," but in the bodies needed to guard them once there.

With the advancing Battalions still getting heavily pinned down under machine gun fire, Colonel Lafluer with A Coy decided to surge out and came under some heavy fire directly in front of them himself. This time though he and his men began a process of systematically reducing and eliminating enemy positions on these higher elevations. They wanted and needed this Olympic Ridge to continue their assault. They kept a "chiselling effect" of battling away at enemy Serb positions until they just stopped firing back. The poor weather conditions creeping in were not helping their cause, it made spotting for artillery fire extremely difficult and the Serb artillery itself was once again falling short or over-firing them into rear areas, which was a blessing for those at the front.

His Btn Commanders had long ago ordered their troops to ensure their machine guns were sighted on interlocking arcs so as the advancing soldiers of the Brigade moved forward to engage the enemy, the Serbs alternately came under fire from one or the other, as it was important to keep the momentum of their advance.

Once in the open now, the men of the Brigade were very exposed and if they failed to reach the distant timberline by failing to move forward, they could suffer immense casualties and Colonel Lafluer did not want the advance to stutter and stumble at this very crucial point in the battle. So, in the face of intense machine gun fire, soldiers hugged the landscape for cover using every crag or gully to inch forward, firing constantly, trying desperately to take out the Serbs' positions who were grouped there and had them pinned down. Eventually though, after taking out all five remaining heavily defended Serb positions, the assault of the Brigade finally reached the higher ground that was the treeline.

Colonel Lafluer and his Btn Commanders had shown great leadership by leading from the front, to which their men all around responded, sharing the danger of death and risking the bullets or shells with them. Receiving reports from the skirmishing perimeter spearhead patrols now, whose FOOs also controlled the fire of the 105mm guns by radioing co-ordinates to the battalion battery commanders themselves, Colonel Lafluer realized quickly that the ground they had just taken on Olympic Ridge had to be dug in and defended in preparation of an imminent counter-attack. Thus moving up to the forward points of the battleground, he saw they still needed to advance *further* at this time. They needed to get into the treeline itself and then upward to guard their heavily won area of the battleground. It was an exposed position left alone so his intent was to put them out of range of enemy fire and to ease up the shelling on his men now, if possible, from any potential enemy artillery and mortar bombardments that may come. So as the day was fading, Sabre Brigade secured Olympic Ridge. The costs were high. Approximately 680 Serbs were dead and close to 2,000 prisoners had been taken, including some 800 wounded. This whole group were now siphoned back to the rear via RSM Whittle and crew to guard and monitor. The Sabre Brigade's casualties weren't quite as high but still no less disheartening. Some 150 men were dead and over 450 wounded.

Meanwhile, as the Brigade went about solidifying their defence of Olympic Ridge, they also moved the fire bases and adjusted them for the placement of the anti-tank missiles to a position closer to their flanks, near the mortar and SAW companies. The silently approaching re-inforcements and newly advancing remainder of the Brigade adopted positions on the ridge out of line of direct enemy fire with the A&A Btn artillery batteries also bringing up the 105mm guns. Colonel Lafleur's fears were that he realized all of the Olympic Ridge was vulnerable. He therefore commanded his 2IC in the battle for it, Maj. Galloway, who also held an exposed position on the outer edge of the mountain promontory toward the left flank to get additional cover for these exposed areas. As well, he gave out orders that the battle-weary men were to dig in once again. In doing so, he extracted himself and moved to a position on the forward edge to talk to his other battalion commanders and to observe.

While Colonel Lafluer was up front in another Chinese Parliament, as ordered, Maj. Galloway took control fortifying the weak outer flanks until they could afford a tighter and more balanced flow and arc of fire. On the most extreme outer edges of this ridge they now occupied, under the view of the treeline, the various troops and companies were readying in a "Forming up Point", a base for the next thrust of their assault. This battle procedure was also being duplicated in a few other locations too. Using ground-to-air radios they let the AirCavBtn know of their location, also advising OPS to pass it on to the soon-to-be arriving next wave of Allied bombers.

"On your maps gentlemen, you will see through these trees is a bridge. I want the spearhead roving patrols to continue on their success and circle round northwesterly, to group up and detach a troop to swoop down and siege this bridge under the devastating fire control of their counterparts!"

"And where are *we* supposed to be while they are seizing this bridge, Sir?" asked some Captain.

"*We* will be advancing through these very same woods of trees, ready to sprint across that bridge and establish our foothold and defence for those who will follow!"

"Little risky, don't you think Sir?"

"This whole operation is risky, but we have no choice men, we have to keep advancing, enough to drive the Serbs off and away, or to kill or capture them all, either way, we have to keep moving forward!"

"Well I haven't heard a better plan and everything's gone well for us so far, so I guess that means we're all in Colonel," said the grinning Captain.

"Just remember to pass on to your men that once over that bridge there's going to be the same pattern and advance bombing waves coming in as cover once more! We've advanced under its umbrella before so we know what to expect, as long as we stay under it we'll be safe, if we stray more than 200 metres either way, or even forward, we're probably cooked, it's pretty dangerous ground out there!"

"Now what's the good news, Sir?" said some joker.

The Col. grinned, "The good news soldier is that you're not out there on the perimeters with the roving spearhead patrols. Plus, I do believe we're slowly winning this battle!"

"How much further Sir?" someone else asked.

"When we get there, you'll be the first I let know soldier," grinning, "Are there any more questions, everyone clear on what they have to do?"

On receiving no reply, the Col. said, "Alright, let's get it done!"

With that command the Battalion Commanders moved off to their separate units again.

Zooming down "Bomb Alley" once more came the jet planes. It was also a signal that brought sighs for the tired and weary soldiers to pick themselves up with urgency, to once again advance under its umbrella of cover. As the Brigade started to advance once more, perimeter spearhead patrols circled wide but dangerously out into the open bombing zones looking for a way to attack the bridge from higher ground. They found their target sitting in a clearing. The Serbs held positions at either end so using their anti-tank weapons and supported and relying on substantial fire from their own SAW teams, their attack went in. Their superior firepower as well as aggressive assault soon destroyed the Serb positions and bunkers which collapsed under the pressure of their sustained assault. They were left with quite a few more prisoners whom all they could do for now was to disarm them and put a watch on them under armed guard. In this way they were herded until they could have others take them off their hands and pass them through channels onto RSM Whittle's crew, whose team's duty was controlling them through a systematic order of permanent search, disarmament and possible Intelligence gathering.

The battalions of men arrived and poured across the bridge like a column of soldier ants and fanned out. Across the clearing they soon noticed fenced-off areas with the remnants of unused mine packing cases and associated equipment. This created a lot of sudden anxiety from the commanders and troops but they had to count on their luck, for they had gotten this far without coming across such an obstacle and all knew that it was bound to be seen sooner or later, all hoping for the later!

Into the radio General Logan yelled, "You have what—a minefield?"

Then holding the mouthpiece away he swore and said again, "No, stay put, I'll get you some Engineers up there immediately!"

While Col. Lafluer was cursing the delay, without his knowing, matters were taken out of his hands, as up at the fence to the minefield some soldiers began following the fence line looking for the corner. Others climbed over the fence and took out their bayonets and used them as mine prodders, digging into the hard ground at angles, just as the engineers had taught them, and would themselves anyway if they were here!

Meanwhile further on up the far side of the bridge, Brigade spearhead patrols saw an exposed area on the right side which had once been the ski slope's housings. They also noticed it was guarded and manned by Serbs with others arriving. Shooting then commenced simultaneously on both sides. There were many casualties before a direct hit from one of the mortars hit the building and knocked it out.

Elsewhere, sections of the main body of the attack that had broken off and followed the minefield fencing, met up with remnants of a much depleted spearhead patrol. Together, they found the corner of the minefield. While the main body of this combined mini force set up a fire team to guard its borders and besides forwarding their info on the radio, a runner was dispatched with haste to the main body of men further back to advise their commanders they had the corner of the minefield now. It would probably be an accessible route to follow, and quicker, as opposed to the logic of trying to breech and traverse the minefield itself.

When the news came back Colonel Lafluer decided that both routes should be followed. Crossing the minefield definitely would give them an element of surprise, but before that could be achieved, a path through the minefield still needed to be breached completely by the Engineers. The trouble with minefields was that a lot of surface personnel mines were usually found and cleared, but the difficult ones were the deep laid mines that were usually ploughed in deep, like anti-tank mines! Ones that the pressure of heavy armour or tracked vehicles travelling over would explode through their extra heavy weight. These were the mines that needed the professional skills of the Engineers to locate and disarm, then remove or detonate. The minefield clearance was also an opportunity to re-org once more, to use that lull in the fighting to evacuate casualties and prisoners and to bring forward badly needed ammo supplies from stores.

On the Serb side, they had just moved their 35mm and 20mm gun emplacements further down the mountain in hopes of being closer and ensuring they reached the ridge.

Colonel Lafluer suggested to his small but effective 'O' group that radio operators try to establish a link to contact General Blavic to allow future negotiations. This was tried, but word soon came from the Serbs that General Blavic would be pleased to accept a surrender delegation from the Brigade. *The nerve of that cheeky bastard*, thought Lefleur. The Colonel advised his radio operator in no uncertain terms to advise the Serbs and General Blavic personally, that he only had two clear choices. The first was complete surrender himself. The second was to accept the consequences of a crushing military defeat from a vastly superior force!

General Logan himself was pleased with the Brigade's progress. After conferring with Colonel Lafluer how things looked from that end, he checked with Colonel Price for his sit-rep and overall slant on things. He decided they needed the bombing raids to continue, to wear the Serbs down, advising Colonel Price to put the call through to the NATO Command in Aviano. So, more bombing runs from waves of war planes commenced, followed by artillery salvoes, and continuing on into the early evening. Noting that the Brigade *didn't* have the surrender of the Serbs *yet*, their only alternative was to stay the course and to continue the advance to overthrow the Serbs and capture Mt. Igman and eventually linking up with Major Lafluer on its sister mountain, Mt. Bjelasnica. Artillery 105mm guns were being flown *up* to Olympic Ridge under the fuselages of the huge workhorse helicopters along with badly needed ammunition and other supplies like food and gas. As the men merged into the darkening light of what remained of the day, they looked for covering ground to occupy in case they had to stand their ground and fight. They created makeshift bunkers purely as cover before moving and using trenches previously occupied by the enemy Serbs not hours ago which were cleared by the Milan "bunker busters" quite effectively. The fighting spearhead patrols had been doing Trojan work throughout this assault. Their scouting recce patrols could always be heard firing on the enemy, sometimes sporadically, but hopefully dampening Serb morale and mobility. Colonel Lafluer was reluctant now to ease the thrusts of their Double Trident attack just yet, allowing General Blavic valuable time to regroup, as he had done not hours earlier that day. Now he did not want to allow him that second chance to get or move more reinforcements onto the mountain before his final surge of assault.

Colonel Lafluer could not and did not know that General Blavic now had neither the men nor the determination to continue this fight with the Brigade. He was vastly out of his league, all his previous battles had been mainly against a civilian population or paramilitaries, not elite combat veterans like the Brigade!

Colonel Lafluer meanwhile called for more reinforcements for the Brigade up to Olympic Ridge. His intentions being, to get as many men as he possibly could into position for their final assault. He knew the planes would be coming now, as he also called for his own helicoptor support on the ground-to-air radios, urging them to transport the troops. Using their night flying aids, the helicoptor pilots conducted their hazardous operations of transferring men of the Brigade as the pilots were able to hug the contours of Mt.Igman pretty low, even though they were filled beyond capacity. The men, having been re-supplied with extra ammunition, 81mm mortars, and other supplies, jumped down out onto the wide ridges of Olympic Ridge. Their LZ not only screened their cover but assisted in holding down the drone of the helicopters themselves.

In the distance, the men of the Brigade on Mt.Igman could see the red lines of tracer arching and ricocheting into the distant fading darkness, followed by the familiar thud and thump of mortar and grenades. For those watching, it was a startling array of lights, this major firefight in progress that they were witnessing. It was being played out under their very eyes, up on Mt.Bjelasnica. It was truly a spectacular sight!

On Mt. Igman troops of the Brigade continued to alight from the helicopters as badly needed reinforcements, soon disappearing into the trenches and behind clumps of grass and rock, anywhere that provided cover. They continued to come and spread out and along the ridge.

Colonel Lafleur's Command vehicle HQ was close to the helicoptor LZ, under cover of the ridge promontory. He himself was getting ready for his final 'O' group, discussing his plans for this next, and hopefully, final surge of the Brigade's assault. He saw Maj. Galloway moving up Olympic Ridge under the cover route to attend his meeting, picking his spots on his way up the steep slope of the area too, moving between cover from trenches and rocks. He arrived for the 'O' group and, with the other company commanders, settled in place forming a tight circle of camouflaged men around their Field Commander, all their faces being set and determined.

"Pretty soon," said the Colonel, "we'll be breaking out, making the final assault to the top to overwhelm the Serbs. That's the good news, the bad news is that Allied Air Command are actually closed in by the weather now so we'll have to provide cover for ourselves. Major Galloway, did you get every available 105mm up here as ordered?"

"Yessir."

"Good, make sure all webbing is worn battle-ready. Have the men now leave their packs in the rear echelon here. Where we're going, they'll just require ammunition and battle dressing and plenty of it!"

"The intensity of the Serb bombardments seems to be easing Sir."

"Yes, maybe they're low on ammunition, if they are, it's going to be our lucky day, for when we get around or through that minefield our infantry will be following the M1 tanks and M2 tracked fighting APCs into an all-out assault."

"How far do we advance Sir?"

"From this assault, all the way relentlessly, no stopping 'til we take it. This is what we've been advancing slowly and building up to, we charge those Serbs with every means available to us until we've taken this mountaintop away from them! Remember to give your machine-gunners as much clear view as cover, if you feel they are compromised, bring them in running, we can't afford to loose them, as if we do, we make it that much harder on ourselves. Go through the proper preparations and battle drills, have magazines full and handy and have the men fix bayonets if they haven't already, it's going to be close-in and hand-to-hand up there at some time in their future. Any questions?"

A young platoon commander called Grafton asked, "Sir, if I place my machine-gunners wide out on the flanks, what about cross-over fire from the other platoons?"

"You may live through this yet soldier," said Col. Lafluer, "As long as you stay to your grid and the other platoon sticks to theirs, your trajectories will 'arc-out' and miss each other, okay?"

"Yessir."

"Any more questions?" And with none forthcoming he continued on, "Okay, you've all done infantry school, you've all practiced this before 'til you can do it in your sleep like clockwork, now put that knowledge into practice, as your men's lives depend on your leadership here today. I know you're all weary, but it's basic stuff you can forget, especially when tired. It takes guts and leadership to lead men into an attack and even their possible deaths, and these men have had a long few days so you have to find a way to get them to continue on for just a little while longer. Clue in your 2ICs and NCOs in case you go down. Remember, once it's on, there's no pulling back under any circumstances, understood?"

Glancing at their vibrant, alive faces, he realized this was the highest honour his men would ever afford him, to put their lives in his hands and allow him to lead them, it was an awesome trust and he was proud of these men.

Returning to their own Btns and Coys, commanders passed hushed orders down the rank and file line, advising sections to group their packs and equipment they were leaving behind, ready and lighter to charge the enemy. Ensuring each and every man's webbing was secure and ammunition and magazine clips were available, they took advantage of their new-found lightness, as these soldiers of the Brigade set off to form up in another Readying Point. The route was poorly marked but aided by sentries, they gathered and found their way through pure instinct. A tacmap would have been of little use to them on this mountainside, especially in this night!

Shortly, word came down over the radios, "Sun Ray, this is Delta Bravo over."

"Sun Ray, go ahead over!"

"It's done, the big bad minefield now has a path through it wide enough to walk my momma through, over!"

"Well done! over."

"Thank you Sir, Delta Bravo out."

At zero hour, the tanks and M2s led off with columns of infantry spread out behind them. The final push was on as the initiative to take and dominate Mt. Igman. The complete capture of the summit itself and nothing less, was the objective and final phase in the overall plan to capture Mt. Igman. Their attack went in with night falling and the weather closing in. The Brigade had to move as expediently as possible for the plan to succeed. Also, the relief was there for everyone when that final order did come down to move, as just standing around waiting under the heavy shelling, was more than enough for fraying nerves.

Their approach to final assault to capture or destroy the enemy took them initially on a northeasterly route to by-pass obstacles. The decision for the main body to go through the minefield instead of around it in the westerly route, was so as not to slow down the route of advance or pass on its element of surprise. The final summit of higher ground was *not* a given! It was clear from the tacmaps and prior intelligence that it was heavily defended by more than three complete Regiments the Serbs had left. They were even reinforced by artillery and armour, plus specialists and snipers from the Serb Guard. Those Serbian snipers could use their Russian image-intensifying night sights just as effectively as the troops of the Brigade.

The feature itself, the summit of Mt. Igman, no longer had the minefield as a weapon, with it being nullified. But the system of bunkers and sangers (trenches) that the enemy Serbs had established from their previous war before the cease-fire, had never been filled. They were now being put to good effect on the final narrow, then wide, edges of this craggy part of the mountain. The Serbs, besides the heavy armour and artillery, supported their position with heavy machine guns and recoilless guns and anti-tank missiles, with each position a defensive firing one, and they expected these Serbs to be prepared to fight hard or long to defend it.

Mt. Igman's summit dictated that it had to be won or taken head on to the north of their own position. With the minefield in the way (even though a path had been cleared, the rest of it was still considered "live") the paths around the two ends, east and west, were known to have enemy positions facing them, but there was no other option besides having the spearhead patrols take them out. This was planned, as they just had to go for it, right through them and the area, to be able to accomplish that feat.

Colonel Lafluer knew that taking the summit of Mt.Igman itself would be witness to some of the most fierce and ferocious battles so far, yet he tried to keep his mind clear and focused on his duty and sense of purpose for what task lay ahead of him and the Brigade. He knew Mt.Igman's immediate summit dominated the open ground around it for hundreds of metres, making even night movement with only the light of the moon hazardous. In addition, the flanking perimeter spearhead patrols were now certain that they had recce'd and identified any and all areas that might hold or contain anti-personnel mines.

Under another O group Colonel Lafluer, with his commanders, now went over the devised "mini" version of the final Double Trident Attack. He knew from Intel that there were five principle defended positions on the summit. These were previously given code names for each individual Btn to decide which company would attack first and which would skirmish. Assigning the two positions to the east, Blue 4 and Blue 5, then assigning the two positions to the west, Green 2 and Green 3, lastly assigning the central position directly due north of them, Red 1. The attack start line which also served as the rear field HQ and report area was directly *behind* the path and route of Red 1. The plan was not complicated, instead, being deliberately kept simple and flexible.

With some Coys held in reserve they began moving along in their mini Trident along their independent routes, with the beefed-up spearhead patrol troops also acting as guides and FOOs. When it began they were to close in onto their objectives, nothing less than the summit of Mt. Igman!

The heavy supporting fire from the Aviano Bombers came screaming in for the final time in one last and final wave. This wave was making their run down "Bomb Alley" and coming out low, with additional fire then as before, coming from the Brigade's own artillery and armour kicking in, only after this final wave had passed over.

The SAW machine guns of the perimeter spearhead patrol troops were devastating, especially in tandem, and this was used throughout the battle with deadly effect, getting help from the mortar platoons and the .50 cal machine guns. The anti-tank teams were doing their stuff, the milan experts clearing bunkers once again, too. The primary role of reserve troops involved here was to move them forward as other troops established key fire bases as well as all around defences on the contours of the ledges, usually by bringing in (once established) more heavy machine guns. Once the summit had been secured it was intended to pass through it and meet up with the rest of the main Brigade on Mt.Bjelasnica to join up the once-heavily defended Serb mountains and in the process, finally free Sarajevo!

The move out from the start line was going well until Green 2 and 3 had to alter their approach up the mountain when a new path of anti-personnel mines was discovered and at about this same time one of the support companies lost contact for a while, causing some further confusion. Included, the added brightness of the moon caused a lot more concern and anxiety, although when flares went up, they anticipated that it would only help their situation and cause. For now, if they kept down low, it was a minor hitch! Platoon Leaders ordered their troops to keep closer to the rocks, keeping it easily available as cover for the thrust and fight as they moved ahead. At the height of their progress, well after clearing the minefield, the attack formations were grouped and moved slightly, adjusting for visual necessity, once better cover and the rocky ground formations were reached.

Now the main branch of their Double Trident, Red 1, was advancing under the volleys of their own artillery, sighted for by their spearhead patrol FOOs. The gunnery officer's commands were shouted loud and clear.

"Batteries 1, 3, 5, open fire! Continue at will."

Similar commands were repeated throughout the artillery. They could be no more than 500-600 metres away from the main groupings of Serb enemy, or more than 1,000 from the overall summit of Mt. Igman.

Men in the advancing flanking battalions were getting injured intermittently now from stepping on scattered anti-personnel mines that had been missed by the scouts. As grenades were now being thrown in their direction and mortars and rifle fire began in earnest, the final stages of battle went in hard and fast.

Serbs opened fire with all they had it seemed, and the result was men were scattered and getting killed or injured, due mostly to the urgency to go in, and thus, leaving what little cover they had behind. Blue 4 and 5 and Green 2 and 3 on the flanks were taking some fierce pounding but in the determined, constant onward movement, they started to lob grenades back themselves, forming up into pre-selected fire teams as they reached the enemy bunkers and ran through.

The Brigade was coming under some accurate rifle fire from Serb snipers as well as the Serb array of automatic fire, mostly AK47s. The Brigade were suffering their own casualties! The Coy Commander of Green 2 had his radio operator asking if he could re-organize and assist to his wounded. The answer was simple, leave them!—and continue on with his assault and move forward to cover Green 3, letting the trailing medics assist his men. It seemed a cruel order, but other men's lives were also at stake.

To the direct north and summit Red 1 was having their own

difficulty for one of its Coys had started to stray and overlap to mingle with Blue 4, causing delays in orders and operational direction. In their advance up to the summit, they themselves were coming under direct and heavy fire from some heavier machine gun emplacements that were difficult to place and were well fortified. These were eventually taken out by the accurate anti-tank platoons, enabling some teams of SAWs to push for the higher ground further up the rock face, but not before they incurred many casualties. As they went to ground but then managed to get in place, more automatic fire and tracer was pouring into their area from further east along the ridge. This resulted in some heroics from the riflemen taking the offending gun out, as well as offering superb, concentrated covering fire. During these urgent mad dashes from the infantrymen it was just about down to its lowest denominator of every man for himself. Soldiers were firing instinctively now, engaging their own targets, not waiting for the next order.

On a plateau close to the actual summit where rocks jutted out proudly, Red 1 was under direct fire from the eastern edges which, in the initial bursts of fire, one of its Btn. Commanders working in C Coy was shot fatally in the chest. His 2IC and signaller kept doing their job, as did all the Coy fire groups, as this and similar scenarios played themselves out. The Serb weapon that brought him down, with one other machine gun, seemed to be sited in a substantial sanger complex and was well protected. It was charged by some platoon leader and some brave men were accurately sighted and killed. While the gun emplacement was not taken out of action on the initial charge, it *was* compromised. A second assault and charge on this emplacement managed to neutralize it. As in other instances, it was then quickly turned into a defensive position, beefed up with Brigade marksmen, a 105mm gun, as well as a heavy machine gun.

Since the Brigade artillery guns and heavy armour had been laid on selected targets throughout the action, firing onto enemy positions was sometimes as close as fifty metres from their own men. Perimeter spearhead patrols also doubling as FOOs along fire lines all around sometimes came under point blank fire from the enemy themselves. SAW teams moved in as quickly as possible to cover the Brigades every advance and to establish covering fire bases. These patrols also advanced ahead and when they were needed, the FOOs gave the coordinates to call down the artillery fire.

Against a radiant sky, battle progressed all through the night. Everywhere it seemed, enemy Serbs were crawling from foxholes or trenches and as they emerged from them, they were piling up their rifles and surrendering en masse. The Brigade got a real surprise for many of these men were from the Serbian Guard Regiment of the JNA which had arrived specifically as reinforcements. As morning arrived, prisoners were formed up and formally counted, there had to be somewhere between 25,000 and 30,000 men. This was a hugely massive logistical problem for RSM Whittle who, by using his initiative, had already contacted some of the reserve personnel to come and take them off their hands.

The final assault ended as the men of the brigade with fixed bayonets charged through the enemy ranks with blood-curdling screaming as they proceeded to clear final trenches or bunkers with a brutal savagery of cold steel and bullets. This soon cracked the nerve and resolve of the Serbian garrison, or what was left who had not fled or deserted Mt. Igman. After a battle action lasting nearly twenty-four hours, eventually the mountain of Mt. Igman was fully taken and controlled by the Brigade!

With the coming of the pale light of dawn, these men of the Sabre Brigade's Double Trident assault had regrouped on Mt. Igman. It was now slowly getting enveloped with a light mist on its summit as Sgt. Major Gunny Ridgeway and some of his men, Iwo Jima style, proudly erected their Brigade flag on its highest point! The price of victory was extremely high. 548 men of the Brigade killed and some 2,073 wounded. The Serb casualties had been even higher, estimated at over 4,900 dead with a casualty count not yet identified, but expected to be in the thousands.

With the big guns silenced and the prisoners transferred through RSM Whittle's prisoner crews back to the rear, Colonel Lafluer did not waste any more time. He ordered his officers in for another O group, including getting the RSM in on it and to substitute one of his Warrant Officers into his present duties. Maj. Galloway was put in charge of matters there at Mt. Igman. Maj. Buxton-Smith on the ground-to-air radio was asked to bring in the big transport helicopters. He asked for the helicopters to start immediately to transfer and start ferrying himself, RSM Whittle, and his relatively fresh reserve troops over to Mt. Bjelasnica.

"Thank you Sir!" said the RSM, "I thought for a moment there I was going to be deprived of all of the action."

"You did a remarkable job RSM. In fact I don't believe any other could have managed it, so don't go under-estimating your contribution just yet."

"Thank you Sir, but I think you know what I mean!"

"I know exactly what you mean RSM, but I assure you, if there's any action left to be had on Mt.Bjelasnica, I'll make sure you are allowed into the fray, is that clear?"

"Thank you again Sir," smiled a contented RSM.

PART 9

That previous day and night other battles had raged as the battle for Mt. Igman was well under way. Over on the other side of it a little to the right, those battles were namely for the Ski-Chalet as well as Mt.Bjelasnica. The battle for Mt.Bjelasnica itself started almost immediately for the Brigade's soldiers sent to recapture it, for when they separated from the main force battling for Mt. Igman along their advance towards the mountain, Major Stacey's 3rd and 4th Btn's being heavily supported, received heavy resistance from outward pockets of entrenched Serb armour posted along the planned route. It required precision firing from the Brigade's heavy armour of M1 tanks and artillery to neutralize this resistance initially, with the similarly-tasked outward patrols of M2 Bradley fighting vehicles and foot soldiers skirmishing and grappling for those positions. Eventually, the superior and more reliable equipment as well as better trained soldiers won the day for the men of his Btn. All the look-out points and observation points along this route were well fought for and there were casualties from both sides.

Finally, as they neared their objective, a rear echelon station of report area as well as combined HQ (Ops) was established as close as possible to Mt.Bjelasnica as they dared it to be. It was to be their staging point of final advance onto the mountain as well as their radio station link to General Logan and Colonel Price at their HQs, not to mention it being designated a field medical station and prisoner holding area.

Sgt. Major Norbert was the man in charge of siphoning and channelling the injured and wounded, as well as prisoners out of the battle zones. It was not an enviable task, but in battle it took someone with great interpersonal skills and communication abilities to control such monumental logistical nightmares. The difficulty factor involved in such a venture was only appreciated by the most professional of soldiers, namely those who understood and had previous battle experience. Not unlike the RSM, Sgt. Major

Norbert had similar battle experiences in this area and the two of them had devised a tentative plan that they both anticipated being able to implement without hindering the advance or momentum of the battle. Something that could easily occur without professional soldiers to control.

Major Stacey wanted a section of Combat Signallers to start establishing a radio relay from the roadside OPs back toward Mt.Igman, with a section of patrolling spearhead patrols themselves as cover against Serb stragglers or Serb ambushes. He considered it essential and practical to start it immediately, giving his orders explicitly, with no area for debate. As to the looming advance upon Mt. Bjelasnica itself, the Major called his Chinese Parliament together at HQ and they set about the debate of their attack, keeping in mind General Logan's Double Trident.

Each and every officer was made clear his command responsibilities and allowed his input, while he constantly stressed to them that they were only as strong as their weakest link so clear heads had to prevail. In the heat of battle he knew from personal experience that the adrenalin rush was high. He kept pounding his facts home, also reminding them that they had their radios and radio operators and not to be shy of using them. It was their only way of monitoring the battle and getting back-up or help to any specific unit that had come up against heavy odds or a difficult part of the terrain.

The FOOs were given a special debriefing all of their own by elements of the A&A Btn and anti-tank and missile officers. It was critical that they had the right equipment in operating order for calling in covering and advancing fire on the enemy, especially if or when the Allied air bombing cover ended. So after as much deliberation as they could afford to muster under the circumstances, the Chinese Parliament was called to an end.

"Gentlemen, if you haven't already, please synchronize your watches to 1000hrs. In exactly five minutes we are scheduled to receive our first covering air fire from the Allied planes which will also be our signal to advance. In addition, I have it on good authority that the noise and bombing you may have already heard coming in the background from a distance are the jets that are flying over Mt.Igman itself. Their battle is already under way gentlemen, so let's now do our part and do our duty. Remember, we're advancing as close as 400 metres behind the bombing and be sure we keep to our Double Trident, are we *all* clear on that?"

Their goal and objective was simple and the same as their sister Btn's on Mt. Igman, to defeat the Serb enemy, remove them from Mt. Bjelasnica, and in that process ultimately free and liberate a city called Sarajevo. As the first Allied planes came screaming in overhead, officers and men of the beefed up 3rd and 4th Btns also advanced in Double Trident formation.

The air was thick with smoke and the acrid aftertaste of cordite, but the thundering gut-wrenching pounding and shaking of the ground, reminiscent of an 8pt earthquake on the Richter scale, was disturbing and took great fortitude and resolve to ignore. Then it happened seemingly all at once as the Serbian big guns themselves as well as heavy and light machine guns and anti-tank weaponry began firing back at the advancing Brigade and the men now knew like never before that the battle was finally on.

The bursts of flame and fire and exploding shells seemed to be everywhere for a moment. It appeared almost overwhelming, but just as suddenly as the Serbs had opened fire when the covering waves of the Allied bombers had passed over and finished their first runs, the tanks and heavy armour of the Brigade took over.

As this battle was commenced and evolving in place, flanking advance troops of roving scout and recce patrols backed by M2s and M16 carrying infantry, plus double SAW teams went into action, taking beads and sighting in on enemy bunkers and OPs.

Unlike Mt.Igman, Mt.Bjelasnica had a little higher elevation but less direct height to its ultimate summit, as it afforded a more open undulating terrain making it more difficult to move under concealment. Their similarities were that they did have a timberline as well as craggy overhangs that gave ultimate concealment and protection from their Serb enemy. As well, there were many more, but they would need to capture those first.

This particular battle for Mt. Bjelasnica continued on for some hours, with men advancing to the enemy Serb positions under constant fire. They took out strategic bunkers or OPs with their anti-tank missile launchers as well as knocking out certain armoured placements. Once they were overrun, secured, and established by Platoon Leaders and their rushing infantry, their own reserve fire teams and artillery were placed there if they found them suitable to their own cause.

White phosphorous, smoke, and the illumination of the flares and tracer could now be seen in the waning light as one big giant fireworks display. Even those men of the Brigade similarly occupied on Mt.Igman wondered, for brief moments, how their comrades were faring.

By 1800hrs that day, their forceful Double Trident assault had managed to take two thirds of Mt.Bjelasnica, but their main centre thrust point here, as opposed to the flanks on Mt. Igman, were receiving the heaviest resistance as well as casualties. Again, it was mostly the Platoon Leaders and NCOs leading from the front who were going down. It was leaving them a little strained in the command positions which could cause potential future problems in the way of leadership, but section NCOs were picking up the slack admirably.

Advancing troops from Capt. Peltier's M&SW Coy were also now skirmishing fiercely in their advance toward Mt.Bjelasnica, a direction that led them away from the Ski-Chalet where Capt.

Peltier was now staying with a rear guard and the rest of the wounded as well as prisoners from their earlier assault.

Lt. Grey was leading the spearhead patrol when it came under heavy fire. In the ensuing firefight he was seriously hit. With disregard for personal safety, to protect his men and taking into account that his wounds were mortal, he charged the enemy machine gun placement that had seriously held them pinned down for so long. In his attack he was shot and knocked down a total of four times as his personal "one man charge" went in!

It was an act of exceptional bravery that would be evident only after all the fighting was over. After the difficult machine gun firepoint was knocked out and scared Serb prisoners were taken, the extent of Lt. Grey's action and ultimate sacrifice and bravery was realised.

The captured Serbian Guard Officer admitted after capture it was a most courageous act of unselfish sacrifice. Sgt. Steele and his comrades tried to attend the wounds of the dying Lt. but were unsuccessful. His final act before dying in their arms was to remove a piece of his epaulet insignia and offer it to Sgt. Steele, saying between his contorted effort to smile and coughing up mouthfuls of blood, "This is a field commission Ben—now you have no choice Lt. Steele—you're an Officer now—lead these men onward to Mt. Bjelasnica!" Then he fell back, never to move again.

*****

Later when this was all over, Lt. Grey would be awarded the highest American Military honour, the Medal of Honour, for his action. He was the first foreign Officer or enlisted man ever to be so honoured. In fact, it was decided that besides a special campaign medal issued by the UN, any other medals issued for the battle Campaign or for bravery would be strictly American.

*****

Meanwhile, back at the action on their quest to take Mt. Bjelasnica, newly promoted Lt. Steele was a little shocked at just how unexpectedly he had risen through the ranks. The other patrols by now had closed in and joined them. As he explained it, Sgt. Major Brassard said quietly and kindly, "He made a wise decision mon ami, now lead myself and these men forward toward Mt. Bjelasnica and into battle with our comrades!"

Adjusting his new insignia, field-promoted Lt. Steele looked at the surrounding men and said softly, "Okay then, Sgt. Major, you take your section out toward the right flank. Sgt. McKay, take your section out to the left flank. The rest of you follow up in my rear and all of you, make sure that your radio operators are in frequency so I can monitor our advance, any questions?"

With confident faces they all replied in unison, "No sir!"

"Alright, you all know your positions, let's take them and head on out of here so we can meet up on Mt. Bjelasnica, heh?"

"That's the way mon ami," said Sgt. Major Brassard.

A few kilometres onward but nearer their destination, they came to a juncture in their route that caused them fits. There in front of their path was a chasm, very deep and at least ten to fifteen metres across, with no possibility of negotiating around.

"How in God's name are we going to get across that, we never bargained for this, I can't even find it on the bloody map?"

"It doesn't matter, all we need to know is it's here now and we need to cross. I'm not quite sure but I think I might have an idea," said the newly promoted Lt.

"Don't be shy then mon ami, share it with us."

"Okay, I was thinking that maybe, just maybe, we could use those ropes and cast them over to the other side so they take anchor, then one of us could crawl across the rope with some other ropes, then secure them. We could form a rope bridge so we can 'walk' across, then relay everyone's backpacks over. How does it sound?"

"That's a pretty scary prospect mon ami," said the Sgt. Major,

"Who in this company here with us has any mountaineering experience as such to do this?"

"There's a few of us left, besides, I wouldn't ask any man to do what I wouldn't do myself!"

"You're seriously not thinking of doing this yourself are you?" asked the Sgt. Major.

"As a matter of fact yes! Look, I've done a lot of mountaineering in the Alps and around the U.K. I'm the most experienced, so I'm going across Marcel!"

"I don't think so Ben!"

"I'm a higher rank than you now remember? It's settled, I'm going across."

The other troops were called and were now gathering after coming in from their outward flanking positions. Lt. Steele took off his field pack and equipment to lighten his load, then went looking for the biggest and strongest man in the unit who went by the nickname of Tiny.

"Well Tiny, do you have that rope and grappling hook, 'cos we need you to throw it across and secure it for us, think you can do it?"

"Do we have any other choice, Ben?"

"Not really mate."

"Okay, then I'll get it done!" he grinned.

He put his M16 aside, took his pack off, and picking up his ropes, went over to the chasm. The men moved aside to give him room after he chose his spot. Tiny hung the end of the rope with the grappling hook to his side and began swinging it gently in an arc, to and fro. It started getting longer and going in a circle as he let the rope slowly out of his hands. As he did this, he allowed the circle to get bigger and bigger until the point when he threw the rope with the grappling hook out across the chasm.

It took him a good fifteen minutes and about three to five throws before it finally reached across, grasped and took hold of something. Pulling back the slack as other men came forward to help tighten and tie it off to anchor it, Tiny grinned, "Well Sir, I just did my part, now the rest's up to you!"

Getting up onto the rope on the dry land section with the men holding onto him in case the rope gave way and couldn't hold his weight, Ben lay his body lengthwise and snaked his leg around the rope and practised pulling himself along. Satisfied that it would hold his entire body weight, he smiled and slid off it long enough to attach a rope to himself in case he fell. As well, he would be carrying two other ropes that would reel out behind him as he made his way across to make the three rope bridge when he reached the other side. The two extra ropes were not light and with the safety rope anchored to him, he was quite laden down with equipment. His movement along the rope was by a motion of coiling a leg around the rope and pulling with his hands while his free leg also pushed. It was an excruciatingly slow process to watch, fraught with severe danger, as the further out he went the more the rope sagged and swung about. On one hair-raising occasion he came completely off, hanging by the sheer strength of his hands. He was able to agilely swing his body back up onto the rope and once more move, but not before composing himself in balance there.

When this happened you saw the tension on their silent faces as the entire troop held their breath until he came back up onto the rope. They wanted to shout or encourage but the Sgt. Major was already on top of it, hushing them but also not wanting Ben to lose his concentration. Later, when he finally pulled his exhausted body up and onto the ledge on the other side, while he was sucking in the biting cold air trying to get his breath back, he turned to see about two-dozen faces giving him the thumbs up sign. When his energy had returned, he quickly set about anchoring the rope he had crossed more securely around the rocks. He did likewise with the two other ropes in a fashion that left the one rope lower, while the two others were a little higher, like arm holds. This was your basic rope bridge and under the circumstances, it would have to do.

To show his confidence in his new Lt., the Sgt. Major picked up his weapon and began the wobbly "walk" across their bridge. Once on the other side all the men now felt secure in its safety and did not hesitate to follow suit. The final four men left behind began quickly belaying across the backpacks of the men in the troop, then came over themselves. With all the men safely on the other side, these men would now follow Lt. Steele into hell after what they had just observed and experienced. They were professional soldiers and did not need much encouragement getting back into the mind-set that they were now heading into an ongoing war zone. Once again getting their orders from the Lt. and Sgt. Major, they began assuming their previous patrol positions as they led out on their march to join up with the forces fighting on Mt.Bjelasnica.

On the mountain, as the battle for control of Mt. Bjelasnica progressed, Maj. Stacey received a signal from the radio op that an advancing patrol from the M&SW Coy that had dropped behind enemy lines the previous night was now advancing toward their right flank—and was being led by a Lt. Steele.

Grabbing the microphone headset, the Maj. spoke quickly, "This is Oscar Charlie, identify yourself immediately, over!"

"Oscar Charlie, this is Alpha one. Lt. Steele here. I'm in charge now. I received a battle commission from Lt. Grey. I'm afraid he is dead Sir. Also, Captain Peltier is back at the ski-chalet wounded, over."

"How many men are you commanding, over?"

"42 over."

"How far away are you exactly from our right flank, over?"

"I would have to say no more than 5 clicks now, over."

"That's excellent, can you continue your advance onto our right flank directly ahead of you, then assist our depleted spearhead patrols that have been skirmishing and clearing the way for us there, over?"

"Yes Sir, over."

"Excellent, then do that soldier, over."

"Sir, one more thing, over," said Lt. Steele into the radio headset. "Sir, this field commission, do you want me to keep it, or relinquish it now, over?"

The Maj. replied honestly, "Listen to me Ben, I have a serious shortage of Officers right now. I am not about to argue with the wisdom of a dying Officer. You hang onto it for now and lead those men as bravely as your predecessor did. There'll be plenty of time later for the Phoenix himself to decide if you should keep it, over!"

"Yessir, over."

"Lt.Steele, one more thing, Sgt.Major Brassard, is he okay and with you?"

"Affirmative, over."

"Good, can you spare him because when you get close enough I would like you to advise him to make his way down to my position, we could desperately use his skills here, over."

"I'll so advise him Sir, over."

"That is all. Good luck, Oscar Charlie out."

Relieved at the prospect of gaining the Sgt. Major, Maj. Stacey turned to his radio operator with new vigour now and said, "Chinese Parliament, at OPs now!"

As the Officers gathered around him the Major advised them of Lt. Steele's position which brought a few raised eyebrows but no regrets, as they all to a man, had the utmost respect for the previous Sgt.

"Captain, what's our Sit-Rep now?" the Maj. asked.

"Well Major, we have taken some losses rather heavily on the eastern flank to our left, but are presently in a lull in the fighting. It seems that overall we're getting bogged down and not making much headway in the way of advance!"

"Do you hear that men?" thundered the Maj. for the very first time, "Are we going to wait here for those gallant men fighting over on Mt. Igman to come on over and save our asses or are we going to suck it up and make our move?"

"We're with you all the way Major, just tell us what you want."

"Well, first I want the artillery brought up to our forward lines here, the Allied air bombings have long ago stopped, we know most of it was scheduled for Mt. Igman but that's no excuse, we have some special heavy armour and artillery here that is more than adequate to cover."

"Do you want us to do a full frontal assault now then Sir?"

"That is precisely what I want!"

These assembled officers of the supported 3rd and 4th Btns attuned their combined thinking to their current field battle tactics. They agreed that to continue the Double Trident they could not let up once it started again.

"I want my left flank code-named red spear 1, 2 and 3, and my right flank code-named blue spear 1, 2 and 3 to bring in their roving perimeter patrols into a tighter arc. I want to advance with as much visible firepower as possible, under cover of the armour and artillery batteries we bring forward, as well as more of our anti-tank platoons. Let your FOOs know that we will be coming in very tight under our own artillery cover. Also, be sure to let the

ground-to-air radio operator teams know to coordinate and monitor the advancing helicoptor troop movement drops with our infantry. I also want every promontory, ledge or overhang, anything
that can afford our men adequate cover from enemy fire, targeted
and taken out first.

"I will be controlling our advance along with the M1 tanks
and armour as before, which is right down the middle gentlemen.
We will be identified by the code-name of White Spear One. If I
go down, Oscar Minor you take over and lead the attack in my
place. I also just received word awhile back from the Phoenix that
Colonel Lafluer has solidified his position and that Mt. Igman has
been taken and secured!" He let the loud and raucous cheers of his
men ring out, hoping this victory would give them incentive to
push ahead with their own assault.

"By the way, the Phoenix has moved up there and the Colonel
with the RSM along with the reserve forces, are heading our way
to assist in the completion of our operation. Let's not disappoint
them by lagging behind, let's give them a battle they can be proud
of, men!"

Before he dispersed the small OPs group and Chinese Parliament, Maj. Stacey as the commander of this part of the Brigade,
reminded them once more that Lt. Steele's men were advancing
rapidly, still behind enemy lines, but would link up to their right
flank, so urged them to be on the look-out.

Giving his men enough necessary time to return to their units
and pass on their respective orders, he soon came over the radio
and announced to Btn Cmdrs that they were to advance. His radio
operator then screamed down the microphone some words in
French, something about a bloody Legionnaire Officer's hand! He
told himself to inquire and find out about that one later!

The artillery thundered once more and the men of the Brigade once again advanced into battle up the side of this still Serb-
held and fortressed mountainside. Then the battle raged on in
controlled deliberate determination.

The road to Mt.Bjelasnica was a long curving S-bend along the ridgetops, but more importantly, it was clear of obstacles. Major Stacey had thought ahead when he had initially left for it, for he had even posted sentries along the route to direct the remainder of the Brigade when they would be able to follow up and assist. It was good foresight, for even though this battle had been raging for hours, the road side direction and check points and friendly patrols helped them travel much faster.

It was still raging when the Col., RSM and relief troops arrived to assist with the fighting. The transport helicopters were arriving with the fresh troops as reinforcements and it wasn't long after they had landed that they were put into the thick of things. The RSM was instantly in his glory it seemed, taking advantage of this final opportunity to get into the fight which was a far cry from his previous duty. He naturally and immediately assumed a leadership role, urging the men on and screaming at the top of his lungs as only he could, "Up an' at 'em, the wankers, kill the bloody bastards!"

Some called the RSM a foolhardy and brave bastard for allowing himself to be seen so openly, but call him what you like, his efforts were having the desired effect on the men's morale. They all found solace, comfort and inspiration in this big looming figure, urging them on shouting out his epithets like he did. Just as he did on the bayonet drills back in Montana where he would shout, "That's it laddie, give 'em the cold steel, they don't like it up 'em, they don't!" A standing joke from a good British comedy, but it had its desired effect.

The Colonel and Major could only look at each other and shake their heads in smiles and wonder at the big heart and bravery of this man. His presence was having a contagious effect all around and they were beginning to rise to the occasion and were now charging the enemy with zest! It was noted by the RSM that it was hard (especially in the cold with all the heavy clothing) to bayonet a man through the body—so he passed instructions—

over his hand-held command radio, that all close in hand-to-hand combat and bayonet charges be aimed at their heads!

The battle held its own momentum, reaching a point where the advance was moving at a rapid pace and the effect of the Brigade's onslaught of taking out the Serb firing positions and heavy armour was demoralizing the enemy as they could be seen rapidly retreating, as they scurried out of their bunkers and high-tailed it for the rear echelons—maybe Serbia itself.

By this time, the newly promoted Lt. Steele had already made contact with the Brigade's flanking roving patrols and had the foresight to combine his patrols with theirs, yet continue on to the assault itself, giving the advancing men of the Brigade as much of a fighting chance for survival as possible, as the goal of all, besides winning this battle, was to do so with as little bloodshed and casualties as possible!

The advance of the tracked LAVs and APCs and tanks were especially eerie sights in the night's stark artillery illuminations. The armour and artillery were doing their stuff, as brilliant flashes of light and tracer lit up the sky in a buzzsaw effect. Big and black, the heavy tracked vehicles came forward coughing and rumbling their powerful engines. Tracks churning up soft bracken while effortlessly tearing great chunks of divot and dirt clods and moss, spewing and spitting it out like ocean spray at the sides of a battleship. Plunging and rocking ahead, these awesome brute machines had a grinding momentum that was a desperate yet disciplined venture toward the enemy.

As the fighting continued into the early hours, dawn's blanket settled, while the weary and battle-fatigued men of the Brigade had now managed to pass through the timberline and were in sight of the higher knoll of the summit of Mt. Bjelasnica.

The final charge was a blood-curdling mixture of screaming from assorted accents, letting the enemy know that they still had enough fight left in them to win this thing. It seemed to work, for it broke the back of the Serbian Guard resolve and they were in total disarray as they came out of reinforced sangers, bunkers, and foxholes, laying down their weapons in piles and surrendering to the UN Sabre Brigade, as only sporadic rattle of gunfire stung the air now . . .

THE AFTERMATH

As the smoke cleared and subdued voices made various comments, the most vocal soldiers were those in the command of Sgt. Major McKay, as they did quick body searches and then funnelled the captured Serbs as well as the injured in an orderly flow back to the rear holding, medical and OPs area, but a lot further down the mountainside now.

The RSM spotted Lt. Steele holding a bloody wrist and walked over to him with some concern, his sub-machine gun at the ready.

"Are you okay there me 'ol son?" he asked worriedly.

"Seems like I got myself a flesh wound RSM."

"Does it look bad, have you seen a medic?"

"I will RSM, but it seems it went straight through without hitting any bone!"

"You just get that seen to, you don't need it getting infected, okay?"

"I will do RSM."

"Now, what's this I 've been 'earing about you getting a field commission?"

"It's the truth, Lt. Grey did it, just before he died!"

"Lots of live witnesses still, I hope?"

"What, you're going to let them make this stand and lose a perfectly good Sgt.?"

Then uncharacteristically for the RSM, he let his guard down just a little and said, "You bet I am you bloody marvelous wanker, now please let me be the first to salute you, *Sir*!" then rocked back on his heels saying, "Serves you bloody right you plonker!"

Grinning from ear to ear Lt. Steele said, "Don't worry RSM, I doubt that the Phoenix will let me keep it for too long."

Seriously now he said, "I wouldn't bet on that me 'ole son, seems he already mentioned that you were being considered for a commission anyway. You keep the rank Ben, besides, I'm sure it will make things all right again with that girl of yours."

"You have a point there RSM, but the thought of going to Sandhurst scares the bloody shit right out of me, worse than this battle we just fought!"

Laughing, the RSM answered, "You know Ben, there may just be hope for you yet, keep them thoughts son, they keep you honest. Now, go get yourself over to a medic, that's an order!"

"Yessir!" laughed Ben.

"Lt. Steele?" shouted out the Colonel.

"You want me Sir?"

"Yes, I got a report of what Lt. Grey did. Just wanted to let you know that under the circumstances it's appropriate for an officer to do that in battle, especially if he deems it necessary to the situation. Also I'm not about to overturn the wishes of a dead officer either, so keep the insignia Lt., as far as I'm concerned, the promotion stands!"

Then he shook his hand saying, "By the way, well done, that was a helluva job you and your men pulled off. First the Ski-Chalet, then getting to here. And oh, we dispatched a couple of troop helicopters there with reinforcements a long time back while you were making your way here, also bringing out the wounded and prisoners."

"That's good news Colonel."

Before he let him go he added, "I want you to know that Sgt. Major Brassard has given me his account already of your bravery in action. When this is all over for us and hopefully handed over to the UN and we return to Montana, there'll be at least one medal coming your way, well done soldier!"

Smiling now, Lt. Steele said, "Only if you give that heroic

bastard, the RSM, one. He seems to think he's bloody well John Wayne!"

Laughing with him now, he said, "Couldn't agree more!"

"What's wrong with your wrist?" as he spotted the Lt.'s wound for the first time.

"I'll be okay Sir, the RSM has already ordered me to see a medic!"

"Well, just make sure you get yourself seen pronto. I'll be expecting a debriefing from you soon as you're able. Carry on!"

Lt. Steele slowly began moving about the mountainside checking on the consolidation of fire positions. As he moved around from one spot to another checking on the battle-weary troops, he spotted the Sgt. Major.

"Hello mon ami," the Sgt. Major said as he approached him.

"Hello Marcel, I just wanted to let you know I had a very enlightening little chat with our Colonel, seems you've been talking out of class again?"

"You are probably wondering about my little recommendation, heh?" grinning.

"That's an understatement, but thanks Marcel and by the way, don't think I will be forgetting your massive part in all of this, trust me, even the Phoenix is going to know!"

"You would do this to me?"

"I think you deserve it! In fact, I am also going to recommend that *you* get promoted for your leadership skills you have shown throughout all of this too!"

"Sacre Bleu," was all he could say, then they both laughed together, some in emotional relief of the hardships they had endured together these past few days. Then, it was the Sgt.Major's turn to spot the blood seeping out of his tunic sleeve and running down his hand.

"Have you had that seen to yet?"

"On my way Sgt. Major!" he said flinching.

"Don't let me hold you up, get going there soldier!"

"Yessir!" he said once again out of order but out of respect and friendship.

During the next few days signallers from the Support Coys had relay signal lines up and established. Bunkers were reinforced with their own reliable artillery, only it looked out away from Sarajevo this time, as it was there to protect it! In addition, from Mt.Bjelasnica onward, the route was being heavily defended now, just in case the Serbs ever did get foolish and decide on a counter-attack, you never could tell with them.

It was decided by the United Nations that all the unused Serb equipment, artillery and heavy machine guns be left in place for the use of the Bosnian Army. Their own would also be left for incoming American peacekeepers that were being brought in, the Brigade would pick up new replacement supplies immediately once they were back in Montana.

General Logan, the Phoenix, as Commander of this task force of the Sabre Brigade, had now based himself back at the main HQ out at Butmir airport along with Colonel Price. They both had an awful lot of logistical matters to contend with still, plus a lot of UN and NATO brass to mollify and pamper. Colonel Lafluer and Major Galloway were still in command out at Mt.Igman, while Major Stacey was left in command out at Mt.Bjelasnica and the Ski-Chalet. They were busy establishing their positions still and deploying and keeping their troops busy rebuilding, hoping to keep their minds off things. Back at Butmir HQ, the Phoenix and Colonel Price were anxiously awaiting the arrival of General Clarke himself, along with his British and French counterparts, who wanted to see firsthand the results of their favourite sons.

As he disembarked from the 767 that had just landed at the International Airport, General Clarke walked over to his waiting subordinate Officers with a huge smug grin plastered all over his face with his first words being, "Every paper in the free world has headlines about the heroes of the United Nations Sabre Brigade—

and the press corps are going to have a field day trying to get to you guys for every last bit of information we're willing to let them have. This is going to be another Gulf War mediafest."

"You're all conquering heroes now Mac, what do you think about that?"

He was grabbing their hands and pumping them up and down in warm friendly handshakes, pointing at the masses of the press coming down the ramps and the remainder of his entourage, including the British and French contingent. Smiling and saying their welcomes, General Logan and Colonel Price could also see what and who was arriving. Wanting to steer well clear of the press, at least until they had managed to give their superiors their own quick and skimpy debriefing, General Logan was the one who said, "Why don't you inform your counterparts where we will all meet later, then let's get the hell away from here, heh General?"

"Good idea son, just allow me a few moments."

Lt. Jane Crenshaw, as a member of the Intelligence Corps assigned to her father's staff, was totally exhausted from the previous few days of late nights, as well as the fact that she was totally distressed with worry and anxiety over the safety of Ben. She had absolutely no knowledge at this present time as to his whereabouts or whether he had come through this safely or not. She only knew that he had jumped HALO behind enemy lines *before* the main battles had started and was also aware that there had been quite a lot of casualties. As she now sat on the edge of her bed in her downtown Sarajevo hotel room and eased the shoes off her tired feet, she couldn't shake the feeling of fear and anxiety that she was feeling for her man. The knot of tightness in her stomach turned to nausea as she ran for the bathroom.

Later, much later, as she lay back on her bed she looked up nonchalantly at the ceiling and tried desperately to search her mind for happier memories of him, wanting desperately to keep his memory and soul very much intact and alive! It seemed to do the trick and have the desired effect, but in the privacy her hotel room provided her, she allowed her defenses to come down and afforded herself the luxury of crying to release her tension and fears as the tears flowed freely down her pale cheeks.

A few hours later she was once again back in her usual role of British Army Intelligence Officer in complete control as she was at her father's side with two other members of his ministry staff. She excused herself long enough to approach a member of the Sabre Brigade's administrative staff at HQ to ask him for a favour. She asked him to go through the list of those still alive and give her a reply as to whether or not that also included a Sgt. Steele.

Besides having his ego stroked at the thought of being asked as well as wanting to please a beautiful lady, he said he would see what he could come up with and get back to her as soon as he could. Well, that was it she thought, all I really can do now is sit back and wait and hurry up and get on with things as is British Army custom (hurry up and wait!).

A day or so later after getting a brief respite, Jane set out in search of the administrative Officer she had seen a few days earlier. Seeing him busy over by a desk with some other obvious men of his Sabre Brigade, she approached once more.

"Hello there Captain, it's me again, were you able to find out any information at all for me on a Sgt. Steele as I asked?"

Looking at her awkwardly, the Captain hesitated and looking around the room said, "As a matter of fact Lieutenant, I checked with post battle statistics that keep track of the dead, wounded and living—and to date, there has been no reported living member by the name and rank of a Sgt. Steele." Stunned and shocked, Jane staggered backward a little and leant against a filing cabinet to steady herself.

"Are you all right there Lieutenant, I do hope this Sergeant is not a relative or something, I'd hate to be the bearer of bad news?"

"Actually, he is someone special, someone I know, but it's not your fault, just took me by surprise," she answered, bowing her head and trying desperately to remain calm. She was feeling a little light-headed and the room was moving on her. Inside, she was in knots as her mind was racing for another question to ask to remain calm.

"Do you think there could have been some mix-up or that all your data is not quite yet in from the field?"

"Unfortunately Lieutenant this information is confidential as you know, but I did double check for you 'just in case'—and I have it on good authority that this list is accurate and up to date!"

Leaning back again but slowly raising her head, Jane asked desperately, "Did it confirm his death then Captain, do your records confirm that?"

The Capt. looked on with a little sadness for her obvious state of distress, saying gently, "I did look into that for you, just in case, I'm sorry . . . " and during the next few seconds of awkward silence for her that seemed like an eternity, the Capt. replied, "He was not on our list of dead, so I'll presume there is a chance he could still be out there as an MIA."

Sagging under the relief, she felt the room go dizzy now, then collapsed at the feet of the Captain. When she came to, she was aware that men were standing over her looking on. Through the initial blur she made out the concerned face of her worried-looking father who looked very anxious.

"Thank you all, I'm quite all right now," she lied, adding, "I would also be grateful if you allowed myself a little privacy with my father, the General?"

"Not at all, sure!" the men and officers mumbled as they moved away.

As she lay there regaining her composure, her father looked on worriedly.

"Jane, this is an awful scare you're giving me, if you were ill you should have said so before we came here," he asked foolishly, just not equating her grief at this time.

With tears welling up in her sad eyes once more, she burst out sobbing and clutched her father's tunic saying, "It's Ben, father! He's presumed dead or missing, they had no record of him being alive," and through her sobs continued, "The Captain told me from my discreet enquiries, it's official!" then she began sobbing some more.

Right now her father understood, he and everyone else had been so engrossed in the much bigger picture that it had completely slipped his mind for just awhile that his daughter would obviously be looking for Ben the first chance she had on landing here in Bosnia. Putting on his best face and lying to her he said, "You know Jane, that Sergeant is just too good a soldier to let something bad happen to himself, especially when he has something to come back to. I'm sure he's out there somewhere."

Hanging on to any shred of hope that she could, Jane looked up lovingly at her father and said, "Do you really think so father?"

"I'm positive of it!" he lied once more, saying to himself, *Heaven help me if I'm wrong!*

Feeling a little more together now, Jane looked at him and said, "I think I'm okay to get up now!"

Helping his daughter to her feet he said, "Look Jane, let me take you to your hotel room so you can lie down, then I promise I'll get on over to that Commander of this unit himself, General Logan, and even *his* superiors if I have to, but I promise you I'll find out myself for you what his status is, alright?"

Receiving a loving hug and kiss on the cheek, the General left the HQ centre and escorted his daughter back to her hotel.

Much later at Butmir, General Crenshaw was a determined man with a personal mission at stake now—to find out the fate of Sgt. Ben Steele for his daughter's happiness and everyone else's, including his own peace of mind. When he entered the hangar, General Clarke himself personally came over to greet him and stated, "This is a surprise. Didn't expect to see you out here until tomorrow General, what brings you here?"

"Well General, it seems that there's a certain soldier in this outfit that my daughter has long ago lost her heart to, I sort of have a preference for him myself!"

Grinning, General Clarke said eagerly, "Yes, I know the very soldier, heard the story myself and after meeting them both I can say that they're a Harlequin romance meant to happen!"

"Be that as it may General, but it seems that we have a little problem and hurdle to get over first, but so far, we have it on good authority it seems that there is a good chance that the Sergeant is either MIA or may actually be dead?"

"What's that you say man?" stammered the General.

Then, General Crenshaw took a chair that was proffered to him and quite exhaustedly himself, sat down and related the story of his daughter and how she gathered her ill-brought news. At that juncture, General Clarke interrupted to say, "Then for once in a war, it seems like I'm the bearer of good news for a change, heh General?"

"What do you mean General Clarke?" he asked all confused.

"Quite simply put my friend, it appears that the good Sergeant has obviously been misplaced and incorrectly categorized—due to the simple fact he is now a Lieutenant!"

"Good God Sir, do you know for sure what you're saying?"

"I sure do!" said a smiling General Clarke.

"Then can you please explain to me how on earth this came about?"

Smiling now, General Clarke related the story that had been told to him personally by General Logan himself, not two hours previously! He also gave General Crenshaw the bad news that his Sgt. but now Lt., had indeed been shot, but it was just a flesh wound to the wrist, which far from hindering the new Lt's. function or mobility, it had not prevented him from rejoining his men in their deployment when he realized that the battles had left a distinct officer shortage and his services could still be used!

"Well I'll be damned," exploded General Crenshaw, "That's absolutely the best news you could possibly have given me General Clarke. I'm forever indebted to you for it!"

"Not a problem old fellow, don't even mention it. I'm just glad, sincerely, that I was in a position to be of help, so why don't

I get you a driver to return you to that worried daughter of yours so you can put her mind at ease?"

"Thank you kindly," replied General Crenshaw, rising from his chair.

"What?" was all Jane could manage to utter at first, while hanging and clutching onto her father's arm.

"You heard me Jane," said her father, "Our Sergeant Steele is alive and well and was promoted to the rank of Lieutenant in a field commission which brought about all this confusion in the first place!"

Slowly smiling through her tears of joy Jane looked up at her father and said craftily, "I wonder how our Sergeant is handling his new role, as an officer I mean?"

"Probably a little embarrassed as well as proud, I know that's how I felt when they did the same to me in Borneo."

"Tell me daddy," said Jane craftily, "Don't you think that Ben now has *no* excuses for setting a date? Being an Officer as well as a Gentleman?"

"Why Jane," laughed out the General heartily, "You're positively and completely your mother's daughter. If he tries to weasel out and away from you now, after all this concern and worry he's put you through, you let me know and I'll be sure to have him removed from the service immediately!"

"Oh, I wouldn't worry about that now father, there's no way I'm letting him get away from me a second time, no matter what!"

The General then did something he hadn't done in a long, long time it seemed. He enveloped his headstrong daughter in his massive arms and gave her a strong and long warm hug as he patted her back affectionately. Then holding her at arm's length he said, "You do what you know is right dear and you know that your mother and I will approve, we already have approved of your choice, not to mention the Sgt. Major and aunt May and your brother and sister, I think things are going to be alright now Jane, yes I do!"

The pilot of the Huey Cobra helicoptor looked at Lt. Crenshaw and repeated his orders again in question to her, just to confirm they were right.

"I have my orders from HQ command and the General's staff Ma'am to fly you up to Mt. Bjelasnica and drop you off—then pick you up in an hour or two—is that correct?"

"Roger!" said an excited Jane as she sat there in her smart tunic of the British Intelligence Officer that she was.

"If you don't mind me asking Ma'am, but what's the purpose of this flight if it's not transporting the press corps or confidential, as I'm usually kept on perimeter patrol up until now?"

Lying to him gracefully, not even considering telling him that General Clarke had pulled strings to allow her into the field of operations, very briefly she replied cagily, "Intelligence work for the General's Staff I'm afraid Captain!"

Nodding his acceptance and resigning himself to this flight which was just a twenty minute hop anyway, he started his rotors and raised his helicoptor into the air slowly as Jane waved to her father and General Clarke who were standing some 100 metres away by the HQ hangar there at Butmir. As the helicopter tilted and rose swiftly to a height of around 600 feet, Jane looked down on the sight of Sarajevo as they banked to the east and sped off in the direction of Mt.Igman. The ride was absolutely spectacular and she tried to imagine what this pilot must have experienced less than a week earlier as he and his crew flew their helicopter into battle. She could only admire their skills as this pilot manoeuvred his craft with seeming ease and dexterity. Hopping over the contours of the mountain and then reaching the timberline of Mt. Igman, they swiftly lurched and were over it in seconds, to now follow the ridge along the corridor to Mt. Bjelasnica—and Lt. Steele.

She knew that the newly promoted Lt. Steele had absolutely no idea whatsoever of her impending arrival, all he knew and expected was that he was to greet *this* helicopter's arrival and escort the officer on board around for an hour or so. As the helicoptor slowed, she instinctively took that as a matter of its impending arrival. Her heart was all in a panic as silly thoughts raced through her mind like, *I wonder if he'll be happy to see me again?* The helicoptor suddenly banked and slowed even more, the pilot's voice came over the headset she was wearing so they could talk above the noise of the rotors and engine.

"Ma'am. if you look down outside your side window you'll see we're there. When we land, one of my men will unbuckle you and assist you out of the helicoptor. We'll still keep the rotors twirling so keep your head down for about fifty metres until you clear their distance, okay?"

"I understand Captain, I've flown in helicopters before!"

Not taking it as a personal rebut the Captain just replied, "Okay Ma'am, then have a good visit, I'll be back in an hour to pick you up as ordered, alright?"

"Roger!"

As she exited the helicoptor she kept her head down as was normal procedure and advanced away from it, toward the waiting group of soldiers. As she moved toward them, she was instantly squinting her eyes against the twirling snow and wind raised by the helicoptor as it was already taking off. She spotted newly promoted Ben to the forefront of the three soldiers standing there— and instantly saw the unshaven faces and grime that was their post battle conditions. She didn't let this deter her as she was forewarned and prepared. She had previously acknowledged that she wouldn't let their appearance disturb her, besides, she had gone days herself out in the field so she knew what it was like to go long periods without a bath!

She slowed her advance and looked at Ben. She saw the look of incredulity grow on his unshaven face, then the penny dropped and he seemed to come completely alive as he hurried towards her. He swept her up in his arms in an instant and said stupidly, 'Tell me I'm not dreaming?"

"Just shut up you big lug and kiss me!"

"That's the best order I've ever been given in all my time as a soldier."

With his two assistants looking on smiling and surprised to say the least, Ben held Jane tightly, as she desperately clung on and kissed him with a passion they never knew they held for each other—until this moment in time. Eventually they separated and she reached a hand up to rub his bristly face with tears of joy.

"They told me you were dead or missing Ben. It was positively the darkest moment of my entire life."

Then she just clung to him again, laying her head against his chest and sobbed. Looking over his shoulder he shouted back to his men, "You can both disappear for now, I have things under control here!"

"I say he does!" they muttered as they turned and moved away.

"Do you still love me Ben?" she asked. "I have to know now!"

"You're bloody stupid or foolish to ask me such a thing, you're the only thing that keeps me going any more in this life, I can't possibly imagine a life without you now Jane, of course I love you!"

After much, much more hugging and kissing Ben turned to her and said, "Now what in the hell brought you all the way out here, do you know just what kind of a shock you just gave me seeing you like that?"

Smiling she added, "Surprised yah, heh?"

"That's a bloody understatement Jane," he laughed, playfully pulling and stroking her hair, then blurted out, "You smell bloody wonderful Jane!"

"Wish I could say the same for you loverboy!" she said, holding her nose and grinning.

"Yes, well a week in the field will do that to a man!"

Changing the subject, Jane looked deep into his haunted eyes as she kissed him gently this time and said the obvious, "What was it like Ben? It must have been sheer bloody hell for you, how awful!"

"War is war Jane, we train for it and this is the result, but I can tell you, there must be a whole city down there cheering us on, as for the first time in years they can *really* come and go from their homes in safety as they bloody well please!"

Throwing her head back and laughing out loudly, Jane said, "A city? There's a whole world out there cheering on the exploits of your precious Brigade!"

Smiling back he said, "Yes, well we did sort of bloody well kick some ass, heh?"

"Sort of—Ben Steele, I'll be damned if that isn't the biggest understatement of this war," then continued on, "Do you realize that besides getting yourself promoted, yes I also know about that, your very own General has informed me that you're getting at least *two* more medals for bravery alone when they decide which countries that will be?"

"How about that," he smiled, then looked at her saying, "Now that *I'm* a Lt. I've got an order for you, let's get the heck away from the open here. I'd hate like hell to lose you to an angry sniper!"

As he led her away into the treeline, she remembered the face of the man fast walking toward them and then realized it was the big RSM Whittle.

"Hello there you two love birds, looks like you finally managed to figure a way to get together. Never figured you'd both manage to do it on the side of a mountain after a battle though, heh?" he laughed.

"That was the plan all along RSM, keep you all guessing!" said Jane.

"You know each other?" said Ben, surprised.

"In a manner of speaking," said Jane, "The RSM was the one who escorted me to your room to leave my care package for you (which brought a flush to her face and a smile to his on remembering) and he was also kind enough to drop by on leave with his wife to let us know that you were doing just fine!"

Looking at the RSM, Ben just smiled and said, "You dirty lying rotten bastard!"

Not taking any offence to that statement the big RSM just shrugged and said, "I'll take that as a compliment, me 'ole son!"

"Oh, let me be the first to congratulate you RSM," said Jane.

"On what?" he said bewildered.

"On the fact that you're also getting some bravery medals when this is all over here for you and your Brigade!"

"Fancy that, trust them to give me more stuff to clean for parades!"

After chit-chatting awhile, Jane said, "Do you wish me to let Mrs. Whittle know you're fine RSM, or do you want to yourself when you get back?"

"Actually Lieutenant, I'd be most grateful if you could find a moment to give the 'ole dear a quick call for me, would you mind?"

"Be my pleasure RSM."

After giving her his wife's phone number he said his goodbye and departed.

"Ben, is it safe for you to walk me over to the trees over there? Away from all these lonely and hungry staring eyes where we can be alone for what remains of our time before I have to return?"

"Not a problem Jane," he said tenderly, "I was just about to suggest it myself!"

Once there in the trees, they just hunkered down in the soft warm carpet of pine needles on the shady side, out of the wind. There they talked about their love for one another and about their plans for the immediate future, but what they wanted desperately from each other, their loving bodies, had to wait. Jane brazenly took Ben's hand and slipped it into her tunic under her blouse and placed it on her warm breast and said tenderly, "Caress me for a moment Ben and close our eyes and pretend we're far, far away from here."

"That shouldn't be too difficult Jane," he whispered pleasantly.

When the helicoptor arrived he said to her, "Jane, your taxi's come to pick you up I'm afraid!"

"Do I really have to go, tell them to bloody well go away and leave me here with you."

"Jane, as much as I would love to do such a thing, you better get your cute little rear in gear and get over there. Besides, I really am worried for you being out here like this, the farther you're away, the safer you'll be and better peace of mind I'll have!"

"Heh, trust you to be the pragmatist!"

They made their way back to the helicoptor landing site in a hurry still holding hands. As they moved, a lot of battle-weary faces wondered that maybe this was some sort of war correspondent that he knew and left it at that, at least letting it wait until later before they started the teasing!

"Remember, I'm down in Sarajevo in the one good hotel that all the war correspondents use, if you get a chance to go their before you leave, I'll be waiting!"

They kissed on the edge of the doorway to the helicoptor which brought a smile and more raised eyebrows from the pilot as he patiently waited to get her in and seated.

"I love you!" she shouted and waved, blowing him kisses.

"I love you too Jane!" he waved back.

He stood there below waving as the Huey Cobra left and was surprised that the pilot banked it and circled for "one more" pass over. He saw Jane crying and waving frantically as they quickly zipped by on their return flight to Sarajevo.

"Was *that* your special mission Lieutenant?" asked the pilot smiling.

Brushing away her tears, Jane said proudly, "Yes it was Captain!"

Looking at her the pilot said, "Well Ma'am, then I'm glad I could help."

Sitting just behind the pilot Jane began to brush away her tears and hugged and smiled to herself contentedly now, for she knew that the battle was over and that her man was safe!

THE SUMMARY

The hardest thing after a battle was the reorganising and solidifying of captured positions and the continuation of incoming logistical needs. Leadership at a time like this was also just as critical and re-inforcements were needed to take the place of those lost in battle. There would be a constant relay and recycling of men in the days to follow, between HQ and those recalled from the "front" to police the town until regular UN peacekeepers could be brought in.

It was also a few more days before Lt. Steele was allowed to get off Mt.Bjelasnica and get down into Sarajevo. In fact he was sent for by an HQ runner who stated that his presence was needed now by General Logan at HQ. As he alighted from the helicoptor with his backpack and personal weapon there at Butmir, he then made his way over to the hangar that had been the overall battle OPs as well as HQ. Entering, he spotted the RSM who had come down the day before and now leant over him to whisper jokingly in his ear.

"They do have baths 'ere old son, smell!"

"The only bath I'm interested in right now is taking the one over in my girl's hotel room RSM!"

As they both laughed uproariously, the Phoenix himself came over and said, "Good to have you here with us Lieutenant. Get yourself cleaned up, showered and shaved, then I expect to see you back here by 0800hrs tomorrow, understood?"

"Yessir."

The RSM walked back over to him, "If you like Ben, I will get one of our corporals from the staff driver's pool to take you directly to her hotel?"

"Thanks, that's the second best offer I've had this entire week," he joked.

"Okay then son, just you take a chair over in my office there and I'll 'ave one of the drivers sent over pronto and 'ave him page you, best of luck!"

"Tom?" said Ben as the RSM was leaving, which made the RSM stop and look back and say, "Yes?"

"Just wanted to say thanks for everything," then added in jest, " 'ole mate!"

Waving him away he added, "You'd do the same for a mate!" the RSM left him there in the entrance. It was five to ten minutes at most when a Brigade Cpl. walked over to Ben, saluted, and said with a big grin, "I'm your driver Sir."

Looking up at the Cpl. now, Ben said, "You can take that grin off your face Jonesy, I'm just going over to a hotel for a bath and to get cleaned up!"

"Pardon me Sir, but by now the whole damned Brigade knows who's staying in that hotel—and who visited you up on Mt.Bjelasnica!"

Laughing only to himself now, Ben said straight faced and matter of factly, "Okay Jonesy, now you all know my love life, just get me the hell over there, will yah?"

Smiling, Cpl. Jones saluted and said, "Be my pleasure Sir."

Ben entered the International Hotel carrying his gear and walked directly to the desk and said to a receptionist, "Can you tell Lieutenant Crenshaw of the British Army that I am here?"

"Who should I say is here?" asked the receptionist in her thick English with a strong Bosnian accent flavouring it.

"Just tell her that her husband is here!" he lied.

"Smiling now, the receptionist looked at him in a different light and said, "Right away Sir!"

He just stood over to the end of the desk and watched the elevator door. It eventually rang as it stopped at the main lobby. He saw Jane come out searching for him. Spotting him in an instant, she walked over and said smiling, "Husband heh?"

"Knew it would get me a faster response—and save your reputation!"

"Not that I care, come on love, let's get you upstairs and bathed!"

"Promise to scrub my back?"

"And more!" she chuckled as she took his hand and led him back to the elevator.

Once in the hotel room, she immediately ran him a bath as she ordered him to change out of his dirty smelly clothes and to put everything in a pile so that she could get it sent out and cleaned for him. As he was doing as ordered, changing in the corner of the old fashioned bathroom, he could see the steam rising from the water pouring from the taps into the pedestaled bathtub.

"How hot do you want it?" she giggled, as she observed him modestly clinging to the towel around his waist.

"Just don't let it be cold so that I shrivel up in front of you and embarrass myself!"

Fighting off fits of laughter, Jane said, "I always wondered about that myth, now you're telling me it's true?"

"Absolutely!" he grinned.

"Well don't worry, I probably made this hot enough to give you 3rd degree burns!"

Throwing aside his towel and with it his modesty, he stepped quickly into the bath and sighed, "Ahh, this is perfect Jane."

"Good, now let's get you scrubbed down, you dirty little boy," she chided.

"Only in my thoughts of what awaits me," he retorted.

So with Jane scrubbing his back and Ben doing the honours on his frontal parts and feet, they set about scrubbing a good few weeks or more of grime off him. After they had finished, there was so much scum and dirt floating, they decided he should take another quick one just as soon as Jane cleaned the tub for him. As soon as this was done, he climbed back in and they did a final rinse. Looking on at Jane now, kneeling next to the tub, he said slyly, "Come up here and let me kiss you!"

"What do you take me for soldier, a fool, if I do that you'll get me soaking wet?"

"Don't worry, I won't pull you in," he lied, "Anyway, you already have most of the water on you if you hadn't noticed?"

"Yes, I am kind of wet here aren't I?" she giggled again, then added, "Okay, but you have to promise, no funny stuff?"

"Scout's honour!" he lied again.

So she stood then leant over to kiss him, as he then quickly grabbed her and pulled her fully clothed into the tub on top of him. Jane squealed and squirmed and finally giving in to his vice-like grip she mockingly chided, "I thought you gave me your best Scout's honour?"

Looking at her mischievously he replied, "Didn't I tell you? I was never a Boy Scout!"

As she laughed with him, she playfully slapped him, then grabbing his head in her two hands she lowered and kissed him fervently once again.

"What do you say we get you out of these wet clothes before you catch your death of cold?" he said, as his eyes twinkled his real intentions.

"Now there's an original idea, what took you so long?"

They laughed and jostled, splashing water everywhere trying to get Jane out of her clothes and naked in the bath with him. When he succeeded, he held her warm body close to him and sighed once more. "Jane, I feel like I just died and went to heaven!"

"Oh I'll take you to heaven soldier, but I have had my share of worrying over whether you have died or not, thank you very much!"

Laughing together, they embraced each other and began to make passionate love, right there in the warm waters of that old fashioned bathtub.

Then later, much much later, they both lay back on the bed naked once more under the sheets. They were feeling a little bit hungry and Jane decided to get some food sent up to her room for them. While they waited, Jane dressed herself enough to greet the bellman respectfully. She handed Ben the clean clothes the room service had returned clean and pressed earlier saying, "Here you are my love, get yourself dressed."

It wasn't until he was eating that he actually realized how hungry he was and how long it had been since he last had a proper meal. Somewhere in-between his final bites he noticed Jane resting her face in her palms and looking on at him.

"I was hungry," he said embarrassed.

"Don't worry dear, I was looking at your features, not judging you for your table manners," she laughed on at him.

Feeling full and happy and relaxed, he came over to her side and drew her towards him.

"How much longer do we have before either of us have to report for duty?"

"Well I have to help father with a press conference for the BBC in about two hours, at about 1600 hrs," said Jane.

"Can I tag along with you, I don't relish the thought of waiting here alone for your return?"

"Of course you can silly, besides, father will be angry if I don't let him greet you soon. He'll not admit it, but he was quite worried for you himself in his own way, you know."

"Good, I kind of like the General too, but seeing it's not for another two hours?"

Laughing she said, "Not again, surely?"

Ignoring her remarks he pulled her toward him and walked backward until they both toppled backward onto the bed. He held her in his strong arms and as they kissed, they both urgently undressed each other as they caressed each other's bodies. He cupped her breast with one hand, then lowered his head to suck and kiss her other. She arched her back in ecstasy as she took his hand and guided it between her legs. Feeling and rubbing her until her excitement was taking over, she in turn rolled him over and straddling him, lowered herself onto his body. As they continued their gyrating and wriggled about on the bed, she dug her nails deep into his back with excitement, but he felt no pain, only the pleasure. Their mouths were locked in a long sensual kiss as they mashed their lips into their teeth while tongues searched out the other, they continued to writhe and make love right there on top of the squeaking bed until they collapsed into each other's arms in a shuddering, shaking climax!

As they both lay heated and exhausted in each other's arms, Jane cried, "Oh my God Ben darling, I think you just gave me a major orgasm!"

"As long as it was as good enough for you as it was for me, I'm happy," he replied breathless. Leaning on his chest she kissed him gently this time and replied, "I think we should get ourselves ready properly now, we don't have a lot of time left to spare?" as she rose naked from the bed and moved into the bathroom. He took this opportunity to gather his own uniform and to dress once again, walking to the bathroom door with Jane's clothing held out in his arms saying, "Do you have another skirt and blouse hanging in the closet Jane?"

"Yes I do, but why?"

"I was just thinking that you may want to wear that instead, as this one is rather creased up, if you know what I mean?"

Laughing she said, "Lucky for you I do, if you don't mind getting it for me then Ben, it's hanging on the right side I think?"

"Found it," he shouted.

"In that top drawer," she shouted again, "You'll find a new pair of panty hose, will you please pass it in to me too?"

Obliging, he walked across the room and returned to the door of the bathroom and passed the item through. When Jane came out, she was once again dressed as the impeccable British Officer. Putting on the tunic top that Ben held out for her, she twirled for him to say "Well, how do I look?"

"Like you're the sexiest most attractive British Army Officer ever!"

"Thank you darling," she said pleased, while kissing him on the cheek, adding, "And I think you're some kind of handsome hero too!"

Hours later, in the former HQ of the United Nations, they

gathered to meet the elite press corps from around the world, but also for the debriefings of the various High Command of the member countries whose troops made up the Sabre Brigade. While General Clarke was busy talking to the CNN T.V. journalists and other members of the Associated Press and like organizations, General Logan was kept in the wings ready to take his cue with Colonels Clarke and Lafluer, to give their overview of how the battle went (Swartzkoff style) and to answer specifics.

When Lt.s Crenshaw and Steele walked into the room many eyes turned and glanced their way as General Crenshaw came over with Colonel Price in tow to greet them.

"My, but you look pretty good for a soldier who just went through a war and came out wounded!" said the General.

"That's all thanks to your remarkable daughter, Sir!" he replied, looking at Jane again with his twinkling eyes.

"In a few moments it'll be our turn to go on the telly in front of the BBC," said the General, "Want to join us?"

"No offence Sir, but not bloody likely."

When the laughing died down he continued, "I'll leave that up to the professionals like yourself and Jane here!"

"What if they want some comments from the real live drama in the heat of battle?" the General asked.

"Well Sir, no disrespect again, but I think there are lots of Officers much more qualified than I am. Besides, I don't quite understand the 'rules of engagement' with the press, camera people and journalists etc., if you know what I mean."

"It's all quite simple my boy, you show them the maps then tell the truth but as little as possible, but I understand. Well, find a quiet secluded place if you can and watch the show from there, then when it's all over we'll get together somewhere for a drink and talk."

Looking at Colonel Price for advice, Ben received a smile and agreeable nod advising him to go ahead.

"Okay Sir, only because you've asked, but I have one request to add?"

"What's that?" asked General Crenshaw.

"Why, that I be seated right beside Jane here?"

The gut-wrenching laughter again from their corner of the room caused the combined press corps to look over in their direction once more and wonder *'just who'* are *that noisy lot?*

"You certainly have a way about you Ben, after all you've put us through it will be my pleasure—and Jane's I'm sure!"

The debriefing Ben had been watching was going really well. He was looking around the room for his favourite reporters, Justin Sidor and Shirley Queen, who worked for the big USA news network. Gen. Logan, with aid from his two Colonels, had been keeping the press enraptured with their professional manner and the whole account of their actions for the past hour or more. Ben and Jane sat quietly with no interruption thankfully in a deserted corner. Gen. Crenshaw meanwhile was seated behind the main table with the UN logo front and centre. It had now become the focal point for the press corps main photo op, so to speak, and for the benefit of the BBC, he did his piece in "classic" British style for all those watching on the telly back home. Most of the difficult and tactical questions were now being asked of Gen. Logan with Colonels Price and Lafluer once more.

The entire press corps sensed the importance of their explanations and soon they were all gathered, not just their own countries' reporters. They had all made their way over to the BBC seating area to see for themselves what this angle was they were newly disclosing. Questions of the battle and how strategy was played out was unfolding, as the entire press corps seemed to be focused now on this drama, that had played out against the backdrop of Mt.s Igman and Bjelasnica.

Eventually they started to wind-down their historic news-briefing for the media by saying, "The real story here folks is the people of Sarejevo and Bosnia."

This reality check worked! The press, realizing and respecting this for what it was, seemed to know their time was getting short. Final questions and details of the two battles and the logistical-related questions of 'show and tell' from their maps, took it from its full swing to a gentle and respectful close down.

When it was all over and the media had disappeared into the night to prepare their respective reports for "on air" status, Gen. Crenshaw turned to Ben and Jane and the small crowd of military escorts and a "few" familiar and friendly British press guests to ask, "Do any of you lot think the bar is open in one of our hotels?"

"Guaranteed!" someone yelled out.

"Then what do you say we all go and have a good brandy or two?" he replied jovially.

"I'm with the General!" said Ben, looking hopefully at Jane.

"And I'm with them!" said Jane, hanging onto his arm and looking up proudly at Ben's face, then her father's. On entering the hotel, it wasn't hard for this seasoned lot to find the right direction to the bar . . .

. . . The following morning at exactly 0800hrs sharp, Lt. Steele was in the Brigade HQ in the temporary office of the Phoenix, Gen. Logan.

"Relax, take a seat Ben!"

Not knowing if the General had remained or hung around long enough back at the press conference to catch his dialogue, in playful but determined grilling, Ben asked him such and enquired of him how he felt it went.

"Yes, excellent! In fact it wasn't as bad as you'd expect. Besides, it will at best give the Brigade a softer and more inspiring image."

"That's great news Sir," he said, genuinely relieved and pleased.

"Now, about that Officer insignia you're wearing. If you want to keep it, then as soon as we land back in Montana, I want you on a plane and over to Sandhurst—that is where you British train your Officers, isn't it?"

"Yessir," grinning.

"Well don't just stand there, go and tell your lady Officer sweetheart. But also I'm afraid Ben, you'll have to tell her that you'll be seeing her for the last time for a while, I have to send you back out into the field now, there really is a shortage of command personnel up amongst our units. We took incredible losses in Platoon Leaders, unfortunately, too many amongst our Canadian friends. I know they felt they had to do more than their share due to lack of numbers, but I just wish they weren't so badly devastated. It will make it all the harder now to get new replacements for them, but regardless, I will still try. They are first rate officers those Canucks Ben, as you know."

"Absolutely Sir", said Ben, smiling an 'All Canadian' grin.

Then it clicked for the Phoenix too. "Ah that's right, you're Canadian too, well maybe we can use that fact in our recruiting campaign, eh?"

"Might help Sir, you never know."

"Anyway", he said rising from his seat, as Ben did the same and put his beret back on too, "Good luck to you Lieutenant, I'm really glad things turned out for you and that you're still here with us!"

Ben came to attention, saluted the Phoenix and left the room . . .

THE RETURN

It was at least another full month of digging in and fortifying over-run and captured positions as well as the other Serb-controlled enclaves around Bosnia before the Sabre Brigade were afforded the luxury and opportunity of passing off their positions and duties to more permanent members from the new United Nations Peace-keeping Mission.

During all that time, from the beginning of their battles to the end of hostilities, these elite soldiers of the Sabre Brigade, as the world now recognised them to be, had also become hardened to the harsh weather conditions living out in the open on the mountains as they had. And if truth be told, many of them had even come to prefer it to the stifling claustrophobic feeling of being cooped up in a room. The luxury of which soon came their way as the separate Battalion Commanders tried to rotate *all* their men for a well earned one week spell of R&R. Even though this was at Butmir, it was well received, as it was mostly to clean up and the get the mud, blood and gore off themselves, their clothing and equipment. Just so that when they eventually were seen in public, they wouldn't terrify the living crap out of people!

General Logan himself directed the RSM to see about getting as many of his soldiers as possible (of whom he was extremely proud) that extra leave so they could actually go into Sarajevo them-selves before they left. He felt *they* alone more than anyone (for it was they who had carried the brunt of hand-to-hand combat etc.) deserved the opportunity to visit and see it for themselves as well as experience and enjoy what favours a freed city could offer their rescuers. Albeit for most soldiers, the only thing on their minds was women, with hefty doses of: booze/beer/wine.

Eventually, on December 8th, the mass take-over of "official" UN Peacekeepers, with a large U.S.A. contingent, was completed. There was not a lot of fanfare but it was another major feat of logistical organization controlled by Colonel Price and his staff, namely the Engineer Officer, Major Biggles. This all thankfully being achieved just before the heavy Balkan snows came.

On December the 11th (under the watchful eye of what seemed like most of the free world's press) the entire Sabre Brigade were being transported out of Bosnia and Hertzegovinia. Some made their own way to the International, as well as Butmir Airport, as their own Brigade transport planes (mostly Hercules) as well as regular commercial 767s were put to task ferrying the Brigade back to Montana . . .

Once back in Camp Fredericks, weapons were put back into the armoury, vehicles into the transport pool and all other equipment cleaned. It was only then all the soldiers of the Brigade were given passes, as well as a deserved Christmas leave, except for a skeleton Guard.

As for Lt. Ben Steele, he was sent with haste back to the Royal Military Academy at Sandhurst, known as RMAS. It was, for what was to be an accelerated training Officer course. It was a hectic time, trying to find time between studies to visit his "home away from home" now at that place known simply as "The Mews", plus to plan a wedding with Lt. Jane Crenshaw . . .

In the spring of that following year, with his training on hiatus, Lt. Steele returned once again to Montana and the Sabre Brigade. He was surprised with the knowledge that to update and fill badly needed officer positions, he would personally receive a further promotion to the rank of Captain. This was courtesy of Generals Clarke, Crenshaw and last but not least, his direct boss, "The Phoenix" himself, General Logan, who was newly promoted also during his absence, to the rank of 2 star General.

The soldiers of Camp Fredericks went about cleaning up their barracks and readied it for a dedication monument and special remembrance parade to recognize their fallen comrades in battle as well as preparing for a special honorary parade. This would require being in full dress parade uniform, complete with medals etc, for they were to receive their Brigade & Battalion Battle Honours. The individual medals would also be presented at this time to those soldiers for their various bravery and actions in battle in Bosnia and Hertzegovinia.

It was known that all soldiers of the Sabre Brigade would receive at least two campaign medals now, a special one newly introduced by the United Nations, as well as one from the U.S.A. Then of course there were the individual medals for bravery! There were a lot of brave and heroic soldiers needing to be honoured this day, many posthumously. It had been decided long ago at a lengthy meeting of the Member States of United Nations as well as Security Council, that to keep some kind of conformity with the Brigade, that only one country would issue the medals for this honouring, and this duty & honour fell to the United States.

The men of the Sabre Brigade had their native countries' Presidents and Prime Ministers and Secretaries of State and Chiefs of the Military Staff in attendance, plus a further abundance of other top military brass from the Brigades represented countries here to present them—as well as relatives and a lot of the International Press and journalists to capture it all on celluloid and still film and print.

The most prestigious medal awarded that day, the "Medal of Honour", was presented posthumously to Lt. Grey for his gallantry under fire at a crucial moment in time during the march from the Ski-Chalet to Mt. Bjelasnica. His widow and children were present to receive their countries and Brigade's flag, presented by Gen. Logan.

Capt. Steele received the Silver Star as well as two Bronze Stars for his courage under fire and bravery in action on more than one occasion. These were the recce of the two mountains prior to the battle, his actions at the Ski-Chalet, and his leadership and daring during the advance to Mt. Bjelasnica.

RSM Whittle refused outright to even entertain any talk of promotion saying, "I'm an enlisted man through 'an' through I am." He did receive the Silver Star and Bronze Star for his courage under fire and leadership and actions on Mt. Bjelasnica though.

Newly promoted RSM Brassard received the Silver Star and Bronze Star for his bravery, actions, and leadership on the recce of the two mountains prior to the battle, and for his actions during the campaign.

Newly promoted RSM Ridgeway (Gunny, who also flatly refused a commission) received the Silver Star for courage under fire on the battle of Mount Igman.

There would be a long procession of many others, of officers and enlisted men alike, who would receive their various medals this day, but these soldiers mentioned were the first of many singled out that warm spring day.

As the soldier raised the standard flag of the Brigade newly received now with their battle honours, a loud cheer went up from the crowd. The subsequent coming to attention with boots ringing off the gravel in unison, followed by all picking up arms, shouldering arms, and saluting crisply the reviewing stand of VIPs and guests was smartly done. The men then marched away proudly from their parade square, just as they had arrived, only this time they marched away with banners and standards gently swaying in the breeze.

As the Sabre Brigade marched off the square, Brigadier Price (he couldn't be left out of the promotions!) leaned close to the ear of Gen. Logan to say, "You do realize we're going to have to go through all the growing pains once more, especially once they all find out that most of the new replacements due to arrive to the Brigade this time will be from the German, Belgian, Spanish, Italian and Australian armed forces."

"Wouldn't surprise me one darn bit!" laughed out Mac, "God, but I love this life."

Then, their brief but spontaneous moment of jocosity was interrupted by the sudden appearance of the indefatigable Cpl. Jones.

"Sir."

"Yes, what is it Corporal Jones?"

"Sir, I have a message from General Clarke, he says he needs to see you both quite urgently."

"Where is he now then, Corporal Jones?"

"He's over in the War Office Sir with the Secretary General."

"I see, please tell them we're on our way."

As Cpl. Jones hurried away, Mac turned to his 2IC and friend David, "Are you thinking what I'm thinking?"

"Yes," said David, "Considering yesterday's message and now this, I'd say it's a good bet that something's in the wind . . . "

THE END

Quote:
"Worse than war is the fear of war."
SENECA, Thyestes